SCORPION TRAIL

Geoffrey Archer is the former Defence and Diplomatic Correspondent for ITN's award-winning *News at Ten* television programme. His work as a frontline broadcaster has provided him with the deep background for his thrillers – the bestselling *Shadowhunter, Scorpion Trail, Eagletrap* and *Java Spider*. A keen traveller, he now writes full time and lives with his wife and family in Surrey.

SCORPION TRAIL

Geoffrey Archer

ARROW

Published by Arrow Books in 1996

3 5 7 9 10 8 6 4

First published in the United Kingdom in 1995 by Century

Arrow Books Limited
Random House UK Limited
20 Vauxhall Bridge Road, London SW1V 2SA

Random House Australia (Pty) Limited
20 Alfred Street, Milsons Point, Sydney, New South Wales 2061, Australia

Random House New Zealand Limited
18 Poland Road, Glenfield, Auckland 10, New Zealand

Random House South Africa (Pty) Limited
Endulini, 5a Jubilee Road, Parktown 2193, South Africa

Random House UK Limited Reg. No. 954009

A CIP catalogue record for this book is available from the British Library

Papers used by Random House UK Limited
are natural, recyclable products made from wood grown in
sustainable forests. The manufacturing processes conform to
the environmental regulations of the country of origin

ISBN 0 09 954941 7

Printed and bound in Great Britain by
Mackays of Chatham PLC, Chatham, Kent

To Eva, Alison
and James

'My father hath chastised you with whips, but I will chastise you with scorpions.'

1 Kings Ch. 12, v. II.

One

The breeze flicked at the collar of his coat. The Highland
airstrip was little more than a grass field with a windsock.
A single-engined Cessna stood in front of a club house.
Sheep grazed beyond the perimeter fence.

The foreboding that gripped Alex was irrational and
sudden.

The risks hadn't worried him before. This sport was
safe. Statistics proved it. So why the sense of panic, the
feeling that some thread binding his world together had
suddenly snapped?

The club secretary was used to dealing with worried
parents. He'd claimed that the Sky Trainer 'chutes had
been used two million times and never failed. Then he'd
shown Alex last month's beginners alighting on the grass
as if they were gulls.

'You see? Nothing to worry about.'

However, as the pilot strode towards the little Cessna,
followed by the instructor and three orange-suited students, Alex had to fight the urge to shout 'stop!'

Jodie, last to board, turned to wave. Trying to reassure
himself, or his stepfather?

Still time to stop him. He could run forward and . . .

Hysteria, that's what they would put it down to.
They'd restrain him gently, take him to the club house
and settle him with a cup of tea so the boy could get on
with his life.

Alex tried a grin but couldn't move his muscles. Arms

like lead, legs like jelly, tongue puffy and useless. Couldn't speak if he tried. Just that sense of disaster sweeping in like a squall.

The boy had wanted to jump since the age of fifteen. Seen it on television, the floating figure in bright, flapping nylon. The goggled grin at the camera. And the swoop away from the lens as the chute jerked the body, jigging and jangling, feet braced for contact with the earth.

The power, the freedom, the sheer sense of *joy*. God knows, there hadn't been too much of *that* in Jodie's young life.

His mother was overprotective, but she had her reasons. She'd blanched when he'd revealed his ambition.

'Never, Jodie. Never, never!' she'd begged.

But 'never' is a word you can't say to a man, and the boy was over eighteen now. Nineteen, even. He had asked Alex for the parachuting course as a birthday present.

Kirsty hadn't spoken that morning. Just stood by the big picture window looking across at the Firth, watching the scurrying clouds and the blurs of rain on the water. Not spoken, because the words, if she'd voiced them, would have been pleas for a change of heart that had already been rejected.

Alex knew what she feared. That history would repeat itself. That she would lose her only child the same way she had lost his father.

'He'll be fine, Kay. Just fine. You'll see.'

His steady, brown eyes gave her the warm look he used to soothe women's worries, his soft voice tinted with the Lowlands inflection he'd adopted years ago as a disguise.

He stood behind her, held her shoulders and brushed

2

his lips against her hair. He could feel the tension shooting through his fingers. He took away his hands.

'Jodie *has* to choose, Kay. You can't control his life for ever.'

He saw her tremble, and a tear mark her cheek like a scar.

'Okay, Alex?'

The prompting was from Jodie standing in the doorway, fearful that his escape from the maternal arm lock might yet fail.

'We'd better get a move on, Alex.'

Always called him by his first name. Never 'Dad', although Alex was the only 'father' Jodie had ever known. Kirsty had wanted it that way, out of respect for the dead.

They drove north over the toll bridge, the morning sun to their right struggling through the clouds and silhouetting the trapezoid ironwork of the rail link across the Forth.

Alex had never been to Scotland before events propelled him there in the 1970s. This was a simpler, more conservative community than he was used to, but he'd wanted nothing else, so long as it hid him from the men who sought to kill him.

He had grown the beard immediately, a full set, but clipped short. The simplest of masks. The job at the radar factory, the minders had arranged. All part of the back-scratching world of Defence, they'd told him. He'd be safe here. No one need ever know his past.

The hard part was being alone. Not used to it. He had always had women in his life, sometimes more than one at a time. Not just for the sex. He needed women to blather with, to lean on. Yet how could he share his life, when his recent past was so dark a secret?

Then he met Kirsty and saw the glimmer of a solution to his dilemma.

3

It was the firm's Christmas dance. She'd been invited by one of the staff to make up numbers at their table.

'The girl's had a tragic bereavement,' the friend confided. 'We felt it time to get her out and about again.'

Married just three years, her husband had been killed in a blizzard in the Cairngorms. Many an experienced climber had died that winter. He'd left her a widow with a nine-month-old baby.

Everything about Dermot, everything about her short marriage to him, Kirsty had locked inside her mind pledging never to forget. The memories were like a sealed room in an old castle; she denied access to everyone. Never talked about Dermot, and couldn't bear others to.

She was a pretty girl. Soft, wavy hair, scrubbed cheeks and blue eyes that glistened with never-distant tears. Alex's heart went out to her.

He began a gentle courtship, hinting that he'd also suffered a tragedy too painful to talk about. As the months slipped by and they became closer, the understanding grew that they both had parts of their lives which must remain private.

'You think she'll cope?' Jodie asked, as they passed the underemployed Rosyth dockyard to the left of the bridge. 'Maybe I'm being a bit selfish.'

'Course she'll cope,' Alex answered, slowing to pass an accident at the junction with the motorway. 'She has to get used to you doing your own thing. Anyway, when you're away at Aberdeen she has no idea what you're up to. It's just a pity she has to know about this particular happening.'

'You're right there!' Jodie nodded. University had been a merciful escape from the over-protection at home.

'I tell you, when you get back tonight, give her a big

4

hug and tell her how great it was. Look, she's terrified because of what happened to your dad. It's understandable, for heaven's sake. But it's something she's got to get through. This jump today could even help.'

'Shock therapy for nervous mothers! I don't think so somehow.'

The rain was holding off. The day before, the instructor had said the weather would have to be appalling to stop the jump. Alex turned off the motorway and pointed the car towards the Ochil Hills.

'Are *you* nervous?' he asked the boy.

A moment's pause.

'Shit scared,' Jodie laughed.

'Think how *I'll* feel, bloody watching you!'

He thought of Kirsty, wondering if she was still standing by that window, staring at the sky.

Theirs had been a marriage of convenience, but a good one. She had needed a man, to support her and her child. He had needed a woman, to share his bed and to help hide him from the predators. Affection and respect was what they'd had, rather than passion and love. A formula that had lasted nearly eighteen years.

It hadn't been easy at first, fighting his way past her first husband's ghost. It took months of wooing before she could even smile without a feeling of guilt. Months more before she let him make love to her.

They'd been out walking in the dunes near North Berwick, just the two of them. Jodie was being baby-sat by her mother. A bright, crystal-clear day in early summer. They'd rested in a clearing in the woods. No one else about. No chance of being surprised. Alex slipped his hand under the soft cotton of her tee-shirt, fingertips finding her nipples already hard.

Then she locked her mouth to his and unleashed the

hunger that had been building inside her for weeks. She pulled him into her, climaxing quickly.

Afterwards, as they lay on their backs, she had cried. Sobs of grief at her final acknowledgement that Dermot was dead.

As Alex swung the car through the gates onto the small airfield, a Cessna pulled away from the flightline, bumping over the grass towards the strip. To their right was the club house and hangar and a small square of hard standing for cars.

'There's Claire,' Jodie said. He wound down the window and gave her a 'thumbs up'. There were as many young women as men on the course.

'What are all these girls trying to prove?' Alex wondered aloud.

'You mean they should all be at home, making babies,' Jodie retorted. 'Come on, Alex! It's a challenge. A big thrill. There's no difference for men or women.'

'I reckon it's a substitute for sex, myself.'

'Shows how little you know!'

Claire was walking across to them as Alex switched off the engine. She had a pretty smile.

'You could do okay with her, if you play your cards right,' Alex teased.

'Piss off!' Jodie reckoned he was already well on the way. Chatted her up in the pub last night, after the day of theory lessons at the club.

Next to them was a Range Rover with two large Labradors steaming up the windows in the back.

'So, what are *you* going to do, Alex?' Jodie was out of the car. 'It'll be a couple of hours before they take us up.'

'Don't know. May wander off for an hour. I've got the "Sunday's" in the car, so I won't be bored.'

'See you later, then.'

Jodie strode towards the club hangar. Claire touched him on the arm and they went inside together.

There were more parents there, settling down to make a day of it. Mums as well as Dads in most cases. A pity Kirsty hadn't come. Might have done her good to see other families coping.

Another lone father nodded him a greeting, wanting to talk. No, thought Alex. One of his golden rules: avoid social contact. He smiled briefly, then got purposefully back into the car and re-started the engine.

He took the main road for a mile, then turned up a narrow lane. Another mile and he was on the crest of a ridge with a view over the airfield. He parked in a gateway and as soon as the engine cut heard the bleating of sheep from the field beyond.

He wound down the window, pulled a pack of Bensons from the pocket of his Barbour and lit up. He didn't smoke much these days; it was banned in the office and Kirsty objected at home.

Golden rules. That's what he'd lived by for twenty years. Had to, so the minders had told him. The terrorists had friends everywhere. One incautious word and they could be on to him. And we wouldn't want that, would we, Mister Crawford?

Crawford. MI5 had chosen that name for him. Jarvis was the one he'd been born with. Alexander Jarvis.

They had given him the framework of a new life. Birth certificate, passport, all falsified in the name of Her Majesty. Even a driving licence, once he had settled his address.

Add the rest yourself, they'd said. Keep it simple; make up a new past to replace the one that could kill. No mixing of fact and fiction. Invent it, fix it in your head until you believe it's true, and stick to it.

And never ever reveal the truth, even to those you make love with.

Rules. He'd made some up himself. Told his neighbours he was obsessed by tyre pressures – an excuse to check under his car for bombs.

Some rules he never revealed. Superstitions. Little things he had to do if the good fairies were to keep him safe. Little things like putting his left sock on before the right. There was the daft, childish 'tide' game too.

Every Saturday, unless the weather was atrocious, he would drive to the Yellow Craig beach west of North Berwick, for a run on the sands. His marketing job at the radar factory near Edinburgh was tedious; that beach, with its huge, wide sky was freedom. Freedom from drudgery, freedom from fear. Freedom to imagine what his life might have been like if it hadn't been for that balls-up in Belfast.

He would run near to the water's edge where the sand was firmer, keeping close to the creaming froth of the waves, but never, ever letting the water touch him. If it did, he told himself, the Belfast gunmen who had his name on their 'touts' list, would find him.

Silly superstitions, but in the part of his mind he had to keep private, they mattered.

From the distant hillside, Alex watched the little plane creep across the airfield and lift into the air. Shafts of sunlight bathed the valley in patches of green gold. Rain streaked a hill to his right. Sunday traffic crawled on the road running south to Stirling. So peaceful. So safe.

'Christ! It's been twenty bloody years,' he breathed.

He'd just passed the anniversary of his escape from Ulster strapped into the back of a Hercules. You'd have thought they'd have forgotten him by now, but not according to the MI5 man he phoned once a month. The IRA still handed old photos of him to new boys going active on the mainland.

He slipped on a pair of half-moon reading specs and browsed the newspapers. His bushy brows bunched into a frown. Always did when he concentrated.

Front pages filled with pictures from hell. The blackened corpse of a child burned alive in a Bosnian village.

Massacre of the Innocents – his two papers shared the same stark headline.

The *Sunday Times* reported over forty killed in a single village called *Tulici*. Moslems, this time. Bosnians, Croats, Serbs – the divisions were confusing. They'd all been Yugoslavs once, in a place people went to for holidays. And now they were killing each other.

It depressed him just to read about it.

He picked up *Scotland on Sunday*. On the front page, a local tragedy. Pictures of a tear-stained Edinburgh mother. Her thirteen-year-old girl had disappeared. Suggestions the child had been seen with prostitutes.

Sad world, he thought. He folded the papers, tossed them onto the back seat and slipped his glasses back into their case. Better take some exercise. He opened the door, got out and locked it out of habit.

He was average height, a little under six foot, with straight, dark brown hair and a sportsman's build. Under the thornproof coat, so stiffly waxed it was like armour, he wore brown cords and a navy pullover. This was how he liked to dress; the business suit he wore on weekdays always felt wrong.

He stuck to the road, striding along the edge of the fields, walking for twenty minutes, his mind on Kirsty and the boy.

Jodie.

'Christ almighty!'

He stopped in his tracks. His stepson's face had suddenly appeared in his mind, sharp and clear as a flash photo. It was the boy's expression. A look in his eyes that wasn't Jodie at all. Terror. Abject terror.

The image was gone again. He shook his head to try to recall it, but couldn't. Most odd. Like a burst of clairvoyance.

No believer in such phenomena, it unsettled him none

the less. He stared across at the airfield, then marched to the car and headed back.

The fear he'd seen in Jodie's eyes spread in him like an infection. His heart beat unnaturally fast. He told himself to stop being daft, to rationalize this irrational sensation. Nerves – parachuting was risky and Jodie was about to do it. That's all it was.

But that wasn't all. He began to experience more weird sensations, as if he wasn't alone in the car. A feeling that Kirsty was there. He glanced behind.

This was getting stupid.

Back at the airfield, no sign of the boy. He barged into the old bi-plane hangar, where used parachutes were being tensioned on the floor for re-packing.

'Experienced jumpers have their favourite packers,' Jodie announced suddenly at his side. 'Gives a sort of feel-good factor.'

'Oh, there you are!' Alex started. The boy grinned at him, clad in an orange jump suit. No fear in those eyes.

'They pay three pounds a time. It's worth learning how to do it. Pack five 'chutes and you've earned enough for a jump.'

'You mean you intend to make a habit of this?'

'Most people get hooked,' Claire announced, joining them. 'I've only done five jumps, and it's like a drug.'

Alex eyed her. Older than Jodie. Early twenties perhaps. A broad face, eyes bright with single-mindedness. Not unattractive.

They looked so at ease, the pair of them, Alex felt his anxiety lifting.

'Oh by the way, Alex this is Claire,' Jodie said awkwardly.

He shook her hand.

There were half a dozen getting ready for their first jump. Several Jodie's age, but two in their thirties. They'd spent the last hour revising drills learned the day before. Jodie had driven himself here on Saturday.

'Two days in which to learn how to survive, falling out of a plane,' Alex mused. 'It'd take two lifetimes if it were me.'

'Time you got kitted up.' The instructor took Jodie by the arm and led him to the racks of parachute packs.

'This is when your stomach really gets going,' Claire murmured to Alex. 'But he'll be okay.'

'What ... what exactly does he have to do?' Alex wanted reassurance again.

'He'll be on a static line. You always are for the first few. It means there's a line attached to the plane, and as you fall away it pulls your canopy open. You don't have to do a thing.'

'Supposing it doesn't open?'

'Always does. But just in case, you carry a reserve parachute on your front.'

'And does that open by itself too?'

'You have to pull a handle ... Look, don't worry. Everybody's so safety conscious here, you just wouldn't believe it. Haven't had a fatality for five years.'

It was her use of that word 'fatality'. He sensed a hand on his shoulder. Kirsty's hand. Not there of course. He shivered.

Jodie waddled back across the hangar, parachute packs strapped to front and back. He pulled a soft leather helmet over his head and eased a pair of goggles into place.

'Cheer up!' he said. 'It's me doing the jump, not you!'

'You look like a phantom rapist, in that gear,' Alex joked, trying to disguise his anxiety.

'Thanks. Found my *métier* at last.'

'How do you feel?'

It was a stupid question. Jodie's face was tense. Nerves, but excitement too.

'They say it's the fear that gives you the buzz ...' he answered. 'If that's true, then I should have a great jump!'

The instructor strolled over.

'Just come over here a minute Jodie,' he said, with practised calm. 'We'll go through things one last time.'

He led him onto the field.

A new emotion now in Alex's chest. Jealousy. He'd been father, brother, teacher and guardian to the boy. *He'd* been the one Jodie had trusted. Now there was someone else. Some jerk in a jump suit.

'Are you excited for him?' Claire asked.

'Of course.' His voice sounded husky.

As excited as their first time together on the stands at a Murrayfield International. As excited as the day he took the twelve-year-old on a day-long crawl through the heather to stalk Red Deer on the Monadhliath Mountains. Landmarks in a life, all as exciting as this, but none so terrifying.

Alex and Claire crossed to the fence separating the car park from the field.

He pulled out his cigarettes again and offered her one. She shook her head.

'Did *your* family come and watch first time?' Alex asked, tugging the smoke down into his chest.

Claire shook her head. 'Didn't even tell them I was doing it.'

Better that way, maybe. Better if neither he nor Kirsty had known.

Claire asked about his job.

'Marketing. Radar. I'm an electrical engineer by trade.'

But possibly for not much longer, he omitted to say. The company was being taken over and the work 'rationalized'. That meant redundancy, probably. Looking for volunteers, and if they didn't get enough, they'd start naming people. He'd not told the family yet.

Maybe that explained his anxiety today. Fear about losing his job, twisted by his mind into fear for Jodie's life. For a moment or two he almost believed it.

An engine purred high in the sky. The club's other aircraft was up with the free-fallers. He squinted at the even greyness above. One. Two. Three and then four tiny figures tumbled from the black 'T' shape. Claire counted aloud to five.

'Five seconds delay! That's my next step. I've done three seconds already.'

One by one, the 'chutes had popped open.

'Great!' Alex croaked. It all looked so easy. Nothing to fear. 'Bloody great!'

They watched the canopies glide and float towards the field, the bodies beneath tugging on the steering guides.

'Ram-air canopies,' Claire explained. 'Like a wing. You can get twenty-five knots horizontal speed on them.'

As they swooped to land gracefully a few feet in front of them, Claire detached herself from Alex's side and went to greet one of the free-fallers. He only realized it was a girl when she removed her helmet and shook free a tress of chestnut hair. Claire grabbed her excitedly by the arms.

Alex lived that moment with them. Faces aglow, the world their oyster. Make the most if it, he thought.

For an instant he was Jodie's age again. In a flash of memory, he recalled a noisy pub in Hampstead and a girl called Lorna Donohue.

Lorna, who'd caught his eye and left him breathless. A golden-haired teenager. Someone who really *had* believed in clairvoyance. They'd been lovers for just a few weeks and she'd told him they'd never be parted. Then she'd dumped him and disappeared back to college in America.

Lorna Donohue. Perhaps the only woman he'd ever truly loved. They'd met again in Belfast a decade later, quite by chance. Once more the chemistry had been instant, so explosive that time it had scarred their lives. The result for him – exile in Scotland. For her? He had no idea.

The memory faded. All in the past. The past he never dared talk about.

The pilot climbed into the little plane, followed by Jodie and the others.

'Alex!'

Jodie waved from beside the doorway.

Alex stared back, unable to speak.

'Alex?'

The boy looked strained, wanting a response.

'Yes!' he managed to shout at last. 'Good luck!'

He clutched the fence, telling himself to be rational. Of course there was a risk. People *had* died, parachuting. But not beginners, not on a static line.

The engine flicked into life. His last chance to run across and stop them . . .

'Don't be so fucking stupid!' he growled to himself.

It was Kirsty's fault. Paranoia must be infectious.

The aircraft began its take-off run. He waved again, a terrible, empty feeling.

It was a tight squeeze in the back of the plane. No seats. Just a bare metal floor and a gaping hole to the slipstream. Jodie was to be first out and had to kneel, gripping a webbing handle.

The Cessna banked and climbed to 2,200 feet. The instructor tapped Jodie's shoulder, then ran his hand along the strap connecting his back-pack to a ring on the floor. All secure, all as it should be. Thumbs up.

'Okay now,' he yelled above the engine and the wind. 'Into the doorway and take the bracing position.' He gave a reassuring grin.

Jodie's heart pounded so hard, he couldn't speak. His mind was blank. He'd forgotten everything. Everything he'd been taught in the last two days. Gone.

Think.

Legs over the edge. Strange how it didn't affect him,

14

looking down at the earth two thousand feet below. Couldn't go more than two rungs up a ladder normally.

Left hand on the sill, right on the door frame.

Good.

Turn to look at the instructor. The man grins again, gives thumbs up, his eyes asking for an acknowledgement. Jodie nods. No going back now.

Go! The signal.

Hesitation.

Go! Go!

Pushes off from the sill and the frame. Airstream hits like a gloved fist at a hundred and fifty miles an hour.

'Aaaah!' The scream choked in his throat by the wind.

Spread arms. Count. One thousand, two thousand, three thou . . .

Bang. The straps jerk under his groin as the 'chute opens.

Shit!

Now what. Check canopy. He strains his head back. That beautiful dome of blue and white.

He feels sick. Doesn't know whether to laugh or cry.

'Hey! This is amazing!'

He laughs.

'Jodie!' A man's voice in his ear. 'Don't forget to steer.'

The radio. He'd forgotten about it. Another instructor was on the ground, watching through binoculars, talking to him on the VHF.

'Is that him?' Alex asked, craning his neck up at the sky.

'Should be,' said Claire. 'He told me he was first out.'

'God! Isn't that great?' Alex's voice cracked with relief.

'Told you it was foolproof.'

'Christ,' thought Jodie. 'Where am I?'

The field was nowhere to be seen. He pulled a line to

15

close a vent on the back of the canopy and began to swing.

'Pull hard on your left.' The metallic radio voice again.

He did and swung the other way.

'Now let go the guides. Straight ahead now.'

At last he saw the hangar and the windsock, and then the orange cross on the grass which was his notional landing point. Miles away, and he was dropping fast. He looked straight down.

Oh, no! That bloody clump of trees they were warned about.

He willed the canopy towards the field. Eight miles an hour forward speed, that's what he should have in still air. But looking at that bloody windsock, the wind was gusting too strongly. Wasn't moving forward at all.

Ground coming up fast.

'If you go in the trees, remember legs together and cover your face. No problem.'

So reassuring, the voice in his ear. All right for him. Done it a thousand times.

O..oh! Here we go.

From across the field, the man who'd spoken on the radio watched from his van as Jodie's legs pierced the dome of green-black branches. Soon obscured by the pine foliage, all he could see was the blue and white canopy snagged and deflated above, and the vaguest hint of an orange suit close to the ground.

'Remember. Don't do anything now. Just wait for someone to come and help you down. Repeat. Don't do anything.'

He picked up the other handset and told the control room what had happened, just in case they hadn't already seen.

The radio in Jodie's ears died when he hit the trees. Twigs snagged the wires. One foot twisted against a branch and he banged a knee. Then suddenly he stopped, a metre from the ground.

'Fuck!'

Heart pounding, he jigged in his harness, trying to shake himself free.

'Hah!' he shouted.

He was stuck but ALIVE! Elation hit him.

'I've bloody done it!'

He looked up through the trees. The plane droned into position for its next drop.

'Hah! Ha, Ha!' He laughed out loud. He'd just come down from there! Jumped from that same little plane. From that little dot in the sky.

Ten feet tall, that's what he felt. A few more jumps and he'd be onto the square canopies, the ones that zipped around like autumn leaves.

He looked down again. So close, yet so far. Except he wasn't far. Three feet at the most. Easy. For heaven's sake, he'd just jumped from two thousand feet all by himself. Couldn't let the last few inches defeat him.

He reached down to his groin and began to unbuckle the harness.

'Shit! He's in the trees!' Alex had taken an involuntary step forward as Jodie disappeared from view.

'That's bad luck. On your first jump,' Claire answered calmly.

'Isn't it dangerous?' he asked, turning to her.

'Should be okay. They tell us it's the softest landing you can get . . .'

'If you don't get stabbed by a branch.'

'See that van down the far end of the field?'

He looked where Claire was pointing.

'They've got ladders and stuff. If he's caught in the

17

trees, they'll get him down in a wee while. He'll just stay dangling until they come. That's what they teach us.'

Alex stared harder at the van. Motionless as a rock.

'Why don't they get a move on?' he growled.

'They have to wait until the others are down. The guy in there is talking to them on the radio as they drop.'

That terrible sense of dread was back. He began to walk.

'They won't want you on the field,' Claire called after him.

Alex heard, but didn't hear. The relief at seeing Jodie's 'chute open had evaporated. Something was wrong; something desperately wrong. *He* knew it, if no one else did.

There was a little gate into the field. An instructor grabbed him as he ran through it.

'Hang on, mister. You canna go through here. There's students jumping.'

'Jodie . . .!' Alex panted, pointing. 'He's in the trees.'

'We know. We know. He'll be a'right. They'll get to him in a couple of minutes.'

'Now! You've got to get him now!'

The jump-instructer saw the panic in his eyes.

'Okay. Okay. We'll go together. But if I tell you to do something – you do it fast. No questions asked, okay?'

Alex nodded.

'Come on then.' They began to run towards the copse. 'It's your son, is it?'

Alex felt a chill descend. Kirsty's son, but his too in all but blood.

'Yep. My boy.'

The jump-instructor kept a hand on his arm and checked the sky as they ran. The last of the novices was on the way down. But they were well clear. No problem.

They neared the trees. There was a smudge of orange between the trunks. Jodie's jump suit. Feet almost touching the ground, but not quite.

18

In the scrub at the edge of the wood the instructor faltered. There was something not quite right. Something about the head . . .

'Jodie!' Alex yelled, fighting his way through the saplings. 'Oh, God . . .'

Nothing. No response. No movement.

They heard an engine revving. The van with the ladders was coming across.

'Jodie?' Alex croaked, the branches slashing his face. The instructor joined him as he broke through to where Jodie dangled.

The boy's body hung twisted in the straps, the harness half on, half off. In the struggle to free himself, a strap had slipped round his neck bending it to an angle that no neck should ever be.

'Oh my Christ . . .' murmured the instructor. 'He's tried to get himself down. You mustn't do that – we tell them.'

Alex stood transfixed by Jodie's startled, indignant eyes, the nightmare image that had come to him on his walk.

'Quick! Take his weight,' the instructor ordered.

Alex gripped the lifeless thighs and lifted. The instructor reached for Jodie's wrist and felt for a pulse. There was none.

'His neck's broken,' he said, but Alex didn't hear him, deaf to the instructor's words, and to those others who rushed to help. Jodie was dead. He'd seen it, and done nothing.

Two

Thursday 17th March

Kirsty's brother helped her from the first of the Daimlers. She wore a navy blue coat over a long, black skirt, her face wraithlike beneath a veil.

Alex emerged from the second limousine and paused on the cobbled ground, watching his wife's alabaster visage turn towards the tower of the kirk. He saw her legs threaten to buckle and her brother grip her more tightly. Eighteen years before, she'd made the same journey here to bury another part of her life.

They stood to one side while the coffin was slid from the hearse. The distance between Alex and Kirsty was just a few metres on the stones, but emotionally a canyon now gaped between them.

On Sunday, when Alex had returned to the house overlooking the Forth, Kirsty had known already, her sixth sense confirmed by seeing a stranger driving their car, with Alex in the passenger seat and a Range Rover pulling up behind.

'You've killed him!' she'd whispered as he opened the door.

Ashen faced, he couldn't meet her look. He'd thanked the people who'd helped him home and bade them leave. Then the dam of Kirsty's feelings had broken.

Her accusations had found their mark. He *could* have prevented Jodie's death. He'd had the premonition after all.

Why hadn't he acted on it? Because he hadn't believed in premonitions, that's why. And anyway, it had been *Jodie's* choice to jump, *his* decision. The boy was nineteen, not nine.

Kirsty had railed at him, her charges growing wilder, beating him with her fists. She kept throwing out Dermot's name. Accused Alex of trying to erase him from her memory. Said Dermot was angry at being forgotten, angry at the way Alex had taken his place as Jodie's father. She'd even claimed Dermot had returned from the dead to take back his son.

Nonsense. Madness. She'd needed help, of a sort he couldn't give. He'd telephoned for the doctor to come, then called her brother to break the tragic news to the family.

Her sobs had cut deep, the pain of her grief compounding his own. They'd been punished, she'd said. Punished for forgetting the past. It was Alex she blamed. No one else. *He* had brought this on them. Nothing would shake her from that belief.

As the hours passed, her anger had subsided, but she'd not let Alex touch her. Their marriage was over, she'd said. It had died with Jodie.

She'd left the house that same afternoon and gone to stay with her brother.

'She doesn't want to see you again,' he'd reported two days later. 'I suppose you know that.' He was visibly distressed. They'd got on well, he and Alex.

'She's talking about moving to a retreat . . .' He'd shaken his head. 'Almost twenty years since Dermot passed away, and she's never come to terms with it. Should have had treatment long ago . . . I'm really sorry. None of *us* is blaming you, you know that.'

Alex had thanked him.

In the small, grey, stone church, Alex sat across the aisle

from Kirsty, her eyes fixed on the coffin below the chancel steps. Most of the mourners knew she'd left the house at Longniddry. Most wished it weren't so, but feared nothing could change the way she thought. The doctor had called it a 'kind of breakdown', but she was refusing further medical help.

She looked to be in a trance. Paper-white face, lifeless eyes. Behind her sat her parents, ramrod-straight Presbyterians, faces as impassive as they had always been, emotions locked away. Kirsty was so much their child. All her pain, all her scars hidden from view.

Outside in the hillside churchyard, they lowered the simple pine box into a newly-dug hole beside the grave of the father Jodie had never known.

Alex bit his lip and swallowed back tears.

Such a waste, he thought. A person, a character that *he* had helped mould, wiped out just as he'd begun to grab what life could give him.

'He's yours at last, Dermot,' Alex reflected. 'But if it *was* you who took him, don't expect the boy to be grateful.'

By the churchyard gate, the family stood in line to receive the condolences of the mourners. There was a set of faces Alex didn't recognize until Claire took his hands and squeezed them. Several others from the parachute club had come with her.

A camera flashed; the tragedy had interested the local press. Alex flinched; he was shy of photographers. Made it a rule to keep his face out of the papers.

He turned away.

The ghastly process over, Alex heard the parachute group talk of heading for a bar. He might have joined them, if only their youthfulness weren't too painful a reminder of what he'd lost.

Kirsty was driven off in the Daimler. Suddenly Alex realized he might never see her again.

'Mr Crawford?' The chauffeur of the second car held

the door for him. Kirsty's parents were already inside. A reception was to be held at the brother's house, but he couldn't face it.

'No,' he answered after a moment. 'No. I want to walk.'

He leaned in, made his excuses, then waved the vehicle away.

The car park emptied. With Jodie in the earth and Kirsty gone from him, seeing the last vehicle rumble down the hill was like watching twenty years of his life drain away.

Earlier that morning, there'd been another blow. As if to twist the knife, a letter had arrived from the radar factory saying he'd been made redundant.

He set off towards the sea, raising the collar of his dark grey overcoat. Four miles of coastal path lay between him and home.

The cemetery was on a hillside. Beyond was a golf-course where many of his neighbours spent their leisure time. Small, bright figures strolled between the greens.

He had never taken up the sport. Golf clubs spelled danger. Too much chat. Too many people asking about his past. Jogging was his exercise. Lonelier but safer.

He seldom met anybody when he ran on the beach. Just one regular, a stocky man walking a Red Setter. They'd exchanged names once. Somebody McFee. An executive with Edinburgh Life. Hadn't seen him recently.

As he cut down through slopes of dead bracken towards the coast, it felt as if the corner stones of his life had been stolen away and he'd been presented with a blank sheet of paper in exchange.

He realized there was little to keep him in Scotland now, other than the place itself. The gentle Lothian hills, the clean coastline and views of the Forth speckled with white sails in the summer had been a kindly hole to hide in, but having isolated himself for his own safety, he had few friends here.

His life had been different before the disaster in Belfast, first as an engineer with Marconi's, and later when he'd worked with the television news. He'd had plenty of friends to drink with then, to chat to and to make love with.

Surely it would be safe to return to some of that life, he thought, despite what the minders said. Not to have to hide any more, that would be something . . .

The tide was ebbing and the Gullane sands stretched far out, their dull flatness broken by strips of sky reflected in pools left by the receding sea.

He saw Jodie everywhere he looked, the beaches so much part of his childhood. Emptiness gnawed at his stomach. There was no way he could remain here. Not when every whiff of seaweed, every caw of the Arctic terns was a reminder of the boy.

Not easy to start again, approaching fifty. Unless he could salvage *something* from the past.

He thought suddenly of Lorna. Always did when things weren't right in his life. She was his 'if only' girl, the one he would have married if events hadn't got in the way.

They'd met in the sixties. Pop and protest, Ban the Bomb.

Lorna was a believer in fate. A sacred thread linked their karmas, she'd told him. That's why they'd fallen in love. When they met again ten years later, it had confirmed her belief.

'There's someone up there making the breaks for us,' – that was the way she always put it.

The trouble was he'd not seen or heard of her for the twenty years since then. And when they'd parted, she'd hated him enough to want him dead.

Where then was he to begin his new life? Have to talk to the men at MI5, if he wanted their continued protection. He could go back to London where he had his roots. Parents were both dead, but he had a sister in Wimbledon. They'd been close once, until she married some detestable stockbroker.

The stones of the coastal path jabbed through the thin leather soles of his black shoes. By the time he reached Longniddry his feet were pinched and sore.

He stood in the porch fumbling with his keys. There was no light inside. As he opened the door the emptiness engulfed him.

A newspaper lay on the mat. He picked it up. It was the local one. The headline caught his eye. They'd found the body of that girl – the thirteen-year-old he'd read about on Sunday.

Poor kid. Poor mother.

He tossed the paper onto the hall table and fumbled in his pocket for a cigarette. He flicked the lighter, then stopped. Not in this house. In his mind the place was still Kirsty's.

The message light winked on the answerphone. He left it. There were people still ringing for Jodie, not knowing he was dead. Or else it would be for Kirsty, and he'd have to explain she was no longer there.

He wandered into the kitchen. It had been his wife's domain. Kirsty's wish as well as his; she'd been old-fashioned that way. He filled the kettle and plugged it in.

The message machine niggled him. It *might* be for him. He brewed his tea then returned to the living-room and pressed the replay button.

'Ah, hello . . .' A man's voice, but not one he recognized. 'It's Moray McFee here. Just ringing you Alex to offer my condolences. Er . . . terrible business. I was very sorry to hear about it. Er . . . I haven't been around much in recent weeks, which is why you haven't seen me up at Yellow Craig in a while.'

It clicked at last. The man on the beach. The man with the Red Setter.

'I'm down in London, as it happens. Something new I'm involved in. Errm . . .'

There was a pause of a few seconds. Alex could hear the muffled rumble of traffic in the background.

'I . . . I wonder if you would give me a ring here. I'd like to talk to you. There's something I think you might be interested in knowing about. I'm staying in a wee bed and breakfast place. Just ask for me, Moray McFee, and if I'm not here, then leave a message and I'll call you back. The number . . . oh, hang on. Ah yes. Here it is . . .'

Alex wrote it down.

Odd. Why should a man he hardly knew take the trouble to find his number and call him?

He hesitated. It was twenty-past five. Perhaps he'd ring him this evening. Or now. Get it over with.

He picked up the phone and dialled. It rang for a while, then a woman answered, her voice heavy with some foreign accent.

She laid the receiver down, and he heard footsteps in a corridor. Then a few moments later, a heavier footfall returning.

'Hello? McFee here.'

'Ah. It's Alex Crawford here. You left a message on my machine.'

'Alex! That's good! I wasn't so sure you would ring. Very presumptuous of me I'm sure, but er . . . I heard about the terrible accident and then . . . then your wife taking it bad. Sorry to be so direct and so on, but em . . . I understand it was in the local papers about Jodie, and then em . . . I was talking to someone else who . . . who knew the family . . .'

There'd been no shortage of gossip in the area, Alex was well aware of that.

'I wanted to offer my condolences . . .'

'That's good of you. It's been a bad time, as you can

imagine. Pretty bloody really. I'm just back from the funeral.'

'Oh, I'm sorry. My timing was not of the best, perhaps . . .'

'That's all right. You said there was something you wanted to tell me.'

'That's right. Look, um . . . I won't go into all the details on the phone, but for various reasons, I've resigned my job in Edinburgh, and . . . well the fact is my wife and I are having a break from one another as well. So, my life is going through a bit of an upheaval, shall we say.'

'I'm sorry to hear that.' Alex began to regret he'd made the call. Had enough troubles of his own.

'But that's not the point. That's just for background. The reason . . . the reason I rang you was to tell you what I've got involved in down here, because . . . well I happen to think you might be in a similar position and might be interested in hearing about it.'

'Go on.'

'You'll have seen on the TV all the dreadful things that are happening in Bosnia?'

'Of course.' Alex frowned.

'Well, I've just been out there as a volunteer to help get emergency food and clothing to children. There's thousands and thousands of them who've been burned out of their homes, and they've got nothing. Nothing at all. And the winter's still biting.

'There's a small charity called Bosnia Emergency that's been set up by an ex-major in the army. They collect stuff here and take it direct to the villages where it's needed. I'm going out with another van-load in a week's time, and they're looking for one more volunteer. I told them I knew someone who might be interested, but I need to give them an answer tomorrow.'

Alex did a double-take. It wasn't something that had

remotely crossed his mind. Bosnia had always been 'someone else's problem.'

'You mean me?'

'Aye . . .'

'But why? Why did you think of me?'

'Look, I've been away from Scotland for a good few weeks now, but I keep in touch with what's going on up there. Em .., I won't mince words Alex, I know your company's in trouble and they're making half the staff redundant . . .'

'Is it half the staff? God, I didn't even know that.'

'And I guessed, just a guess mind, that you might have been sent a letter through the post. The money's good, I'm told. And that's important. Because you wouldna get paid for this Bosnia business. Just living expenses.'

'I see.' Alex felt distinctly uncomfortable that a stranger should know so much about him. 'You seem remarkably well informed . . .'

'Years of listening at keyholes, that's all! Well. Are you interested or not?'

'I don't know . . .' He was thinking hard. It was bound to be interesting. Worthwhile too. Might be the break he was looking for. 'I'll need to think about it . . .'

'Aye, well, as I said, there's not a lot of time. I have to tell them tomorrow one way or the other. But from my point of view it'd be grand. I'd much rather work with someone I know than a complete stranger.'

'Well, yes I can see that . . .'

Alex glanced round the living-room. A stack of Kirsty's *Good Housekeeping* magazines on the coffee table. A pile of Jodie's CDs on the audio system. The silence that echoed.

Someone up there making the breaks for him . . .?

'Well, thanks Moray. Yes, I'll do it.'

Three

Three men and a woman sat at the light oak conference table flicking through the thin file which had been presented to them by the Data and Records Section. The words it contained were clinical, but they described a calibre of human savagery most Europeans believed had died out with the end of the Third Reich.

The Yugoslav War Crimes Tribunal was open for business but it was early days. No prosecutions were yet in prospect, and many of those who paid lip-service to the need for a tribunal suspected there would never be any. Politics, they thought, would get in the way.

The office smelled of new paint. There was a hammering in the background. Carpenters putting up shelves.

All four round the table were from different countries: a Dutch police inspector, a lawyer from Senegal, a French investigating magistrate, and Caroline Zander, a legal officer from the British Home Office.

Communication between them alternated between French and English.

'It's thin,' Ms Zander complained, tapping at the paper.

She was in her mid-thirties, a career woman with short, brown hair and a look in the eye that warned others not to waste her time.

'Plenty on the crime, but not much on the criminals.'

The War Crimes Tribunal had been set up the previous summer by the UN Security Council. Seen politically as 'the right thing to do', the UN had found its member nations reluctant to finance it, however. The Tribunal's rented space in a former insurance office in the Hague was short of equipment and staff.

The woman from the Home Office turned back to the cover page of the file.

'The Tulici Killings – March 11th,' she read again.

'Victim Total: 44.

'Women: 18

'Children under sixteen: 21

'Men (elderly): 5.'

The first inside page gave the background:

'The village of Tulici consisted of twelve habitable dwellings and a small mosque. A further two houses had been rendered uninhabitable recently; their occupants, Catholic Bosnians, referred to as 'Croats', were expelled from the village during the widespread "ethnic cleansing" perpetrated by all sides in recent months.

'Tulici is on the northern slopes of the Lašva Valley in central Bosnia, where the community has been of mixed religions for many years. The battle lines between the BiH (Bosnian) army (mostly Muslim) and the Bosnian-Croat Hrvatsko Vijeće Obrane – HVO (Catholic) are constantly changing, according to UN observers. At the time of these murders Tulici was at the edge of the area under BiH (mostly Muslim) control, but was not believed to be of strategic importance to the other side. It had been left undefended, apart from the presence of a few elderly men armed with hunting rifles and shotguns. All the younger men of the village had been enlisted in the Bosnian army and were manning defences elsewhere.'

Caroline Zander picked up a pen and gently chewed its end.

'At approximately 14.15 hrs, an unknown number of assailants (the UN Protection Force UNPROFOR estimates twelve) approached the village from the south. An unmade road passes east-west through Tulici. Sniper positions appear to have been established at each end of the hamlet. Six of the women and nine of the children killed were shot at the eastern end as they tried to flee.

'At 14.55 hrs, an armoured patrol from the UNPROFOR base

at Vitez saw smoke from the village and went to investigate. Before reaching Tulici, they came under attack from a mortar and withdrew. One hour later they returned and succeeded in entering the village.

'In an orchard at the western end they found the bodies of five men, described as elderly. All had been shot several times. UNPROFOR believes the men had been rounded up in the village and brought to the orchard to be murdered.

'Along the road through the hamlet the bodies of seven women and six children were found. All had multiple gunshot wounds. Two of the children also had their throats slit.

'Every house in the village had been set on fire, apparently to ensure that anyone hiding in them would also die. Some had been attacked with grenades. The charred bodies of four women and six children were recovered from cellars by UNPROFOR soldiers and the men from the village who had arrived back at the same time.

'The last victim was discovered in a cow shed behind one of the houses, a young woman, said by her father to be nineteen. She had been shot in the head and chest, and stabbed several times. The clothing had been stripped from her lower body. An UNPROFOR medical officer was present; he reported that blood smears in the area of her vagina and anus suggested she had been subjected to multiple rape.'

Caroline Zander smacked the pen down onto the table and chewed her lip. She'd seen many reports like this in the past three months, but it didn't make them any easier to read. She pressed on.

'The bodies of the victims were buried the next day in a field next to the mosque. No autopsies were carried out. There are no known survivors of the attack, and no one witnessed it at close enough quarters to provide any description of the assailants. It is assumed however that they were affiliated in some way to the HVO.

'The UNPROFOR Colonel in Vitez lodged a strong protest with the HVO commander and demanded that he carry out an investigation. The latter reported back that after interviewing all his subordinate officers, he could find no one who had any knowledge of

the incident. The UNPROFOR Colonel has described the HVO chief as a "pathological liar".

'Inquiries by a representative of the UN Centre for Human Rights, based in Zenica, produced "hearsay" evidence only. The men of Tulici who had been absent at the front, are convinced that the attackers were from a neighbouring Bosnian-Croat (Catholic) village. In particular they have named one man whose own family had been made refugees by the war with the Muslims. The man is called Milan Pravic, aged about thirty. He is known to have worked in Germany for several years, but had returned to Bosnia to support the HVO. He has acquired a reputation for being a tough, ruthless fighter and is said to have a deep hatred of Muslims.

'All efforts to trace Pravic through the HVO have failed. They claim that on the day of the massacre Pravic was fighting on another front.

'Without some direct evidence of his culpability, we have at this stage no case against Mr Pravic. The Bosnian forces however are convinced that he was in overall command of the attackers. Any extra resources the Tribunal is able to provide in trying to secure an interview with Mr Pravic would be most valuable.'

Ms Zander smiled wryly. Extra resources? The money the UN had budgeted would scarcely cover the rent and the wages of the small staff until the end of the year.

At times she despaired of the work she was doing. Yes, the politicians mouthed support for the Tribunal every time the television showed new horror pictures. But more money? Oh no.

'I'm not sure we can get far with this one,' she confided. 'What do you all think?'

'We have a name. That is a beginning,' the Dutch policeman insisted. 'We can alert EU countries to watch for him at their borders.'

'I agree, but so far there's no *evidence* against him,' the French magistrate pointed out. 'Unless we can find him and persuade him to confess.'

The Englishwoman snorted with laughter.

'Fat chance.'

The Senegalese lawyer began to stir. His command of English was poor and it had taken him longer than the others to read the report.

'The place ... where they kill...' His voice was laboured and slow. 'The UN soldiers ... they are British?'

Ms Zander nodded.

'Then maybe the British ... they can do something? Ask the questions ...? Maybe British military police ... can find this Pravic.'

'It's not in UNPROFOR's mandate ...' she explained.

'I know, I know. But unofficially ...'

'Undercover, you mean? I'm not sure about that.'

For a moment there was silence round the table.

'Mind you, we could make something of the fact that this man's a Bosnian *Croat*,' she conceded.

The others frowned. She wasn't making herself clear.

'As you know, some politicians think putting Bosnian war criminals on trial will undermine the peace process,' she explained. 'Because most of those we've identified so far are *Serbs* ... They're scared Milosevic will accuse the world of bias and pull out of the talks.'

'But most of the criminals *are* Serbs ...' the Frenchman insisted.

'I know, I know ... But if we can persuade our government that prosecuting Mr Pravic, a *Croat*, would balance the books, it *might* encourage them to give us the help we would need to dig up enough evidence against him. I mean, my Foreign Secretary has called the Tulici massacre a *stain on the conscience of humanity* ...'

'Ooph, such strong words ...' the Dutchman mocked.

'Caroline is right. It could work.'

'But Bosnia is a sovereign state,' the Frenchman objected. 'We have no right to go and investigate there unless the Bosnians give us permission. This is not like Nürnberg.'

'*Permission . . .*' the Englishwoman pondered. 'Of course that's not something the intelligence services worry much about, is it? And I can't imagine Britain has two thousand soldiers out there without a few spies watching their backs.'

She stood up and grabbed her copy of the Tulici file.

'Let me talk to my friends in London and see if I can pull a trick or two, gentlemen.'

Berlin

Lufthansa flight 3227 from Moscow was late. Due at ten to three on this wintry afternoon, it was after five when the 737's tyres kissed the tarmac.

Kommissar Günther Linz of the Bundeskriminalamt, BKA, had been assured the two men were on the flight. Germany's secret service had a man on board who'd radioed through. What they didn't know was the precise nature of the stuff in the men's bags, nor how dangerous it was.

This was a public place. Innocent people everywhere. Couldn't afford to slip up with the snatch. No chances being taken – sharpshooters on the balcony and, just seconds away, a medical team from the Bundeswehr's nuclear protection unit.

A tall man, with salt-and-pepper hair and close-set, hazel eyes, Linz wore a dark green raincoat and carried a Duty Free plastic bag. He was uneasy – always was when the security people set up a 'sting'. If the two men he was about to arrest *were* committing an offence, it was because the intelligence services had put them up to it.

The blue tail of the jet lined up with the gate. Linz began to sweat.

As airports went, Berlin-Tegel was one of the best for arrests. Baggage collection, immigration, customs – all at the gate itself, and just a few metres beyond the barrier a door to an access road where police vans could wait.

The first passengers emerged from the pier and lined up for the passport check. Linz watched his four BKA detectives mingle by the carousel.

The two Italians stood apart, one in a business suit, the other in leather jacket and brown trousers.

They're good, Linz thought. Not a hint they're together. Not a sign of concern. Natural gamblers. The contents of their cases could make them rich, or put them behind bars.

A buzzer. The carousel about to move. Linz watched the plain-clothes men close in on the couriers. Near enough to move fast, but not so close as to be noticed.

The Italians watched the bags emerge. Linz guessed they planned to travel separately to the hotel where their 'customer' was waiting.

Leather Jacket grabbed a Samsonite then aimed his trolley for the exit. The Suit checked customs didn't stop him, then took his own bag from the carousel.

Two broad-shouldered BKA officers followed the first man out, and two more took position behind the second.

Leather Jacket passed through the automatic doors. The Suit began to follow.

Linz scratched his chin. The customs officer acknowledged the signal and stopped an African laden with boxes. The Suit found his way suddenly blocked. Linz saw fear flicker at this untimely delay.

Outside in the concourse strong hands wrenched Leather Jacket's arms from the bar of the trolley and pinioned them behind his back.

'*Che cosa fai . . . ?*'

A tobacco-stained hand clamped his mouth. He saw his trolley and Samsonite disappear through the doors.

Then his feet lifted from the floor and he hurtled after them.

In Linz's earpiece, a whispered voice. All was well. A scratch at his cheek this time – the customs man waved the African through.

In the concourse, the Suit looked round for his companion, but for less than a second. Then he too felt metal cuffs, and his dream of wealth vanished like steam from a kettle.

Across the airfield a small hangar had been cleared for operation Black Gold – *Schwarzes Gold*. Black-clad snipers from the anti-terror unit watched, while the two Italians sat in separate vans seething.

On trestle tables in the centre of the hangar, stood the two suitcases. X-Rays had shown they might be booby-trapped.

Linz watched from a distance, while the bomb experts did their stuff. He puffed at a small cigar. Then a technician beckoned him over. They'd cut through the sides of the bags, to by-pass the locks.

'They live well, these Italians,' he quipped, holding a large tin of Russian caviar.

Linz pulled on plastic evidence gloves.

'Let me see.' He spoke in a low mumble. He took the can, which felt too heavy for caviar.

'Plutonium probably,' the technician suggested. 'Twenty times as heavy as water. Permission to open it, Herr Linz?'

The Kommissar handed back the tin and glanced at the truck-load of sophisticated gear they'd brought from headquarters.

'But do we have a can-opener?' he asked laconically.

Heads shook. There was a ripple of embarrassed laughter. Linz sent someone to find the kitchens, then wandered onto the apron again to relight his cigar. He limped slightly, the result of an old gunshot wound when he'd been on the Drug Squad. He was joined by a man shorter than himself, whose shiny baldness looked premature.

'Hardly worth opening the cans,' Linz scowled. 'I suppose you know what's in them already.'

'Of course we don't. We only baited the hook. You never know what kind of fish you catch until you reel in the line.'

The smaller man was from the internal security service BfV. This was *their* sting.

'Where did you find these two types, anyway?' Linz needled.

'If you know the right bars, they'll come to *you*,' he replied. 'One of my colleagues looks like an Arab. Said he had a rich friend who would pay a fortune for enough of the right stuff. And, what do you know? Up jumped the Mafia.'

'And when they get before the judges, they'll claim enticement . . .'

'But, Herr Linz, does that matter?'

Couldn't see the bigger picture, policemen, the BfV man thought. Too focused on detail.

'It matters to me!' Linz growled. 'Catching criminals and locking them away is what I'm paid for.'

'*Na schön!* But what we need at this moment is *information* about the plutonium trade. And if you want to learn if there are poachers out there, you must wave a rabbit.'

Behind them someone cleared his throat.

'We have the can-opener, Herr Linz!'

The policeman and the intelligence agent walked back to the hangar. Linz squeezed the glowing end from his cigar and put the rest in his pocket.

They began to open the caviar, snapped by a police photographer.

'What do all these things do?' Linz asked, pointing to devices set up around the can.

'They detect neutron radiation. Plutonium 239 is what people want for bombs, but it's contaminated with 240, which gives off neutrons,' explained the technician crisply.

'So what will these toys tell you?' Linz pressed, still confused.

'Whether it's dangerous to handle, and whether this stuff is weapons grade.'

Linz grunted and let them get on with it.

Gingerly they removed the cleanly cut lid. Inside, was layer upon layer of polythene sheeting, cut into discs to fit the can. A technician tore off a strip of Scotch tape, crumpled it then used it as a sticky handle to lift them out.

'Polythene absorbs neutrons,' the technician explained.

As the last of the plastic was removed, he pointed the neutron detector into the can. There was a rise in the whine emitted by the machine.

'That's okay. The levels are safe. This stuff is high grade.'

Black powder beneath the plastic.

'Everything suggests weapons-grade plutonium,' Linz was told. 'We'll know more tomorrow after we've analysed it fully.'

'Morning, I hope?' the BfV man queried, adding as an aside to Linz, 'the press conference is planned for three in the afternoon.'

The press conference had been scheduled since yesterday. That's what Linz hated about this whole affair. Little to do with crime. Just politicians wanting Brownie points.

'About midday,' the technician confirmed.

The second can of 'caviar' revealed the same contents as the first.

'Tell me something,' Linz said, grabbing the white-coated technician by his sleeve. 'Someone could make an atom bomb with this stuff?'

'*Jawohl*.' He held out the can so Linz could see more clearly. 'But you must convert the powder to metal and machine it to the right shape.'

'Just this much? What we have here?'

'No, this is a sample. You'd need eight kilos for one bomb.'

Linz let them pack away their equipment. Just a sample. But in the wrong hands one that could lead to death and misery for millions.

He looked at the vans where the Italians were being held. Small fish. Couriers. Might not even know who was pulling their strings.

'Come on then,' he said, taking the BfV officer by the arm. 'Let's see what your two jokers have to say for themselves.'

Four

Sleep, in the empty, ghost-filled house at Longniddry, was almost impossible. Alex's mind raced like a toy train on a loop line. Even though he knew Jodie's death was an accident, he couldn't forget that the boy would still be alive if he'd acted differently.

His decision to join the relief effort in Bosnia had lifted his spirits a little. Helping people who'd suffered more than himself had to be a good thing to do. Yet he knew too that to some extent he was running away, avoiding decisions he couldn't face. Like whether to try again to reconcile things with Kirsty or to accept the defeat of letting it end this way.

He tossed and turned, unable to shake off the feeling that he was *responsible* for Kirsty – and for Jodie, even though he had been old enough to vote.

Funny thing responsibility. Get it wrong and it stays with you for ever. Like the time he'd taken Jodie deer stalking and the boy had been traumatized by the bloody gralloching of the carcase. Hadn't realized how sensitive a twelve-year-old could be. The worry that he might have harmed Jodie's mind never left him.

Alex had loved watching the deer, and accepted the need to hunt them for the cull. He'd identified with the way the beasts used cover to avoid detection, but had been chastened by how often they rewarded the stalkers' patience with a fatal mistake. A warning not to drop his guard against those who were hunting *him*.

It was after three a.m. when he finally nodded off. Then at six-thirty the alarm went. He staggered from the bed to make himself a mug of tea. There was much to do still.

He'd telephoned Kirsty's brother last night to say he'd be away for a few weeks. Told him about the redundancy, but not about Bosnia. Just said he was going to London to look up old friends. Better to keep it vague. Old habits – born out of twenty years in hiding.

There was a train at twelve-thirty that would get him into London at five p.m.. Had to get everything sorted by then.

He opened the refrigerator. Kirsty kept it well stocked. Eggs and bacon should get him going. Hadn't often cooked his own breakfast. She'd seen it as *her* job.

After he'd eaten, he showered, dressed and packed a couple of holdalls with the few things he thought he'd need. Warm clothes, his walking boots and a strong torch. Moray had said to bring a sleeping bag. The only one in the house had been Jodie's. Couldn't bear the thought of using that, so he resolved to buy a new one in London.

He phoned the local taxi company and booked a car for eleven-thirty. Then he sat at the kitchen table with a notepad and pen. His first letter was to the firm where he'd worked for twenty years, accepting their terms and telling them he'd not be back. Citing personal reasons for his sudden departure, he asked to send best wishes to his colleagues and for the redundancy cheque to be paid into his bank.

Then he took another sheet.

Dear Kirsty . . .

He sat for ten minutes, unable to write. What should he tell her? That he loved her? True enough, even if he'd never been *in* love with her. That he wanted her back? That was the hard part. He wasn't sure it could work again.

41

He screwed up the page and threw it in the basket.

He wrote cheques for the handful of outstanding bills, found some stamps for the envelopes and took the letters to the box a short distance down the street. On the way back, a neighbour who'd been Kirsty's closest friend popped her head out to ask how things were. He told her he'd be away for a few weeks, asked her to keep an eye on the house, and said she should help herself to the contents of the 'fridge.

The car came five minutes early, but he was ready. With a lump in his throat, he didn't look back as they headed west along the coast towards Edinburgh.

At Waverley Station, police were putting up posters of the thirteen-year-old girl who'd been murdered nearby. A woman sergeant with a clipboard asked Alex if he'd been in the area the previous week. He shook his head.

He bought a one-way ticket to London Kings Cross, a newspaper and some sandwiches. Having breakfasted so early, he was hungry again.

Then, one important call from a pay phone to an address he'd never known, where MI5's 'C' Branch ran the minders who kept an eye on his back. He'd put off ringing them until now, knowing they'd urge him to stay where he was and not break cover.

'Don't think it's a good idea, this, Mr Crawford,' the voice at the other end told him. 'Understand your predicament, but you'll be on your own. We can't keep an eye on you if you're moving around all the time. Haven't got the staff.'

'You think the risk's that great any more?' Alex queried.

'File says you're still current. Tell you what, give me another ring from London before you leave the country would you?'

Then he found a window-seat in the smoking section and settled down for the journey.

The train pulled out five minutes late. He stared out of

the window watching the Lothian landscape that had concealed him so hospitably for twenty years, slip past with increasing speed.

His eyes moistened, his heart ached with a deep sadness. If only he could wind back the clock . . .

Beyond the border, he slept, his overstressed brain lulled by the rhythm of the wheels.

He'd not been to the capital for twenty years. He'd expected change, but the crush of traffic and the sullenness of the packed Underground came as a shock.

Born and brought up in London, his roots were there, although the Security Service had done its best to cut them off. They'd stopped him attending his father's funeral ten years ago. *The IRA will be watching* . . .

Died just a few months into retirement, after life in a smoke-filled broker's office selling insurance. Consoling his mother had been left to a secret meeting in Birmingham two weeks later. Then last year *she* had died . Didn't hear about it until after the funeral . . .

He found his way to the Bed and Breakfast in Acton where Moray McFee was staying, a house that smelled of dead air and bacon fat.

McFee was waiting for him in the TV lounge, a short, stocky man in his mid-fifties with crinkly auburn hair, thinning on top.

'Welcome, welcome,' he said. 'Can't tell you how delighted I am.'

He hardly knew the man, but it felt like being greeted by an old friend. A friend in need . . . Both in that category, he suspected.

'It was good of you to remember me,' Alex replied.

After settling his bags in his room and washing off the grime of the journey, McFee took him to a pub. Alex had a thirst and went for bitter; McFee drank whisky.

'Let me fill you in about Bosnia Emergency,' he began,

pulling out a pipe and thumbing St Bruno into the bowl. They'd settled at a corner table. 'It was set up by a guy called Major Mike Allison who'd served with the UN in Bosnia and then got made redundant under the defence cuts. He used his gratuity to get the charity running.

'An old army contact found him a disused warehouse in Surrey. Then he recruited volunteers, many ex-military, or army wives. They collected old clothing and stuff. He's also got drug companies to give him medicines nearing their sell-by dates, that sort of thing. And with money raised through appeals on local radio he bought baby food and disposable nappies at cost price.

'Then he got really lucky. Inherited a couple of old bread vans from one of the big bakeries. Just needed a few new parts, and they were fine. What happens is the volunteers at Farnham stuff one of them with goods, then we drive it down to Italy next week and over the ferry to Split in Croatia. Then, because the vans can't make it on Bosnia's roads, we transfer the gear to an old Bedford four-tonner for the drive up to central Bosnia. Mike supplies body armour and life insurance. I've checked it by the way and it's good. He pays for food, drink and accommodation, but that's it. The rest of your reward's in heaven!'

Body armour? Insurance? The realities of what he was in for suddenly sank in.

'You make it sound a bit like a scouts' outing, Moray,' Alex joked, awkwardly. 'But it looks terrifying on TV. How dodgy is it?'

'Not for the faint-hearted, d'ye ken!' McFee answered. 'But you'll be fine. It's dangerous, but just keep reminding yourself that there are hundreds, thousands of aid workers, UN people, even journalists going in and out all the time, and most of them survive okay.'

'Did you get shot at?'

'There's shooting going on all over the place, but it's

not often *at* you. I'll tell you something though; it's what they call a "sharp learning curve" out there. I've just made the one trip – with Mike Allison, but by the time I got back here again, I felt like I'd done an assault course.'

'And passed, I take it.'

'Aye,' he laughed. 'Hope so. You'll find out in a few days' time!'

Alex told McFee he had to take a leak. The pub had filled up. He had to elbow his way through to reach the toilet.

When he returned he saw McFee talking with a young woman. He thought he recognized her as one of two tarty creatures who'd been sitting at a table near them. As he approached, the girl saw him and moved towards the door.

'Who's your friend?' Alex asked.

'Oh, er . . . just a local lass,' McFee answered, avoiding his eye. 'There's a few of them collecting clothes for Bosnia Emergency. I was chatting them up the other evening, regaling them with tales of my exploits out there, and they've got pretty keen. You know, if you tell people about the suffering in Bosnia they usually want to help.'

'Good for you,' Alex answered. For some reason he sensed McFee was lying.

Later, back at the boarding house, they watched the evening news – fresh fighting between Bosnia's Croats and Muslims in the town of Gorni Vakuf, houses ablaze, women and children running for cover, and UN soldiers battened down impotently.

'We drive through that place on the way up to Vitez,' McFee commented.

The pictures were scaring, but Alex felt excitement too. He was about to return to the thick of things after two decades in a backwater. His veins buzzed, just as they had on the troubled streets of Belfast in the nineteen-seventies.

He turned from the screen to find McFee staring coldly at him. Suddenly he sensed he was being used, although he didn't know how.

'No problem,' McFee muttered, flashing a grin. ' "*Nema problema*" as they say out there.'

The bulletin ended and they decided to call it a day.

In the unfamiliar bed, sleep still proved elusive, his mind haunted by Jodie's face dangling at that impossible angle in the trees.

He heard every train which ran nearby. Then around one in the morning they stopped. He was on the verge of sleep when he heard the click of the lock on McFee's door just along the landing. A loose board creaked as the Scotsman made his way downstairs, then another click as the front door opened and closed.

Odd man, Alex thought. He must have dozed off after that, because he didn't hear him return.

Frankfurt, Germany

Martin Sanders ambled down the long, anonymous concourse of Frankfurt Airport, looking forward to the prospect of a couple of days in Germany. Many of his formative years had been spent in the cat-and-mouse world of Berlin, and he'd had a spell as liaison man for the Secret Intelligence Service at the British Embassy in Bonn.

His flight from London had arrived on time. Carrying just hand-baggage he joined the line filtering through passport control, then headed for the exit. Sanders was fifty-two, fair-haired and wore a grey business suit. He had the broken nose of a rugby player. Instinctively he mingled with other, similarly dressed travellers and walked at their pace.

Years of good SIS fieldcraft.

At the car hire desk he told the girl he wanted to upgrade from the VW Golf that he'd booked, to a Renault Espace. She seemed rather tickled by his story that his wife and young children were joining him on the trip at the last minute. Englishmen, in her experience, usually came to Frankfurt to escape their families and visit the sex-shops.

'They're on the next flight,' he explained when she looked past him for some sign of them.

'Second family,' he shrugged as her eyes suggested he was rather old to have small children.

Driving out of the airport, he turned onto the Autobahn A3 in the direction of Würzburg.

Martin Sanders had no family. He was a bachelor. But he was attending a meeting of the Ramblers, a select, highly secret international gathering. Just four intelligence men in attendance, one of them had the task of renting an Espace or a Previa. This time it was his turn. Doing a last minute upgrade reduced the risk of anyone doctoring it beforehand.

It was Rudiger Katzfuss who'd made the hotel arrangements this time. Every six months when the four met, they took turns to play host in their own country. The last time in Germany had been two years ago; Sanders remembered how their French colleague had complained about the sweetness of the Rhine wine. This time Rudiger had chosen the Franken region because the wines were dry.

Like many a businessman whose work is deadly serious, when away from home the Ramblers felt they had the right to 'play' a little. Modestly – these were cautious men – but a glass or three and good food somewhere pleasant helped create the bond which would be vital in a crisis. Even if their governments fell out over foreign policy, it was important that the four intelligence services kept contacts sweet.

Autobahn driving was the one part of the process Sanders didn't like. Narrow lanes of traffic moving excessively fast. Rudiger had faxed a map showing the way to Sommerhausen.

There was a newcomer to the group this time, Jack Kapinsky of the CIA, who'd taken up the job of Director of the European Division. Sanders had met him three times before. A dry character who drank cold tea. A man eager to make his mark.

Taking the Würzburg exit and heading south, the ground rose sharply to the left, hillsides combed with neat lines of vines still just visible in the early evening gloom.

'One of Germany's best-kept secrets' is how Katzfuss had described the region. Sanders was surprised Germany had *any* secrets left after the Cold War penetration by moles from the East.

The signpost to Sommerhausen led him into a pretty, red-roofed wine village of grey, yellow and half-timbered houses. Along the narrow main street, locals carried home shopping and tourists strolled, glancing at menus in the Weinstube windows which glittered in the dusk. Third turning on the right, Katzfuss's note had said. Sanders eased the Espace down a narrow lane.

The Gästehaus zum Mönchen had been chosen for its inconspicuousness. A modern building, but in traditional Bavarian style, with a dozen small bedrooms, it was cheap and simple – a room with breakfast. The couple who ran it expected to see little of their guests.

Rudiger Katzfuss was waiting in the tiny reception area, a big man with a face so deeply lined it looked crumpled. Katzfuss was Director for Europe with the BND, the Bundesnachrichtendienst, Germany's secret service.

'*Mein lieber Martin!*' he purred, grasping Sanders' hand.

'Always first to arrive. You're so efficient. I think perhaps you are secretly a German . . .' Then he roared with laughter.

'I've been many things, Rudi, but not that. Not yet,' Sanders chuckled.

The Ramblers' cover story was that the four men were partners in international marketing, each managing an office in his own country. They only met twice a year, so used the occasion to relax, taste wine and explore new countryside.

Sanders filled out a registration form with the usual false address. They would pay cash for all their bills.

He took his key from the manageress and declined her offer to show him upstairs.

The room was clean and plain, walls papered in featureless beige, a pine wardrobe and matching bed covered in a plump, white linen *Federbett*. Sanders hung a pair of trousers in the wardrobe, had a quick wash, then heard a tap at his door. He let Katzfuss in.

'You have everything you need?' Katzfuss asked. 'Small, but functional – are those the words, I think?'

'Your grasp of English idioms is faultless, Rudi,' Sanders answered. 'But if you're offering extras, what about a popsie!'

Katzfuss raised an eyebrow. The word had beaten him.

'Never mind . . . ,' Sanders smirked. 'What's the plan this evening?'

'Well, I think that when the others are here, there is a *wery* nice Weinstube where we can start. And then dinner. I have booked us for eight o'clock.'

Marcel Vaillon of the Direction Générale de la Sécurité Extérieure turned up next, a stocky man, going bald; then Jack Kapinsky, tall, thin and bespectacled, minutes later. By the time everyone was settled, it was after seven.

They left the hotel together, glad of their coats. The

air nipped. The village smelled of wood smoke and cooking, the place busy with weekenders from the cities.

In the Weinstube Kapinsky removed his glasses to polish them. They'd steamed up, coming in from the cold.

'I'll take a coffee, thanks,' he replied, when asked what he wanted to drink.

'That can be bad for the liver, you know,' Vaillon remarked.

'I'll risk it,' the American replied. 'Now, Rudi, what've you got fixed for us? Is this the hottest spot in town?'

'Almost! I told them we would eat here this evening, but tomorrow we can be somewhere other, if you like.' Katzfuss spoke English with only a slight accent. 'In this part of Germany the food is supposed to be good.'

A look of disbelief creased the round face of the man from the DGSE.

There was no official language for these gatherings, but with two English-speakers always present, theirs was the tongue that dominated.

Relations between their four agencies were rooted in suspicion, but since the end of the Cold War, they'd discovered a new common cause – a wish to preserve the ability to act quickly and independently when the need arose, free from the dithering of politicians.

They believed a myth had arisen in the minds of the general public that the end of the Cold War meant the end of the threat to the West. Governments were using it, they felt, as an excuse to cut budgets and curb their powers with demands for greater accountability.

So the Ramblers had been formed as a bypass to the political process. A group that could take action in the interests of their joint national security, without the politicians being told anything about it. Direct action – such as assassination.

Secrecy was all. Their meetings were never minuted. The existence of the group was known only to the chiefs of each nation's intelligence service and the four representatives themselves.

Jack Kapinsky fiddled apprehensively with his cup of unpleasantly bitter coffee, his glance flitting between the faces of his more relaxed colleagues. He barely knew these people yet his brief was to trust them and agree a plan that could get him jailed if its details were ever made public.

This at a time when some Congressmen were demanding the CIA be disbanded for incompetence . . . Not the wisest moment to get involved in dirty tricks, he'd suggested. His Director had countered with a quote from Edmund Burke – *the only infallible criterion of wisdom is success*.

Rudi Katzfuss had left little to chance in the process of ice-breaking which this first evening was intended to accomplish. The Gasthof was renowned for its cooking and its *Gemütlichkeit*. He ordered two flat-sided bottles of Frankenwein so their tasting could begin.

'They call these *Bocksbeutel*,' he explained. 'They say the monks who made the wine found this shape easy to hide under their cloaks. You must try the Müller-Thurgau and the Sylvaner. The earth here is *Muschelkalk*. You know what is that?'

He was met by frowns.

'From the mussel. Millions of years ago this land was under the sea.'

'Instead of prattling on, Rudi, why don't you pour the bloody stuff . . .' Sanders remarked. 'I don't care how pretty the bottles are, wines are for *drinking* . . .'

Katzfuss peered at the labels and chose the one nearest.

'First the Müller-Thurgau, I think . . .'

He filled the four glasses.

'Tastes great,' Kapinsky announced.

'*Aimable*, but I prefer Chardonnay,' the Frenchman commented.

51

The waitress brought menus and the food followed swiftly. Even Vaillon was satisfied. Soon the conversation veered to politics.

'You know, I can't understand why our system allows so many dough-heads into the White House,' Kapinsky exploded. 'For a sophisticated democracy we've had some pretty ignorant presidents. And the one we've got now . . .' He shook his head in despair. 'He couldn't even find Bosnia on the map . . .'

'Nor can most people,' Sanders remarked curtly.

'Okay. But this creep is on a learning curve so steep it's almost vertical. European history is not his strong point. We keep showing him the mess you guys have got in over Bosnia and tell him America won't do any better. So, what does he do? Gets involved – then backs off. Just one more indecision for the *New York Times* to write about.'

'We call that "learning on the job". That's the British way of doing things,' Sanders offered.

'But he was strong on war crimes,' Katzfuss added. 'He backed the UN tribunal in the Hague.'

'Waste of time,' Sanders snapped. 'Might get a few tiddlers, but the big fish'll end up running the place.'

'It's the feel-good factor,' Kapinsky continued. 'Makes the politicians look as if they're doing something. Kids the voters.'

'I'll tell you something about the Hague,' Sanders added. 'They're hardly up and running there and already getting cheeky. We got a request from them yesterday. Do we have someone we could send to Bosnia to do a bit of detective work? I ask you.'

'Tulici?' Vaillon checked. Sanders nodded.

'Pictures on the television . . .' Vaillon shrugged.

They knew what he meant. Europe's policies on Bosnia had been driven by public reaction to TV news broadcasts.

The conversation drifted dangerously towards the sort

of gossip that shouldn't be overheard. The place was too public.

'Shall we call it a day,' Sanders suggested. 'Make an early start in the morning?'

Those with brandies drained their glasses. They settled their bill with cash, then the four headed back to the hotel. On the way Kapinsky stopped at a phone box to ring Washington. Not to discuss Bosnia – hardly a serious matter for intelligence agencies – but for an update on the real nightmare preoccupying the Agency.

Iran – poised to acquire an atomic bomb.

The morning dawned bright and dry, although rain was forecast.

At the breakfast table, Katzfuss ostentatiously spread out a walker's map of the neighbourhood.

'There is a path that will give us good views and take us to a fine *Kneipe* for lunch.'

They were all dressed for the part in hiking boots, thick socks and warm clothes. The overnight frost had been heavy.

Sanders went outside to warm up the Espace. It was a ten-minute drive to the start of the 'ramble'.

The CIA man was last to climb into the vehicle.

They didn't talk as Katzfuss navigated. Mist clung to the valley of the River Main which looped round the hills and the vineyards. A pale sun struggled to burn it off.

Soon they were at a small Schloss reputed to produce the best local wine. There was a car park for visitors.

'If there is time later, we can *wis*it here,' Katzfuss gestured.

The path began as a farm track leading diagonally up a southwest facing slope, terraced with vines. The winter pruning had been done and the plants looked stunted and dead.

They walked for five minutes. Then the path levelled

out and began a gentle descent, the sun, where it pierced the mist, glinting on the river below.

'Okay, gentlemen. I guess we should start our business.' The CIA man was tense, finding it hard to reconcile the informality of the setting with the seriousness of their purpose.

Katzfuss glanced round. No one else about, crazy enough to be walking this early.

'You know the agenda,' Rudi began. 'As chairman, I think best I report you first about *Schwarzes Gold*.'

'Thursday's arrests in Berlin?' Sanders checked.

'*Ja.* Exactly. Two Italians caught with four hundred grams of Plutonium 239, which was eighty-five per cent pure.

'As you know, this was a trap by a BfV agent pretending to be from the Middle East. The Italians had Mafia connections in Russia.

'The aim was to learn if such material is possible to buy . . . We know now the answer is yes. And that it came from a Russian laboratory, Chelyabinsk-70. The scientists there have not been paid since last year.

'We don't know how much can be bought, or if it is enough for a weapon. And the BfV don't know who wants to buy it – apart from themselves,' he added wryly.

'Yesterday the *Kriminalpolizei* made a press conference, and the German government asks Russia to have stronger control over these materials.'

'Sounds like your boys have been having a bit of fun,' Sanders told him. 'If MI5 pulled a stunt like that, there would be howls of protest in parliament.'

'I think that same noise is just beginning here . . .' Katzfuss confessed.

Jack Kapinsky held out his arm for them to stop. Walking and talking was not his scene.

'Look, let's discuss this in the van. I've had enough scenery. And there's something big we've got to decide on.'

They turned and walked back the way they'd come.

'And I'll tell you something,' Kapinsky continued, 'when the Russians trade seriously in this stuff, they won't do it through Germany, particularly after all this high-profile police activity.'

Back at the Espace, Sanders wrestled with the floor clips and spun the two front seats round to face the rear two. Then he unfolded a small table. Their conference room was ready.

'Now look . . . *we* have something new on this nuclear business,' Kapinsky explained.

He had their full attention.

'First, let me say that in Washington we don't believe those labs like Chelyabinsk will leak enough material to feed a bomb programme. We don't believe either that there's a terrorist organization out there able to make a bomb from the sort of stuff your guys picked up in Berlin, Rudi.'

They had one of the windows open for ventilation. Far away they heard a tractor start up, and to their right a flock of pigeons took to the air startled at the sound.

'The people chasing Russian plutonium are the same ones who've been trying to produce their own stuff for years,' Kapinsky continued. 'Iran, Iraq, Libya, to name but three. And what they've got their eyes on is all those warheads being taken apart under the disarmament agreements. There are two thousand a year being dismantled, and all that plutonium's just being put on the shelf. You can't destroy the stuff. At Nizhnaya-Tura and Svatusk and Penza there's enough for thousands of bombs.'

'That of course we all know,' Katzfuss chipped in defensively. 'And in principle that must be the greatest danger. But in the BND we believe the risk of that material getting on the market is . . .'

'It's minimal,' Sanders agreed. 'Jack, you know that too. The 12th Main Directorate has those places stitched as tight as a duck's arse. For plutonium to leak from there you would have to have a total breakdown of military authority in Russia. I mean, they've plenty of problems, but we're not seeing anything like that yet.'

'A few days ago, we would have agreed with you . . .'

Kapinsky's words floated before them like a mine.

'We've just learned that the Iranians think they've cracked the problem.'

'*C'est incroyable!*' Vaillon spluttered. 'What source do you 'ave?'

'I don't know that. *Humint* of some sort. But it's grade one.'

'What exactly *do* you know?' Sanders asked.

'The Iranians believe they're in contact with a group of middle-ranking Russian officers who control security at one of the storage sites. They say they can supply twenty kilos of ninety-three per cent Plutonium 239.'

'Jesus wept!' Sanders breathed.

'I am not the *technologue*,' Vaillon ventured. 'What does that mean?'

'Sufficient for maybe four bombs . . .' Katzfuss explained.

'And what is the price?' Sanders asked.

'One hundred million dollars.'

'The Iranians will never pay that much!'

'Maybe not. But that's how much the Russians are asking. Foreign bank accounts, the lot.'

'How do they plan to do it? Twenty kilos? That's a hell of a lot to handle.'

'We don't know the plan,' Kapinsky explained. 'Only that the Iranian who is running the show is due to meet the Russian go-between pretty soon. The Russian has to show a sample to prove it is from a warhead stockpile.'

'Where's the meeting to be?' asked the Frenchman.

'That's the trouble. We don't know that. Not yet. We think maybe somewhere in the Balkans. Bulgaria, Romania, who knows.'

The mist had cleared but the sun retreated behind a cloud. Across the valley they could see the first streaks of rain.

'Have you talked to the Russians about this?' Vaillon asked, uncertain how much co-operation they could expect.

'We're doing it now,' Kapinsky answered. 'I know what they'll say; that their security measures are as tight as they can be and such a leak of materials is impossible.'

The tractor they'd heard earlier appeared on the brow of the hill behind them and approached rapidly.

Katzfuss opened an attaché case and handed them each a small schnapps glass. As the tractor slowed to pass their van, they raised the glasses in a toast to the driver. He mouthed the word *Prost!*

When the tractor was gone, the four bunched together again.

'The Iranians have been flirting with nuclear power for thirty years,' Kapinsky continued. 'When the Shah had control he launched a thirty billion dollar civil programme that would give him plutonium as a spin off. That idea died when the Mullahs came in. The two plants being built at Bushehr were abandoned, and then in 1987 the Iraqis bombed the shit out of them just to make sure.

'But in eighty-nine, Rafsanjani said Iran couldn't ignore the reality of nuclear power. He meant military power. Since then they've set up a cadre of technicians at the Nuclear Fuel Cycle Research Centre at Isfahan. And they've built a secret weapons development centre near the Caspian Sea at Moallem Kelaieh and another in the desert near Yazd.

'Our source is very close to the top. The man who's made the breakthrough with the Russians is a Dr Akhavi. Speaks Russian and did a year in Gorky in nineteen-ninety.

'Akhavi's connections are entirely personal. The guys

in the Russian military who claim to be willing to supply, know him and no one else in the Iranian hierarchy. He's the only one they trust.

'Our proposal is this – remove Akhavi from the equation, and the whole deal should collapse.'

Sanders stroked his chin. He knew what was coming next.

'My people in Washington believe that if some way can be found to stop this trade, we should take it,' Kapinsky declared. 'My chief wants *us* to agree a plan. A plan to eliminate the problem.'

They all knew what that meant.

Murder.

Something they hadn't involved themselves in since the Iraqi Supergun affair.

'We'll need a lot more information,' Sanders stated blandly. 'What are you proposing, Jack?'

'We don't have a proposal. I guess that's for the four of us to work out. But it seems to me if we eliminate Akhavi *and* the Russian go-between, we've won.'

'For this time,' Katzfuss commented. 'As long as there is a market, there will be others.'

'Oh, sure. The long-term solution lies with the Russian military keeping the stuff locked up. We're just in the business of crisis-management on this one. But the immediate crisis is that Iran looks dangerously close to a deal.'

They sat in silence for a while, staring out of the windows.

'You trust your source a hundred per cent?' Sanders asked.

'I guess.'

'But you've got nothing from the Russian side?'

'Nope. You neither?'

The three Europeans shook their heads.

'You think you'll get notice of when and where this meeting is to take place?' Sanders queried.

'If we don't, then we can't even start anything . . .' Kapinsky shrugged.

'Quite.'

'Our hope is that we would get maybe two or three days' warning. What we have to do is set someone up who can move fast. A freelance. Someone who'll do it without asking why, or who's paying.'

'Always remembering the Ramblers' eleventh commandment . . .' Katzfuss warned.

Kapinsky frowned, not understanding.

'Thou shalt not get caught . . .' Sanders explained.

Five

The breakfast news on the television at the Acton boarding house reported more fighting in Bosnia and the death of a French photographer, killed when his Land Rover was hit by an anti-tank rocket.

Alex expressed some concern but McFee assured him it wasn't as bad out there as it looked.

They were leaving early the following morning. McFee was to drive them to Farnham, and leave his car at the warehouse. Then they'd collect the van filled with supplies and be on their way to Dover, the Continent and Bosnia.

Alex had been introduced to Major Allison on Saturday. The Surrey epicentre of Bosnia Emergency's activities had been chaotic, but impressive. Stacks of old clothes, tinned food and basic medical supplies being sorted into boxes by a handful of volunteers. The place throbbed with goodwill. Allison had shown Alex photographs of the villages and villagers they'd helped.

The warehouse was on an industrial estate, deserted at weekends. Alex had never driven anything as large as the former bread van he and McFee were to take to Split.

McFee, who for some unexplained reason had acquired a Heavy-Goods Vehicle licence when he was younger, showed Alex the ropes.

'By the time we reach Ancona, you'll be an old hand,' he'd declared.

'What about a licence?'

'Ach . . . tell them it's in the post.'

Less than twenty-four hours to go, and Alex felt far from prepared. He still had to buy that sleeping bag. But first there was a phone call to make.

The voice at 'C' Branch answered at the second ring.

'Ah! So pleased that you called,' the man wheedled. 'There's someone upstairs who's very keen to talk to you. Says he's an old friend.'

Alex's heart sank.

Roger Chadwick. It couldn't be anyone else. It was thanks to Chadwick that he'd spent the last twenty years in hiding. They'd gone to the same school and the man had used that flimsy connection to suck him into his world of betrayal.

'I'm not so sure I want to talk to *him*,' Alex growled. Chadwick spelt trouble.

After a slight acquaintance at school, they'd met again on a nuclear disarmament demo in the sixties, quite by chance. Alex had been marching with Lorna Donohue. Chadwick was a new boy in MI5 then, trying to make a name for himself by spotting the anarchists in CND.

'He's booked a table at the Monteverdi Restaurant in Church Street Ken for one o'clock today,' the voice said. 'Is that all right?'

'Oh, I suppose so,' Alex sighed, suspiciously.

'He says it really is essential you meet. Says he owes you a lot and has something for you.'

'Like what?'

'Sorry. There's nothing more. Monteverdi at one. I'll tell him you're on?'

The outside of the restaurant needed a lick of paint. A window box filled with bone-dry earth held the remains of some pelargoniums, cause of death unknown.

He checked the name sign again, then pushed open the door.

'For one, signor?' asked a weary waiter, eyeing his casual clothes and marking him down as a tourist.

'No. I'm meeting someone.'

'Name?'

'Dear boy!' The shout came from the back of the restaurant. A large, dark-suited figure arose from the gloom, flapping a hand at him.

Chadwick had put on weight. A good two or three stones heavier than when they'd last met in Belfast.

'Alex! What can I say . . .?'

He reached out with both hands.

'Roger . . .! It's been a long time. And you don't look a day older,' Alex lied.

Chadwick's laugh boomed out. He examined Alex up and down.

'Sorry if I'm a bit scruffy,' Alex apologized.

'Not at all. But I'm glad you're having trouble with the waistline too,' he chortled, patting his gut. 'The beard suits you, by the way. Gives you the wiry look of a Border terrier. Pulls the birds, does it?'

Chadwick gestured to the chairs.

'Only the nesting kind,' Alex retorted. 'Had to cramp my style, Roger, as you well know . . .'

He stroked his chin.

'Anyway, I think I'll shave it off. Too many grey bits showing through.'

'Keep it. Particularly if you're intending to "come out", as they say.'

Chadwick grinned, then switched quickly to an expression of sympathy.

'So sorry about your son.'

'Stepson, actually.'

'Of course. But I know how you felt about him.'

Did he know? Had he been watching him *that* closely all these years, with those small, conspiratorial eyes behind the horn-rimmed spectacles?

Alex told him about Kirsty's breakdown and then

stumbled into talking about the accident itself, and the sense of guilt that still followed him like a cloud. Hadn't meant to open up like that. Not always a safe thing to do with Chadwick. But he felt better when he'd finished, realizing he'd needed to tell someone.

'It was an accident, my friend. That's all. Not your fault in any way,' Chadwick assured him.

'I know, I know. Anyway, you didn't invite me here to talk about *that*.'

Chadwick pursed his lips.

'Not entirely . . . You know me too well. I do have some business in mind. But later. Later. Let's have a drink and pick something from this magnificent menu!'

It was pizzas and pastas. The restaurant had been chosen not for its cuisine but for the wide gaps between the tables and the muzak which would prevent their voices being overheard.

The waiter delivered bottles of Corvo and San Pelegrino.

'Never cold enough,' Chadwick complained, feeling the wine. 'Never mind. If we drink it quickly we won't notice!'

He filled their glasses.

'Cheers! A toast to . . . to putting the past behind us?'

His eyes seemed to be pleading. Alex guessed this was the closest Chadwick would ever get to saying sorry for the pain he'd inadvertently caused him.

'To the future,' he replied, simply.

They drank.

'So, what are you up to these days,' Alex asked. 'Still in "F" Branch, chasing subversives?'

'What a memory! No. I'm up in the rafters now. Director of something or other. Paper-clips, I think. But I've always kept an interest . . .'

Alex's eyebrows bushed into a frown.

'An interest in your well-being, Alex, that's what I

63

mean,' he growled. 'You did us . . . did your country . . .
a great service twenty years ago, you know.'

Alex doubted that. 'I helped you kill three IRA men. It
didn't exactly stop the war, did it?'

'They were three top-drawer murderers, Alex and
don't you forget it. If their jail break had succeeded,
there'd be even more police and army widows now
crying in their pillows. You paid a heavy price, that's
what's unfortunate about it. And that's why I insisted
"C" branch took such good care of you for the past
twenty years. It was *personal* for me, Alex,' he added,
overtly sincere. 'That's why I knew about Jodie, you see.
Anything new, anything bad, "C" Branch had orders to
tell me.'

Too smooth, too much oil, Alex said to himself.
Chadwick was after something. Better keep his wits
about him, and play for time. He asked Chadwick about
his own family.

'Children both at University now. Amazing how time
passes. And my wife's quite remarkable. Hardly a cross
word in twenty-five years! Amazes me how she puts up
with my life . . .' he added, patronizingly.

The first course came and went and they were into the
second before Chadwick finally turned to the purpose of
their reunion.

'So, you're off to Bosnia, then. To do good deeds,' he
began. 'Nasty place. D'you know where you'll end up
precisely?'

'Vitez.' McFee had shown him the map at the
weekend. 'Where the British troops are based. It's the
safest place to be, I'm told.'

'Exactly, Exactly,' Chadwick mused. 'Sounds all terribly worthwhile and rewarding. And very brave.'

'Don't know about that . . .'

'You always did have a lot of guts, Alex. No false
modesty, now . . .'

He could feel Chadwick slipping the ring through his

nose, just as he had when he'd persuaded him to identify troublemakers on the CND rallies. Just as he had too, a decade later in Belfast.

'Okay, Roger,' Alex sighed, 'what is it you want?'

Chadwick poured the last of the wine.

'Does the word *Tulici* mean anything to you?'

Alex scratched his beard.

'That's the village . . .?'

'Exactly. Forty people massacred there, ten days ago. All Muslims. Mostly women and children. No known witnesses, but the word is that a man called Milan Pravic led the gang of killers. Spelt "vic", but pronounced "vitz", I'm told. He's a Bosnian Croat, vanished without trace, of course. Well . . . the UN War Crimes Tribunal in the Hague want him found and delivered to them for trial.'

'I'm not surprised. Shouldn't be too hard, should it? The place is crawling with UN personnel.'

'They have no police powers, Alex. The UN can't go round investigating, or arresting people. They're there to get the food through. The Brit commander in Vitez has done his best. Tulici is on his patch. In fact he reached the village when it was still burning.

'The local Muslims say Pravic is a well-known psychopath. They're convinced he did it, but the evidence is only hearsay. Not enough for a prosecution.

'So there are two problems, my dear Alex. No accused, and no evidence! And that's where *you* come in.'

'Surprise, surprise! What are you getting at?'

'The Hague Tribunal's asked Britain to help. And when we learned that *you* were heading there, we thought you might be prepared to do your bit to help the nation again . . .'

Alex frowned and narrowed his eyes.

'From your beetled brow I can see you think I'm going to land you in it again,' Chadwick continued, looking a little pained. 'But all you'll have to do is keep your ears open and ask a few questions. That charity of yours takes food parcels all over the place – Muslim villages, Croat villages. They'll have interpreters. People everywhere are *talking* about the slaughter at Tulici.'

'You amaze me, Roger,' Alex declared wearily. 'The last time I helped the nation as you put it, I had to spend the next twenty years in hiding.'

Chadwick narrowed his eyes. 'That was just bad luck . . .'

'Which wouldn't have happened if I hadn't spied for you,' he retorted. 'No. After what I've been through, I can't think of any good reason for helping you out again.'

'Well, I can think of two, actually,' Chadwick retorted. 'One – gratitude for the very considerable resources devoted by your countrymen to keeping you alive for the past two decades.'

'What?'

'And two – because you like the excitement.'

'I don't believe this,' Alex breathed.

'Come on, Alex! You are by nature a *chancer*, you know that. Taking risks – you love it. Let's cast our minds back to Belfast for a moment.'

Alex flinched.

'Nineteen-seventy-three. There you were, an electrical engineer with a good degree and several years of success in industry behind you, and you'd chucked it all up to become a sound recordist with a television news team! Why? Because the idea of running round Ulster dodging bricks, bottles and bullets gave you a big stiffy.'

'Now hang on . . .'

'And that wasn't the only thing that got your willy all hard, was it? Remember the lovely Catherine?' One of Chadwick's eyebrows arched alarmingly. 'Now, *she* wasn't one of those old Belfast bangers the TV crews used to pick up to nuzzle between riots. No. *You* had to choose someone really special, didn't you? Someone so dangerous that every time you bonked her you risked a

66

knee-capping! Catherine McNulty, the bored wife of one of the IRA's most powerful godfathers . . .'

'Okay, okay. But I didn't know that, did I? Not at the start . . .'

Alex felt the ground shifting beneath his feet.

'And then, when your old flame Lorna Donohue turns up, instead of ditching Catherine, you were screwing them both on alternate nights! Talk about walking a bloody tightrope!'

'Oh, shut up!'

He *had* been pretty wild in those days, but he didn't need reminding of it.

Chadwick raised his hands in a truce.

'Sorry. I didn't mean to rake all that up. Come on, I'm not getting at you. I'm not putting the squeeze on. Not on an old friend. I mean, sod it Alex, we were at school together . . .'

He pulled an avuncular grin.

Chadwick had been senior to him and they'd hardly known each other as pupils. By the time Alex left school, Chadwick had already graduated from Cambridge and joined MI5.

Excitement? He couldn't deny it was why he'd gone along with Chadwick at first. Any impressionable eighteen-year-old, asked to help his country flush out hotheads bent on destroying democracy would have got a thrill from it.

'Just thought you'd be interested in helping to get a mass murderer locked up,' Chadwick continued, pithily. 'The last twenty years have been bloody hard for you. Particularly the boredom.'

'It hasn't *been* boring,' Alex protested. However much Chadwick had kept an eye on him, he could have no idea how full his life had been.

'But that's all over,' Chadwick went on. 'The Scottish chapter is closed. Tragic circumstances of course . . . but you're ready to put a bit of a thrill back into your life, no?'

Alex was startled at his bluntness.

'I mean, no one goes to *Bosnia* for a quiet life . . .' he added in exasperation.

'No. Okay,' Alex answered defensively. 'But *I'm* going because I want to do something useful, to help those poor sods out there.'

He regretted the words as he spoke them, knowing they'd propelled him into Chadwick's trap.

For a moment Chadwick's gaze focused above Alex's head, as if searching for a halo.

'Doing something to help, Alex? Don't you see, that's exactly what I'm proposing? Look. Delivering parcels for Bosnia Emergency may stop people dying from cold and hunger. But by delivering up Milan Pravic to justice you'll help stop the revenge killings that are fuelling the whole war. If you do this little thing for us you could be helping millions of people, not just a few hundred.'

This was the way it had always been.

Give us the names of the anarchists or you'll speed the death of democracy.

Betray Lorna's secrets or have the deaths of more soldiers on your conscience.

And now – *help us find a mass killer or you'll be prolonging the bloodshed in Bosnia.*

Chadwick smiled confidently. He knew he'd won.

'But I'm way out of my depth,' Alex protested. 'I don't know the language, the country, the people, the issues . . . nothing.'

'Don't need to. Have a natter with the Colonel when you get there. We'll let him know that you're more than just an aid worker. And then chat to people as you do your rounds. See what comes up. Keep in touch with us. I'll give you some numbers to ring here. You can use the army's communications, I'll arrange that.'

Alex had been suckered again, and he knew it. There

was always something addictive about Chadwick's offers. The chance to be at the heart of things.

Chadwick beckoned and the waiter appeared at the table.

'Large espresso and a Grappa, suit you?' Chadwick asked.

Alex shrugged. He pulled out his cigarettes.

'Why not?'

It was a double answer. To that question and the unspoken one. Chadwick had tickled him like a trout.

Six

The security guard on night duty rubbed his eyes and stepped out of his warm, smoke-fugged office for a last tour of the Faculty for Veterinary Medicine before handing over to the day shift. A light dusting of snow had fallen; he hoped it wouldn't settle because the weekend was coming and he had his in-laws to visit two hours' drive away.

Most of Leipzig's University had seen better days. This faculty of drab, turn-of-the-century laboratory blocks and ramshackle animal shelters had the look of a run-down farm.

Rounding a corner by the Department of Hygiene, the guard stopped in his tracks.

'Scheisse!'

Lights, in the Infectious Diseases Laboratory. Could have sworn he'd switched them off. Certain of it.

He reached the door and tried the handle. Locked. He fumbled with the huge ring attached to his belt, screwing up his eyes to identify the key he needed. He'd left his reading glasses in the office.

He opened up and crept along the corridor.

'Aahh,' he sighed, reaching the lab's glass-panelled door. 'Should've guessed.'

Chief Technician Kemmer. Not yet seven a.m. and the man was there, in his white coat, busy as a rat in a treadmill. The guard shook his head and stomped back along the corridor to the exit.

Poor old Kemmer! Turned up here at all hours, even weekends. They said his wife had died the day before German unification and he'd hardly known what to do with himself ever since.

Siegfried Kemmer's world consisted of pipettes, glass flasks and gas burners, the equipment of a microbiological kitchen. In it, the art of brewing lethal substances had become, to the initiated like him, a matter of routine.

Kemmer opened the incubator and peeked through the inner glass panel at a single Petri dish a few centimetres across. Hands sheathed in surgical gloves, nose and mouth masked, he eased open the panel, extracted the dish and carried it to a safety cabinet. Setting it down beside five flasks of yellow liquid, he closed the cover and switched on the internal fans that kept the bacteria from escaping.

Then he froze. Footsteps in the corridor. His head craned round.

The wheeze of a dry spring and the bang as the front door closed. He turned to the window, terrified someone else had come in early.

He saw the guard walk into view. The man waved. Kemmer acknowledged him, then sat on a stool to let his heart recover.

Siegfried Kemmer had been at Leipzig University for as long as anyone could remember. A pale, bespectacled man, hair the colour of wet sand, his closest colleagues would have found it hard to describe him, if asked.

None of the students or lecturers he served was sure of his age. Few cared. If they had, they'd have discovered he was approaching his pension.

The unification of Germany in 1990 had brought him little joy. His wife was dying and so were all the tenets he'd been taught to believe in.

In 1945, when Hitler shot himself, Kemmer had been

71

a frightened ten-year-old, his mind etched with memories of the suffering Fascism had brought upon Germany. Easy meat for the conquerors from the East who told the vanquished that socialism was their salvation.

He'd accepted its deficiencies and its corruption as the price for living in peace. Until the day the Wall tumbled in 1989, the day that became known as *die Wende* – the change. Then, all the people he'd once respected as knowing what was what, had stood up one after another and announced that the world he'd been taught to believe in was a chimera.

Sweat trickled down Kemmer's forehead. He pushed the spectacles back up his nose. His hands shook.

Setting the chair in front of the safety cabinet, he slipped his hands into the rubber gloves which projected inside like dead men's arms.

He picked up the Petri dish, removed its lid and tilted it towards him. Colonies of the bacillus that had developed overnight stood out as brown blobs against the jelly of agar and sheep's blood on which they'd fed.

Dangerous pathogens were strictly controlled here, but as Chief Technician, Kemmer had unfettered access to the refrigerators where infected blood and tissue were stored. It was his job to provide the students with samples for their diagnosis experiments and to monitor safety.

And the dangers were terrifying. The Institute was in a residential area next to Leipzig's International Trade Fair. A release of anthrax, borne on the wind, could kill thousands.

Siegfried Kemmer was a man in whom the University's elders had put their trust.

A trust which he was now in the process of breaking.

One millilitre of infected cow's blood was all he'd taken. Too small a measure to be registered as missing. He'd done it last night, after the last student had left. Mixed the droplets with the agar and let them incubate overnight at blood heat.

Two nights ago, the plodding predictability of Kemmer's life had been shattered. A man who called himself 'Herr Dunkel' had arrived unannounced and unbidden at his lonely apartment in Leipzig-Lindenau.

Dunkel was a man from the past. A cold warrior who'd worked for the former communist nation's Ministry for State Security. An officer in the Stasi, whom Kemmer had expected and hoped never to see again.

During those post-war years of national isolation, Kemmer had believed the Party's lies about the 'threat from the West'. Believed the capitalists were out to take away his guaranteed home, his guaranteed job and his free health care. So, when Herr Dunkel had first approached him a decade ago, wanting lethal potions to use against the enemies of the State, he'd obliged.

His loyalty and support had been quietly recognized. The fourteen year wait for a new Trabant had been slashed miraculously to months.

But then the world had changed. His countrymen smashed the chains of communism, Kemmer's own daughter joining the thousands cramming Saint Nikolai's Church for the Monday prayers for liberty. She'd been there too on the Leipzig Ring Road, clutching a candle in the procession that had brought down the regime in 1989. She'd wanted her father to join her, but he'd used the excuse of his wife's illness to stay at home. It was fear that kept him there, however. Fear of what would happen in the future to people like him who had supported the lies of the past.

Hands steady in the thick gloves, he picked a bacterial cluster from the gel with a fine wire loop, then lowered it into the first of the flasks. He twizzled the wire to disperse the anthrax bacteria in the yellow liquid, then repeated the process until the growth medium in each bottle had been inoculated. Then he capped each flask with a loose lid of foil. :

He pulled his sweating hands from the cabinet-gloves and wiped them on his white lab-coat.

Five flasks. Five flasks of death.

Kemmer choked back a sob. How could he be doing this evil thing?

He crossed the floor and lifted the lid on the shaker-heater. Then one by one he took the flasks and placed them on the vibrator platform. He closed the lid and switched on.

He removed his glasses and dabbed his eyes.

Not too late to stop this monstrous process. Maybe Dunkel's threats had been bluff. Things were supposed to be different now.

Not for Dunkel, though. He was still working, still murdering for 'someone up there'. Wouldn't say who. But no bullshit about 'ideology' this time. Blackmail had become his only weapon of persuasion.

Kemmer had said 'no' at first. Refused the outrageous request. Then Dunkel had picked up the silver photo-frame from the coffee-table, a picture of Kemmer's wife and daughter in happier days.

'I saw Erika, yesterday . . .'

The words had dribbled from his mouth.

'A fine woman, your daughter. Fine baby too. Grandson is it?'

'Erika?' he'd gasped. A chill finger had run up his spine. She'd moved West when the border opened in '89. Married an engineer in Heidelberg.

'So vulnerable, babies of that age.' Dunkel's voice like slime. 'Accidents happen so easily . . .'

Kemmer's resolve had crumbled. So little left in his life. Just his daughter, his grandchild – nothing must be allowed to happen to them.

Dunkel had promised it would be the last time he would trouble him.

That, Kemmer had resolved, was a promise that one way or another Dunkel would be forced to keep.

Seven

Moray McFee was in the driving seat as they drove Bosnia Emergency's old bread van into the Italian port of Ancona. He pulled confidently at the wheel, hunched forward like a gorilla.

Alex's trepidation at what lay ahead had eased during the journey, his mind distracted by the business of learning to be a truck-driver – nowhere near as simple as McFee had said. Now however, the Adriatic Sea stretched in front of him and the knowledge that war was being waged on the other side set his pulse racing.

The port police waved them through onto the long, broad quay.

'How's that for timing, eh?' McFee purred. 'Ferry leaves in a couple of hours.'

Behind the docks the grey-pink walls of the medieval city rose up, glowing softly in the dying sunlight. To their left lay the terminals, two ferries and a container ship.

They'd been driving for four days.

'I'm bloody knackered,' Alex wheezed.

'Wait 'til you see the road facing you on the other side,' McFee cautioned. He swung the wheel hard left and pulled into a space in front of the main terminal.

'I'll just away in there and get the tickets. Will you keep a good eye on this lot? You know what Italians are like.'

While McFee went inside, Alex climbed down from

76

the cab to stretch his legs and smoke a cigarette, not straying far from their load of survival boxes.

The journey south had been painfully slow. They'd ceased to be strangers, but Alex had come no closer to understanding what made his companion tick. McFee had talked a little about his life in Edinburgh, saying he'd reached fifty-five that summer, and taken early retirement. At the same time, he'd split from his wife. Their marriage had been a formality for years, he'd said.

He'd joked about the similarity of their situations, threatening to paint a sign on the side of the truck saying – *Danger! Mid-life Crisis Inside.*

Alex had begun to suspect there was a perfectly simple reason why he'd been asked along. McFee's life was a mess and having a companion in a similar state made him feel better. The Scotsman, however, made Alex feel uneasy. Something contrived about him. Not a man to confide in.

'All hunky-dory!' McFee announced, clutching the tickets. 'We can drive straight on and start getting the beers down!'

'Sounds good to me,' Alex concurred.

McFee backed the van away from the terminal and drove it over some railway tracks to where the stern of the ferry *Gloria* loomed.

A cursory check of the paperwork by the Italian customs – and they were waved on board. The first vehicle to do so, they drove the full length of the garage deck and parked by the bow doors. Then they climbed to the passenger decks and were allocated a two-berth cabin.

'I hope you don't have any curious nocturnal habits . . .' Alex muttered as they walked down the corridor to deposit their bags. He'd never liked sharing rooms with other men.

'Should have thought of that earlier . . .'

A few minutes later they located the deserted bar. A

harassed steward washing up glasses told them they'd have to wait another half-hour.

Out on deck the air was pleasantly mild, compared with the icy March winds that had buffeted them in the English Channel. Alex hardly needed the thick, green pullover he'd put on.

Behind them to the west, the memory of a sunset lingered on the horizon; ahead, the cathedral on its hill above the harbour floated like a floodlit phantom.

Alex began worrying about Kirsty again. There was something about a sea crossing, about gazing back at the shore that made him think about what he'd left behind.

Still that sense of guilt at leaving her, despite the certainty there was nothing he could have done to get her back. He resolved to phone her brother to see how things were. Maybe there'd be time on the other side.

He shivered. The 'other side' was an unknown quantity.

Diesel fumes rose from the quay as trucks bustled to board. Customs men glanced at their watches. Departure hour was near. Time for them to go home to their dinners.

'A lot of heavy stuff down there,' McFee remarked. 'Some of it's aid, some just commercial. Thing is, life's pretty normal over in Split, as you'll see. Croatia's fine. It's only when you drive up into Bosnia that it gets shitty.'

A bus pulled up on the quay and disgorged a stream of fair-haired men in mud-green uniforms.

'Swedes probably. Or Danes. With the UN. They come over here for a bit of R and R,' McFee explained.

'Does all the aid for Bosnia come through here?'

'Oh no. Not at all. A lot of the NGOs drive down through Austria. And the UN brings stuff in by ship.'

'NGOs?' Alex queried, still struggling with the terminology.

'Non-governmental organizations. Like us. Charities and so on. You'll soon get used to it.'

Patronizing sod, Alex thought. The man had only been here once before, yet he made himself out to be the world's greatest expert.

The last of the trucks was aboard and the loaders began to lift the ramp. Suddenly headlights appeared from behind the terminal, bobbing rapidly towards them. The deck crew didn't notice, until alerted by the frantic blaring of a horn.

A white-painted Toyota Land Cruiser skidded to a halt at the edge of the ramp, the driver leaning from the window waving her papers.

'Typical bloody woman! Late as usual,' McFee sneered. There was venom in his voice.

'Who d'you think she works for? The UN?' Alex asked.

The Toyota driver was a blonde. Alex caught his breath, reminded suddenly of Lorna Donohue. Couldn't say why. Too dark to see her clearly. Something to do with the toss of the head. The woman seemed to be apologizing.

'Probably not UN,' McFee guessed. 'Might be Red Cross, anything. You'll find those dinky little motors all over the place. There's a "designer set" in Bosnia, who drive round in the trendiest off-roaders, wearing immaculate white jump-suits, and are sod-all use to anybody.'

'Hmm. Well, they're letting her on,' Alex murmured. There was definitely something about the woman . . .

'Shall we try that bar again,' he heard himself suggest.

As they headed below, the sea boiled at the stern and the ship shuddered with the rumble of the diesels.

'Oh hell! Look at this lot,' McFee moaned.

The young UN soldiers had got to the saloon first, scrabbling at the bar and coming away with fistfuls of beer cans.

'Told ye they were Swedes! Ah, well, faint heart ne'er won fair lady . . .'

McFee torpedoed the throng of giants. Alex spotted

two unoccupied chairs at a table and made a grab for them.

He studied the faces of the soldiers. Jodie's age, most of them. Some scrubbed and innocent, farm boys perhaps, out of their depth. Others noisy, leery, brought up in a harder school. None drunk yet, but the night was young.

Across the saloon two Italians in business suits pressed themselves against the window, hammering words into their portable phones before the ship got too far from land.

Alex kept a curious eye on the door in case the blonde woman came in.

McFee returned with two cans each.

'They don't run to glasses. Not with this load of hooligans.'

They peeled back the rings and raised the lagers in a toast.

'Here's to a safe trip,' McFee declared.

'And to a useful one.'

'Aye, indeed.'

Alex peeled open a new pack of Marlboros and lit one. McFee fiddled with his pipe.

One more look, that's all he wanted. Just to be sure that in the glare of the lights the blonde did *not* resemble Lorna. That his mind, fazed by the uncertainties ahead, had simply been triggered by a hand movement into seeking comfort from the past.

The sound of reedy singing cut through the growl of the bar. The music of hymns and prayers, coming from the passageway outside.

'Sounds ominous,' Alex remarked. 'Do people know something about this ship that we don't?'

'Sit tight a minute . . .'

McFee weaved through the crush and disappeared. He returned a minute later, grinning.

'Italians. They're sitting in a little circle out there bloody praying!'

'Christ! What are *they* going to Bosnia for?'

'To pray for peace, I suppose. Worth trying. Nothing else works.'

The ship's public address system began to buzz. A bilingual announcement that the restaurant was open.

'Come on,' McFee ordered. 'Grab your tins and follow me. Last time I was at the back of the queue and missed out.'

In the dining room they took their plates of steak, chips and salad to a window table. The pin-pricks of the shore lights were disappearing fast.

Alex half turned, checking faces. The pilgrims or whatever they were had secured an alcove to themselves. Most had brought their own food. Bread was broken and blessed. Men and women with ugly, pious visages.

Then he saw her. In the alcove next to the pilgrims. Sitting with a man. The tilt of her head, the half smile. The cascade of blonde hair.

The shock that it *was* her thumped through his body.

No doubt, even after twenty years. Hair a bit shorter now, but the same magical eyes he'd twice fallen for. The same earnest hunching of the shoulders as she made a point.

Lorna Donohue.

He twisted away from her, blanching with panic. She mustn't see him. Not yet. He'd waited twenty years, but now the moment had come he wasn't ready.

'Hey, what's up?' McFee demanded. 'You've gone grey, man. Are you sick or something?'

Alex waved dismissively.

'Is it the ship? Canna be. It's like a mirror out there.'

'No.' Alex pushed the tray away and shielded his face. 'There's someone over there, someone I know.'

McFee peered past him.

'Ghost from the past, eh? Which one is it?'

'The woman in the alcove beyond the pilgrims. But please don't . . .'

81

'Aha. Blonde hair? Not bad. Want me to bring her over?' he needled.

Alex waved a finger of caution and glared at him.

'I think that means no . . . More of a skeleton than a ghost, eh?'

'We were both eighteen when we first met,' Alex explained reluctantly.

'Oh, a lovely age, a lovely age . . .'

'Don't . . . don't let her see you looking . . .' Alex fussed. 'I don't want her to recognize me.'

'My! What did she do to you all those years ago?' McFee asked, eyes burning with curiosity.

'It wasn't then. It was ten years later,' he added, embarrassed. 'We met again and . . . and it's what *I* did to *her* that's the problem.'

McFee whistled softly, intrigued.

'Naughty boy, were you?'

Alex's mind jumped back to the last day in Belfast. Lorna, eyes smeared with tears, pounding his chest with her fists after she'd found out he'd been two-timing her.

Sure, he'd been naughty, but there were reasons. And if she'd given him half a chance he would have explained them to her. Could have explained the second betrayal too, the one she hadn't known about then. The betrayal that had put a price on his head and must've set Lorna baying for his blood.

At the time, Lorna had been a courier for the IRA's American bankers and had brought cash to Belfast to fund a jail break. He and she had literally bumped into each other at a funeral. *Lorna* had been walking with the Republican mourners, *he* with a TV crew filming it.

When they'd met that second time, they already had a 'past', a teenage romance in which they'd pricked their fingers and bonded their lives in blood. To meet again like that could not be coincidence, Lorna had insisted. It was the 'guy up above, making the breaks for them'.

She'd given him everything after that. Her body, her

soul – and her secrets. She'd told him of the jail break plan.

Then Chadwick had turned up to put the squeeze on him and he'd betrayed her to MI5. Never had the chance to tell her why.

Now, she was sitting just metres away and he hadn't the words or the nerve.

'She's standing up,' McFee whispered. 'Coming this way, with the bloke. No sign she's seen ye.'

Alex felt his neck burn as she passed behind him.

'All clear. I should have one of those sirens they blow when the bombers have gone,' McFee chuckled.

Memories. Painful memories flooding back.

The fractured ribs after McNulty's men had slipped into his hotel room and beaten him senseless for sleeping with the IRA man's wife.

The escape on an RAF Hercules, with Chadwick watching over his stretcher.

The news a day later, that three IRA escapees had been shot dead by the police. Three men killed because of him.

'How's about a wee nightcap?' McFee offered, snapping fingers to wake Alex from his dream. 'Look as if you could do with a dram.'

Alex's mind returned to the present.

'Moray, you're dead right.'

Then he hesitated.

'I suppose you want me to go ahead and check *she's* not in there?' McFee growled.

Alex grinned sheepishly. McFee shook his head in mock censure.

'Some people I know will pull any old trick to avoid their round!' He stood up. 'If I'm not back in one minute, it's all clear, okay?'

'You're a pal!'

Alex let out a gust of a sigh.

'God, what's happening,' he croaked.

Jodie dead, Kirsty gone, and now Lorna. What game were the gods playing? Was this Lorna's beloved Fate at work, or just some perverse, bloody coincidence?

In the saloon some of the Swedish soldiers were worse for wear, ready to make a night of it. All the tables were taken. Alex and McFee leaned on the bar with their whiskies.

'So, what about this lassie of yours then?' McFee pressed, unable to restrain his curiosity. Over his checked shirt he wore a fawn jerkin with pockets. His pipe stem protruded from one of them. He hooked a thumb into another. 'What would she be doing here?'

'Don't know. She was driving that Toyota. The one that nearly missed the ferry.'

'Thought as much. The chances are she's heading for the same place as us, then!' His eyes twinkled.

'You think so?' Alex caught McFee's look. 'You're enjoying this aren't you, you bastard!'

McFee's face split into a grin.

'Well, there's not a lot to laugh about where we're going. And you should've seen your face in there . . .'

'You're an evil sod!'

'Och, come on! You'd do the same in my shoes.'

'Probably.' Alex burned his throat with the remains of the spirit. 'That's it. I'm turning in.'

'What? Are ye no going to talk to her? You'll have to, some time or other.'

Maybe McFee was right. No time like the present. For a moment Alex considered taking a stroll round the ship. Bumping into her casually might be the simplest way to break the ice. But she'd probably gone to her cabin with that man she was with. Tomorrow would be better.

'Not tonight,' he announced. 'Need to get my act together . . .'

Away from the hubbub of the bar, the long, beige passageway to the cabins was silent but for the hiss of the ventilation.

McFee let them in with the key and closed the door behind them. Alex took off his trainers and jeans and climbed onto the upper bunk.

'I suppose you'll be lying awake all night thinking about her . . .' McFee joshed.

'That would not surprise me . . .' Alex sighed, knowing sleep would be almost impossible.

'Waste of time, if you ask me. Still, it's your life.'

'Yes . . . That's just the trouble,' Alex muttered.

'Good night!'

McFee turned out the light and within minutes was snoring softly.

The cabin was on an outside deck, with a window. A soft, grey luminance filtered through the thin curtain. Nearly a full moon. He could hear the swish of the wake. In the ceiling above him an air vent rattled. He reached to adjust it and the noise stopped.

Lorna. Marriage to Kirsty had pushed her to the back of his mind, but she'd always been there.

Chadwick's minders had warned him contact with Lorna could be contact with death. And now she was here, maybe just centimetres away. He touched the partition, imagining for a second she was just the other side, breathing, sleeping – making love even.

He'd been transfixed the first time he saw her, back in 1962. It had been celebration night in a Hampstead pub, a crowd of eighteen-year-olds just finished with school, the wider world beckoning. His attention had been caught by the snick of a billiard ball and there she'd stood, resting her cue, blonde curls tumbling about her face like water over pebbles, blue-grey eyes cocky with confidence.

For Alex it had been like honey to a bear.

He'd soon discovered they were from different worlds. In Lorna's, money was taken for granted. In his own, every penny had to be counted. She was from the sort of old, American stock that had shaped the New World. Alex's ancestors had slipped through life unnoticed.

Living then with her English mother, Lorna had mixed with the Hampstead smart-set of socialist lawyers and academics who rode the nuclear disarmament bandwagon. Alex's circle had been on a different plane where talk was of motorbikes, football and beer.

Lorna had dressed like Ché Guevara, navy beret over her blonde curls, and taken Alex on protest marches. She had also introduced him to some 'angry' friends – anarchists and Trotskyites who favoured revolution through violence. It was *their* names Roger Chadwick had been after. He'd filled Alex's ears with stories about 'people in high places' fearing British democracy could be destroyed by these thugs.

Nearby on the ferry the sound of shouts and doors banging pierced the ventilator hiss. Alex lifted his head from the pillow, straining to hear.

Italian voices. Not hers. He lay back again.

From the lower bunk, McFee's snores turned to grunts, followed by a jabber of gibberish as he talked in his sleep. Sounded like 'chirrup' repeated over and over again. The noise subsided into a mumble and a moan, then suddenly erupted in words that were sharply clear.

'Shuddup! Shuddup will ye!'

Then a sob.

McFee snorted. He'd woken himself up. There was the rustle of bedding being rearranged, then silence. A shutter had opened on some torment in his soul, then closed again before Alex could guess what ghosts had frightened the man.

He returned to the spirits of his own past.

Betrayal, he thought to himself. That's how it had been each time with Lorna. Never a betrayal of *her* though, just of her friends. And there'd been good reasons each time.

Those anarchists were nothing to do with CND.

They'd just wanted to throw petrol bombs at the police. And in Belfast, the men he'd helped get killed – they'd been killers themselves. No reason to be ashamed of what he'd done.

The trouble was, Lorna's hunger to follow the action kept leading her out of her depth. She'd hate to hear him say that, but it was true.

He was remembering so much now. When they'd first kissed, her body was taut as a violin, electric with intensity. He'd had other girls before, but it was Lorna who taught him to love, taught him there was an *art* to touching a woman.

Her breasts had been firm and small, hardly filling the palms of his hands. One night on the sofa at her home, her mother safely in bed, Lorna had taken his fingers and guided them to the moist, warm pip between her thighs that unlocked her ecstasy. He'd come in his pants.

He was becoming aroused at the memory of it.

Bloody stupid to be lying here like this. Should've spoken to her in the restaurant. Should be putting the bad bits of the past behind them and reliving the good ones.

So long ago, yet still so close, so vivid. The perfume of her creamy skin. The half moan, half cry of pleasure, her cheek against his, sticky with sweat, as she came and came under his humping in the Belfast hotel room.

Damn Lorna! For thirty years she had lodged in his soul. She'd warned him she would. Told him she *knew* their lives would always be linked. That one day even, he would weep by her grave.

Load of rubbish. The fantasy of a fanciful mind. Yet, it hadn't been rubbish . . . She *was* still with him.

What would it be when they came face to face again? There was so much to forgive. Too much to forget. Would it be war, or peace?

He turned on his side. Had to get some sleep. McFee's

snoring had subsided to a murmur. The ship was rolling a little. The wind must have got up.

Had to think what to do, what to say. Above all, he had to decide what he wanted to happen.

That wasn't hard. He wanted to turn back the clock.

Eight

The *Gloria* berthed at Split at seven a.m. No breakfast
offered, just a bleary-eyed scramble down to the chilly
vehicle deck. For Alex, making contact with Lorna now
assumed top priority. Pulling on his brown thornproof
for warmth, he peered back through the tightly-parked
cars in the half-lit hold. Then the ramp crashed down
and McFee started the engine. No time to look for her on
board.

They were first off, first to the barrier, but the
Croatian customs officials were not to be hurried. Alex
drummed his fingers, anxiously watching the other
vehicles drive from the ship. On the quayside, trucks
were being separated from cars.

Suddenly there it was, the clean, white Toyota scoot-
ing towards a free-flowing exit.

'I'll be right back . . .' Alex gulped, pushing open his
door and jumping to the ground. He propelled himself
towards the fast-receding Land Cruiser. Then a rough,
official hand grabbed his arm. Alex spun round to
protest, but the policeman reached for a pistol with his
other hand.

'There's someone I've got to talk to . . .' Alex protested, pointing with his free arm. The policeman shook
his head and hustled him back to the truck.

'Shit!'

He closed the cab door. McFee sucked his teeth

noisily. He was slumped low in the seat as if trying to avoid being seen.

'I don't think they appreciate impetuous behaviour here,' he drawled. 'Tend to shoot first . . . And telling them you're in love won't help, either.'

'Fuck off, Moray!'

He saw an arm in a green anorak reach out from the Land Cruiser and take back the passports after their inspection. Lorna's arm.

Shit! Shit! Shit! How stupid not to speak to her last night. Twice in a matter of days he had failed to act when he should have done. The Toyota disappeared.

McFee was anxious. He hadn't done these formalities on his own before.

'Let's hope their wives did the business with them last night . . .' he muttered sourly, as the customs men returned with their documents. 'If they're frustrated they'll insist we open every sodding box.'

They were waved through within minutes.

'This could be our lucky day,' McFee chortled. 'Now all I have to do is remember the way out of town . . .'

At the end of the road from the dock, market traders folded back striped rain-covers from their stalls. To the left a palm-lined promenade edged with cafés and restaurants faced the harbour, golden in the morning sun. Beyond, a marina with its fretwork of rigging.

Split wasn't quite what Alex had expected. No sign that a war raged nearby.

'Pretty, don't you think?' McFee remarked. 'Used to be packed with tourists. Now the hotels are stuffed with refugees.'

They headed out of town, along a wide dual-carriage-way lined with slab-sided apartment blocks. Signposts pointed to the airport.

'All we do today,' McFee reminded him, 'is get everything out of this truck and into the Bedford which is parked at a UN depot near the airport. Need to get you some accreditation too. And some fuel and food. By the time we're done it'll be too late to start the drive to Vitez. Canna risk getting stuck on the mountain in the dark. There's a Lada jeep out at the depot, which we can use as a runabout, and rooms booked in a hotel for us tonight.'

Alex listened silently, miserable at his own ineptitude, his own inability to get life back under control.

Lorna Sorensen had no reason to linger in the Adriatic port. She took the road that climbed from the surreal blue of the Dalmatian coast towards the tortured hills of Bosnia. Her Land Cruiser was stacked with boxes – vaccines and antibiotics mostly.

Lorna shifted confidently through the gears. She'd driven the four-wheel-drive into Bosnia three times for CareNet. Beside her sat Josip, a Croat from Zagreb with a surname she'd never learned to pronounce. He didn't offer to drive; his efforts the first time she'd hired him as translator had resulted in two scrapes within minutes of each other.

To Rescue Children From Darkness – that was the mission statement of CareNet of New England, an organization backed by Evangelical Christians, and directed by a computer freak. Their original intention had been simply to supply aid where it was needed, but the 'statement' was now being interpreted literally. Lorna's mission was to find an orphaned child and smuggle her to America. Under Bosnian law that was an illegal act.

For the first three hours the road north was tarmac, the only hold-up a pause for fifteen minutes at the Croatia/Bosnia border.

Ever since Belfast, uniforms had made Lorna shudder. But if she was scared now as the sour-faced official fingered her American passport, it would be on the way *out* of the country that she'd be truly quivering.

Uniforms. Down the years they'd been the signposts to

the causes she'd embraced. The London police breaking up anti-nuclear protests; the American military committing war crimes in Vietnam; the British soldiers crushing Irish freedom. She'd challenged all those uniforms, but the fear of them was as strong as ever.

Her therapist had told her it was all because she'd had a tyrant for a father . . .

The border guards waved them through. A country at war, Bosnia looked no different at first. Then, the first sighting of a blackened house and further on a couple more.

At Tomislavgrad, a Bosnian Croat bastion much shelled by Serb artillery, huge baulks of timber shielded windows and doors from shrapnel. Men in drab uniforms of green and brown gathered on street corners, faces sallow, eyes that smouldered. She drove past a home-made troop carrier, a slab-sided, steel armadillo, smeared with camouflage.

Lorna turned east to the mountains, their wooded slopes blanketed with snow. Dark, swirling clouds hid the peaks through which they would have to thread their way. Small UN signposts marked this the only route into central Bosnia that was safe from Serb guns, a potholed lane at first that sliced through yellow-green meadows half-flooded with melt water.

Lorna grimaced at the threatening sky.

'We're going to need those snow chains, Josip,' she declared.

The Croat grunted. He supposed she'd expect *him* to fit them.

Lorna shivered. Not with cold but with fear. They were driving into a wilderness where the veneer of civilization that curbed man's nastier instincts elsewhere had long since crumbled.

A squat, gun-toting man in grubby, olive-brown fatigues stepped into their path and held up a rough hand.

Josip cranked down his window.

'*Dobro jutro . . .*'

The Croat HVO militiaman pushed him aside to look in the back of the vehicle.

'Medicine . . .' Lorna announced.

He pulled his head back to eye her. She showed her UNPROFOR pass and tried to smile pleasantly. Not easy. The man and his Kalashnikov looked inseparable, his stare was bloodshot and lustful.

He made a coarse remark to Josip, who laughed throatily. They were waved on.

'Asshole!' Lorna hissed, imagining the innuendo.

A convoy of trucks lumbered down from the mountain towards them, their tarpaulin covers crusted with snow.

'Shit! Look at that!' Lorna said. 'Chains, Josip. Here, I'll help you.'

They pulled to the roadside and grappled with the heavy steel links in the cold mud. Between them it was done quickly. Lorna shivered again – the wind this time. She zipped up her dark green parka and wished she'd remembered to put on long johns under her jeans.

She knew it was mad to keep throwing herself back into Bosnia. 'A misplaced devotion to the underdog', one friend had called it. 'An obsession with good causes', her sister had said. 'Might be a *fatal* obsession one day . . .' Thanks Annie!

But she'd had no choice. Not when the appeal for help had been so direct; not when a child risked being murdered if she refused.

Route Triangle. That's what the UN called this lifeline into central Bosnia. Formerly a narrow logging track, now made useable in all weathers by the muscle and machinery of the British Army's Royal Engineers. The way had been widened with dynamite and diggers, its surface toughened with stones and hardcore.

The Land Cruiser jolted and rattled up the fierce gradients. Controlling the slithering machine took grit and concentration. Lorna enjoyed the driving. It took her mind off the terrors she suspected were to come.

The track climbed through dark forests, their pine branches burdened with ever-thicker layers of snow. A blizzard swirled, forcing the Land Cruiser to a crawl. Soon they were halted by a line of trucks, stationary in the white and brown slush.

'Hell! This is all we need,' Lorna snapped.

'In this weather there will be many stops,' Josip assured her gloomily.

'I hope you're wrong, Josip.'

Melancholy bastard.

'I'm gonna go take a look.'

Her green Goretex boots sank into the icy gunge. She tucked her hair into the hood of her parka and leaned into the driving snow, glad of the thick rollneck she had on under the coat. Diesel fumes from the idling truck engines polluted the wind. Small flags painted on the doors told her the convoy was Danish. Young soldiers in their warm driving seats, plump and squat in body-armour and blue helmets, looked down at the slight, middle-aged woman with amused curiosity.

She reached the rim of the rise where the track curved sharply to the left and down an incline.

'Oh, God!' she breathed.

A dark green bus had slewed sideways across the track. Standing around it were dozens of militiamen, stamping and shivering. A UN tractor had hooked to the front and was trying to pull it straight.

'Shouldn't bloody be on this road in these conditions!'

The voice beside her was Yorkshire. She could still recognize the accent, despite not having lived in England since the age of eighteen.

Under his blue beret the engineer's face was pale apart from the red tip of his nose.

'Who are those guys?' she asked.

'HVO. We build this road so we can feed the victims of their war. *They* use it to get more guns in. Net result? More victims for us to feed. Bloody daft really. If we closed this road the war would stop within weeks.'

'But innocent people would starve,' Lorna reminded him.

The soldier gave her an old-fashioned look.

'Innocent? Who's innocent in this place . . .?'

He stomped across to the tractor, yelling at the driver to watch out that the bus didn't topple on its side. The driver ignored him and with a fierce tug pulled the vehicle straight. A muted cheer rose from the militiamen who piled back inside.

British soldiers. Strange to hear their voices here. Lorna remembered them painfully well from Ireland. Still thought of them as the enemy. Couldn't help herself.

She hurried back to the Land Cruiser.

'Not long now,' she announced.

Josip had wound down the window to smoke. The man was invaluable to her as a translator but nothing else. Like any male, he imagined she had bodily needs which she secretly longed for him to satisfy. She'd seen the calculating look in his eye.

Lorna sat back in her seat to wait. It'd be a few minutes yet before the road would be clear enough to move.

She dreaded the stretch beyond the mountains, where they'd need to don their body-armour. One shattered town after another. Villages whose houses were blackened skeletons. Front lines to be crossed, marked by barriers of land mines. And the risk of some madman tanked up on brandy, taking a shot at her with his Kalashnikov.

At the end of the journey awaited the dead, steel town of Zenica, cold and silent, blacked out by power cuts. She knew what it felt like there; like being in a trap. And the crazy thing was she was spending nine hours battling to get *into* it.

The HVO bus that had blocked their path emerged slowly over the brow of the hill, then crept gingerly past them, the driver grimacing with the effort of avoiding a repeat performance in the slush.

'Okay, guys,' said Lorna, 'let's get this show on the road again.'

Josip finished his cigarette, threw the butt into the snow and wound up his window.

Inside the bus, thirty-seven men slumped back in their seats, rifles wedged between their knees. They'd just come from hell. A fortnight in the icy trenches north of the Makljen Ridge. Two weeks of pounding from mortars and twenty millimetre cannon. Fourteen days and nights preventing the Muslim-led Bosnian army seizing their strategic positions.

Sleep, when it had come in the trenches, had been brief and fitful. Only when exhaustion had so blurred their vision they could no longer shoot straight had they been taken out and replaced with fresher men. Their reward – a respite from the war zone, a few days of R & R.

One man in that bus however had not been in the Makljen trenches. He sat at the back, speaking to no one, head resting against the window, the stare in his eye as cold as the glass he looked through.

His journey had already been longer than the others', and it would take him further. In his case it wasn't exhaustion that had merited a ticket from the battle zone, but an excess of zeal.

Clean shaven, in his early thirties, with untidy fair hair, he had eyes of ice blue and a hawkish nose. Put him in a suit and he could have sold cars or insurance. Put him in uniform, however, and he had killed. Killed again and again. Killed with such relish and with such disregard for the 'civilized' rules of war, he'd become an embarrassment to those he fought for.

Getting him this far had not been easy. The Vitez 'pocket' where he'd served the Bosnian Croat militia was surrounded by Muslims. Crossing the lines had meant hazarding precious assets, but to his superiors getting him out of there had been worth the risk.

He could remember every detail of that day in Tulici. The terror in the old men's eyes, the snivelling of the children, and the off-white flesh of the young woman whose warm but lifeless orifices he'd filled with his seed.

No remorse. How could there be when the killings had been so long overdue? Why pity such creatures after what they'd done to him, his land and his people? What else could they expect after opening their doors to Islam's foreign savages?

'You've played your part, Milan. Time for others now' – that's what the HVO had told him.

Others! Some of those he'd led into Tulici couldn't look him in the eye afterwards. One man who'd been with him there had cracked up. When Pravic had heard the UN were asking for names, he'd had to shoot him dead to ensure no one talked.

He'd left his country once before, along with thousands of others seeking an escape from poverty. Most of the burned houses in Bosnia had been built with money earned abroad. However, when the war here had started in 1992, he'd returned from Germany to fight the Serbs. Then as the months passed, the Muslims who'd once been his neighbours became the new enemy in the struggle for land.

He had a sister living now in the Croatian capital Zagreb. He would stay there until things cooled. Maybe he'd go abroad again for a while.

This war that had started as a scrabble for land

however, was turning into the endgame of a struggle begun centuries before.

He'd be back.

Nine

Dieter Konrad, a one-time assassin with the Stasi, the former East Germany's secret police, was anxious. Time was short. He drove fast up the A2 from Leipzig to Berlin, keeping a lookout for police cars. With enough anthrax in the boot of his Merc to kill the inhabitants of a small town, the last thing he wanted was to be stopped by the law.

The murder he'd been forced to arrange was just seven days away, the location – Zagreb. There was one man, and one man only who had the skills he needed for the killing, and so far he'd not been able to find him.

Konrad was nearly sixty, a slack-faced, weary man too old for this business. It should have ended for him when the Wall came down, but he'd been trapped by his past.

The Mercedes traversed the flatlands south of the Elbe, a landscape of cabbage fields and dead industry. It would be dark when he reached Berlin, and the traffic heavy, but he could still make the meeting with Fräulein Pocklewicz at six.

Gisela Pocklewicz. A Berlin hooker, she alone knew where to find the creature he needed. The man in question had once been her lover and protector. Konrad had never probed their relationship, but he knew her clients were people who got their pleasure through pain.

The woman was one of the last of his old underworld contacts still prepared to take his money. *Dunkel* was the name he used with her, as he had with the scientist

Kemmer in Leipzig. It meant *darkness*. During his Stasi days, the satanic quality of the name had appealed to him.

It had broken Siegfried Kemmer to do him this last service today. Meeting in a deserted wood, the biologist had given him the bottle of bacteria in a shopping bag, his eyes dead as buttons.

Konrad had taken no pleasure in threatening violence to Kemmer's grandchild in order to secure his co-operation. Ideology and duty had worked in the past, but the world had moved on.

One hundred and thirty-six kilometres to Berlin, it said on a road sign, and just five to Dessau, where he had some shopping to do.

When the Cold War ended, so had Konrad's privileged life with the Stasi. Not everything was lost however. He'd skimmed a profit from the money for his missions abroad and bought a house in the Harz mountains. He'd hoped to retire there, to fish and hunt boar, but his wife refused to leave her friends and the opera in Berlin.

Next exit Dessau and the huge D-I-Y warehouse he needed. He swung the Mercedes into the tight slip road. The car park was half full. He pulled in beside a Trabant which wallowed under the stack of goods on its roof-rack.

Inside, he made for the aisles marked Tools and Safety Equipment, looking for protective masks. He prodded through the packaging to reject those that were flimsy, choosing a type that covered the full face, made of soft rubber. He took two from the rack and headed for the tills.

Just before the Stasi headquarters were stormed by East Berliners in January 1990, Konrad had tried to find and destroy documents detailing the murders he'd carried out for his masters. He'd suspected he'd not been totally successful.

For months he had lived in fear of arrest, hiding out at the house in the Harz. One day, walking in the woods, he'd been approached by a tall man he'd never seen before who had a face like crumpled leather. *Schiller* was the code name he'd used. He'd claimed to work for the BND.

Schiller had revealed that amongst the Stasi papers uncovered in Berlin, they'd found enough evidence against Konrad to get him jailed for life.

He had offered a deal. Konrad could avoid prosecution on one condition – to continue to kill, but for *him*.

Konrad had had enough of executions, but prison was no option for a man of his age. He'd accepted.

That had been three years ago. Since then, Schiller had paid him a regular retainer but had made no demands – until a week ago.

The contract was to eliminate an Iranian and a Russian. A poisoning, Schiller had said, because death must occur after the victims had returned to their own countries. It had to be an untraceable murder – something Konrad was skilled at.

He had demanded half a million marks for expenses, and to his astonishment was told he could have it.

Schiller wouldn't tell him who he was acting for, nor why the men had to die. But Konrad read the newspapers. He reckoned he could smell plutonium.

On the Berlin ring road the traffic thickened. It was just before four p.m. He'd made better time than he'd expected. There was one more purchase he needed to make, at a small shop in Kreuzberg. Might just get there before it closed.

He joined the long queues on the Mariendorfer Damm. Berlin had become a building site in the rush to reinstate it as the nation's capital. Diggings pockmarked every crossroads.

He squeezed the car into a small space near the Kottbusser Tor, then pressed a neatly trimmed, false moustache onto his upper lip, using a mirror from the glove locker to ensure it was straight. He slipped on heavy-rimmed spectacles then set off on foot.

This was a quarter for night creatures, the air scented with Döner kebabs. Bars stayed open here until dawn and between open sites razed for redevelopment, tenements were homes for squatters and refugees.

A little further, and the cafés were interspersed with galleries and craft stores. He pushed on the door of a small shop with easels in the window.

'*Guten Abend!*'

A thin-faced young man with a diamond stud in his nose emerged from a back room.

'I wanted an air brush,' Konrad began. 'I telephoned.'

'Of course. Yesterday evening.'

The young man turned to a shelf, glancing back. Not many of his customers wore business suits and overcoats.

'It's for my nephew,' Konrad explained. 'A birthday present.'

The assistant turned back to the counter holding two boxes.

'What does he want to use it with? Inks or acrylics?'

'Acrylics probably. That's quite a thick paint?'

'Well, he'll probably have to thin it, whatever he uses. You'd be safest to buy a few nozzles of different sizes.'

'That sounds best. Can you show me how it works?'

The salesman cut the tape seal with an obscenely long fingernail.

'You attach this can of air to the brush with a plastic tube. Then fill the jar with paint and plug it into the socket at the front. Then you just press the button. Simple as that.'

Konrad picked up the components. It wasn't really a brush at all, simply a precision paint sprayer. But in *his* hands a precision weapon.

'Fine. I'll buy it.'

Back at the car, he drove north again, crossing what used to be the Wall at Prinzenstrasse. More building works. *If there's a gap, fill it* – that seemed to be the motto of the developers.

By the time he'd found another parking space near Rosenthaler Platz it was twenty-past-six. Fräulein Pocklewicz would complain at his lateness.

The bar *Zum Weinberg* had fewer than half a dozen customers, and Gisela was not one of them. He panicked instantly. He was too old for this game. Even the tiniest hitch unsettled him.

He sat and ordered a *Weisse mit grün* – a wheat beer with a dash of liqueur. He sipped gently so as not to wet the fabric backing of his moustache.

Twenty minutes passed before the whore appeared.

'So sorry to be late, Herr Dunkel!' Always formal with a man twenty years her senior whose real name she'd never known.

Gisela Pocklewicz was short and overweight. She had a round face, dark, butch hair and the eyes of a victim.

She asked the waitress for a Coke, then flashed Konrad a smile.

'We're in luck, Herr Dunkel! That's why I'm late. It all happened at the last minute.'

'Go on,' Konrad pressed.

'As you know, I rang Zagreb yesterday, but they had no idea where he was. And I phoned again this afternoon. Then this evening, just as I was coming here, *he* called *me*!'

'Aaah,' he sighed. 'And?'

'He asked what it was about of course, but I couldn't tell him . . .' she fished.

'What did he say?'

'He wants a passport. In another name and another nationality. Says he needs to hide up for a while. Here in Germany.'

She smiled. If this worked out she'd have a reunion with the only man she'd ever come close to loving.

'Did you ask why he has to hide?' Konrad asked, fearing the reason might affect his plans.

'Of course not. Can't trust the 'phone.'

Konrad took another sip of beer. So he wants a passport. Easy enough in the old days, he thought. The Stasi's Normannenstrasse building had housed some of the world's best forgers. He had to get one from somewhere.

Acid burned in his gut. He dared not fail.

'Fräulein Pocklewicz, if we are to find a passport in time, I fear it'll have to be stolen. Can you put the word out?'

She looked pained. She had no intention of taking any more risks than she had to.

'I don't know people like that any more,' she lied. 'I'm legit. I pay taxes. My clients wouldn't like it if they thought the Kripos had their eye on me.'

Konrad wet his lips. He couldn't get used to people saying no.

'I'll do one thing,' she added, seeing his discomfort. 'I'll give you an address to go to. Talk to the woman who runs the house there. Some of *her* girls are thieves.'

She tore the top off a cigarette packet, then wrote down a name and a street number.

'It's not far from here. Sorry, but it's the best I can do.'

'One more thing,' Konrad whispered, leaning forward. 'Tell your friend in Zagreb to send some passport photos tomorrow by air courier. Collect them and give them to me. Tell him if all goes well I'll bring the passport when I join him before the end of the week.'

'And you *will* bring him to Berlin after the job's done?' she asked, doubtfully.

'Oh yes, I'll bring him back from the war for you.'

Ten

Sunday dawned with a steady drizzle smearing the window of Lorna's bedroom. The cold of the concrete floor penetrated the stained, threadbare carpet that covered it. She tried the bathroom faucet to no avail.

And she'd forgotten to fill the tub last night when the water *had* been on.

'You're a shit-head, Donohue.'

Still called herself by the name she'd been born with, even though she'd been married for fifteen years to Rees Sorenson. Nice guy but a mistake.

She pulled the soft nightdress up over her head and dropped it on the bed.

'It's so-o-o cold . . .' she shivered, crossing her arms tightly, hands cupping her small breasts. Nipples like bullets, goose-bumps everywhere.

'Too skinny, that's what's wrong with you . . .' She mimicked the whine of her sister, who was the same height, but at least thirty pounds heavier.

She caught a look at herself in a wall mirror as she reached into the suitcase for underwear. Okay, so what if her ribs did show, at least she didn't have stretch marks. Five children Annie had had. Not a pretty sight in the buff. She and Joe must do it in the dark nowadays.

She pulled on some clean cotton panties, tucking her light-brown pubic curls under the elastic. Then she reached behind her back to secure the straps of the bra.

Didn't really need one, but with Josip around, the less cause he had to misinterpret things the better.

In the bathroom there was at least electricity this morning. She switched on the light, looked in the mirror and pushed at her hair. The good thing about being a little frizzy was that it didn't need a wash every morning. She moved closer to the glass. They weren't going away, those crow's feet beside her eyes and the deeper lines round her mouth. Ought to be flattered that Josip fancied her, she supposed.

Her thin face and high cheekbones went with the small frame of her body. She'd always thought her nose a little too big – wouldn't have minded one of those petite, turned-up numbers. But men liked the strength it gave her face; she'd never been short of admirers. Just a pity most of them weren't her type.

A little warmer in jeans and walking boots, a thick green pullover over her white rollneck, she clomped down four flights of stairs to the dining room. If anything it was even colder there. Josip sat alone at a table drinking coffee, his leather jacket draped over his shoulders. His dark hair was greasy and his jaw grey with stubble.

'Morning,' she said briskly, sitting opposite him. 'Sleep okay?'

'Mmm . . .' he wobbled his head, gave her a look that was intended to smoulder, then smiled. 'Could be better.'

'Is there anything to eat?'

'Some bread. The coffee is okay.'

She glanced round. No sign of a waiter. Warming himself in the kitchen, no doubt. Two other tables were occupied. UN people, she guessed.

Then a girl appeared at her elbow. Lorna ordered tea.

First call that morning was to be at the office of the Co-ordinating Committee for Refugee Problems, run by

106

staff from what was left of Zenica's civil government. It was from there the call had come which had brought Lorna scurrying back to Bosnia.

Not an official message; the bureaucracy would never have condoned it. The proposal had come from a woman called Monika, who'd befriended Lorna last time she was here. It was Monika they now had to find.

The Land Cruiser was empty. The hotel had given them a store-room for their boxes of medical supplies. Lorna had to find out today where the need for them was greatest.

The town looked like any drab east European city except for the lack of cars. What little fuel there was in Bosnia was reserved for the war. The only vehicles moving belonged to the BiH Armija – the Bosnian government army – or to the UN and the aid agencies.

The streets were filled with people, wandering in the middle of the road as if cars had never been invented. Where did they go, she wondered? Nothing to buy in the shops, yet they still went to look. Nothing to drink in the cafés, but they still sat down for a chat.

No sign of Monika at the office, they were directed instead to a refugee centre near the silent steel works that dominated the town with its dust-coated mills and furnaces. BiH soldiers guarded the gates to the plant. Their 3rd Corps had its headquarters inside.

Opposite was a school where the refugees lived behind timber blast-barriers and windows of polythene sheet. They parked in the former playground.

A man carrying a tray of loaves led them down a dark corridor that smelled of boiled vegetables. The power was off again. An old woman shuffled past, holding a plastic bowl, her head covered by a black shawl. Two small children prodded one another in boredom.

In the huge gymnasium every square metre of floor was covered by mats or rugs, each one occupied. One rug, one family. Toothless grandfathers. Widows in black. Mothers, fathers, children, babies.

'Oh, my! This is full!' Lorna exclaimed.

The air smelled of urine and unwashed bodies.

'*Lorna! Lorna!*'

A woman in her thirties with dark, straight hair and eyes that had seen too little sleep grabbed her by the hands. She babbled in Serbo-Croat.

'Monika, hi!' Lorna grinned.

'She says . . . well she says she's glad to see you,' Josip translated simply.

Looking uneasy, Monika hustled them from the gym. She had the frenetic manner of someone for whom the day was always too short.

She led them to a part of the building where a shell had blown in the front wall, replaced now with polythene which bowed and flexed in the wind.

Monika turned to Lorna and spread her hands in despair.

'She says sorry about the room,' Josip explained, 'but we can be alone here.'

The Bosnian woman began talking at length. The only word Lorna could make out was *Tulici* . . . She let her continue for a while before nudging for a translation.

'She say at first they think no survivors at Tulici,' Josip interpreted. 'But when Armija search, they find girl, twelve years, called Vildana Muminovic. She hiding in a cellar. She say she saw her mother being shot, and the soldier who did it was a man she knew. He used to live in next village. She say his name is Milan Pravic . . . Later, Armija bring girl here to Zenica. But then some men come asking about her. Monika think they Croats . . .'

Josip raised an eyebrow. He reckoned Bosnians believed what they wanted to believe.

'Monika think HVO want to kill the girl because she can identify this man Pravic.'

108

Lorna nodded understandingly.

'Where's Vildana now?'

Josip put the question.

'She say maybe take you see her tomorrow. She asks, do you understand she afraid?'

'Sure. But she wants me, wants CareNet to get Vildana out of the country and find a family to look after her?'

More Serbo-Croat. Lorna winced. It was understanding the *way* people said things that mattered as much as the words.

'She asks whether you have plan yet?'

Had to be careful what she said.

'About getting her out of Bosnia . . ? I still have to talk to some people. Finding a family for adoption is no problem however . . .'

'*Nema* adoption . . .' Monika replied, wagging a finger. A flood of words followed.

'She says Bosnian government not allow foreigners adopt orphans, because sometimes they do bad things.'

'Tell her my agency is plugged into a network of Americans who are all top grade professionals, all checked out . . .'

Rain spattered against the polythene wall.

Josip sighed.

'She says be careful. If anyone ask, say it is just so the girl can be safe until war is over. Then Vildana will return here . . .'

Lorna hesitated. A temporary arrangement like that could be harder. Most couples on her network were desperate for families.

'No talk of adoption, then, okay? Tell Monika we understand each other,' Lorna declared. 'But first I must see the girl and find out what she needs . . .'

Tomorrow then. Monika would come to the hotel and they'd go together.

For Alex the drive over Route Triangle was a nightmare. Fog obscured most of the mountain road and a thaw had turned it into a mud slide. Handling the Bedford four-tonner in such conditions had taxed McFee's experience.

Twice the front wheels of the lorry had slipped into a ditch, once perilously close to the edge. They'd travelled with a British UN convoy all the way up from Split. Without help from an army tow-truck, they'd have been stuck on that mountain.

It was on the long run down from the Makjlen Ridge to the contested town of Gorni Vakuf that the engine gave up.

'Fuck! Fuck! Fuck!' McFee screamed. 'Don't *do* this to me.'

'What is it?' Alex fretted.

'It's fucking died, that's what!' McFee yelled, punching the switch for the emergency flashers. He pulled onto the verge.

'Fuel?'

'I don't fucking know.'

McFee got down to the ground. They'd been at the tail of the convoy; behind them just the tow-truck and a Land Rover, both of which halted beside them.

'What's up, mate?' The soldier's chubby face peered down from the truck.

McFee had the engine hood raised. 'Water in the fuel maybe,' he ventured.

A young officer walked over from the Land Rover.

'Can't stop here for long, I'm afraid,' the voice brayed.

A woman's voice. Alex contained his surprise. Blonde hair up under her UN helmet. Horsey but pretty. All of twenty-three, and so bloody confident in this spooky place.

They were near the bottom of a pretty, wooded valley. Could have been Austria, if it weren't for the crump of explosions from somewhere ahead of them.

'Party-time in Gorni,' the lieutenant remarked. 'Supposed to be having a cease-fire.'

'Where are we?' Alex asked nervously.

'Pretty well on the front line. HVO in the woods all around us. BiH in the town about a mile down the road.'

'BiH? That's the Muslims?' Alex queried, still confused by the acronyms.

'Bosnian government army. Mostly Muslim.'

She stepped back and peered up the road with binoculars.

'Pretty vulnerable here . . .' she murmured. 'If you've got helmets to go with your body armour, I should put them on. Corp'l Baker? We've got to move on.'

She strode to the front of the Bedford.

'The convoy's halted down the road, waiting for us . . .'

McFee was squeezing the rubber bulb on the fuel line to drain off the contaminated diesel.

'Hey, Alex. Get us a jerrycan off the back o' the truck,' he called over his shoulder.

'Look, I'll tell the company in Gorni to send a Scimitar up to look after you,' the lieutenant announced. 'But we've got to get on. Let's go, Corp'l Baker.'

'Sorry mate,' the soldier apologized. 'You okay now?'

'We'll manage.'

The towing vehicle growled off down the road, the Land Rover following.

Soon they were alone.

'What a place to break down . . .' McFee muttered.

An eerie silence had descended. Alex strapped his helmet tighter, but it gave him little comfort.

Crack! A rifle shot zinged over their heads.

'Shit! Get down.'

They flattened themselves on the wet grit.

'Where'd that come from?' Alex breathed, his heart pounding.

'God knows. They're all around us here.'

Then they heard a distant laugh.

'Bastards!' McFee swore. 'Fucking playing games wi' us.'

'What the hell do we do now?'

'I don't bloody know. Suppose it depends if the sods decide to come and thieve the stuff out the back o' the lorry.'

They lay still. All they could hear was their own jerky breathing.

'Can't stay here all day,' McFee hissed. He stood up and stuck his head back into the engine compartment. Alex raised himself to a crouch.

Two more rifle shots thwacked overhead like a double whiplash.

'Oh, fuck!'

Both flat on their bellies again.

'I think we're in a wee spot o' trouble here,' McFee panted.

Then from down the road came the growl of a high-powered engine and the slap of track pads on tarmac. Alex craned his neck. A small, white tank with a long, slim gun on its turret sped up the hill towards them.

The Scimitar bobbed to a halt, its Jaguar engine burbling unevenly. Its commander peered from the top hatch at their prostrate bodies, then jerked his head back inside. The turret turned slowly, the gunner scanning the woods through his sight. It swung back and stopped. Then the machine inched past the Bedford, to get an unobstructed view.

After a couple of minutes, a soldier climbed out and crouched beside them.

'They've bogged off,' he told them. 'About six of 'em. Could have been nasty. Looked like they intended to 'ave you. You're okay now. They won't risk getting an HE round up the rectum.'

'God . . . thanks,' Alex croaked, easing himself upright

and brushing the dirt off his coat. He swallowed to wet his throat.

'Problem?'

'Fuel contamination,' said McFee. 'Another five minutes . . .'

'Okay. We'll hang about.'

Alex stood up gingerly. The last time he'd been under fire was twenty years ago – Lenadoon Avenue in Belfast. 'Scares me shitless, this place,' he said.

'Aye, me too,' McFee concurred.

He worked on for a few minutes then told Alex to pour the fresh fuel into the tank.

'Moment of truth,' he muttered, hauling himself up into the cab.

The engine churned, churned again, then rattled back to life.

'Good stuff,' the soldier shouted. 'We'll lead you into Gorni and pass you on to "C" Squadron at the bottom of the canyon. Okay?'

Alex gave a 'thumbs up'.

The Scimitar rotated on its tracks then scooted ahead. McFee slipped the clutch and they were on their way again.

Smoke rose from the centre of town. A shell whistled overhead then exploded somewhere unseen.

'Some bloody cease-fire,' McFee growled.

They reached a crossroads. The Scimitar stopped, and the soldier waved them to the right across a bridge. A muddy river trickled beneath it.

Two figures ran at a crouch across the road in front of them, clutching assault rifles. The truck bumped and jolted over mortar craters.

'Be out of this madhouse in a minute,' McFee muttered through clenched teeth.

The destruction was unbelievable. House after house blasted to rubble, roof timbers shredded to matchwood.

Another right turn and they were into woodland.

Ahead, amongst the trees, another UN vehicle. McFee stopped the truck beside it and wiped his brow. A soldier came up to the window, encased in a thick flak jacket and a blue helmet which almost covered his eyes.

'Convoy went through just a couple of minutes ago,' he shouted. 'If you're quick you can tag on the back of it.'

'When's the next one due?' McFee asked.

'Haven't a clue. Hours maybe. They never tell *us*.'

'Okay, okay . . .' McFee deliberated whether to wait. The next stretch of road was a hangout for bandits.

'Couple of minutes you said, the convoy up ahead?'

'Yeh. Just now.'

'Okay. We'll go for it, eh?' He looked across at Alex for confirmation.

'Up to you. I've never been here before . . .' Alex wished McFee inspired more confidence. He had no idea what lay ahead.

'Aye. That's the trouble . . . The thing is you're not supposed to go up the canyon on our own.'

He had a sudden idea.

'Can you call on your radio and tell 'em to hang on for us?'

The soldier looked doubtful.

'Yeh. I'll give it a try. If it's fuckin' workin'.'

He turned back to his Scimitar, putting a fist up to his ear in a gesture to his signaller.

McFee crashed into gear and they lurched forward. 'Dodgy bit of road, this . . .'

Alex gripped the dashboard as they bounced up the rough track, the band of his helmet squeezing his temples. They were entering a gorge, the road hugging a limestone rock-face, twisting and turning in company with a raging stream.

'With a bit o' luck we'll catch sight of the convoy round one o' these bends,' McFee suggested without conviction.

Sweat broke out on his brow as he wrestled to keep the

114

wheels in the ruts. He was driving dangerously fast. To the left of the track was a sheer drop into the river.

'Is it long this bit of road?' Alex shouted.

'About twenty minutes . . . There's a straighter stretch round the next bend, I think. Should get a bit of a view . . .'

'Whose territory is this? Muslim or Croat?'

McFee was silent. For the first time he looked seriously frightened.

'Have ye heard of the *fish-head gang*?'

Alex felt a hard lump in his stomach. The lower rim of the body armour pressed heavily on his thighs.

'Didn't they murder some Italian aid workers once?'

'Aye . . .'

'Here?'

'At the fish farm. A couple of miles further on.'

The road straightened. Nothing. Not a sign of the convoy.

'Oh, fuck . . .' McFee breathed.

There was a brain-jarring crash as the left wheel hit a hole McFee hadn't seen.

He cursed again.

'Take it easy, Moray,' Alex soothed. McFee was losing his nerve. 'Don't wreck the truck.'

McFee recovered his grip and eased the throttle. The road narrowed, the top of the lorry threatening to catch on the limestone overhang.

The engine roared. Wheels spun in the mud. The canyon seemed endless. They lurched round another corner.

'Sh . . . it! Look at that,' McFee screamed.

Ahead, a blue Volkswagen Golf was slewed across the track. From the far side climbed a man in grubby green, the lower half of his face obscured by a chequered scarf. He steadied his arms on the roof of the car, aiming a pistol.

Alex felt the blood pound in his ears. He tried to shrink

below the dashboard, but his body armour pinioned him to the seat.

McFee panicked, swerving wildly. Alex clung on, transfixed by the dull grey of the gun. He saw it jerk and flash. Then the bang as the bullet punctured the windscreen.

'Stop! You've got to stop!' Alex screamed. Ears ringing, he put his hand to his head, thinking he'd been hit.

McFee stamped on the brake. The Bedford halted yards from the gunman. Arms rigid, hands clamped to the automatic, the man stepped from behind the blue car. Above the mask, the face was dirt-smeared. Green eyes darted from Alex to McFee, alert, dangerous eyes.

He hissed something unintelligible.

'What's he want, what's he want?' McFee gabbled.

'Don't know,' Alex replied through closed teeth. Stay calm, he told himself. Avoid eye contact. He'd read that somewhere.

'*Mish . . .*' the gunman repeated, closing steadily, waving his weapon to his left.

'He's pointing over there,' McFee mumbled. 'A track into the forest. He wants us to drive up it.'

'No way,' Alex snapped. That was the road to certain death. He'd better try talking to the bastard.

'Do you speak English?'

He opened the door to get out.

The next shot deafened him. Seemed to explode in his head.

'Christ!' he heard himself yell.

'Are ye all right?'

The bullet had punched a hole in the roof inches above him. The gunman pushed the smoking barrel into Alex's face, hot against his mouth. The green eyes were ready to kill.

'Okay, Okay! Do as he says, Moray!'

Then suddenly the nightmare ended. The bandit

twisted round and backed away, lowering his weapon like a guilty child. Alex didn't understand. Then he looked up. A huge, mud-spattered UN Warrior was thundering down the track from the opposite direction.

The gunman sprinted for his car, the driver gunning the engine. The VW spun round and darted up the side track into the trees.

'Whoo-ay!' McFee bellowed. 'Fifth Cavalry to the fucking rescue!'

A grin slowly spread across Alex's face, but he couldn't speak.

Four soldiers burst from the back of the APC, sprinted behind rocks and tree trunks and took up firing positions.

A sergeant ran across to the Bedford, eyeing the bullet-crazed windscreen.

'Anyone hurt?'

Alex sucked air into his lungs and wiped a sleeve across his face.

'No,' he gulped. 'No injuries. Just need a change of underpants.'

Plain luck had brought the Warrior down the track at that moment. No radio message from the patrol at the foot of the canyon.

'Radios are sodding useless in these mountains,' the sergeant explained. 'Designed for the north German plains. We can escort you to the top of the hill, gents. You'll have no problem after that. The cease-fire's pretty good everywhere except Gorni.'

The sergeant looked at their frightened faces and shook his head. He wiped the mud from the logo painted on the side of the Bedford. Hadn't come across Bosnia Emergency before.

'First time out here?' he asked wryly.

'No,' replied McFee defensively.

'Then you should have bloody known better than coming up the canyon on your own!'

'It was your bloody soldiers down the bottom! They said there was a convoy just a couple of minutes in front!'

'Couple of minutes?' the sergeant frowned. 'More like thirty! I'll have a word with those buggers later. Anyway, let's move on.'

He yelled at his infantry section to get back in.

The thirty-four tons of armour gouged new ruts as it turned, then headed up the track, the sergeant in the turret glancing back to ensure the Bedford was following.

From the top of the hill they were on their own again, running down through lush green valleys and villages, Muslim at first, then Croat, where children grinned and waved at them.

The sudden tranquillity of the landscape enabled Alex to unwind. They'd survived their first brush with death. He'd learned a lesson too – not to rely on McFee's judgement.

The drama of the past few hours had wiped Lorna temporarily from his mind. Now she was back. Time to work out how to find her.

An hour later, they rumbled into the outskirts of Vitez. It was the end of the day, and UN armour ground in from all directions, packing the old school yard which was the main British base in Bosnia.

The sky had cleared, just a few streaks of cloud turning pink as the sun went down. It was a broad valley, hills on either side bathed green-gold in the evening light. Villages studding the distant slopes were pockmarked by the burnt shells of homes, 'cleansed' to make each hamlet ethnically pure.

'This is it,' McFee announced. 'This is our billet.'

He stopped the Bedford beside a two-storey house with a chalet roof, set back about twenty metres from the road. A pair of low, wrought-iron gates closed off access to a gravel drive.

McFee had been subdued for the last part of their

journey, still rattled that the decision he'd taken had nearly got them killed.

'There's an old couple live upstairs. We have the ground floor and their garage to put our boxes in,' he explained. 'Andrej and Dragana, they're called. Don't speak any English. Most nights Andrej has to put his uniform on and take his rifle down the trenches.'

'They're Croats, right?'

'Aye. They call this the Vitez pocket. Croats surrounded by Muslims. Those villages acorss the valley are Muslim. The daft thing is both religions got along fine here until two years ago. Ludicrous really, if it weren't so bloody tragic.'

He unlatched the metal gate and led the way down the drive.

'We'll just say hello, before we drive the truck in. Can't leave it in the road; the bastards would have everything out of it by morning.'

'*Dobro vece!*'

An elderly woman of indeterminate age called a greeting as she descended an outside staircase from the upper floor. A scarf covered her head; the rest of her clothing was thick, rough and woollen. The smoke from a wood fire blew down from the chimney.

'*Dobro vece!*' McFee replied. 'Dragana, this is Alex, who's come to help me.'

The woman's hand felt rough and prickly.

With no common language, communication was by smiles and gestures. McFee pointed to the truck and waved his arms.

'*Da! Da!*' she said.

'Okay, let's back the truck in. Can you do the gates, Alex?'

Soon they had the supplies secured in the garage, and took their bags into the house. Clean and tidy, rugs covering varnished floorboards, Alex was impressed.

'I think they did B&B before the trouble started,'

McFee explained. He led the way through the hall. 'There's a bedroom which you can have; I'm okay on the sofa in the lounge.'

'Are you sure?'

'Oh, aye. Anyway, it's warmer in there, with the stove!'

He pointed out the bathroom, where the water flowed only in the early mornings. He flicked a wall switch.

'Power's off as usual. I brought a load of candles. Some for us, some for Dragana.'

He looked at his watch. The cookhouse in the army camp a hundred metres down the road would be about to serve supper.

'Let's get some food. I'm starving.'

As they stepped outside again, the still of the evening was broken by the noise of military generators powering the camp and the houses the UN rented. The moon had not yet risen. Somewhere out there, Alex thought, is Lorna, unaware their tracks were converging. So too perhaps was the man Milan Pravic, whom Chadwick had asked him to find.

'Colonel lives there.' McFee indicated a home two doors down. 'And the next house is P. Info. The press office. Their evening briefings aren't bad.'

A spotlight dazzled them at the entrance to the camp.

' 'Scuse me sirs, could I see your passes?'

The voice came from inside a sandbagged, wooden guardhouse, what the military call a sanger. The soldier's breath steamed in the evening chill. His torch lit up their UNPROFOR cards and then their faces.

'Okay, sirs. Enjoy your teas.'

They walked on, picking their way through pools of mud, past rows of freight containers filled with stone chippings to protect the base from shrapnel.

'It's unreal . . .' Alex whispered. 'Like a wild-west fortress.'

The camp had been a school until the war started.

Now the sports field in front of it had been gritted over to make a Portakabin village and parking for trucks, Land Rovers and armoured vehicles.

'Here we go.' McFee pushed through the doorway into the cookhouse. 'Have to sign your name on the visitors list, then pay at P. Info.'

The large, warm dining-room steamed, the windows opaque with condensation. The mud-smeared floor glistened. About a hundred men and a few women sat at trestle tables. There was a separate, partitioned area for officers. Soldiers queued at hatches for steaks, curries and puddings, then took their foil trays to any space they could find, stopping to fill paper cups from dripping tea urns.

'Bloody good grub, this,' McFee proclaimed, heading towards some spare seats he'd spotted.

'Who are the people not in uniform?' Alex asked, looking around. 'Other aid workers?'

'And press. There's a couple of TV crews there, look. Never go anywhere without their cameras. So they can film themselves being blown to bits!'

Alex noted the equipment on the ground at their feet and peered at the faces. Would he recognize someone? It was a long time since Belfast but one never knew. He turned away, glad he'd not shaved off the beard that had helped hide him since then.

McFee had been right about the food. Alex had a passion for bread-and-butter pudding with custard. If anyone was starving in Bosnia, it wasn't the UN.

'Evening.'

They were joined by a man and woman in jeans and anoraks, who introduced themselves as working for Feed the Children. McFee picked their brains about where to find the neediest refugees.

Alex was only half listening, preoccupied.

The couple from Feed the Children stood up again and left.

'Oh . . , Moray,' Alex began. 'Where would I find the Colonel? I promised a mutual friend I'd say hello to him.'

'Oh aye? *You* know the right people then!' McFee snorted sarcastically. Then he shot a glance sideways. Someone had caught his eye.

'He-llo!'

A young woman with straggly dark hair and the bewitching mouth and eyes of a gipsy had paused at the end of their table, smiling.

' 'Ow you, Mac?' she pouted.

'Well, we . . ll!' McFee looked mildly flustered. 'Still here then?' he asked her.

Then without looking Alex in the eye, 'See the sort of people *I* know?'

The girl was dressed in a baggy pullover, long blue cotton skirt and thick, knitted stockings.

She said something in Serbo-Croat and laughed, exposing teeth that looked as if they'd been aligned by a drunk.

'This is Illie. *Hello* is about all she knows in English,' McFee explained. 'Works in the kitchens. Scrubs things . . .'

'*Laku noć*. See you . . .' The woman smiled at Alex with her eyes and continued her progress towards the door, glancing back just once.

'*Dobra, dobra.* See you later, Illie,' McFee waved. 'Lovely lass. Does almost anything for a couple of Deutsche Marks.' His eyes darted about, as if frightened they'd given something away. 'Not that *I'd* know, of course,' he added hastily.

'Of course not.'

'Now, where were we?' McFee looked broody. 'The Colonel? He's probably in there,' he said, pointing to the partitioned area. 'But if you want to say hello, best to fix it through P. Info. Talking of whom, if we get our skates on, we'll catch their evening briefing.'

Alex noted the television crews had already left. He and McFee took their foil trays and stuffed them into a plastic rubbish sack by the door.

The temperature outside had tumbled since dusk. They walked briskly back towards the road and the houses. The still, cold air smelled of wood smoke and manure. Above the generator hum came the deeper drone of aero-engines high in the sky. NATO planes, Alex guessed, heading for their drop zones, parachuting food to Muslim towns cut off by the Serbs.

Huge resources were being poured into Bosnia, yet with the effect of a sticking-plaster. And now he was part of the process.

There was a smoky fug inside the P.Info house, about a dozen media people on benches, lining the walls of a bare-floored room.

The Major in charge of PR introduced himself as Alan Clarke-Hartley. He briefed the journalists on the day's fighting around Gorni Vakuf, and mentioned that an aid truck had narrowly escaped being hijacked. No one should travel on that road unescorted, he told them.

Afterwards, as the media dispersed, he singled out Moray McFee.

'I saw your ears burning, just then,' he quipped.

'It was all your chaps' fault . . .' McFee growled. 'By the way, this is my new partner Alex Crawford.'

'How d'you do?'

They shook hands. As they exchanged pleasantries, McFee fiddled with the stem of his pipe, then made an excuse about having something to sort out, and left them.

'First time out here?' Clarke-Hartley asked, offering him a can of beer.

'Thanks. Yes it is. I wanted a word with your Colonel,' Alex replied. 'A mutual friend suggested I look him up.'

'You're out of luck, I'm afraid. He's in Sarajevo for a few days with General Rose.'

'Oh, that's a pity . . .' It was a setback. He'd been relying on the Colonel for advice. 'When's he returning?'

'Not until the end of the week. But I can fill you in on things. Come over here and I'll give you the new boys' tour.'

He pointed to a wall map and described their area of operations. He indicated the canyon where Alex had been ambushed, then moved his finger north to the Laśva Valley.

'This is Tulici, where the massacre was two weeks ago . . .'

'Were you there?'

'Yes. I went with the Colonel. Bodies all over the place. Appalling carnage. Quite bestial. And no survivors that we could see.'

'Any idea who was responsible?' Alex asked innocently.

'The Bosnian army, which is mostly Muslim, are blaming a man called Milan Pravic as the chief villain. But the whole thing must have had official HVO backing. One of our patrols had seen houses in flames earlier on, but when they tried to reach the village they got mortared. Heavy weapons, mortars. Not the sort of thing carried around by some mad freelance.'

'Have you tried to trace this Pravic?'

'Not our job really. We made a few enquiries, but didn't get anywhere. *Pravic? Pravic? Never heard of him* – you know the sort of thing. The Colonel went and slagged off the HVO for allowing their animals to go around murdering women and children. But they just shrug it off. It's another world out here.'

He pointed up a few more details on the map, then they wandered towards the door.

Outside on the steps, he cupped a hand to his ear.

'Hear that?' He pointed up into the blackness. An aero-engine again, but this time the beat of rotor blades.

'A UN helicopter?' Alex inquired.

'No fear! That's a Croat "Hip". They use it to ferry people and ammo in and out of the enclave. Bloody risky, flying at night. Shows how desperate they are.'

'Is that the *only* way the Croats can get out if they have to?' Alex asked, thinking suddenly of Pravic.

'Just about. As I showed you on the map, the Muslims control a circle of land around here. Beyond that it's Croat again. The chopper is their air bridge.'

Alex was about to bid him goodnight, when he had an afterthought.

'Oh, by the way,' he asked, trying to sound casual. 'Have you ever come across a woman called Lorna out here? Surname could be Donohue. Blonde hair. Some sort of aid worker.'

Clarke-Hartley frowned.

'Can't say I have. Why?'

'She's an old friend. Thought I saw her on the road today.'

'Could have been heading for Sarajevo, or Zenica. That's where a lot of the refugees are.'

'Of course,' Alex acknowledged. 'Goodnight.'

Crunching down the gravel path, his torch picked out the sparkle of frost. In the distance he heard the whine of the helicopter taking off again. They don't hang about, he thought.

Who was it this time? Another killer who'd overstepped the mark?

Eleven

Zagreb, Croatia

Irena Pravic tucked the soft pink sheet under the cot mattress. Only the head of the baby was visible, sucking rhythmically at her dummy. Maša was fourteen months old and slept through most nights, without disturbing Irena and the man she lived with.

Irena half turned at the click of the front door closing. Too early for Goran. A rough coughing told her Milan was back again. Her brother had descended on them last night without warning, smelling of smoke, sweat and slivovitz, and saying he'd be staying for a few days.

Goran, with whom she'd lived for three years, was all for throwing him out. But blood was thicker than water. Even bad blood.

She caressed her daughter's head, then slipped from the tiny bedroom and closed the door, leaving just a crack to hear any crying.

Milan had slumped on the sofa with his shoes dropped beside him on the beige, shag-pile carpet. Irena picked them up and took them to the hall.

It was a small apartment. One small bedroom, a living room, kitchen and bathroom, all they could afford. The sofa was where Milan had to sleep.

He'd not explained why he was here. But then he never had explained anything.

'Irena! Bring me a beer!' She heard the television go on.

He was up to something. Phone calls for him from

Germany, then turning up out of the blue. She'd seen the butt of a pistol poking from his bag.

There had been three children in the family, Milan the youngest, she in the middle and Tihomir her elder brother. A rough, village upbringing it had been, in a house that had always seemed dark. Eventually she had gone to college in Sarajevo, Tihomir had entered the priesthood and Milan the building trade.

She looked in the refrigerator, then closed the door again.

'There are no beers,' she carped, returning to the living room. 'You've drunk them all. Should have bought some while you were out.'

He ignored her, as always. Couldn't remember a time when he'd looked her in the eye. She returned to the kitchen. Had to think of something for them to eat.

She'd met her partner in Sarajevo, studying medicine, while she learned English. Golden days then, the city a hub of culture and no cares about religion, but as soon as the fighting started they'd fled. Goran had finished his studies in Zagreb and was now a hospital intern working more hours than there were in the day.

She crossed to the window and folded her arms. Their sixth floor flat overlooked an identical grey block, twinkling with lights. A dreary place to live, but they'd been lucky to get it.

Milan unsettled her. Couldn't concentrate with him around. Never knew what he was thinking. She drifted back to the living room.

The Croatian news was on. Pictures of Bosnia. 'Muslims breaching the cease-fire', they said. Always the other side at fault. The tragedy was people believed this propaganda.

He'd cut his fair hair short like a convict, having arrived with it long and lank. He'd wanted some passport photos. Definitely up to something. He'd bought some spectacles too. She'd seen him try them in front of a mirror.

Milan had been pretty as a child. Almost blonde in those days, with eyes she remembered as luminous blue. Their father used to call him a cissy.

A brute, their father was. Ran a garage and tyre repair station. Used to come home drunk on occasions, crashing about the house, shouting obscenities. Their mother would barricade the bedroom to keep him out. Then in desperation he would snivel into the children's room. Irena would listen for him and scurry into Tihomir's bed for protection. Her elder brother had the guts to stand up to their father and kept a stick under his pillow to clout him when he groped for them in the dark.

Milan however got no such brotherly protection and it was *his* bed their father would end up in, often as not. Having once been dragged from underneath it and beaten black and blue, the boy had stopped trying to hide.

It was a *body* their father wanted. *Any* body. Irena used to cover her ears to shut out the grunts and whispers. Milan never talked about those nights, but his face was always tear-smudged in the mornings.

'Milan!' she shouted, fed up with him ignoring her.

He appeared not to notice. The news was still on.

She'd often wondered if he was backward. Always withdrawn, always sullen, but there was cunning there. And cruelty. He'd caught a stray cat once, pinned it to the ground with his boot and crushed its head with a crowbar.

'Milan.'

He turned his head a quarter of the way, still not looking at her.

'Milan, do you know how long you'll be staying? Goran's asking . . .'

'A few days.'

'Oh. And then?'

'Germany.'

'Are your friends finding work for you?'

The calls had been from a woman called Gisela in Berlin.

'Mmm.'

He'd worked five years in Germany. Then came home two years ago, to fight for his country, he'd said. Heard nothing of him until now. Secretly she'd hoped he'd been killed. Terrible to wish that of your own brother. But something in her heart told her the world would be a safer place without him.

She gave up trying to communicate, and returned to the kitchen. There was minced meat in the fridge. She'd make *ćevapcici*.

Zenica, Bosnia.

Lorna had spent the afternoon delivering medical supplies, some to the main hospital in Zenica, others to Muslim villages up to thirty minutes away. She'd kept some boxes back to give to the Croats. In this country where aid workers crossed front lines daily, survival depended on even-handedness.

Now it was evening in the dimly-lit hotel and she was weary. But it was still only eight o'clock – too early to retire to the cold darkness of her room.

She and Josip sat at a table together alone, the restaurant half full of Scandinavians working for the UN High Commissioner for Refugees. She kept the conversation with her translator as superficial as possible, resisting his efforts to make it personal. Not hard to achieve, because her mind was elsewhere.

Her work was beginning to worry her; not the danger

– that she was more or less used to. What concerned her was the motivation of CareNet.

She had no problems with the Medical Aid side of things, but her employer's increasing interest in arranging child adoptions disturbed her.

CareNet's intention was simple, and laudable enough – to give war orphans a better life. But there was an evangelism at the heart of the organization which brooked little argument over how to achieve that. Their assumption that the children would *always* be better off in America was not, in Lorna's view, a safe one to make.

The first step in CareNet's adoption business had been taken on her last visit. She'd been instructed by her Boston HQ to check out the 'supply situation'. Her boss, a born-again Christian who'd made a fortune from computer software, was using information technology to organize 'the market' for adoption.

On this trip he had given her a notebook computer and a satellite phone, so she could send details of the Tulici girl and any others she might find to a bulletin board he'd set up on the Internet.

But children, Lorna felt, should not be a 'business'. Her anxiety had deepened that morning at seeing Monika's nervousness about the adoption issue.

Josip had been heavily into slivovitz that afternoon. Everywhere they'd delivered their medical supplies, the bottles had been brought out in gratitude. Lorna hadn't touched the stuff; just the smell of it made her want to throw up. But Josip had drunk all that was offered, 'so as not to offend'.

This evening he'd persuaded the waiter to produce one of the hotel's few remaining bottles of good Croatian wine. It had cost him twenty Deutsche Marks in bribes, but he'd told himself if it helped unfreeze Lorna, it would be worth it.

After half an hour of his meandering suggestiveness, Lorna felt her fuse shortening. Her instinct was to unman him with some cutting remark, but she feared he might walk out on her. Without a translator in Bosnia she simply couldn't work. So she stone-walled wearily.

Suddenly her lack of response got through to him.

'Why you don't want me to make love to you?' he blurted out, mouth turned down like a child denied sweets.

'Oh, God,' she thought. 'This I can do without.' She'd never imagined he would come straight out with it.

'Josip!' She feigned surprise. 'I had no idea . . .'

Had to be careful. She looked at his sad, moist eyes, his cheeks flushed with alcohol and frustration. He wasn't *bad* looking. A little gaunt. Too Balkan, maybe. But he was fifteen years younger than her and there'd be plenty of women over forty-five who would grab at the chance.

'Hey, I'm so flattered. I mean Josip, you could have *any* woman . . .'

'You have no husband now,' he blurted out. 'Last time here, you told me you were separate from him.' He shrugged, as if the lack of a man was justification enough for her to sleep with him.

'Sure. But that doesn't mean . . . Look, what is this, Josip? You and I we *work* together. Office rules – you don't have a relationship with someone you work with . . .'

She saw his eyes light up. Josip had taken it as encouragement. Rules, after all, were there to be broken.

'Anyway, maybe I don't like sex . . .' she flustered, fiddling with Rees's white gold wedding ring which she still wore.

He shot his arm across the table and grabbed her arm.

'That is joke. You *love* sex! I always know if a woman will be cold or warm. Your eyes, the way you move . . .'

He pulled her fingers to his lips.

'Your body, Lorna – it would be like violin in my hands . . .'

'Oh, for Christ's sake!' She whipped her hand free.

131

'And I suppose you'd play Brahms' Concerto on my tits!' Diplomacy was getting her nowhere.

Josip's face crumpled like a paper bag. He made as if to stand up.

Oh dear. The wound had been deeper than she'd meant. Men were like kids. She prayed she hadn't blown it.

'Look, if it makes you feel better, I *do* have a guy. That's the reason . . .' she said hurriedly. 'And I don't cheat on him . . .'

He sat down suspiciously.

'It's someone I've known a long time,' she continued, realizing the story needed a little embellishment.

'How long?' he demanded.

'What? Oh, most of my life.' She spoke without thinking. Had to say something.

'So, you knew this man before your husband?'

'Well, yuh.'

'He was your lover *then*?'

'Mmmm.' What was she *saying*?

'And now you . . . you are separate from your husband, and he is your lover again?'

Josip's face was a picture of disbelief.

'Yuh . . . sure. But look I don't want to talk about . . .'

'Why not?' he pressed, drawn by her defensiveness. 'You *love* him. I want to know what kind of man that is.'

What kind indeed. Fiction or fact?

'I guess . . . I guess you could say we're sort of soul mates,' she heard herself say.

What was this crap? What thread from her past was Josip unwittingly loosening?

'*Soul mate*? That means like a brother?'

No. Closer than that, she thought. Like an integral part of you. So that when you're wrenched away from him you think you're going to die.

'Sure. Like a brother. Sort of incestuous . . .' she teased. Time to make a joke of it.

132

'But you didn't marry your soul mate?'

No. She married Rees, because she needed *someone* to be a father to her child . . .

'Yup, well, you know how it is. Things got in the way. Things . . . like the Atlantic Ocean.'

She'd said enough. This had to stop.

'What his name?' Josip pressed.

'Uh?'

'He has a name, this soul mate?'

Yes. But a name she'd not spoken lovingly of for twenty years.

'Dan. Dan Samson,' Lorna lied, crossing her arms. 'And that's it, now. You keep your nose out of my personal life.'

Her tone snuffed out the last flicker of light in his dream. Josip shrugged. His cause was lost. Game over.

Suddenly he felt unpleasantly sober.

'Maybe I have some brandy . . .'

Lorna pushed back her chair.

'Not for me. I'm going to bed. Alone!'

Josip looked round for the waiter, ignoring the rebuke.

'Goodnight, Josip.'

'Sure,' he replied dismissively.

She closed the door to her room and slipped the chain. After a couple of brandies Josip might yet try again.

She sat on the edge of the bed, pulled off her boots, then fell back onto the rough blanket that smelled of smoke. How the hell had she let herself get into that? Inventing a lover to put him off was one thing, but all that soul mate stuff?

Just slipped out, your honour.

And just because 'soul mates' was the way she and Alex Jarvis used to think of each other, it wasn't necessarily *him* she'd meant. Who said she still thought about him?

'*I* say. That's who.'

Her voice echoed flatly in the cold, half-lit box, with its seedy wallpaper and plasticky furniture. A bedroom that smelled of strangers.

Why, though? Why could she still think of him with love as well as with hate?

Belfast 1973. A long, long time ago, but still sharp in her memory.

On a scale of 1 to 10, what Alex had done to her there was 11+ for shittiness. A monstrous betrayal after his beautiful words and after the love-making that was so much more than just sex.

All that stuff about her being the 'spark that had been missing from his life'. Sure, she'd said those things about him too. The difference was *she* had meant them.

She had fled home from Belfast and then discovered the hard Irishmen in Boston wanted her dead for 'touting' the secret of the jailbreak. They'd planned a little 'accident' for her, but her father was tipped the wink and bought them off. Being one of the richest Irish-Americans in New England had its advantages.

Then, and this was the worst part for her, Lorna had found herself back in her father's pocket, saddled again with the burden of filial obligation it had taken her years to shake off.

She and her sister knew it as 'The Gratitude Trap' – never being able to say or do anything to contradict their father in case it was seen as lack of appreciation.

A sense of failure and guilt had been pummelled into their brains since birth through paternal rebukes at any flaw in their performance and ridicule at their juvenile opinions.

Lorna shivered. She'd crossed into adulthood devoid of self-esteem, conditioned to believe her only value was as her father's vassal.

Then she'd met Alex who'd told her she was just wonderful the way she was. He'd called her a star –

clever, witty, beautiful. She! Lorna! No wonder she'd loved him so much.

She'd felt a star, too, whizzing around Hampstead on the back of Alex's BSA. A rebel, with Alex as James Dean. A little rough in his voice and manner, he would not have won Papa's approval, which had served to heighten the thrill. The first challenge to her father she'd ever made.

Her parents had been separated by then. Her mother, born in Britain, had brought her to London for a taste of English education and culture.

Alex. He'd given her the strength to stand up to the old man – then thrust her back into his debt by betraying her.

Alex. She remembered his smell when they first met. Almost feral. Something to do with the leather jacket he wore. But it was his eyes she'd fallen for, dark and tempting as chocolate. And the feel of his body. She'd nicknamed him Samson.

Samson! Dan Samson! That was the stupid name she'd given Josip for her fictitious lover.

Shit! Shit! Shit! She leaped from the bed.

Had to wash all this stuff from her head. She tried the bathroom tap. Water. A miracle. Warm too.

She turned on the shower, tossed her clothes at a chair, then climbed over the rim of the tub. The water smelled funny, but beggars couldn't be choosers.

She shampooed her hair then spread the foam down her soft skin; the water threatened to lose its heat. She rinsed herself quickly in case the flow died altogether, then huddled under the spray to savour the last of its warmth. Crossing her arms over her breasts, her fingers felt the nipples grow and harden.

It was a while since she'd been with a man. Only once since leaving Rees, a divorcee she'd met at a party. Not a night to remember. He'd had the hands of a butcher.

Alex's hands had been something else.

Damn! She hated the guy, remember? He'd screwed up her life. She recited the litany in her mind.

After buying off the IRA, her father had forced her into hiding, to take a job with a law firm he knew in an out-of-the-way New England artists' colony.

All because you betrayed me, Alex!

There, after years of frustration at her exile, she'd bedded some careless pot-thrower she didn't even like, who had gotten her pregnant. Her contract with the law firm precluded motherhood for seven years, so she'd had to leave her job.

Your fault, Alex.

Two choices had faced her. To become a single parent and depend on her father for an income, or find someone to marry.

No choice, Alex.

The potter was out of the question, but there was someone else. A partner in the firm called Rees Sorenson. So keen was he to make her Mrs Sorensen, that this deeply Christian man overlooked the fact she was already pregnant.

After what you'd put me through, Alex, maybe I deserved such a saint.

The baby was born. They'd called her Julie.

After a few months they'd realized something was wrong. Autism, the doctors called it. The child couldn't communicate.

For twelve years Lorna had cared for Julie, battling to break through to her, but when the girl reached puberty things had gotten out of control.

Rees put Julie in a home for the mentally disturbed, Lorna had a breakdown, and their marriage disintegrated.

All your fault, Alex! Every little part of it!

Suddenly the bathroom went black.

'Oh, hell!' she screamed. 'Damn! Damn!'

She groped to turn off the taps, then felt for the rim of

the tub. Where was the frigging towel? She banged her toe on the doorframe and cursed again.

Somewhere she had a flashlight. She felt her way into the pitch-dark room. The power failure was total; no light spilled in from the window.

She stooped forward and felt the edge of the bed, her heart pounding. Suppose Josip had gotten in while she was in the shower . . .

She held her breath. All she could hear was the pumping of her own blood. What if he *was* there, holding his breath too?

Silently she felt along the bed. Please, God, let the flashlight be on the bedside table.

It was. She fumbled with the switch.

'Thank you Lord,' she breathed, waving the pale, orange beam round the room. It needed new batteries.

Back in the bathroom, she rested the torch on the shelf so she could dry herself quickly before it died altogether.

A quick teeth brushing before the water gave out, then her nightdress on and into bed.

She bit her lip. What the hell was she doing in this crazy place?

'I hate you Alex! I hate you,' she moaned.

Twelve

The roadway between Dragana's house and the UN
camp opposite was lined with heavy vehicles, engines
rumbling like ruminating beasts. Exhausts steamed like
cattle-breath in the crisp morning air.

A convoy of empty supply trucks was forming for the
long drive to Split and a pair of Warriors twisted on their
tracks, to bracket three white, armoured Land Rovers
with 'TV' marked on their sides in black tape. The
journalists were being taken on patrol along the cease-
fire lines. In public they expressed hope that peace would
last, but privately they knew that only fresh violence
would guarantee them a place on the evening news.

Alex coaxed the Bedford out of the drive and turned
left onto the road. He was glad of his boots and Barbour
and had pulled on a tweed cap to keep his head warm.

This was the first full day of his mission. With a little
luck by the end of it he would have picked up the trail of
at least one of the people he was looking for.

As they headed northwest he looked across flat
meadows glinting silver in the watery sunlight. Beyond,
rose a snow-capped mountain range, a ski-centre in
happier times. It reminded him of frosty mornings in the
Highlands, out on the moors before dawn, waiting for
the deer to leave their valley feeding grounds for the
safety of the hills.

'It's beautiful here!' he murmured.

'Yes. Took me by surprise,' McFee concurred. 'You

138

don't expect it somehow, after all the butchery you see on TV. You think the place'll be one big shit heap.'

The road wound through hamlets, scarred by the occasional burned-out shop or house.

'And then you see that sort of thing,' Alex commented.

'Beauty and the beast . . . eh?'

Grey-faced young men, wearing the drab camouflage of the HVO, ambled wearily home, eyeing the truck for a lift.

Swerving to avoid a mortar crater, they reached a road juntion and a chicane made of rusting tank-traps and a burned-out bus. To the left the UN's Route Triangle led to the mountains and the coast. Straight on was to Travnik.

'It's eerie,' Alex breathed. 'Not a soul in sight. You feel you're being watched.'

'Aye. We've just crossed the front line. There's probably a dozen rifle sights looking at us, so keep smiling.'

'Bit dodgy on our own, isn't it?' Alex snapped, not wanting a repeat of yesterday's nightmare. 'Shouldn't we have a UN escort?'

McFee bristled.

'Look, when I left you at P.Info last night I dropped into the officers' mess,' he blustered expansively. 'They said Travnik's wide open. No probs.'

Officers' Mess? Sounded like bullshit. But McFee had been out *somewhere* last night. Hadn't got back to the house until after Alex was asleep.

And another thing, he thought. They had no translator. How the hell was he going to ask questions about Milan Pravic if he couldn't communicate.

'Wouldn't it be handy to have a local with us,' he needled, 'someone who speaks the language?'

McFee pursed his lips.

'Which local, that's the problem. A Croat couldn't

come in here with us. And a Muslim couldn't come back with us to Vitez.'

'How do the UN manage?'

'Och, well, they pay them good wages, stick 'em in a uniform and give 'em a nice wee plastic UN pass. But Bosnia Emergency hasn't the money.'

He ruminated for a moment.

'But it's something to work on. If we found a volunteer, maybe the UN could get her a pass.' The thought that it could be a woman set McFee brooding.

An ancient hilltop castle towered over the approach to Travnik. Beyond were minarets. Old shell cases littered the roadway.

'This place has taken a pasting,' McFee remarked, guiding Alex through the shrapnel-scarred streets of the old Muslim town. At a small park, dug up for fresh graves, women laid flowers. The road was full of men in uniform.

'The bearded ones are Mujahedin,' McFee mentioned under his breath. 'Iranians, Palestinians, you name it.' He shot a glance at Alex. 'With that fungus on your own face, you'd better watch out they don't recruit ye!'

Alex manoeuvred the truck over a narrow river bridge and into a school yard, then swung down onto the tarmac. From behind barred windows faces peered, most of them blank with despair. Parked closer to the school entrance, its rear towards the door, was another white-painted truck.

'Looks like Feed the Children have beaten us to it,' Alex remarked, spotting the line of refugees passing aid boxes into the building.

'Oh, hello, there.'

It was the Englishman who'd shared their table in the cookhouse last night.

'They've plenty of supplies here just now. But have a word with the director. She knows some other places.'

'Thanks.'

Inside, class-rooms were stuffed with beds, mats and the meagre belongings of families. Weaving through the crush, Alex bit his lip. It was the first time he'd touched and smelled the human tragedy of Bosnia.

They entered an office. Desks stacked with paperwork, half a dozen women struggling to make sense of it. Clucking about them like a mother hen was a matron in fawn cardigan and what looked like a Hermes scarf.

She smiled and affected to recognize McFee when he introduced himself.

'Full. No more room,' she explained, brown eyes wide with astonishment. 'Enough food for a week, maybe.'

'You know somewhere else we could take our stuff?' McFee asked.

'Yes, yes!' Her eyes lit up. 'Some people came last week but no space. They go to village near Guca Gora.'

'Maybe you could send someone with us as a guide,' Alex chipped in. 'Someone who speaks English.'

'Maybe. Perhaps . . .' She looked at her watch. 'Moment.'

She bustled from the room shouting a name. Two minutes later she returned, leading a fair-haired youth with eyes of bright blue.

'This is Ivan. He is refugee. He learn English at school. You bring him back?'

'Of course,' Alex assured her.

They walked out to the truck, Ivan shooing away children unpicking the tailgate tarpaulin.

They drove slowly through the town using the same road they'd come in on.

'How old are you, Ivan?' Alex asked. Squeezed between him and McFee, the boy's diffidence reminded him so painfully of Jodie.

'Seventeen. But if someone ask, I am sixteen, okay?' There was fear in his eyes.

'Okay,' Alex frowned. 'But why?'

'Huh. If seventeen, they put me in army! Then I dead like my father.'

He drew a finger across his own throat.

Back past the castle and out onto the Vitez road again, Ivan directed him up a lane that climbed through bare woods of birch and chestnut. They reached a muddy village, slowing for a pony-cart piled with silage.

Then, round a bend, the Bosnian Army flag drooped above a café. Bearded soldiers lounging on chairs followed the truck's passing with suspicious, unwavering eyes.

'No stop! No stop!' Ivan gibbered. '*Mujahedin* . . .'

Alex put his foot down. Out of the village, the ground fell away steeply to the right.

'I thought the Mujahedin were on your side,' he checked. The boy was pale with fear.

'Crazy peoples. Arabs. Not Bosnians . . .'

A little later, Alex asked how much further it was. Ivan counted on his fingers.

'Three more village, I think.'

It took twenty minutes to reach the scruffy hamlet of Duba. Ivan leaned from the window and asked an old man directions.

'He say the refugees are in the school. I show you.'

Always the schools, Alex thought. War had wrecked so many aspects of life here. Outside a dismal pre-fab a crowd milled, elderly men in caps and women in shawls, but young families too, some decanting from a mud-spattered bus, hugging the few belongings they'd seized in their moment of flight.

As the Bedford pulled up, faces turned as one, and the mob descended on them like gulls on a rubbish tip.

'Christ!' Alex yelled. 'They'll take the truck apart!'

'Ivan!' McFee growled. 'Find the person who's in charge of this place.'

Alex switched off the engine and pocketed the key.

142

'Come on, Moray,' he barked. 'Let's see if we can hold them off.'

The truck was surrounded.

Alex squeezed to the ground, pressed to the side of the vehicle by the throng. Some youths had already undone the tarpaulin at the back.

'Now, hang on a minute, chaps!' McFee's bellow rose up from the midst of the crowd. 'Ooof!'

Hell! Someone's thumped him, Alex thought.

He elbowed his way to the tail-gate. McFee leaned against the rear wheel-arch nursing his chin. A scuffle had broken out. Whoever had hit McFee was being restrained, and punched in return.

Boxes poured out of the back of the truck. Some in the crowd ripped them open where they stood. Others clutched them in their arms like trophies and elbowed their way back to the school.

Suddenly a shot rang out. Alex dropped to the ground. Then came the rattling crack of automatic fire. Women screamed. The crowd melted away at a crouch.

A middle-aged man in Armija uniform strutted towards the truck, blasting Kalashnikov rounds into the sky. Close behind were two other soldiers, and Ivan.

'Good lad,' Alex breathed, clutching the boy by the arm.

'Your friend. He is hurt?'

'You all right, Moray?' Alex asked.

'Oh, aye.'

The middle-aged soldier helped McFee to his feet and dusted him down. He babbled away in Serbo-Croat.

'He says "sorry for what happened",' Ivan translated. 'These people have no food for three days.'

'Tell him we understand,' Alex soothed. 'I'd have done the same.'

'He say the people of this village not want refugees,' Ivan continued. 'They tell them "go away". Give nothing to eat. Only for themselves.'

'Well, tell them they're welcome to all the stuff we've brought,' Alex replied. 'There's food and warm clothing. But ask him to make sure it's shared out fairly.'

Ivan turned to the officer to translate.

'*Da. Da.*' He nodded, gesticulating at his juniors. They scurried off to muster a gang of box-handlers.

Alex began collecting the broken boxes into a sack, vaguely aware that another vehicle, a white jeep of some sort had pulled up outside the school.

'I'll gi' ye a hand in a minute, Alex,' McFee called. 'Just get my breath back.'

From some of the boxes the contents had already been looted. Alex bent to gather up the torn cardboard.

Suddenly in front of him he saw a pair of green Goretex boots. Small feet – belonging to a woman . . .

Slowly, very slowly, he straightened himself up.

Lorna Donohue.

The passage of time had scored lines in her face, but to him it still radiated magic.

Her mouth dropped open.

'Alex?' she gasped.

His chest felt as if it was about to explode.

'Lorna,' he gulped. 'It's you.'

'And it *is* you!' Her voice rose an octave. She pointed at his face. 'The beard. I didn't . . . I don't believe this . . .'

She felt she was going into shock. He reached an arm out to her, but it didn't quite connect.

'I thought I saw you the other day,' Alex spluttered. 'Coming off the ferry at Split. But this is amazing!'

He wanted to grab her, hug her, kiss her. But he didn't dare.

'Twenty goddam years!' she mouthed, her face a mask. There was no invitation there.

Didn't dare show him her feelings. Didn't even *know* what they were. She spun away from him and ran her hands through her hair.

'My God!' she murmured. 'This isn't happening.'

'It's amazing,' Alex repeated, his hands flapping. He felt like a kid on his first date, weak at the knees with wondering what to say.

He became conscious of McFee watching them.

'This is Lorna,' he gestured. 'The one on the ferry . . .'

McFee leered, as if to say, 'not bad'.

Unsmiling, Lorna turned to face the man who'd once meant everything to her. She felt sandbagged. Had to play for time.

'What are you doing here, for heaven's sake?' she asked, looking at him opaquely.

He waved his hand towards the Bedford.

'Endeavouring to be useful, I suppose. You too?'

She nodded, eyes hard, trying to show that whatever she felt about meeting him again, it wasn't necessarily pleasure.

He told himself to get a grip and moved a little closer. 'You look fantastic, Lorna. Haven't changed at all. Astonishing . . .'

'Older,' she replied. 'And wiser . . .' She raised one eyebrow.

'Aren't we all.' He could see she intended to give him a hard time. 'We . . . we've got a lot to talk about, I guess.' He reached out to touch her, but she backed off.

'We certainly do.' He saw the hurt in her eyes. She let out a long, deep breath. 'We sure do, Alex!'

She felt she was clinging on by her finger tips. Time for a smile, she thought. Mustn't let him see she was floundering.

'Well! Well, well . . . So this is your truck? What have you got there, food and clothes?'

'Yep. Bosnia Emergency is the name of the charity. Oh, and this is Moray McFee. Moray? This is Lorna . . . *Donohue*?' he checked.

'Donohue will do. Nice to meet you, Moray.'

'This chap Crawford tells me you go back thirty

years . . .' McFee ventured. Lorna darted Alex a suspicious glance – his name had been *Jarvis* when she'd last seen him. Her name change had a simple reason – but his?

'Thirty years! You'd have been in nappies when you met, surely?' McFee grinned.

'If only,' she laughed, thawing a little. 'But thanks for the compliment.'

McFee spotted the Nikon on a strap round her neck.

'Here, gi' me that camera! It's a moment of history, this.'

She faltered but handed it over.

'Stand together, now. Alex, put your arm around her for God's sake!'

McFee's request brooked no refusal. For a moment Lorna leant uneasily against Alex.

She forced a thin smile. McFee snapped off a couple of pictures, before handing back the camera. Lorna was grateful to break off the unsettling contact.

'I'll leave you to reminisce for a moment,' he offered, backing away. 'Don't worry, Alex. I'll do the boxes.'

'So . . . What's all this *Crawford* stuff?' she snapped, businesslike again, as McFee went over to the Bedford.

He took her arm and led her out of earshot.

'I've been using the name since Belfast. I've had to hide. The Provos wanted to kill me, you know.'

'You and me both, kiddo.' She pulled her arm from his grip. Why was he standing here like this, bold as brass? He should be on his knees begging for forgiveness.

'Look, I got work to do,' she said brusquely. 'I guess this isn't the place to talk. Where are you staying?'

'Vitez. You?'

'Zenica. The International Hotel.'

She wasn't going to suggest they should meet. Leave that to him.

'And who do *you* work for?' he asked, unnerved by her coolness.

'Have you heard of CareNet of New England?'

'Nope.'

'It's a disaster agency that helps kids. We hand out medical supplies, and find homes for war orphans.'

'People to adopt them?' he frowned.

'Sure. You don't approve?'

'It *is* rather controversial . . .'

'And *that* is an old-fashioned, English understatement.'

Her blue-grey eyes softened. She wasn't altogether disagreeing with him.

Alex glanced towards the truck. The remaining boxes were being unloaded in an orderly relay. Better to steer clear of the past for now. Keep talking about the present.

'And what are you in *this* village for? Medicines, or orphans?' he asked.

Questions, questions, the biggest one inside her own mind. Why was he really here? But he'd just asked her something . . .

'This one's special. There's a kid here in real danger. You've heard of . . .'

She stopped in mid-flow. Hell, she thought. I'm doing it again. Telling him things. It's those soft brown eyes, and the way he listens as if he cares.

She slipped her mask back in place and looked at him out of the corner of her eye.

'Last time we met . . .' she began, 'you were a spook. MI5 wasn't it?'

He began to sweat.

'We've got to talk about that, Lorna. Let's work out when we can meet . . .'

'Do you still do that?' she interrupted. 'Are you still a spy? Out *here*?'

'Give me a break, Lorna.'

'*Gimme a break!* You watch too many soaps. *Is* that why you're here?' she demanded.

'No, it's not.'

It's happening again, he thought. Lying to her because the truth's too complicated.

'I told you, I came here to help . . . and to get away. I had problems at home. You know what I mean?' he added, appealing for sympathy. He saw pain in her eyes.

'Sure,' she nodded. 'I know what you mean.'

A couple approached, the man in a leather jacket. He had dark, greasy hair and jealous eyes.

'Lorna . . .' Josip snapped, irritated by her intimacy with this stranger. 'Monika – she say we must hurry.'

'Okay, okay!' Lorna replied. 'Just give me a minute.'

This time she took Alex by the arm and led him a few metres away.

'He's my translator,' she explained. 'I've got to go. There's a kid here who lost all her family in a massacre.'

Massacre. He had an eerie sensation of a window opening.

'All right, but let's meet up somewhere. I'm staying opposite the UN camp in Vitez. Any chance you could get there?'

'I don't know. I've got a lot to fix . . .'

'That massacre,' he asked, ignoring her prevarication, 'was it Tulici?'

'Uhuh,' she acknowledged warily. 'Were you here then?'

'No. It's just that the way I'd heard it, there weren't any survivors.'

'Mmm. That's what most people think. It's safer that way.'

'What do you mean?'

Lorna swallowed hard. Nobody was supposed to know Vildana was in this village.

'Because if there's a survivor, she might be able to identify the guy who did the killings. And if he knew there was a witness, he'd want to kill her too.'

She'd said enough.

'I've got to go.'

148

'Hang on!' Alex gripped her arm. 'If this girl can identify the killers . . .'

'I didn't say that,' Lorna protested.

'But if she can identify them, then the UN must be told. They want to put the Tulici killers on trial. Did you know that?'

'Not my problem! All I'm concerned about is the safety and future happiness of a twelve-year-old.'

'She's here in this village, you say?'

Questions. Questions. Just like Belfast.

'I must go.' Yet she couldn't. Not without fixing to meet him again.

'Can I come with you?' he pleaded. 'To see the girl?'

'You have to be kidding,' she protested. 'Do you know what it took to persuade Monika to bring *me* here? No way.'

'How long will you be? I'll wait.'

Lorna shrugged, exasperated. 'I don't know.'

'I'll wait.'

She hurried after the others. Monika led them briskly up the street to a half-built house less than fifty metres away.

Suddenly Alex looked over to the truck. Children riffling the cab for anything consumable.

'Hey, get out of there!' he yelled, sprinting across. He grabbed at the squirming bodies and yanked them out.

Ivan appeared and shouted in Serbo-Croat.

Alex climbed onto the driving seat. A couple of packs of Marlboros that he'd left on the dashboard were gone.

'They have nothing . . .' Ivan explained in mitigation.

'They have *now*.'

He looked over to the school. The last of the boxes was being carried inside. McFee started weaving through the crowd towards them.

'Lots of happy faces in there, now,' he beamed, when he reached them. 'Where's your lady-friend?'

'Up the road somewhere.'

He cocked his head on one side and studied Alex's face.

'So how was your big reunion? Cut your dick off, did she?'

Alex smiled. 'Not quite.'

'Okay. We'd better get a move on. Young Ivan here needs to get back to his folks.'

'We can't go yet.'

'What d'you mean?'

'I have to talk to Lorna again, when she's finished doing whatever she's doing.'

'Oh, great! And how long's that going to be?'

'I don't know, but not too long.'

McFee didn't disguise his annoyance.

'Couldn't you have arranged to meet up this evening or something? A little tête à tête in the Vitez cookhouse, maybe.'

'No.' He wasn't going to explain. 'I'll keep a lookout for her, now you're back to guard the truck.'

He gave him the keys, pushed open the door and dropped to the ground.

Monika hustled Lorna down a path of broken bricks at the side of a house. The building was made of unrendered breeze-blocks and a concrete frame. The tiled roof was intact, but the windows were polythene.

Inside, a young couple wearing pullovers and tracksuit trousers stood awkwardly beside a small kitchen table and two plain, wooden chairs. It was the only furniture in the room, which had a bare concrete floor and rough, plastered walls.

Lorna's head spun in disbelief at what had just happened. Suddenly she feared it had been some extraordinary fantasy and wanted to run back into the road to check he was still there.

Then she saw the fear on the faces of the Bosnian

couple and jerked back to reality. Monika introduced them with names she didn't catch.

'This man is cousin of friend of Vildana family,' Josip translated. 'Friend who live in Tulici . . . Also dead.'

The woman of the couple began talking volubly, all the while dabbing her eyes with a handkerchief.

'She say Vildana very . . . well, shocked, I should say,' Josip explained in a whisper. 'She eat and sleep little. Every time she hear gun, she cry and looking somewhere to hide, like animal.'

'Poor little thing,' Lorna breathed. A child *that* traumatized might be hard to place.

The woman put a hand to her mouth and spoke lower.

'Vildana has something on mouth,' Josip whispered. 'Some mark . . . Boys threw stones because of this. She always running away. That's why she alive the woman say. She know all the place to hide.'

Lorna sensed an abyss opening up. This was no normal child.

'Monika, we need to talk to the kid,' she pressed, gently. Josip relayed her words.

The woman dried her eyes and blew her nose. Then she opened the door into the next room. A double mattress and a smaller single one lay on the bare floor. Blankets and bedding were scrunched up at the end of each.

At first Lorna thought no one was in the room. Then she realized that what she'd taken for a pile of clothes in a corner was in fact a child. In bright red pullover and yellow trousers, a multi-coloured scarf draped over her head, and hands covering her face, this was Vildana.

'Vildana?' the woman coaxed. She walked across and knelt before the cowering girl.

A tang of salt burned the back of Lorna's throat as she swallowed her welling tears.

The small hands slid cautiously down the face, exposing dark-brown, frightened eyes. Vildana kept her mouth covered, however.

The woman talked to her softly in a sing-song voice.

'She explain who we are,' Josip whispered, resting a hand on Lorna's shoulder and putting his face close to her ear.

She flinched as the stubble of his chin brushed her cheek and she caught the smell of his hangover breath.

'Ask Monika if Vildana knows that we're planning to get her out of the country,' she told him brusquely.

Josip obliged. Monika bobbed her head from side to side as if to say 'yes, but . . .'

How much of *anything* did Vildana understand, Lorna began to wonder.

She crossed the room and kneeled on the rough concrete a few feet in front of the child. Twelve years old. About the same age as Julie was when she'd had to give up caring for her.

'Hi, Vildana. I'm Lorna,' she said, forcing a smile.

The dark eyes wouldn't look at her. The grubby hands still covered her mouth. Twelve years old and still so much a child. Julie had developed a woman's ways by this age.

'Vildana? I want to help you if I can. If you'll let me.'

She beckoned Josip over to translate.

'Do you want me to help you?'

Josip let the translation slip softly from his tongue.

The girl's eyes looked up for guidance. The woman who'd been caring for her nodded.

'Will you tell me?' Lorna pleaded. 'I want to be your friend, Vildana.'

Slowly Vildana pulled her hands away from her mouth, eyes watching for the look of distaste which, experience had told her, would flit across the visitor's face.

A strawberry birthmark. A big one. Poor kid, Lorna

thought. Such a pretty face otherwise. Maybe the surgeons could fix it.

Fighting for self-control, Lorna let nothing show. Just smile, she told herself. She'd done it for Julie, she could do it for this girl.

She reached out. Vildana's cheek felt hot and moist.

'Do you know where America is?' Lorna coaxed.

Josip relayed the question. Vildana nodded.

'Would you like to go live there?'

She shook her head and the eyes began to fill with tears.

The woman looked desperate. She hugged the child, then whispered something to Josip.

'She say they cannot look after her much longer. They only marry few months, and Vildana not their family.'

'And there's no one else? No uncles, aunts, cousins?'

'She say no. Vildana father killed months ago, and the rest of her family die at Tulici.'

Monika beckoned Lorna and Josip to the other side of the room.

'Well, she say there is nothing for this girl in Bosnia,' he explained.

They both glanced at the damaged creature in the corner. The problem was how to get her out of the country. Apart from anything else she'd need a passport.

Lorna turned to the girl again, an idea forming in her head.

'Vildana, can I see how tall you are?' She held out her hands and beckoned the girl over. Hesitantly Vildana obliged.

She can walk at least, Lorna thought. Looks more normal standing up. She held her lightly by the shoulders.

'Monika, can you explain to Vildana that we'll try to find her a nice family to live with, in a place where there's no shooting?'

Lorna watched the girl's face as Monika talked to her.

'Tell her she'd have her own room, lots of nice clothes and things.'

She was determined to find something that might bring hope to those tragic eyes.

No response.

Hell! This was like walking a minefield, but she'd give it a shot.

'Josip,' she whispered in an aside, 'tell Monika to say to Vildana there'd be doctors in America who'd make her mouth better. She could look as beautiful as a movie-star and have all the boys begging for her to smile at them.'

Josip coughed.

'You're sure you want me translate?'

'Whisper it to Monika. See if she thinks it's a good idea.'

He did so. Monika's tired eyes seemed to grow in their sockets. She looked across at Lorna as if to say 'how *could* you?'

Then the girl's eyes darted from one face to another.

'She heard you,' Lorna whispered.

Vildana's voice when it came was a husky squeak.

'She ask if it true,' Josip confirmed.

'Then we're getting somewhere. Josip, bring Monika next door, would you?'

Lorna walked back into the room with the kitchen table. The other two joined her a moment later.

'Maybe Vildana will be happy to go with me,' Lorna began. 'But the first problem is how to get her out of here. Would I be able to take her through the check-points on the road to Split, without any papers?'

Josip make a 'tchk' sound.

'Impossible. Armija could shoot you for steal child, and HVO shoot *her* because she Muslim.'

'So how do we do it? Ask Monika what's happened in the past.'

Josip conferred.

154

'She say sometimes UN fly children from Sarajevo, but only when television makes big story. Anyway, it impossible to take Vildana to Sarajevo. No. Monika say the only way is to hide her in a white truck. There are many go to Split empty.'

'Hmm.'

Alex! He had a truck.

It was as if spring had arrived. Maybe *this* was the reason they were suddenly meeting again. Somebody up there making the breaks – like they'd done before.

She grabbed Josip's arm.

'Hang on here Josip. Get Monika to keep up the persuasion. I got to go see someone.'

She ran back down the path of broken bricks into the road. Two bearded men in fatigues watched her with cool curiosity, rifles slung lazily across their backs.

The truck was still there, just beyond her own Land Cruiser. Alex lounged against it. He spotted her and came her way. She slowed to a walk, hurriedly composing her thoughts.

'The girl's okay?' he asked, seeing the concentration on her face.

She stopped a few feet away, hands behind her back and chin thrust forward in that intense way she had when there was something important to say. Her blonde hair stuck out spikily as if electrified by the energy inside her head.

'Are you taking that truck back down to Split?'

He read her mind.

'Well, yes, in a day or two. When we've handed out all the supplies we brought up.'

She nodded, her whole body rocking with the motion of it. *Dare* she trust him again?

The salt and pepper grizzle on his chin might have changed his appearance, but his eyes had the same directness she'd fallen for in that Hampstead pub.

Oh hell! She *had* to trust him. No alternative.

155

'When you and I . . . all those years ago . . .' she began hesitantly. She held out her right hand, fingers cupped as if holding something precious.

'Ye-es,' he answered, worried about what was coming.

'We . . . we shared something, didn't we?'

She saw his frown and nearly gave up.

'This sounds crazy, but I'm talking about *fate* Alex. You remember,' she floundered, unable to look him in the eye. 'Things that are *meant to be*? We were believers, weren't we? God, I must be mad standing in the middle of all this shit and talking such stuff . . .'

'Go on. I'm listening.'

'Well, you've got to admit it's one hell of a coincidence, that we both end up here, doing the same sort of job?'

'It certainly is,' he nodded, his mind racing.

'Okay. Here it is. In that house up the road, there's one totally traumatized twelve-year-old child called Vildana. She needs psychiatric treatment, she needs surgery, and she needs to be gotten away from this place where there are people who want to kill her.'

'I see,' he nodded, listening intently.

'But for a Muslim girl with no papers, there's only one way you can get out from Central Bosnia.' She pointed at the Bedford. 'Hidden in the back of an aid truck.'

'Ahh . . .' He'd guessed right.

His pulse quickened. Maybe *he* would start believing in fate. This twelve-year-old girl could be the catalyst to bring him and Lorna together again. And she might lead *him* to Milan Pravic.

'I'll have to talk it through with Moray,' he answered cautiously.

'Can you do it now?'

'It'd be better tonight. Over a drink.'

'Okay, okay. I've got a lot of things to fix, anyhow. Now, look. How do we meet up tomorrow? Where do I find you?'

'Come to Vitez in the afternoon. We're in a house opposite the UN camp. Ask for Bosnia Emergency in the P.Info, that's the press office. They'll show you where.'

Behind him the Bedford coughed into life. McFee was making his point.

'Okay. I'll get there.'

They stood just inches apart, unable to bridge the gap, staring at each other awkwardly.

'Tomorrow, then.'

'Bye.'

He turned on his heel and pulled himself into the cab through the door that Ivan held open.

Thirteen

Central Bosnia

McFee simmered silently for most of the drive down from the village. Then, after they had dropped Ivan at the Travnik refugee centre, he let fly.

'Look chum, there's rules in this place. And thanks to you we just broke a whole set back there!'

'What d'you mean?' Alex snapped, angry at McFee's high-handedness.

'That village was dead dodgy. *Muj* all over the place. The rule is *get in, get the stuff off, and get out fast.* It's not the time to hang about so's you can chat up old girlfriends!'

'Christ, Moray! If you'd met someone you hadn't seen for twenty years, what would you have done?'

Alex bit his tongue. Not a good time to pick a fight with McFee.

McFee weaved past the junction with Route Triangle. Ten more minutes and they'd be at the house. It was late afternoon.

'I suppose the lassie will be warming your bed for ye, tonight,' he needled sourly, hunched over the wheel, grubby and frayed.

Alex guessed they both looked like that by now. 'I should be so lucky . . .' he snorted.

They jolted on.

'Women, eh?' McFee mused bitterly. 'Nothing but trouble . . .'

'Yeh . . . Don't know why we bother . . .'

McFee seemed to want to get something off his chest.

Alex decided it might pay dividends if he were to play along.

The Scotsman whistled tunelessly for a second or two.

'All that hassle for a few moments of pleasure . . .' he sighed.

Alex sensed the imminence of a torrent of misogyny.

'It's a matter of luck,' he answered vaguely. 'Some you win, some you lose.'

'Me? I *lost* . . .' McFee continued, bitterly. 'Picked a woman who was no use to *any* man, and waited too long before doing anything about it.'

'How long were you married?'

'Sixteen years. Didn't get hitched until I was nearly forty.'

'No kids, you said?' Alex checked.

'She lost a couple. Miscarried. Then refused to try any more. Pity. I really love kids. And after that, she didna want to know about sex . . .'

'But you stayed with her sixteen years?'

'Aye!' McFee shook his head in disbelief. 'Must want m' head examined.'

'But now you've split up for good?'

'Oh aye!' he chuckled. 'She'd take a carving knife to me now, if she could . . .'

'Why, what did you do to her?' he asked, then wished he hadn't.

McFee laughed awkwardly.

'Well if a chap doesn't get his oats at home, he has to go somewhere else.'

'Ah. A girlfriend, eh? Nothing so dreadful in that.'

McFee didn't answer. He looked as if he wanted to open up but there was something stopping him. They reached the outskirts of Vitez.

'Quite a lot of "somewhere elses", that was the trouble,' he mumbled eventually. '*Ladies o' the night.*' There was a glint in his eye, almost like pride.

'Sounds expensive,' Alex remarked lamely.

'Not at all,' McFee answered. 'It costs plenty if you take a lassie to a nice restaurant because you want to fuck her after. And she may not even oblige. My way costs the same, but removes the doubt . . .'

A grubby argument for self-interest that sounded well rehearsed.

'And since you're paying, you call the shots. Don't have to worry about whether the earth moves for them . . .' he added, his mouth twisting.

So, Moray was into hookers, Alex thought. Not often you met someone who'd *admit* to that. He couldn't help a sense of disgust.

He began to remember things. The girls McFee had chatted up in the London pub the evening he came down from Edinburgh. Must have gone with one of them when he slipped out of the boarding house in the middle of the night.

'And as you said last night, I suppose out here the tarts come pretty cheap,' Alex prodded, thinking of the woman from the camp kitchens with the gipsy eyes.

McFee bristled. 'What I said's between you and me, okay?' He reversed the truck into the driveway to their house. 'I don't go telling everyone. Some people can take against you.'

The Scotsman looked flushed, as if fearful he'd said too much already.

'Fine.' Alex had heard enough.

Inside the house, McFee put the kettle onto the heat. Alex decided it was time to talk business.

'So what's the plan for the next few days, Moray?' he asked, trying to sound casual.

'It's the Croats tomorrow. We'll find a home for the other half of our supplies. Then we might head for Split the day after. There should be another bread van out from England soon. I'll check at P.Info to see if there's been a fax for us.'

The landlady came in with fresh bread and home-made curd cheese.

'*Dobar dan, Dragana,*' McFee greeted her.

'*Dobar dan, Dobar dan!*'

They brewed the tea and ate the food.

Alex noticed McFee looked preoccupied, as if the man regretted letting even a small amount of daylight shine on the dark secrets of his sex-life.

He cleared his throat. The issue of Lorna's orphan could wait no longer.

'If we join a convoy on the way south,' Alex began innocently, 'do we get much hassle? Road blocks, searches and so on?'

McFee seemed not to hear. Then he began to focus.

'Er . . . well I've only done the trip once,' he reminded him. 'Had a clear run that time. Why?'

No point in prevaricating.

'So if there was a good reason to smuggle someone out of here through the front lines, in the empty truck, it should be possible . . .'

Too blunt, Alex thought. Damn!

McFee raised an eyebrow, startled.

'Oh aye! And if you wanted to smuggle grenades in with the supplies on the way up, that should be possible too. Only you'd never do it. Because if you got caught you'd be dead. And every aid organization in Bosnia would become suspect. You'd screw it for everybody.'

'There could be exceptions though, like a child who would die if she didn't get medical treatment?'

McFee looked at him suspiciously.

'What are you on about? It's yon lassie, isn't it? Yon Lorna.'

'Well, yes, actually. She's got a big problem on her hands and needs our help.'

'God almighty! You only spent a few minutes with the woman and already she's got you jumpin' through hoops . . . What's this all about?'

This wasn't going the way he'd intended.

He told McFee about the girl Vildana. The Scotsman's eyes seemed to fill with mist.

'And all of this came out when you bumped into Lorna this afternoon?'

Alex nodded.

'I wonder! You sure you didn't fix all this up before? I'm beginning to think I'm being set up by you twose.'

'Come off it, Moray!'

'Well, whatever . . . The answer's no. Major Mike would go through the roof. It's just not on, chum.'

'There's no reason Mike should ever know about it . . .' Alex pressed.

'Don't even think about it! It's too bloody dangerous. For us, for the kid and for Bosnia Emergency. You'll have to tell the lassie to try it on in her own car.'

'There's not a lot of room to hide in a Land Cruiser,' Alex responded.

McFee was adamant. 'There's no way, Alex. No way.' His scowl warned not to press the point any further.

He sat hunched on the sofa, the troubled look back in his eyes. He jiggled his foot nervously. Suddenly he stood up.

'I'm just off out for a minute,' he said. 'I'll see if there's any messages and find out where's the best place to take the stuff for the Croats tomorrow. See you later.'

Alex raised a hand. He watched McFee amble to the door, seeing him in a new light now. For some reason it was hard to respect a man who had to pay for sex.

There was a roundness to McFee's shoulders, a bit of a stoop. He had the look of someone living amongst shadows.

Alex pulled out a cigarette, tapped it on the arm of the sofa, then lit up.

He felt angry with himself. Should have handled things better. Smuggling the girl out was something he *had* to do. It wasn't just *her* future that depended on it.

But McFee had the power to block him. He was the boss out here. Unless Alex could think of a way to change that . . .

163

Fourteen

Dr Hamid Akhavi sat in the back of the Nissan as it turned out of the security gates and headed for Yazd down the service road built by engineers from the Revolutionary Guards. He removed his black-framed spectacles and polished the lenses.

Dasht-e-Lut is the name given to the expanse of sand-blown hills and plains in the heart of Iran, a place of lingering death for any life caught under the blast of the summer sun. An isolated, lonely place, six hundred kilometres from the nearest neighbouring state, as far from an enemy attack as it is possible to get – the reason it had been chosen as the site for a nuclear bomb factory.

Everything around him was the colour of sand – the long, concrete-capped laboratories with their deep, underground workshops; the accommodation block where he lived with his wife and child; even this car taking him to the airport.

Just sand – that's what they hoped the spy satellites would see, and the pilots of the Israeli planes if they ever braved such an expanse of hostile airspace to attack the plant.

The bomb meant 'power'.

To the east, possession of it had made equals of Pakistan and India. To the west, the Jews believed it guaranteed their survival, and fear of its acquisition by the madman in Baghdad had struck terror into the hearts of the Americans and the fat sheikhs in the Gulf.

164

The nights were cold here at this time of year. Icy even. It was late afternoon and the sun had warmed the air to a comfortable twenty degrees. Hamid's wife hated life in the desert compound; nothing to do but talk to other mothers and watch television. She'd asked to be given work at the site even if it were only typing, but the guards who controlled everything had refused. Security grounds, they'd said.

Hamid looked out of the car window at the hostile, grey-brown landscape. He'd resolved one day to live somewhere green, with water and flowers always in sight. But not yet. Not until the regime released him from the burden they'd placed on his shoulders.

Thirty-three years old now, with black hair and a thin moustache, he'd been just eighteen when the mullahs overthrew the Shah. On television, the world had watched the mob choke Tehran's streets to welcome Khomeini back. He'd been in that crowd, a passionate believer in change from the corrupt old ways.

Later, at university, his brilliance had shone. The Islamic leaders decided he had a talent they could not afford to lose. They had inherited a nuclear programme from the time of the Shah – reactors at Bushehr, only half built. Publicly they'd stopped the programme, proclaiming it 'unislamic', but privately Hamid and a cadre of others were coached in the art of the atom, ready for the day when the priests recognized where power truly lay.

He'd been sent to Russia to learn to handle and machine nuclear materials, an isolated, often lonely life in Gorky, but one which had relieved him of his obligation to fight on the bloodstained frontier with Iraq.

To get the bomb before Iraq – that's what sustained him through these difficult days in the desert. Soon all his years of study, all his assiduous contact-building would pay off. Hamid was on the threshold of a deal that could give his nation that bomb within two years.

His elation was tempered with fear, however. Fear

that the mullahs would still be in power when his bomb became a reality. Like most of the educated in Iran, Hamid had long since ceased to believe that power was safe in clerical hands.

That Iran should become a nuclear power – he was a believer. So long as the bombs were used for power-play and not to kill. But whether the mullahs would embrace such constraints – that was the question he couldn't answer.

He slipped off the jacket of his clerical-grey suit, hung it on the door-handle hook, then loosened the collar of his white shirt. Over an hour's drive to the airport at Yazd, another hour for the flight to Tehran. There'd be a day or two to wait in the capital before the military jet took him out of the country. They'd not told him the date he would travel. Security again.

He was excited by his mission, but afraid too. The authorities had placed absolute trust in him, but if he failed, their revenge would be uncompromising.

A month ago he'd confided his worries in his sister in Tehran, breaking all the rules of security. He'd told her about his work, and about the Russians with plutonium for sale. Told her so that if he disappeared one day, someone could tell the outside world why.

Unfortunately for Hamid, in a careless moment she already had.

Sheremetyevo Airport, Moscow

It wouldn't be cheap making the Iran deal work. Colonel Pavel Kulikov already had six people on his payroll at the weapon dismantling site near Sverdlovsk, and the advance payment he'd squeezed out of the Iranians would soon be exhausted.

In his late forties, with hair the colour of brushed aluminium, he strode purposefully across the departure concourse in his smart, grey *biznisman* suit, looking up at the indicator board for word on the flight to Zagreb. His baggage trolley bore a suitcase whose contents could get him court-martialled.

He had no qualms about what he was doing. The nuclear genie escaped the bottle long ago. Nothing could stop its spread. Thanks to him it might happen faster, that was all.

In his world, it was every man for himself now, loyalty to the State a thing of the past. Loyalty to oneself was all a Russian could afford these days.

He knew of many, hungry scientists tempted to do the same as him, many who craved the dollars that would transform their lives. Some had resorted to the Mafia to find a market for their nuclear materials, but ended up being cheated.

Kulikov had no need of intermediaries. He had access to the tons of plutonium removed from dismantled missiles, access to the American-financed plants where the cores were sliced to prevent reassembly. And, above all, he had the means and the skills to run his own sales operation.

Most of his military career had been spent securing special weapons – nuclear and biological – protecting the sites where warheads were stored and where they were made.

He'd befriended the young Iranian while assigned to the All-Union Research Institute for Experimental Physics near Gorky. Communism was meeting its nemesis at the time. The two men had debated revolutions and political corruption, topics they understood well.

After Hamid returned home to Iran, they'd remained

in touch, each thinking the other might be useful one day, even if at the time they didn't know how.

Kulikov lifted his heavy suitcase from the trolley and presented it to the check-in counter. Heavy because it contained a segment of plutonium the size of a thin wedge of cheese.

Sweat chilled his upper lip. The next few minutes were dangerous. If the case was opened and examined he'd be in deep trouble.

The clerk took his ticket and passport and tapped at the computer. The travel papers stated Kulikov was on an official visit to UNPROFOR headquarters in Zagreb. They'd cost him five hundred dollars.

Full of *angst*, he watched the suitcase disappear. Would the idiots send it to the same place as him? Disastrous if they didn't. Disastrous!

He'd weighed the risks carefully, though. Putting the sample in his hand baggage would have meant greater danger. The X-rays at every airport, the searches. Hold-baggage would be safer; it was seldom checked.

Unsmiling, the clerk thrust him the boarding pass. Kulikov joined the queue for passport control.

Berlin

Parking near Oranienburgerstrasse was hard in the early evening. A rash of arty cafés and restaurants had opened in the old Jewish quarter of east Berlin since unification. Dieter Konrad, alias Herr Dunkel, left the Mercedes half a kilometre away, and walked to the brothel.

He nodded at the policeman guarding the synagogue. Neo-nazis had threatened bomb attacks. The papers that

168

morning had reported gravestones defaced in a Jewish cemetery.

At the junction where the road forked, the first whores were out. Early birds, dressed like fantasy creatures. Huge blonde wigs, thigh-length, black leather boots, flesh-coloured tights, topped by crotch-hugging briefs and lurid bomber jackets. They stood in the road, offering themselves to passing cars.

'*Guten abend mein Herr!*' one of them called to Konrad, her voice like a caress. '*Möchten Sie ein schönes Geschäft mit mir machen?*'

So open, so blatant, the offer to 'do business'. He ignored her. In communist times they'd have been jailed for this. Prostitution had had to lurk underground in those days, in the backstreets nearby. A small, criminal community open to exploitation. Particularly by people like him.

He looked the part for this area – a man on his own, in a raincoat. Not very tall, a little overweight and a face with withdrawn, watchful eyes, hiding behind spectacles. An average punter. Even the stick-on moustache would draw little attention here. The whores were used to men with hair that wasn't their own.

He turned left off the main street, past a couple of cafés and then right to where the small neon sign winked above a doorway. He pressed a bell and the door clicked open automatically.

It was an ordinary apartment building, this entrance and staircase serving four floors. Two flats on each of the upper floors, two rooms per flat, twelve girls altogether, he reckoned.

The 'madame' whose name Gisela had given him emerged from a ground floor doorway and welcomed him with a handshake. Heavily coated with cosmetics, she looked in her sixties. Too old for work, she'd moved into management.

'Herr Dunkel! You're back again, so soon.'

She led him into her plush living room, all soft sofas and walls adorned with pornographic paintings.

'You want Karina I suppose?' she asked. 'She's a little busy just now. You'll wait?'

'There's somewhere private?'

Last time he'd been shown to a lounge where customers sat, avoiding each other's gaze until the girl of their choice came free. To be avoided at all cost. He wanted as few witnesses as possible.

'You can wait here if you like, until . . .' The sound of the door-buzzer stopped her. 'Perhaps not. Come.'

She led him along a short passageway to a bedroom that smelled of Chanel.

'This is my own room. You won't be disturbed,' she smiled, touching him softly on the lapel.

'Thank you. I'm a shy man.'

She nodded understandingly.

'I hope that Karina is . . . everything you expected? I think her talents were what you were looking for.'

'First impressions were good,' Konrad nodded. 'For the rest . . . we'll see.'

'She won't be long. I'll let her know someone's waiting. There's a little green light in her room which I can switch on from down here.'

She waddled back along the corridor.

Konrad's pulse raced. The girl upstairs had better not let him down. Time was running out.

Ten minutes passed, broken occasionally by the sound of the door, and by footsteps on the stairs. Then suddenly a petite, pale face with straight black hair like a doll's poked round the bedroom door.

'So, it's you.' She didn't smile. 'I thought it would be. Come with me.'

Karina led the way up the main staircase. A low-cut, white Lycra slip clung to her torso, stretched taut by the nipples of her big, firm breasts. Her disproportionately narrow hips were sheathed in an absurdly small skirt made of shiny red plastic. Konrad was mesmerized by the outline of her cherry-like buttocks as she minced in front of him.

The room was small and the air stale. A large four-poster bed took up most of the space. There was a dressing table with a flat-backed hairbrush, and a curtained opening led to a bathroom.

Karina closed the door and spun round to face him. Her painted lips smiled, but her eyes didn't. Communism might be dead, but she had a lingering fear of the *Horch und Guck* – the 'listen and look', as the Stasi were known.

'So,' Konrad began. 'Do you have it?'

The girl was so young, the bed so blatant, he wasn't here for sex but felt a tightening in his trousers none the less.

'*Jawohl!* But it wasn't easy. And it will cost you more, darling.' Her voice had the huskiness of a heavy smoker.

'We agreed a price,' he snapped. 'One thousand marks.'

'It's not enough, *mein Lieber!* It took time. I lost business here, finding the right type for you.'

Her nut-brown eyes were as hard as pebbles, but he could see she was scared of him.

Konrad seethed. They always did this, these creatures from the gutter. Cheating was a habit.

'Let me see it.'

'Let me see your money first. Two thousand marks!'

'No way, you bitch! No way I'll pay you that much. One thousand, or I'll go elsewhere!'

She could see he was bluffing, see too from his mushy eyes that he wanted more from her than he'd said.

'Fifteen hundred then, and I'll suck you for free.'

He flinched at her crudeness.

'Ach, show it to me and stop wasting my time,' he growled.

'Money on the table . . .' she insisted.

171

Petulantly he took an envelope from his coat pocket and slapped it onto the bed.

'There's a thousand in there. We'll see about the rest.'

Karina fixed him with her eye. She'd decided beforehand to make him sweat if she could. Slowly she undid the zipper on her skirt, while humming 'the Stripper'. Konrad swallowed.

With the waistband of her skirt loosened, she slipped her fingers down the front of her black panties, retrieved the slim booklet she'd concealed there and held it out to him.

Konrad took the passport. It felt warm.

Rzeczpospolita Polska was marked in gold on the grubby, blue cover. It was creased as if its owner had kept it in a back trouser pocket.

Konrad opened it. *Marek Gruszka* was the name next to the photograph inside. Born 1962 in Wroclaw. It looked perfect but he wasn't going to let *her* know that. He frowned.

'It's good, yes?' she asked anxiously. 'It's what you wanted. What you told me.'

Konrad fingered the document, held it up to the light and ran a finger-nail round the edge of the plastic covered photograph.

'The man was here in this room when you took it?' he asked disparagingly.

'Course not. I don't nick stuff here. I'd be out on my ear. Anyway, the punters would know where to find me. I'd get my pretty face slashed.'

She moved close to him and put her hands on his shoulders.

'And you wouldn't want that, would you darling?'

She pressed her naked midriff against him. She could tell he was almost hard. Konrad pushed her away.

'Where then? Where did you get it?'

Scowling, she pulled up her zip again.

'What's it to you? I got what you wanted, didn't I?'

He grabbed her wrist.

'Just tell me!'

She winced at the harshness of his grip.

'The Tiergarten, of course. That's where the Poles go. They park up between the Grosser Stern and the Brandenburg. Some like to do it in the bushes. This one had a bed in the cab of his truck. Two nights I hung around there. *Scheiss kalt!* I was about to give up and find somewhere warm, when this trailer truck pulled in. The bloke wound down the window, sitting in his bloody shirt sleeves with the heater turned full up. I was so cold I'd have paid *him* to get in.

'In his shirt sleeves, with his jacket hung up next to him. And that little sweetheart poking out of a pocket.'

She pointed at the passport, then screwed up her face with distaste.

'Dirty bastard. Stank like a butcher's shop. And thirty marks was all he was going to pay. I said he could have hand relief or nothing.'

Her small mouth widened into a smile again.

'But I made it a bit special! Took my knickers off and laid them on his face while I tossed him off. So when I grabbed his passport, he couldn't see!'

Her description of the act shrivelled Konrad's tumescence.

'All right. I'll give you another two hundred,' he snapped, eager to be away from this place. He stuffed the passport in an inside pocket.

'No way! I missed two nights in this cosy hole to get it. That's worth a thousand at least. And don't you try and sneak off.' She darted to the bedside and held her finger over a bell-push. 'There's a bloke as big as a wardrobe who will be waiting for you at the bottom of the stairs.'

'*Arschloch!*' he snarled.

Konrad was beaten. He extracted his wallet and counted out five hundred marks. The girl took it and

173

then checked the contents of the envelope on the bed. All correct.

'A pleasure doing business with you,' she said, moving close to him again. 'Sure there's nothing else you want?'

She fingered his genitals.

Her flesh seemed to emanate warmth; her perfume tantalized his senses. Then Konrad thought of her in that truck on the Tiergarten.

'*Aufwiedersehen, Fräulein Karina.*'

He shook her hand. An automatic gesture, but one he instantly regretted. As he descended the stairs he wiped his palm on his coat.

Fifteen

Zenica, Bosnia

The power was on at the International Hotel in Zenica. Lorna hurried to get things done before it blacked out again. Since returning from the village of Duba, she'd hardly stopped shaking.

Her bedroom window faced southwest, as she'd requested. She opened the glass and positioned a bedside table under the ledge. No obstructions. A clear view to the Atlantic sky.

The evening air made her shiver and she put her anorak back on.

She placed the digital satphone on the table, unfolded the flat antenna and adjusted it for elevation and azimuth. Luckily there were no tower blocks in the way.

She powered up the equipment, fine-tuned it for signal strength, then connected the modem lead from her portable computer and switched on.

'This is where I start praying . . .' she muttered, not too hot on technology.

Laurence Machin, the computer-wizard who'd founded CareNet had coached her in how to use the equipment, but would she remember it right?

The screen of the portable flickered and flashed as the software loaded, then settled on the 'Cityscape' navigator software. She clicked on the 'dial' button with the mouse.

'If this works it'll be a miracle,' she whispered.

The modem purred and bleeped, then the screen prompted her for her log-in name and password.

'Wow. I sure am getting the breaks today . . .' she grinned.

From the Internet menu she picked ‹Usenet›, then ‹alt.childadopt.agency›. Another menu appeared. She chose the item ‹children available›.

She was now connected to the electronic bulletin board used by Machin as a 'hyperspace' adoption agency.

She typed 'ADD', then the screen cleared for her message.

Urgently seeking foster home, 12-year-old Vildana from central Bosnia. This child must be evacuated for her own safety. Badly scarred mentally, after seeing her family murdered, and with a mild physical handicap, she will need extensive psychiatric therapy and medical attention.
This one's a real 'toughie'; the girl is in bad need of an 'angel'. If there's one out there, please reply to this as soon as possible.
For legal reasons, adoption cannot be entered into immediately, but it can be a long-term intention.

Next she switched to e-mail and sent a longer, more detailed message to Machin himself, explaining how she was planning to get the girl out of Bosnia.

There were no messages in her own box, so she logged off.

That was it. Thirty million people could now read her words, people in what Machin termed 'the grade one market' of academics and businessmen who used the Internet. Just the sort of people who had the drive and the financial resources to make the adoption of problem children viable. In theory.

Lorna powered down the equipment. So impersonal this idea of computerized child adoption. What she'd fired into the ether wasn't key-strokes. It was a life.

She folded the antenna and closed the window.

God, it was cold! She removed her boots and lay on the bed, her legs under the blankets, shoulders propped against a pillow. She'd keep the anorak on until the room warmed up again.

Across the room on the dressing table sat her Nikon. Inside it was Alex – a picture of him at least. With his arm round her. Just like old times.

She still found it hard to believe. The beard had thrown her. She'd never liked facial hair. Soon get him to sha . . .

Hell! Slow down!

She'd been vilifying the man for two decades, how could she even *consider* a new relationship with him? Didn't know anything about him any more. He'd said he'd been hiding. Where? Married? Kids?

She closed her eyes, trying to visualize him in that house near Vitez. Half-a-dozen in his team, she guessed. Drivers, organizers, a mechanic and a translator. Probably with their own generators and satcoms. You'd need that sort of set-up to function long-term in Bosnia.

The translator could be a girl. Maybe he desired her. Maybe they were lovers even . . .

She opened her eyes wide to stop the racetrack of her mind. Fate had brought Alex back to her for one purpose and one purpose only – to get Vildana out of Bosnia.

The cookhouse was crowded. Alex and McFee squeezed in amongst shaven-headed French soldiers who'd stopped for an evening meal on their way to Sarajevo.

Alex hadn't mentioned Vildana again. He planned to wait until later when the Scotsman had a few whiskies inside him. McFee looked tense and thoughtful, his mind elsewhere. He kept glancing over his shoulder.

'Bloody great this apple dappy,' Alex remarked, spooning in the sticky pudding.

177

'Oh aye. But it makes you droop, that stuff,' McFee joked absently. He had eaten little that evening.

'Tell you what,' he went on. 'I've an idea. Why don't *you* go to the P.Info briefing on your own? I'll wander round the camp a bit and see if I can pick up a bit o' gossip. Always useful.'

'Sure. Why not?' It wasn't *gossip* McFee planned to pick up, Alex reckoned.

They took their trays to the bin.

'See you later, then, eh?' McFee said, out in the darkened Warrior park, expecting Alex to head straight for the Press Office.

'I'm going to take a leak first.'

His feet crunched across the hardcore to the white portakabins which accommodated the soldiers. The floor of the toilet was mud-stained and wet.

He headed back into the darkness, annoyed at having left his torch at the house. He paused to let his eyes adjust. To his right, pans clattered in the cookhouse, to his left, a diesel Land Rover rattled past.

He set off again, once his eyes could make out the boards that would get him safely through the mud on the camp perimeter. Had to hurry or he'd be late. The planks passed between rows of containers. From somewhere amongst them he heard hushed voices arguing. A woman, then McFee.

The man's a sex junkie, Alex thought. He squelched into deep mud.

'Shit!

His boots were caked. Reaching the tarmac at last, he stamped and scraped until his feet felt lighter again. At the door to P.Info he paused to wipe off the remains of the slime. On the way in a corporal was inspecting the journalists' feet.

'You're a house-proud lot,' Alex remarked.

'So would you be if you lived in this 'ouse,' the soldier replied.

Major Clarke-Hartley had little to say that evening, other than that the Bosnian Army third Corps was having trouble getting its Mujahedin elements to obey the cease-fire.

'How many of them are there?' asked a man from the BBC.

'Don't know for sure. A couple of hundred, maybe. But they're a determined bunch, as many of you know.'

There was a murmur of assent. The Muj hated journalists and they'd all had brushes with them.

The briefing over, the Major nobbled Alex as he was about to leave.

'Hi. Tell me, how's old Mike Allison?' he asked amiably. 'He was in my regiment, you know. Splendid chap.'

'Really? Well I've only met him once. Seemed pretty switched on.'

'He certainly is.' The Major seemed eager to chat. 'So . . . where've you been today then?'

Alex struggled to remember the name of the village.

'Place called Duba?'

'Oh, ye-es. Lots of Muj up there. We did a patrol through the area first thing this morning.'

'And tomorrow we're going to Busovaca,' Alex continued. 'There's some village near there with a lot of Croat refugees, apparently.'

'Balancing the books, eh? Well if there's anything I can do, do tell me.'

The man from the BBC had returned and hustled the Major away.

Alex wandered back outside. Heading for Dragana's house he suddenly noticed two armed men watching from the darkness on the far side of the road. Their eyes followed him as he turned into the drive, making the skin crawl on the back of his neck.

He opened the door to the house and called out. No reply. Just the crackle of logs in the stove. McFee must still be doing his business. Could the man *really* get a thrill by paying some slag to serve him behind a container filled with ballast?

In the living room, a single candle flickered. Alex lit another to brighten the place up, opened a can of beer and pulled out his cigarettes.

Sod it! How was he going to persuade McFee to smuggle the girl out? He took in a lungful of smoke.

Blackmail? Tell him he'd reveal his sordid sex life to the world? Hardly . . .

He closed his eyes and thought of Lorna, remembering how good it had felt to be near her even if only for a moment when McFee had taken the photograph. Sounded stupid, but it had made him feel *complete* again. He'd never had that sort of closeness with Kirsty. He wondered how she was. There'd been no news when he'd telephoned from Split.

He felt cosily comfortable with the gentle popping of wood on the fire, and the candle flames still as a painting. His eyelids drooped.

After a while the sound of footsteps on the gravel stirred him from his doze. McFee returning?

Two pairs of feet. Wouldn't bring the whore back here, surely? He glanced at his watch. Just after ten. Late for visitors.

A firm knock on the door. Alex took a candle to answer it.

'Good evening, sir!' A voice like a rasp. More announcement than greeting. Two UN soldiers with armbands.

'Good evening. What can I do for you?'

'Would you be Mister Moray McFee?'

'No. He's not here at the moment.'

The soldiers glanced at one another.

'Would it be okay if we came in and waited for him?'

'I suppose so. . .'

As he let them in, he saw the initials M.P. on their arms in big, red letters.

'Can I ask who *you* are, sir?'

'Alex Crawford. Moray and I work together. What's this all about?'

He gestured towards the velour sofa and they sat down, looking stiff and awkward. They laid their SA80 rifles on the carpet beside them.

'A personal matter, sir. Can't discuss it.'

The one who'd done the talking had a sergeant's stripes. His companion was a corporal.

'I see. Well, would you like a beer?'

Again, the policemen eyed each other.

'That'd be grand.' The accent sounded northern. Probably Liverpool.

Alex retrieved the last two cans from the box in the corner.

'Running low. I suppose I can get some more at the camp?'

'No problem. Talk to my mate round the back of the NAAFI shop. He'll see you right. Cheers.'

They nattered for a while about beers, about the food at the camp and about the craziness of the Bosnian war. Then the sergeant looked at his watch.

'D'you know when Mister McFee will be back?' he asked.

'No, I don't. Don't even know where he is.'

Alex felt the sergeant's eyes boring into his head. Disbelief was written on the soldiers' faces.

'What's the outfit you work for? Bosnia Emergency, is it?'

'That's right.'

'Just the two of you here?'

Alex nodded.

'And you don't know where your mate is at half-past ten at night?'

'Sorry. No I don't.' It wasn't his business to tell them

181

McFee was with a whore. 'He told me he was going to hang around the camp and pick up some gossip. Are you sure *I* can't help?'

'Not unless your name's McFee and you come from Edinburgh,' the sergeant scowled.

'Edinburgh? Something to do with his wife?' Maybe she'd had an accident.

The corporal snorted. 'She weren't old enough to be anybody's wife . . .'

Alex felt a chill descend on him. These soldiers were *policemen.*

'What d'you mean?'

McFee's uneasiness that evening . . . the hunted look. The feeling that the man had said more than he'd meant to . . .

'There's just some questions we want to ask him . . .'

Alex recalled the headlines in the Edinburgh paper on the day he left home. The police with clipboards investigating the death of a girl . . . The appeal for witnesses.

'You've not come to arrest him?' Alex asked incredulously.

They shook their heads in unison. The sergeant's eyes were like bullets.

'Just some questions. On behalf of Edinburgh constabulary.'

Stony faces that suspected he knew something.

'Something to do with a girl?' A nod. 'Not the one found dead in Edinburgh ten days ago?'

'What was that then, sir?' The well-practised look of surprise.

'We're both from Edinburgh. That's where we met. It was in the papers when I left, about the girl. A thirteen-year-old found dead. Some suspicion she'd been caught up in prostitution?'

The sergeant nodded slowly.

'Ever talk about it, you and him?'

'Never. But . . . *is* that why you're here?'

The sideways glances again.

''Sright, sir.'

'But surely you don't think Moray . . .?' he gasped.

They stared blankly, letting him flounder.

'Anything you want to tell me, Mr Crawford?' The voice was softer, cajoling.

'I can't believe . . . I mean, I hardly know the bloke,' Alex stammered. 'Met him a couple of times on the Lothian coast, that's all. I used to go running on the beach there, and he walked his dog.'

'Yellow Craig, was it?'

The words jabbed at his guts. The dunes . . . No one went there at night. Not at this time of year. He knew what was coming. He nodded.

'That's where they found the girl, sir. She'd been strangled.'

Alex shook his head. McFee's words in his head – *since you're paying for it, you call the shots*. . .

'She'd been a virgin, until that night . . .' the corporal added.

Silence. Just the fire crackling. Then a short burst from an automatic some distance away.

'Cleaning the barrels . . .' the corporal muttered. ' 'Appens most nights. They can't seem to kick the habit round here.'

The sergeant nudged him to be quiet.

'Moray McFee *killed a child?*' Alex gasped. He needed them to spell it out.

'That's right. At least, that's what the boys in Edinburgh say.'

'Jesus . . . ! But what evidence have they got that it's him?'

'Don't know, sir, but they sounded pretty certain. Must be if they're involving *us*. Are you sure there's nothing you can tell me?' the sergeant pressed. 'You must have some idea where he is.'

Alex clamped his hands on his head. His brain felt as if it were about to explode.

'The last time I saw him was in the camp, after supper,' he whispered. 'Round where those containers are. With a woman from the kitchens.'

'What, Illie?'

'I think that's the name, yes.'

'Tch! She's the camp bike,' said the corporal.

'Well ... if what you're saying is right, maybe ... maybe she's in some sort of danger ...' Alex spluttered. 'I mean, Moray must be a nutter ...'

His mind raced. Why had McFee rung him on that day of the funeral? Why had he picked *him* to come out with him? As an unsuspecting smokescreen? Or because he'd been wanting to talk all along, and thought for some reason Alex would listen? He was good at listening. People always told him as much. Jodie, Kirsty – Lorna.

'Shouldn't you go and search the camp?' he suggested.

'Done that just now. We know all the places. We'll just wait.' They sat in silence, Alex staring at the floor and the soldiers staring at *him*.

Maybe McFee had been on the point of confessing ... Maybe that's why he'd begun talking about his 'somewhere elses'.

'Don't mind us if you want to turn in,' the sergeant said before long.

Alex looked at his watch again. After eleven. He stood up and moved to the window, the neighbouring houses of the village dark and silent in the grey moonlight. McFee was out there somewhere. A hostage of the night.

'All right with you if we sit it out 'til he gets back?' the sergeant asked.

'Mmm? Yes of course.' He turned back to face them. 'I think I *will* head for the sack.'

'Just before you do, sir, can I have a quick shufti round?'

The sergeant propelled himself to his feet and flicked on a pocket torch.

'Always like to see how the other half lives . . .'

Alex bristled at the implication he was hiding McFee, but followed him to the bathroom then the bedroom.

'Satisfied?'

'Not a bad little place, sir. Got the landlady upstairs, have you?'

Alex nodded. He wanted to be on his own now.

'No more beer, I'm afraid,' he said, heading for his room. 'But help yourself to tea and coffee. If I'm asleep when he comes back, you'd better wake me.'

'Certainly, sir. 'Night.'

Alone, Alex sat on the divan with his head in his hands. For over a week he'd been cheek by jowl with a man who'd raped a child, then stolen her life – and he'd known nothing about it. He couldn't believe it.

The MPs would *have* to arrest Moray. Ship him back to Scotland so the Edinburgh CID could get to work on him.

He sat motionless for a stretch, stunned and incredulous. The man had seemed so normal most of the time. 'I love children', he'd said. God Almighty! How could McFee *live* with himself? And he'd talked so gloatingly of his *ladies o' the night* . . . The man was sick.

After a while Alex suppressed his feelings. Had to think about what it meant for *him* – the practical problem of carrying on the job without McFee.

There was the delivery to the Croats in the morning. And there'd have to be a phone call to Mike Allison in Farnham.

Then the journey through the mountains back to Split, driving the Bedford all the way by himself . . .

It hit him.

Without McFee, there would be no one to stop him smuggling Lorna's orphan out in the back of the truck . . .

Sixteen

Alex was woken by the sound of tank tracks outside. He held his wrist away from his face, trying to make out the figures on his watch.

Five past seven. Jesus! He'd slept, despite everything. Was McFee back? He had no idea.

He tugged down the zip of his sleeping bag and extracted his feet, still wearing yesterday's socks. It was icy cold in the room. He pulled on his long johns, jeans and a pullover.

Gruff voices as he stumbled into the sitting room, and rifles on the floor. The soldiers who'd come for McFee last night were still here.

'Morning,' he mumbled, startled. 'Where's Moray? Didn't he come back?'

The sergeant raised himself from the sofa and rubbed his eyes.

'Nope. Can't have done.' He looked at his watch. 'We both 'ad a nap. Took it in turns . . .'

They stood up and shook the stiffness from their legs.

'Where the hell is he, then?' demanded Alex. 'Something must have happened.'

'Yeh. Must've. We'd better put the word out.'

'You're going to search for him?' Alex pressed, anxiously.

'We'll look round the camp anyway. There's a limit though. We're not the law around here.'

'Shall I come with you?'

186

'No, ta. Better you hang on here in case he turns up. Can I trust you to let us know?'

'Don't you worry . . .'

The soldiers picked up their rifles, straightened their berets, and left.

Alex stared out of the window trying to get his sleep-befuddled brain thinking again. He turned to the stove, swung the kettle to check there was water in it, then placed it over the heat. A mug of tea was what he needed.

Last night when the soldiers told him what McFee was accused of, he'd felt revulsion for the man. Now in the light of day, he was worried for his safety.

With the tea inside him, he began to think straighter. Perhaps there was a simple explanation for his disappearance. Moray could have spent the night in Illie's bed, wherever that was. Maybe he would turn up for breakfast in the cookhouse.

He pulled on his walking boots, left foot first, still ruled by the silly superstition he'd cultivated during his Scottish exile.

There had been a dusting of snow overnight. He hurried down the road to the UN camp, took his breakfast tray to an empty table, and scanned the faces around him. McFee's was not amongst them.

As he was finishing, he spotted Major Clarke-Hartley emerging from the partitioned-off section for officers. He hurried over to catch him.

'Morning Alan!'

'Alex. Good day to you.'

They stepped into the fresh air, a crisp astringent after the cookhouse fug.

'I've got a problem on my hands,' Alex began.

'Yes. You bloody well have.'

'You've heard?'

''Fraid so. The MPs dropped in when they left your house this morning. What's your chum been up to?'

187

'Nothing good. But we've got to find him. Could he have been taken hostage d'you think?'

'*Anything's* possible in this place. We'll send someone to badger the HVO this morning.'

'Thanks. In the meantime I've got boxes to deliver to the Croats. Don't even know how to find the place.'

'We'll send a recce patrol with you. And we'll lend a pair of hands to get the boxes into the truck.'

'Terrific, Alan. I'm most grateful.'

'Look, when you talk to Mike Allison today, as I'm sure you will, do make the point that you're a bit thin on the ground. You need a full-time liaison bod and an interpreter. I know it's to do with money, but tell him all the same. And say it came from me.'

'I will,' Alex muttered. 'Couldn't agree more.'

The call to Farnham would wait until later. McFee might have turned up by then.

After half-an-hour, Clarke-Hartley sent round a corporal to help Alex load up. Then a pair of Scimitar light tanks scurried up the road from the camp.

The lieutenant in command checked the grid reference of the village they were bound for on his hundred thousand scale map.

'Right,' he called from his turret. 'All set?'

'Yes, but not too fast. I'm still a bit green with the driving.'

The truck seemed bigger with just himself in the cab, but with one white tank in front and another behind, at least he felt safe.

The road crossed the battle zone along what was now a cease-fire line. Huge water-filled craters, bullet-spattered houses, and a mosque minaret broken like a spear bore witness to the intensity of the fight of recent weeks. Somewhere in the hills to his left was Tulici, Alex remembered.

The route followed the line of the Lašva river, a pretty

torrent under a pale blue sky, spoiled here and there by the detritus of war.

Thirty minutes later they reached the Croat village up a muddy track just wide enough for the Scimitars. Children in anoraks and bobble hats ran to greet them.

An HVO soldier waved the vehicles towards a barn. The ground sloped. Alex pulled on the handbrake, cut the engine, but left it in gear.

No crowds surging forward like yesterday. Just dozens of watchful faces emerging from houses, alerted by the noise of the engines. And, striding towards the Bedford, a priest in a black cassock.

'*Dobro jutro.*'

'Good morning,' Alex replied, jumping to the ground.

'English?'

'Yes.'

'I can speak. Welcome. I am Father Pravic. I am priest here.'

Pravic, Alex gulped.

'I'm Alex Crawford. My organization's called Bosnia Emergency.'

Did he say *Pravic*?

'You bring food, or medicines?'

'Tinned food and clothing. Mostly for children. You can use it?'

'Of course. Everything needed here. Come. I show.'

The crucial question hovered on Alex's lips.

The priest led him into the barn. The cows had been chained at one end to make space for humans. Dozens and dozens of them.

'One hundred twenty refugees came when their village was attacked,' the priest explained. 'Ten people killed.'

Tired, defeated faces. Same as yesterday, just Catholic, instead of Muslim.

'I have some boys ready to help,' said the priest, directing him outside again.

'Good. Let's get started.'

'You speak excellent English, Father...' Alex remarked as they walked to the truck. 'But I'm sorry, I didn't catch your name.'

'Pravic. Tihomir Pravic.'

Alex's heart missed a beat. Just coincidence?

'I live one year in America,' the priest explained. He spread his arms. 'We need many things here. Food, blankets, cookers, pots. Plates and cups ... Everything.'

Four uniformed teenagers clambered onto the open tailboard.

'Do you have medicines?' the priest asked forlornly.

'Not this time. Maybe the next truck that comes from England,' Alex answered distractedly, his mind on the priest's name.

'It's not for here, but at my church, which has become hospital. Doctors need much things.' The priest turned his pudgy face towards him – small, tired eyes behind rimless spectacles. 'You want to see? Come.'

He strode off across the grass, deeper into the village, Alex at his side.

'Excuse me asking Father, but your name ... Is it a common one around here?'

The priest stopped and looked at him with suspicion, wondering why this Englishman should react to his name if he were merely the aid worker he claimed to be. 'Why you ask?'

'It's just that I thought I heard the same name the other day. Someone involved with the HVO?' From the priest's expression, Alex knew he was on to something.

'It is possible,' the priest sighed. The same questions. Always the same. He marched on.

'*Milan* Pravic? Not your brother, perhaps?'

The priest looked away in irritation. He was Milan's brother, yes, but not his keeper.

'UN soldiers already ask,' he snapped. 'A major from

Vitez come here. I tell him I not see my brother for many years . . .'

'But he *is* your brother?' Alex spluttered. 'The man they say was responsible for the massacre at Tulici?'

The priest sighed again. The village and its name had come to haunt him.

'I *have* brother called Milan, yes. But I do not know where he is, or what he has done.'

The church was modern, in concrete and steel. A huge Red Cross banner hung above the main entrance.

The priest pushed open the door. The smell hit them instantly, disinfectant mingling with sweat and vomit.

To their right there was still an altar, covered in an emerald green cloth and topped by candlesticks, but the church itself had become a casualty ward with pews as beds. On them lay the injured and the sick, some prone and still, others propped on elbows, watching and waiting.

Father Pravic beckoned Alex through swing doors into a small seminary. A vestry served as an operating theatre.

'I ask doctors for list of things they need,' he said, indicating Alex should wait. He disappeared behind a door, re-emerging moments later with a thin-faced medic in a stained, white coat.

'The doctor has only few minutes,' the priest explained. 'But he tell you what he need. Maybe you can help.'

'I'll try, but I can't promise anything,' Alex cautioned. The doctor looked as if he'd had his fill of well-meaning foreigners who didn't deliver.

'You have a cigarette?' he asked in guttural English.

Alex pulled a pack from his pocket.

'Keep them if you want,' he said. 'I have more.'

'Just one, thank you.'

Alex lit it for him. The doctor had a notepad and pen.

'I write what we need. But it's all, all. You have brought something? Dressings?'

'I'm sorry,' Alex repeated. 'Next time, maybe.'

The doctor drew at the cigarette and began to write, shaking his head.

'I was specialist in micro-surgery at Sarajevo.' He scribbled away, his list getting ever longer. 'We have excellent medicine before war. Now it is *primitif*, like one hundred years ago . . .' He blew smoke through pursed lips, then held out his list.

'I'll try, but as I say, I can't promise,' Alex reiterated, folding the list and putting it in a pocket.

The doctor gave him a weary look and retreated behind the door.

Then Father Pravic led Alex into a small sitting room, half a dozen plain armchairs ranged in a semi-circle.

'Sit, please. You like drink something?' he asked. These foreigners who came to Bosnia were an enigma to him. They had the power to stop the killing, yet all they did was watch.

'No. No thank you,' Alex smiled. He knew this priest held the key to finding Milan Pravic, but would he be given it?

'Father, I find your country very confusing,' he began, fumbling for a way through his defences. 'I've only been here a few days and I simply don't understand what's going on.'

The priest's face remained sphinx-like. He knew he was being played with.

'I mean, *why* are people killing each other, like this?' His question was deliberately naïve.

'It is our history,' the priest shrugged. 'You must know that.'

'Yes, but your brother Milan for example . . . did he *really* slaughter those women and children?'

The priest pursed his lips and tapped his finger nails on the wooden arm of the chair.

'I tell you, I do not know about Milan. The UN come.

They ask the same question. My brother, how you say. . . ? He is chalk, I am cheese?'

'But you know what sort of person your brother is,' Alex insisted, frustrated by the priest's prevarication. 'You must know if he *could* commit such a crime. And anyway, it's too easy to blame it all on *history*.'

Pravic stopped tapping. Time to play the Englishman at his own game.

'Why have you come here?'

'Sorry?'

'Why you come to Bosnia? I ask *you* question.'

'Well, because I wanted to help. Because of all the suffering we've seen on the news.'

'No.' The priest shook his head. 'Why you come to Bosnia? Other reasons.'

Alex's brain raced. Did the cleric think he was some sort of spy?

'Well, since you ask, I did have some *personal* reasons too . . .' he floundered. 'There was an accident, you see. My son was killed. And then my wife left me . . .'

'You see?' the priest beamed. The response had been as rewarding as a confession. He tilted his head sympathetically. 'I'm sorry. But you see, there is never *one* reason for anything. You come to Bosnia to help *us*, yes, but to help *you* too. To make you feel better.'

'Oh, I wouldn't say . . .' Alex didn't complete the sentence. The priest was right.

'So, you ask why there are massacres here.' His lips puckered as if he were sucking on a straw. 'There are also many reasons.'

He held up a finger.

'Muslims attack Croats here in Lašva valley. So, we fight for our villages, our homes, our lives. *That* a priest can say is righteous.'

He held up a second finger.

'Then, people want revenge for what has been done to

193

them, just now and in history. That the church can understand, but not support.'

The third finger.

'Then there is what you call "personal reasons". A man – his sister is raped, his wife her throat cut, or . . .' A long pause. Whether to continue. . . ? 'Or it is done . . . for pleasure,' he added finally. 'By a man who has black heart . . .'

He flattened his hand on the arm of the chair and looked down at his bitten nails.

'You mean your brother?' Alex asked quietly.

The priest thought of how he'd always hated his sullen, animal-like sibling. How he'd refused to protect him from their father's abuse in the way he'd looked after his sister. And how, once he'd realized what a monster his brother had become, his own soul had been gnawed by guilt at having abandoned him.

'We all make mistakes. Even God. *His* was to allow my brother into this world.'

Alex gaped at the admission.

'You're saying your brother kills because he likes it? He's a psychopath?'

The priest nodded. There was no point in disguising it.

'Haven't you tried to stop him? I mean, you're a priest as well as his brother.'

Father Pravic bristled. Why didn't these people *understand*?

'I told you, I do not meet Milan,' he said, his voice raised, smacking the arm of the chair. 'Not for long time. And *how* I can stop him? *I* have no power. *God* has no power. Only a . . . a *bullet* has power.'

The priest's words hammered home.

'That's pretty strong . . .' Alex breathed. 'You're saying you think your own brother should be *executed*?'

Pravic pursed his lips again, saying nothing.

'What about the HVO?' Alex asked. 'What do they think?'

The priest shrugged. 'In war, armies make good use of men who like to kill . . .'

'But if the UN could do something to stop him, could put him on trial, get him locked away, you'd support that?'

Pravic smiled at his innocence.

'The UN are like you. Here to make *themselves* feel better. But yes. If I knew where Milan was, then I would tell the UN.'

'But you've no idea?'

None that he was prepared to impart. He shook his head.

'You see, my brother knows well how to hide. When he was little, he was weak. Others in our village make fun of him. Then he grew stronger and other children they became afraid. They keep away. And there is a name they gave him . . . I do not know in English. A creature that stings, with its tail above its head . . .' He curled a finger.

'A scorpion, you mean?'

'Scorpion, yes. They call him Scorpion. Because they would not see him, then suddenly he would be there and make them cry . . .'

A man with a lethal sting, with Bosnia for a playground, Alex thought. Anywhere else and the police would be out in droves trying to catch such a creature.

'Where would he hide now, Father? Here in Bosnia?'

'Who knows? Maybe here. Maybe he go back to Germany. He live some years in Berlin. But perhaps he don't go there, because UN will ask German police to look for him.'

Alex saw that the priest was getting restless.

'Do you have a picture, a photograph of him?' he asked quickly.

'No. I have no reason to have one . . .'

'What does he look like, then?'

Father Pravic shrugged.

'He is not tall, not short. He has light hair, blue eyes, like many in Bosnia. But there is something. His eyes . . .' He screwed up his face. 'They never look at you, unless . . . unless he is going to hurt you.'

Alex shuddered. The priest stood up. He'd said enough.

'I think they finish with your boxes now.'

'Yes. Yes of course.'

Back in front of the barn, the tailboard of the Bedford had been closed, the Scimitar commander looked impatient to be off.

The priest shook his hand. 'Thank you for help,' he said coolly.

'I'll try to get medicines for you,' Alex assured him, though he had no idea how. 'One other thing. Your brother . . . what do you think he might be doing now?'

The priest hesitated, his expression hard to divine. Fear? Guilt even?

'To kill will be like drug for him. He cannot stop. Any person can be his victim. Here, it is Muslim peoples. But it could be you or me. There will be more. Many more. Give him the power . . . and the weapon . . . then what he did at Tulici will seem like nothing.'

He turned and walked away, his words rooting Alex to the spot.

Then came a shout. His UN escort was eager to move. Alex waved and climbed into the cab of the Bedford.

On the road back to Vitez, the priest's words churned round in his head.

A killer called the Scorpion, with dozens of deaths to his credit, dozens more in prospect, and no serious attempt being made to stop him. The situation was mad.

Back at the house he was startled to see two TV teams filming him as he reversed the Bedford into the drive.

McFee. Something had happened. Something terrible.

As he climbed from the cab, the camera crews were held at bay by the two MPs who'd spent last night on his sofa.

'Gi' the bloke a chance. He don't know about it yet,' he heard one of the soldiers say.

The sergeant took Alex by the arm.

'Can I suggest we step inside a minute, sir. There's some news, and it's not good.'

They hurried through to the living room without speaking. The stove had gone out and the room was cold.

'What's he done?' Alex snapped, ready to condemn the man. 'Tell me.'

'I'm afraid your mate's been found dead, sir.'

The soldier's emotionless words sandbagged him.

'Oh my God . . .'

He felt the blood drain from his face.

'Where . . .' he heard himself croak. 'What happened?'

'It was in a derelict house about half a mile from here.' The MP's look warned him to expect the worst. 'Someone shot 'im . . .'

'Christ!'

'And I'm afraid I must ask you to identify the body. We collected it this morning. The HVO tipped us off.'

'But . . . but *why* was he shot?' he stammered, fearing the answer. 'What had he done?'

The soldiers glanced at each other.

'It's a right mess, sir, I warn you . . . You know that business in Edinburgh – well, we think he was up to the same tricks. The HVO say someone caught him doin' it to a young girl. He'd paid her fifty Deutsche marks, which is a small fortune round 'ere.'

'God! I can't believe it . . .' He sank onto the sofa. 'The evil bastard!'

He remembered the two armed men whose eyes had followed him back into the house last night – the locals must've been on to McFee already.

'Who shot him, the HVO?'

'They're not admitting it. Claim they don't know who did it. But whoever it was killed a woman last night too . . . Illie.'

'Oh, no . . .' Alex groaned.

'They found another fifty Deutsche Marks in her pocket. The suggestion is that your chum paid her to procure the little girl for him . . .'

Alex felt sickened. To come to Bosnia on the pretext of helping people, and then do *that* . . .

'It's . . . it's unspeakable . . .'

'Course, we can only go on what the HVO tell us. It could be a pack o' lies. But bearing in mind what we was told by the Edinburgh police, it's more 'an likely true. They think the dead girl up in Scotland was new to the game and didn't like what was happening to her. Someone heard screaming. They think he strangled her to shut her up.'

It came back to him suddenly – the night on the ferry from Ancona – McFee shouting 'shuddup' in his sleep.

'It's unbelievable.' He shook his head. The man was a monster and he'd had no clue . . . 'And the TV people know everything I suppose? It'll be all over the bulletins back home tonight.'

'And on Sky which can be picked up here. The camera crews were around when we brought the body back in. They'd got the gory details from the HVO.'

'Well, they'll get nothing out of *me* . . .' Alex snapped, thinking of the pain McFee's widow must be going through. Then the sergeant's words caught up with him.

'What gory details?'

Again that annoying glance between the two soldiers.

'The press know about it, so it'd be better if you did too,' the sergeant began. 'They er . . . they mutilated the

198

body of your friend, I'm afraid. Hacked his knob off and stuffed it in his mouth.'

'And *then* they shot him . . .' the corporal added.

Alex voided the contents of his stomach when they showed him McFee's yellowing, blood-smeared corpse. The Scotsman's eyes had been open when he died; they still were, in rigor mortis – the eyes of a man who'd seen the flames of hell.

The MPs drove Alex back to P.Info, where they gave him tea with whisky in it, while he tried to get through to Farnham on the satellite phone. It took an hour; Mike Allison had already learned of McFee's death from the lunchtime news. He was horrified, fearing the goodwill Bosnia Emergency had built up in its short existence would be wiped out by the scandal. He told Alex to get himself and the Bedford back down to Split as soon as he could, and to ask for army protection.

'Peel the logo off the side of the truck,' he'd suggested. 'Just in case some nutter thinks you're *all* perverts.'

Back in the house, Alex sat forlornly on the sofa watching Dragana make up the fire and dab at her eyes with a handkerchief. He felt numb, unable to think straight.

The TV teams had hounded him on his way up to the house. What was McFee like? You must've had suspicions? How do you feel? – all the standard, stupid questions he remembered from when he himself had been on the other side of the cameras.

He'd said nothing and had tried to shield his face from the prying lenses. Twenty years of concealment from the IRA blown out of the window. Just the beard and the different surname still yielding some patina of protection.

'Hello? Alex?' A shout from the hall. The voice of Major Clarke-Hartley.

'In here.' Alex levered himself to his feet.

Dragana scuttled away, handkerchief to her mouth.

'Brought you a friendly face,' the Major told him. 'Tells me she's known you for yonks.'

Lorna walked in. He'd totally forgotten she was coming.

'Hi, Alex. I'm so sorry.' Her voice cracked. 'Alan's just told me this stuff about Moray. It's too awful. I can't believe it!'

He felt tearful suddenly and embraced her with more intensity than he'd intended. She resisted for a moment, then moulded to the shape of his body.

'I, er ... I'll get out of your hair,' the Major stammered. 'Just wanted a word about tomorrow, Alex. Mike's called me personally to ask us to protect you on the way down to Split. What I suggest you do is join our regular logistics convoy heading south at eight in the morning. There'll be a relay of Warriors to get you from here to Gorni, then after that there should be no problem. You'll be well beyond the range of any of the local hoods.'

'Sounds good,' Alex replied, recovering. 'Thanks. Eight o'clock you say?'

'Yes. And I've had another thought . . .' Clarke-Hartley flinched at what he was about to suggest. 'Would you mind . . . I mean, d'you think you could possibly take the body bag with you?'

Alex caught the alarm in Lorna's eye. It was a living passenger they'd planned to put in the back.

'It's just that there's an RAF Herc leaving Split on Thursday that could take it back to the UK,' the major explained.

'Well, I . . .' Alex faltered. Then Lorna nodded imperceptibly. 'I suppose that makes sense. Where . . . where and when would we collect it . . . him. The body bag?'

'I don't know. Should we say half-past-seven in the camp? You can drive the truck to the medical centre, and then form up afterwards with the rest of the convoy on the road outside.'

'All right. We'll do that, then.'

'Good. I'll alert everybody to expect you. Well, I'll leave you to er . . . to talk about happier times. See you later.'

''Bye.'

Alex stared at his disappearing back and watched the front door close. Then he turned to Lorna. Her face was taut with concentration.

'O . . . h,' he murmured, 'I can't tell you how glad I am to see you.' He hugged her like a life raft.

'Poor Alex,' she whispered, 'it must have been the most awful shock.'

'I can't take it in. I've been with him all the time for the last ten days and I never had a clue . . .'

At that moment she felt a strong urge to sit him beside her, put his big, square head in her lap and run her fingers through his hair. But there wasn't time and anyway she'd determined not to give in to *feelings* again.

'He seemed a normal, likeable guy . . .' she murmured.

'That's just it. He was, quite.'

'So what does it all mean?' she checked, easing herself from his embrace. 'You *can* take Vildana tomorrow?'

'I suppose so.'

'Then we have to move fast.'

'Is tomorrow too soon for you?'

'No, No! It'll be okay. Josip and I have just been up to the village again. The girl – she's real ready. *Wants* to go to America, now. They've filled her head with promises of non-stop Disney and Coke.' Her face twisted into a look of disapproval.

'Monika's moving her to the refugee centre in Travnik tonight. We'll have to fetch her from there early tomorrow morning. Like six-thirty? So we can get her hidden

201

in the truck before you go into the camp to load the body.'

She was on overdrive, rattling off the plan as it evolved in her head.

'Lorna, hang on a minute. Can we really put her through that? A traumatized child huddling in the back of a truck for eight hours next to a corpse?'

'I know,' she winced. 'It's dreadful, but we don't have any alternative. This is her only chance. And anyway, she'll never know the body bag's there. We'll make a little house for her in the truck and hide her in it before you drive into the camp.'

She saw the alarm and disquiet on his face.

'I know it's a long time for her to stay boxed up, but believe me this is a kid who's spent much of her life hiding. . . .'

'And what then? What happens to her in Split?'

'I don't know yet. Maybe we have to hang around a few days until we find the right home for her. All that's being taken care of over in the States.'

She crossed her fingers behind her back. She had no idea if there'd been a response yet to her appeal on the Internet last night.

'And if there's a problem with that, we'll just start praying . . .'

Praying. Alex remembered the priest.

'Hey, I've got to tell you,' he said. 'Something else happened this morning.'

She was only half listening.

'I met the brother of the killer who led the Tulici massacre!'

'You what?'

'A priest, would you believe . . .'

He explained.

'He wants him stopped. Killed if necessary. Said he'd help if he could. You see what this means? With the priest as a witness, telling what he knows of Pravic's psychopathic past, and your Vildana telling the court what she saw in Tulici, we've got him! We can get him locked up for life!'

'*We?*' Her jaw dropped. 'What do you mean *we*, Alex?'

He frowned, unsure what she was getting at.

'What are you doing here, Alex?' she demanded, eyes like darts. 'Who do you work for?'

'I told you. Bosnia Emergency.'

'Which nobody's ever heard of . . .' she retorted. 'Leastways, nobody *I've* spoken to.'

'It's only been going a few months, that's why.' Her venom puzzled him.

She spread her arms in disbelief.

'And this is it? This is your *organization*? An old army truck and two guys, one of whom's a murdering paedophile and the other's a spook? Shi-it!'

'What are you saying? I don't understand . . .' But he was beginning to.

'Oh yes you do. You haven't changed. Still the guy with two faces . . .'

He saw pain and disappointment in her eyes. Belfast was biting back, like a knee-capping, never to be forgotten. She'd winded him.

'Lorna, you're wrong,' he pleaded.

The speed of her mood switch made his head spin. Her mask of sympathy over McFee's death had split to reveal the anger which had smouldered in her for decades.

It was the moment he'd dreaded from the instant he'd spotted her on the ferry from Ancona, but the crisis had come out of the blue. Its outcome would decide whether their extraordinary crossing and re-crossing of paths would end well or in bitterness.

He faced a critical choice. He could try to bluff his way out of a corner like before, or admit everything this time in the hope of stopping history repeating itself.

Whether she accepted his explanation would depend on one key question. Did she still want him as much as he wanted her?

'Lorna, listen. Listen to everything I say. Then make your judgement.'

'Don't lie to me again, Alex,' she warned, folding her arms. Her suspicions deepened.

Truth. It had to be.

'I'm not a spy,' he insisted. 'Not a "spook" as you put it. But . . . I *am* trying to help the UN find some evidence against Milan Pravic so they can put him on trial for the Tulici massacre.'

'You're telling me you work for the UN? Where's your blue beret?'

'Yes. No, not exactly. Look, ten days ago, the UN war crimes people in The Hague sent a message to the British intelligence services, asking if they had somebody out here who could help them trace the man who led the Tulici killings. Well, they didn't have anyone. The only Brits in Bosnia were soldiers or aid workers. Anyway . . . the intelligence people wanted to help the UN if they could. So they had to find someone at short notice . . . and picked me, because they happened to hear I was coming out here as an aid worker.'

She stiffened. '*Why* did they hear that?'

'Because for twenty years I've been on the run. If it weren't for the security people I'd be dead. The IRA would have put a bullet in my brain. You know why. Everywhere I went, I had to tell the MI5 minders so they could watch my back.'

He paused for breath. Her jaw was set, the corners of her mouth tugged down. It wasn't working.

'Anyway Lorna, all they've asked me to do out here is keep my eyes and ears open,' he added desperately. 'That's all.'

'But you *do* still work for them!' She bit her lip. 'So you *lied* to me yesterday!'

'I've helped them three times in thirty years for God's sake! Nothing since Belfast, I promise. Until now. And I don't *work* for them. They've never paid me. I've just given them information when it was right to do so.'

Lorna's face erupted with anger.

'When *you've* felt it's right, huh? Like in Belfast when you decided it was right three boys should be shot down like dogs! Who d'you think you are? Jesus Christ?'

He raised his hands in a gesture of surrender. Everything about Belfast had been a disaster. He should have told Chadwick to piss off, and he hadn't. Should've said to Catherine McNulty, the IRA man's wife, that he loved Lorna, not her, but he couldn't do it.

'Look. The rights and wrongs of what happened in Belfast we can argue all round the houses. But this is hardly the time . . .'

'No? Why the hell not?'

Nothing could stop her now. The dam had broken.

'You *lied* to me in Belfast, Alex! You said such beautiful, *loving* words in my ears. Then as soon as I left your bed . . .' Her face screwed up in disgust. 'You cheated on me! You did the same things, said the same words . . . with an IRA man's wife. And not just any . . .' Her voice caught in her throat.

Alex looked at her, begging for understanding. This wasn't the day to go into all this.

'I didn't *want* to, for God's sake!' he moaned. 'You remember what Catherine was like. I'd been seeing her for months before you turned up. She wouldn't let go. I tried to tell her I was ending it but she said she'd kill herself if I did.'

'And you were so naïve as to believe her? Oh *come on*! You reckoned you were man enough to decide three kids should be shot, but didn't have the guts to tell a loopy lady to get lost?'

He'd lost control of things. He turned his head away.

'Look, let's get it straight what happened in Belfast.

MI5 *blackmailed* me into betraying you. The message was that unless I got you to tell me what you knew about the jailbreak, they'd make sure *you* found out about Catherine, and Catherine's husband found out about *me*. I'd have lost you, and probably have got a kneecapping as well. And don't forget, Lorna . . . those guys who were to be sprung from Long Kesh, they were convicted killers. It was *right* they should stay inside.'

Lorna's hand clamped over her mouth in disbelief.

'*Stay inside,* I said,' he stressed, defensively. 'I . . . I never thought they'd *kill* them. Naïve perhaps, but I just thought they'd put them back behind the wire.'

Lorna turned on her heel and stood by the window staring out. Josip was leaning against the Land Cruiser, twitching with impatience.

So *that* was the excuse she'd waited twenty years to hear. Blackmail. Did she believe him? Did it make any difference?

She shuddered, remembering the cataclysmic night in Belfast when Alex's double-dealing had been exposed. McNulty was the Provos' Belfast quartermaster, and her IRA contact. She'd been friendly with both him and Catherine. Over a drink at their home one evening, bubbly and excited with her love for Alex, she'd told them his name . . .

In her mind now, she could still see Catherine's face, beetroot with fury and pain. Then the earth had opened . . .

She looked at her watch. Had to get to Travnik to warn them to have Vildana ready first thing.

'I have to go,' she said flatly.

Alex stood up. She turned round, avoiding his eye.

'Look, forget the past for the moment,' he pleaded. 'What we're involved in now . . . it's much more important. We're both after the same thing, don't you see? You want to save a girl's life. So do I. Your way is to get her out of here to a place she'll be safe. My way is to nail the man who wants to kill her. We're in this together, right? This was *meant* to happen – you said it yourself, yesterday.'

She crossed her arms tightly, as if trying to hold herself together.

'I have to get a move on,' she said.

Seventeen

Wednesday 30th March
Vitez, Bosnia

Alex stuffed the last of McFee's possessions into the battered, soft-sided suitcase. He'd picked gingerly through his belongings, half expecting to find bizarre sexual aids, or used condoms.

He'd packed his own bags last night, after taking the Bedford to the REME garage to tank up with diesel.

He downed the remains of a mug of tea then went into the hall to pull on his boots and coat. It was six o'clock. Lorna would be arriving any minute and he still had to prepare the hide in the back of the truck.

Last night in the junk-filled garage where they'd stored their aid boxes, he'd found a home-made workbench, a sturdy table one-and-a-half metres long with legs made of 'two by four'. Using sign language he'd indicated to Andrej that he wanted to borrow it.

Outside, the temperature had turned milder overnight. It was overcast and raining, water dripping rhythmically onto the stone path from a broken gutter. If the weather was like this over the mountains, the drive south would be messy.

He unlocked the doors of the driver's cab, then walked to the back of the truck, undid the tailboard hasps, and released the flaps of the tarpaulin. The truck was empty apart from four spare jerrycans of diesel strapped to rings on the floor.

He hoisted himself into the back and shone his torch around to find fixings for the table that was to be

Vildana's house for the coming day. Stout string should do it. There was a roll of it in McFee's tool bag.

He heard the purr of an engine, and looked out to see the Land Cruiser pulling up, raindrops glinting in its headlamp beams. Lorna got out, her face tense, her blonde hair bristling like a hedge. He doubted if she'd slept much last night.

Josip still looked sullen. Did the man ever smile?

Alex jumped down from the tailboard looking for some sign as to how things stood between them that morning. He saw none.

'Okay?' he asked.

'Sure. You ready?' she answered, brisk and business-like.

'I need a hand with something. Josip? Could you help me please?'

He led him to the garage and between them they carried the heavy workbench out to the truck and hoisted it into the back. They placed it against the end nearest the driver's cab and Alex secured the legs firmly.

'She can sit under that,' he explained. 'Need some cushions or bedding, and some cardboard or a tarpaulin to cover the sides.'

'Maybe they'll have a spare blanket at the refugee centre,' Lorna suggested.

'Good thought. Shall we get moving?'

Six-fifteen. Pretty much on schedule.

Lorna led the way into Travnik, the streets of the old Muslim quarter almost deserted at this hour. They drove into the playground of the school and parked out of sight behind it. The easterly sky was fringed with the soft, grey glow of dawn.

'Monika stayed the night here with the kid,' Lorna explained under her breath as they went inside. Now the moment was upon her, she seemed nervous about the responsibility she was taking on. 'Josip will have to help me play Mom, unless Vildana learns English real fast.'

'So that's why he's looking so sour,' Alex commented.

'One of the reasons . . .' she replied enigmatically.

There was a clinking from the kitchen as the early risers prepared tea and coffee.

'I told her to be ready for us,' Lorna fretted. 'But where the hell is she?'

'Let's try the kitchen.'

The two of them were sitting there, pale and drawn, beside one of the wide cookers, Vildana's short, dark hair freshly washed, her fearful brown eyes like pebbles dropped in snow. Monika had her arm round her shoulder and held her close.

Lorna took Josip's arm. 'Earn your money, Josip,' she whispered.

'Hi, Vildana!' Lorna grinned, crouching in front of the child. Josip also dropped on his haunches.

There was a minute or two of words in Serbo-Croat, with Monika chipping in.

'Well,' Josip translated, 'I explain her she stay hide in the truck, until I say she come out. I tell her we look after her, and she will be . . . safe.' He shrugged.

'And she's ready?'

'I think.'

'Just one thing,' Alex added. 'We need to finish off that Wendy House of hers. There must be loads of empty cardboard boxes here. If we stack a pile round the workbench, it'll disguise it beautifully.'

'Good. Maybe Monika knows where they keep them?'

Twenty minutes later the job was done. Vildana's determination not to cry collapsed when Monika gave her a final hug. Then, with a bed made from blankets and Alex's sleeping bag, she took up residence in the hide, clutching a bag of bread and fruit and a bottle of water.

Lorna led the way back to Vitez, this time driving the

Land Cruiser on her own. Josip sat in the Bedford cab with Alex.

Past the junction with Route Triangle, they crossed the invisible line separating Muslim-led forces from Croat. HVO soldiers dawdled with their Kalashnikovs, more relaxed now the cease-fire was taking a grip. Alex wondered what they'd do if they knew the truck carried a Muslim child, the only witness to the Tulici massacre.

Nerves made his gut churn. He breathed deeply to steady them.

The pole was down across the entrance to Vitez camp. A squaddie checked their UN passes, lifted the barrier and waved them in.

Seven-twenty-five. Going like clockwork. The truck clunked in the potholes which had been ground out of the hard core by Warrior tracks.

'Hope the kid's hanging on tight,' Alex said.

'I think it is nothing to what will come on the mountain road,' Josip answered gloomily.

Alex stopped the Bedford by the medical centre and dropped to the ground. He told Josip to stay with the truck.

Inside the portakabin, a couple of bored corporals were playing cards, one dark-haired, the other ginger.

'About bloody time,' the dark one growled. 'We've been up all night waiting for you.'

'Wha-at?' said Alex. 'The major told me seven-thirty.'

The ginger soldier stood up with a grin. 'Take no notice of 'im. Winds everyone up. It is Mr McFee yer after, is it?'

'That's right.'

Ginger switched on an expression of concern. ''E was your oppo, was 'e sir? Your mate?'

'We worked together,' Alex replied tensely. 'Are you ready? I've got the truck outside.'

'Yessir.'

They stepped into a back room and emerged a few

seconds later struggling under the weight of a dark green body bag.

At the sight of it, Alex felt a moment's queasiness, knowing the messy remains that lay inside.

'Good strong bag this, sir. Keeps the pong in,' the dark-haired soldier remarked.

Josip had the Bedford's tailboard down and was standing on it protectively.

'We'll need two of us at each end to get 'im up there,' said the ginger corporal.

Alex hoisted himself onto the tailboard and with Josip took hold of the foot of the bag, leaving the soldiers to bear most of the load. They heaved it into the centre of the cargo platform and set it down between two sets of attachment rings.

'Got enough straps and that, to tie it down?' asked Ginger.

'Yes. We're okay.'

'Then, we'll leave him with you, sir.'

'Fine. Thanks for your help.'

He set to work with string, tying the handles of the bag to the rings on the floor. Josip crawled forward to the hide and whispered words of reassurance to Vildana.

'I tell her it is some equipment,' he explained.

'Good. She okay?'

Josip nodded.

Poor kid, Alex mused. She'd got a hellish day ahead of her. He stood back and checked his work. All secure.

Both men jumped to the ground and re-secured the tailboard and tarpaulin. While Josip climbed back into the cab, Alex sprinted to the cookhouse to pick up ration packs for the journey. Then he drove the truck out of the camp to where the rest of the white vehicle convoy was lining up, and the crews were donning their body armour.

It was ten minutes to eight.

The convoy snaked up Route Triangle, one Warrior at the front and another at the rear, the Land Cruiser and the Bedford tucked in amongst the empty container trucks that had shuttled supplies up from the coast to keep the British contingent of UNPROFOR fed and watered.

He'd had no opportunity to talk to Lorna alone that morning. No chance to find out if she'd accepted what he'd said about Belfast. No occasion to discover if she was for him or against him.

They crossed from one militia's territory to another and back again, with sentries watching their progress from makeshift bunkers, sheltering from the rain which pummelled the roofs of the vehicles. The massive bulk of the Warrior at the front deterred any thoughts they might have of stopping the convoy to check it.

'You've worked many times with Lorna?' Alex asked, casually, deciding he'd try to get to know the translator better if they were to spend the next eight hours together.

'Three times before in Bosnia. Always they pay me to fly to Frankfurt to meet her. Then we drive to Split.'

'Frankfurt? Why Frankfurt?'

'I think because CareNet medicines come from America on Air Force planes. They have big military base at Frankfurt.'

'Really? Didn't know the US Air Force was involved.' Maybe Lorna was planning to get Vildana to America by Air Force jet.

'And you?' Josip said. 'You are old friend with Lorna, she tell me.'

'That's right. Known her most of my life, on and off.'

'You are perhaps like soul mates?'

Odd words to come from Josip, Alex pondered. More like Lorna's words. How much had she told him?

'I don't know about that . . .'

The convoy slowed for a hairpin bend in the midst of a village. Children streamed from the houses, defying the

213

rain in the hope the drivers would throw sweets to them. Blonde eight-year-olds ran perilously close to the wheels of the Bedford.

Minutes later the convoy slowed to a halt on the crest of a wooded ridge. The Warriors that had brought them this far were handing over to another pair that had come up to meet them from the next base at Gorni Vakuf.

Ahead, the unmade road dropped into the canyon where three days before Alex's mission had so nearly come to a premature end. He shuddered at the recollection of that squat automatic pressed against his face.

'Hullo again!'

A breezy, female voice at the window of the cab. Alex looked down. It was the same lieutenant who'd escorted them on the way up, rain dripping from the rim of her blue helmet.

'Well, hello! Fancy seeing you,' he said. 'Not going to leave us in the lurch again I hope.'

She gurgled with laughter.

'No fear! You're on my orders this time. Got to keep a close eye on you.' She smiled toothily. 'Sorry you had a bit of trouble on the way up. But you were just hangers-on then. Different today. I say, I'm terribly sorry about your companion . . .'

'Yup . . .' Alex pointed over his shoulder to the back of the truck.

'I know . . .' she said. 'Look, we're just going to bat on down the road. There shouldn't be any hold-ups – there's no fighting anywhere, so they tell me. Could be a delay on the mountain road, of course. Can't predict that. But the only time we do stop officially is at the border with Croatia. Have to, legally. They usually wave us on p.d.q., but it's possible they'll want to look inside. Just so you're prepared for that.'

'Okay. Thanks for the warning.'

'Oh, and watch the road. It'll be a mud slide up the top.'

She gave a loose salute and strode back to her Land Rover at the front of the convoy.

They set off down the canyon track, windscreen wipers struggling against the brown spray kicked up by the trucks in front, every pothole a tureen of mud.

Gorni Vakuf looked more desolate than ever in the foul weather, its streets deserted, apart from an old man picking through the rubble.

Beyond the town the escorting Warriors waved the convoy past. They'd cleared the conflict zone. It was Bosnian Croat territory all the way to the border.

Josip glanced through the rear window.

'D'you think she's all right?' Alex asked. He thought of Vildana clinging on as the truck bounced and jolted.

'I hope. It is pity we cannot speak with her.'

There was a gap between the rear of the cab and the cargo space. No way of even tapping messages through.

'Perhaps I should have sat with her in the back,' Josip wondered.

'There's no seat. You'd have been knocked all over the place,' Alex assured him. 'We'll try and stop somewhere and check she's okay.'

Lorna shifted into third gear as the convoy weaved through the HVO checkpoint on the Makjlen Ridge, dodging the land mines that reminded her of upturned dinner plates. The Bedford was a few metres in front.

Every sighting of the Croat militia made her shiver. She knew they suspected convoys like this one secretly ferried men and arms to their Muslim-led enemies. Two vehicles without UN logos, hers and the Bedford, would not go unnoticed.

Supposing one checkpoint got awkward? Supposing they searched and found Vildana? Would the girl lieutenant and her three soldiers protect them? No way.

Have to pray for the 'slivovitz factor'; that the men on the checkpoints were too boozed-up to care.

The back of the Bedford jolted and swayed. Poor kid, she thought. Hope to God she's not been sick.

She pictured Alex wrestling with the wheel. Last night she'd lain awake thinking about what he'd told her, smarting that he had lied about still working for the intelligence services. Eventually she had cooled on that, however, convinced he had been honest in the end.

By the time she'd dropped off to sleep in the small hours, Alex's rationale for sabotaging the breakout from Long Kesh in 1973 had begun to seem more acceptable. Her own support for the Provisionals, unquestioning then, had been undermined not long after by their Boston backers' uncharitable wish to end her life.

What she could not yet accept or forgive was Alex's duplicity over Catherine. For twenty years, deep down, she had longed to make things good with him again, a longing she had never admitted to, even to her sister Annie. But that desire had been balanced by an even stronger yearning – that he should *suffer* for what he'd done – suffer like she had.

Eventually they would be reunited, she was certain of that. The dream she'd had when they'd first met had been too vivid to be anything other than a premonition. The dream of her own face in an open coffin and Alex weeping by the grave.

The long, steep hill wound down into Prozor, an evil place from where the Muslims had long since been ethnically cleansed. An HVO garrison town, from where camouflaged buses packed with soldiers shuttled to and from the trenches up on the ridge.

The UN convoy slowed to a snail's pace to negotiate the narrow street. Then they were through, climbing past a string of villages towards the Ljubuša mountains.

The tarmac ended by a lake, its chalky waters grey and choppy. The vehicles in front pulled in to the right.

'We're taking a break, by the look of it,' Alex remarked. 'Gives us a chance to see how Vildana is. And for a pee.'

'I think, I go look in the back,' Josip agreed.

'Don't let anyone see her.'

The translator looked at him coldly. He didn't need to be told that.

'Hi. How're you doing?' The lieutenant had stopped by the cab.

'Fine. How long are we stopping for?'

'Could be ten minutes. There's a Canadian convoy coming down off the mountain. No point in moving until that's out of the way.'

'Good. Time for a leak, then.'

'Huh! All right for you *boys*! I just have to keep my legs crossed.'

She moved on to talk to Lorna in the Toyota. Alex climbed down and scuttled off to the right, where a line of drivers were already relieving themselves against a rock face.

When he'd finished, he found the tailboard down and Josip already up on the cargo platform. Lorna got out of the Land Cruiser and came across.

'How is she?' she asked, looking round to see no one was close enough to hear.

Alex lifted the tarpaulin flap. The body bag was still secure. Beyond it Josip crouched by the camouflaged hide, talking and listening.

'Seems all right,' Alex replied.

Josip loped back to the tailboard.

'She say she feel sick,' he announced. 'I tell her to eat some bread.'

'Poor kid. Has she thrown up?' Lorna asked.

'No. Just *feels* sick. She okay, I think.' He jumped down and re-secured the tarpaulin.

Alex strolled with Lorna towards the lake.

'Are you all right?' An all-purpose question that could cover as much or as little as she wanted.

'Sure. I like driving.'

Giving nothing away, a hand's breadth shorter than Alex, Lorna cocked her head on one side, looking at him pensively.

Extraordinary, she thought. The man had been such a part of her life, yet she had only spent a few weeks with him in the flesh. Never had the chance to find out who he really was . . .

'What I was saying yesterday,' Alex began, fumblingly, 'Belfast and all that . . .'

'I heard what you said . . .' Her tone was flat and she turned back towards the convoy, showing this wasn't the time to pursue the issue.

'The lieutenant said they may search the trucks at the border,' Alex went on, sticking to safer ground.

'Oh? I'd hoped that with the UN we'd drive straight through,' she said, alarmed.

'Maybe we'll be lucky. Anyway, what's your plan once we're in Split? I have to get Moray's body to the airport.'

'Let's stop somewhere when we're safely across the border and there's nobody about. We'll get Vildana out of the truck and into the Land Cruiser. We're going to stay at the Hotel Split tonight.'

He looked at her, wondering for a moment if it was an invitation.

'I'll see you there then,' he smiled. The words slipped out.

Her eyes chilled. 'Don't get any ideas, Alex.'

She took a pace back from him.

'It's not the same this time,' she warned, walking away, a touch of pink suffusing her concave cheeks.

Alex smarted at the rebuff. He'd make a fool of himself if he didn't watch out.

Down the hill towards them came a long line of huge,

articulated trucks. The Canadian UN convoy was on its way through. The drivers of the British vehicles climbed back into their cabs and Alex hurried to the Bedford.

With puffs of blue smoke, the diesels revved and the convoy bounced back onto the rutted track. There'd be a good three hours of this. Three hours to cover fifty kilometres of one of the worst truck highways in the world.

It was only ten-thirty, yet it felt like lunchtime. He reached into his ration bag and pulled out a sandwich wrapped in cling film.

'Undo this for me, would you, Josip?'

'Sure.'

He peeled off the film and passed it back. Alex bit into it hungrily.

'Where's home, Josip?' he asked.

The translator wobbled his head.

'Many place. My father live Zagreb, my mother in Split. I have lived Sweden, Germany, Paris, Belgrade, Zagreb.'

'You don't have an apartment somewhere? Not married?'

'I have many girlfriend. I stay in their apartment.'

Alex nodded. He didn't believe him, but it wasn't worth pressing.

'Fine.'

'You? You're married?' Josip asked.

Hard to answer. He didn't know any more.

'Yes. Married, but not, if you know what I mean.'

The answer seemed to set Josip thinking. He sat in silence for a minute or two.

'You fuck with Lorna?' he asked suddenly.

Alex coughed. Stupid conversation. His fault for starting it.

'No,' he answered. 'What on earth makes you think that?'

The road wound higher and higher, hugging the red

219

sandstone of the mountain. On one of the tighter bends a trailer truck lay in the trees below, a victim of the winter ice. After an hour the surface began to improve, where the British army engineers had widened and strengthened it. Every few kilometres huge earth-movers shovelled hard core into the potholes.

They passed checkpoints manned by HVO but attracted little interest. Away from the front line, tension had eased. On right-hand bends Alex checked in the door mirror to see that Lorna was still behind.

At the highest point, snow lingered on the branches, but on the roadway it had melted into a slush that clogged the wipers.

Eventually, after long pauses to let convoys pass in the opposite direction, the road dipped steeply down through the trees towards the plains of Hercegovina.

'I fear we've got a very sick child in the back by now,' Alex remarked.

Josip grunted agreement.

They rattled and bounced a few more kilometres, then the tyres hummed on tarmac.

'Thank God for a proper surface,' Alex breathed, stretching one arm at a time to shake the fatigue from his shoulders.

They cut through the outskirts of Tomislavgrad, then picked up the main road for Split.

'How far to the border, Josip?'

'Maybe forty minutes, I think.'

As they sped on down the road, Alex's eyelids began to droop. All that driving after a night of little sleep had taken its toll. He kept shaking his head to keep awake.

Suddenly there was a roadside sign. The border was just five hundred metres ahead. Alex tensed up. He had no idea what to do if the Croat guards found Vildana. Have to bluff their way through.

'Fingers crossed, Josip.'

The road border between Bosnia-Hercegovina and

Croatia amounted to a string of prefab huts manned by a handful of officials in dark blue uniforms.

The convoy halted and the lieutenant strode to an office clutching the passports of the UN personnel. The rain had stopped and a chill wind broke up the cloud layer.

'I guess we just sit tight,' Alex muttered.

The border guards idly scanned the line of trucks. Then a couple wandered wearily towards them. One was a woman with curly hair and red lipstick. They made first for the Toyota.

In the door mirror Alex watched Lorna hand out her passport and UNPROFOR card. The woman took them to the office. The male officer walked round the Land Cruiser, looking through the windows.

Suddenly he turned to the Bedford, and stared at the back, low down where the number plate was.

He strolled round the side and appeared at the window, eyes full of suspicion.

'*Paso!*' he said gruffly.

'He want passport,' Josip translated, unnecessarily. He passed his own across too. Seeing he was Croatian, the official fired questions at him.

'He says we do not have UN plates on this truck. He asks who we are.'

'Well, tell him. Say we're a British aid agency called Bosnia Emergency.'

Josip translated.

The official's dark eyes were deeply suspicious. He jerked a thumb towards the back of the truck.

'He wants to see inside,' Josip gulped.

Alex climbed down from the cab and walked calmly back, Josip shadowing him on the other side.

'Explain to the officer that we have a body in the back, Josip. Tell him it's of an Englishman who was shot dead by accident.'

221

As Josip translated, he could see the official believed none of it. ·

Alex unpinned the hasps and lowered the board on its chains. He lifted a corner of the tarpaulin flap to reveal the body-bag. The official peered in and then turned on them, shouting.

'He say where are papers for the dead man.'

Papers? McFee's *passport*? Hadn't thought of that.

'Tell him I'll get them.'

Alex pulled himself up onto the tailboard. McFee's suitcase was strapped to the floor next to the boxes that concealed Vildana's hide. He clicked open the bag and searched through the dead man's clothing with his fingers.

A vile smell pervaded this end of the truck. A smell of vomit. Suddenly he heard laboured breathing and a stifled whimper.

Not now, Vildana! Just a few more minutes, for God's sake!

His fingers touched and he plucked the passport from the case.

'Here it is,' he called, thumping his feet on the steel floor. Noise, that's what they needed. Lots of it to drown any sounds Vildana might make. He crouched on the tailboard, clearing his throat as loudly as he could.

'You know, it never occurred to me a dead man would need a passport, Josip,' he said loudly. 'Did it you? I mean a corpse is just another piece of cargo really, isn't it?'

Josip understood what he was up to.

'Yes. I did not think so either that a passport is needed.'

'But I guess they have to know who the dead person is,' he continued.

The official interrupted, swiping his hand to indicate a zip opening.

'He say he want to see face,' Josip explained, darkly.

222

'Tell him it's not a pretty sight,' Alex replied, standing up again.

The official hoisted himself into the cargo space. Alex and Josip banged about on the steel floor. The fat end of the body bag was towards the middle of the truck. Alex pulled a handkerchief from his trouser pocket and pressed it over his nose.

'I'd advise our friend here to do the same,' he suggested.

The official's attention had been caught by the pile of boxes at the far end of the truck.

Alex grabbed at the heavy zip on the body bag.

'Here,' he said. 'Take a quick look, I don't want this open for long.'

The zip incorporated a rubber seal and took a sharp tug to get it to move.

McFee's face was pinched and yellow, hardly recognizable. The sour smell from the bag penetrated his mask, and made him gag.

The official positioned himself beside the corpse, then held out the passport to compare the photo of the living with the face of death. He screwed up his face in disgust, then nodded that the bag should be closed again.

The official's attention returned to the boxes. Alex followed his gaze. A black smear of water was trickling from under the cardboard along the grooves in the floor.

Jesus! The kid's wet herself and the bastard's going over to look!

Alex dropped to his knees, retching violently. It wasn't hard to simulate with the ever-growing stench.

He'd fallen deliberately between the official and the hide. Josip fussed around him, adding to the distraction. The gut-heaving noise and the smell had their effect; the official stumbled to the back of the truck and climbed out, sucking in great gulps of air.

Josip and Alex followed quickly, closing up the

tailboard. Alex leaned against the side of the Bedford, panting.

The official pulled Josip to one side and began berating him. Josip shrugged and shook his head.

Alex glanced at Lorna who'd remained in the Toyota, pretending she was nothing to do with them. She studiously avoided his gaze.

'O-hh,' Josip sighed, 'this man, he says we must have paper to bring body into Croatia. Special paper.'

'What sort of paper, for Christ's sake? Tell him the body's going to be flown back to England tomorrow by the Royal Air Force. Tell him it'll only be in Croatia for a matter of hours.'

Josip tried again. This time it was the official who shrugged and shook his head.

Alex saw the Logistics Corps lieutenant watching from fifty metres away. He made a face at her as if to say 'can you help', but she turned away. They may have been awarded a UN escort, but they weren't UN business.

Josip grabbed his arm and led him back to the driver's cab.

'You have some Deutsche marks?' he demanded.

'Some. Why? You're going to bribe this guy?'

'I think it is best. Maybe two hundred will do. Give me three hundred, if you have.'

Alex pulled his wallet from his thornproof and placed it on the driving seat, shielding it from view with his back.

'Here you are.' He folded the notes and slipped them into Josip's hand. 'For God's sake handle this right.'

Josip walked the official away from the truck and the hut where the red-lipped woman was waiting. There were smiles and pats on the shoulder, then the almost imperceptible passing of the money.

There was an art to bribery. A Balkan art.

Josip returned with the passports. The officials waved and the convoy moved on.

'Fucking brilliant, Josip! Well done.'

The translator chuckled.

Ten minutes down the road, the convoy halted again, pulling off onto what had been a restaurant car park in the days when Yugoslavia had a tourist trade.

'Okay, now?' The lieutenant was at the window again.

'Fine.'

'Just thought I'd say goodbye. We don't go into Split itself, so I expect you'll want to drop out of the convoy here.'

She reached up and gave a surprisingly feminine handshake.

'Bye. Thanks for your help.'

She paused briefly by the Toyota, then strode back to her Land Rover, and the army vehicles moved on.

On their own at last, Josip and Alex banged down the tailboard.

'What was all that about at the border?' Lorna asked.

'I'll tell you later. Let's get Vildana out,' Alex replied.

All three climbed into the truck. Alex clawed at the tape holding the boxes in place, while Josip spoke soothing words in Serbo-Croat.

'Oh, my God,' Lorna gasped. 'The smell! Poor baby.'

The boxes fell away. Vildana lay across the sodden sleeping bag that had been her bed. Her face was grey, her eyes sunken, and her cheeks caked with vomit.

'Oh, you poor, poor sweetheart,' Lorna whispered, dropping to her knees and lifting the girl's head. Josip took her legs, and between them they carried her to the rear of the truck, shielding her face so she wouldn't see the body-bag.

Lorna sat on the tailboard, dangling her legs over the edge and placed Vildana beside her. She hugged the girl gently and stroked her face. So helpless, she thought. So like Julie.

'All over now. All over,' she murmured.

Alex jumped to the ground.

'I'll get some water so we can clean her face,' he said.

Lorna's blue-grey eyes sparkled with tears.

Two and a half hours later Alex drove the Bedford into the UN depot next to Split airport. It was just after five. A lowering sky and the first spots of rain spattered the windscreen as another front moved in. It would be dark soon.

He'd been expected and was guided to the corner of a huge vehicle garage.

'The Herc goes at ten in the morning, sir,' a Logistics Corps sergeant told him.

Four soldiers lifted down the body bag, while the sergeant saluted. A corner of the floor had been marked off with tape. They laid the bag next to a small vase of flowers.

'Hope you approve, sir,' the sergeant breathed, snapping his hand to his side.

'Oh yes. Thank you.' Standard procedure for corpses, he guessed, whatever their history.

Alex stood for a moment, hands clasped in front of him, suddenly sad. He wanted to believe that McFee hadn't been a total monster, that his other motive for coming out here *had* been to help.

'There's a message from Major Allison, sir,' the sergeant whispered. 'From Farnham. Said he's arriving on a plane getting in at eight this evening, and could you meet him. You've rooms booked in the Park Hotel.'

'Mike Allison? I didn't know he was coming out.'

'Said something about needing to sort out the mess, sir.'

'Mmm.' Sounded like head-teacher was on his way down with the cane.

'You'll be leaving the truck here sir, as usual?'

'Yes. Yes, I suppose so.'

'Need any transport into Split?'

'Umm.' He thought for a moment. 'No. I've remembered there's a Lada Niva jeep here somewhere. Belongs to Bosnia Emergency. Moray and I used it last weekend, when we were loading up.'

'Got the keys in my office, sir.'

After driving the four-tonner, the Niva felt like a toy. Forty minutes it would take to get into town, then a quick shower and he'd find Lorna. Lurking at the back of his mind was a sneaking fear she might just disappear now she'd got what she wanted from him.

Lorna kneeled on her bed in the Hotel Split, rubbing Vildana's damp hair with a towel. She sang softly.

The girl had locked her out of the bathroom when taking her shower, the click of the bolt a painful reminder of her own daughter's indifference to love and affection.

Josip was in the room next door. She'd get him to take Vildana to a restaurant for a meal once they were both clean and dressed.

'Mmmm, you smell so good, sweetie,' she said. She hugged her, rocking from side to side, then kissed her on the cheek just beside the livid strawberry mark.

'You're going to be okay, Vildana. That's a promise.'

The girl had understood none of what she'd said, but decided it would be wise to smile.

Lorna bit her lip.

In the bag Vildana had brought from the refugee centre, there was a clean pair of jeans and another pullover.

'Tomorrow, sweetheart, we're going to get you some new clothes. Something real pretty.'

Vildana pulled the towel wrap tighter and took the clothes back into the privacy of the bathroom to put them on.

Then it was Lorna's turn under the magically hot jets. For several minutes she stood motionless letting the stream rinse the tension from her neck and shoulders. Then she washed quickly and reached for a towel.

Half-an-hour later, Alex drove over from the Park Hotel and walked into the reception area.

'Lorna Donohue?' he asked at reception.

The middle-aged woman behind the desk frowned. 'Not here. No one that name.'

'An American woman. May have had a young girl with her.'

'Ah, yes.' The receptionist riffled through a stack of passports.

'Mrs Sorensen. And her daughter called Julie Sorensen.'

'Daughter?'

'Yes.' The receptionist held up a second American passport.

'Oh. I see. And their room number?'

'Two-three-seven.'

'Thank you.'

Daughter! So that's how she planned to get Vildana out of Croatia. On her own child's passport. And she *was* married. Or had been.

He waited for the lift, but when it gave no sign of life, took to the stairs, passing signs for the UN and the EC Monitoring Mission which used the hotel as a base.

Two-three-seven. On the right. The door was closed. He tapped.

Nothing. He tapped again.

'Who is it?' Lorna's voice, tetchy and distant.

'Alex.'

Silence.

'Hang on a minute.'

Two minutes later the sound of feet scuffing carpet. She pulled open the door.

'I'm on line to the States . . .' She darted back to the

writing-table and the glowing screen of her laptop computer.

'I'm impressed,' Alex said.

'Just got to download my e-mail,' she explained.

He stood right behind her and watched. She smelled of shampoo. Her hair was soft and fluffy, her shoulders round and bony under the clean tee-shirt. He badly wanted to caress the soft curve of her neck, but dared not touch.

'Sit down. You're making me nervous,' she told him.

He perched on the edge of the bed.

She typed 'EXIT', the computer screen flickered and cleared. Then she thumbed the roller-ball to enter a new Windows file.

'Just got to read this stuff again . . .' she murmured. 'But it seems like it's all fixed.'

She grabbed a notebook, then scribbled down names and phone numbers read from the screen.

At last she logged off and powered down the computer.

'It's Germany,' she told him, swinging round in her chair. Her eyes burned excitedly. 'They've found a family in Germany. An Air Force colonel and his wife, two kids of their own, and would you believe, a Yugoslav child nurse. Isn't that amazing?'

'An American colonel?'

'Sure, sure. His tour of duty finishes in a year and then they go back to Milwaukee. Vildana will go with them, if it all works out.'

'And you got all that out of your computer?' Alex asked, astonished.

'On-line, through the phone, to the Internet. CareNet runs a bulletin board for families who want to adopt. I posted a notice there two days ago, and it's all happened lickety-split.'

'Sort of shopping by computer? Kids off the peg.'

She looked wounded.

'I know it sounds like that. But believe me every subscriber gets checked out real good.'

'In just two days?' he asked incredulously.

'Look. Larry Machin, the guy who runs CareNet, he's got a million contacts. He knows loads of people in the Air Force, the church, in politics. He wouldn't have said this family's okay if he had any doubts.'

But she wasn't that certain. He could see it in her eyes. She turned away. You just had to trust people sometimes. And she trusted Machin.

Alex glimpsed at his watch. It was an old Swiss wind-up Lorna had given him in Belfast. Twenty-past-seven.

'Christ I'm meant to be at the airport. The guy who runs *my* organization is arriving at eight.'

He took hold of her hands.

'Lorna, we've *got* to talk some more,' he said.

'Sure. But not now,' she answered, giving his hands a light squeeze, then pulling hers free. 'There's too much still to fix, and anyway you've got to be going.'

'I'll come back later, okay?'

'I'm not sure . . .'

'When are you going to Germany?'

'Tomorrow if there's a ferry to Ancona. I've got to check.'

'With Vildana travelling on your daughter's passport?'

She froze and stared at him. How did he know that? Then she remembered the receptionist had their documents.

'Sure. On Julie's passport. She has dark hair too, and I can cover Vildana's birthmark with make-up,' she declared defiantly.

Alex thought for a moment. He could see a problem. 'But Julie's passport doesn't have an entry stamp . . .'

Lorna looked unsettled. She hadn't thought of that.

'You think it matters?' she whispered.

'If your passport has the stamp and hers doesn't, they

may ask questions. And when they find your "daughter" only speaks Serbo-Croat . . .'

'Maybe Josip can bribe someone, like he did today.'

'Risky . . . I may know a better way. I'll ring you later, when I've sorted things out.'

'No. Vildana's going to be sleeping in here. I don't want her woken up. I'll call *you* about eleven.'

He gave her his room number at the Park Hotel.

'Got to go.'

He held her by the shoulders. She felt frail.

He kissed her dry lips. She pushed him away, looking at him from the corner of her eyes, as if to say *don't try it.*

Eighteen

It was a grey, wintry morning in the Croatian capital. A
damp mist of pollution contaminated the streets. On
people's faces there was weariness, and a lurking fear that
the day could not be far away when war would return to
their part of what used to be Yugoslavia.

Milan Pravic slipped out of his sister's apartment in
Novi Zagreb without a word. Living there was getting on
his nerves. He would strangle that baby soon if it woke
him with its crying any more. Only a few days to go and
he would be gone, thank God.

He pressed the lift button. No green light. Stuck again.
Some stupid bastards had left a door open probably.

He took to the stairs. Going down six floors was fine,
coming up wasn't so funny.

On the way he passed pale women dragging toddlers
up with them. Everyone looked pale living here in these
tall damp towers.

'Broken down *again*,' one of them complained, as if *he*
was responsible. 'Four times in a month. It's too much.'

He ignored them. Wasn't *his* fault the lift didn't work.

The message from Dieter Konrad said to meet him in
the bar of Hotel Dubrovnik on what he still called
Republic Square, despite the name change after Croatian independence.

The tram that would take him there stopped five
minutes' walk away. Plenty of time.

He still didn't know what Konrad wanted. A 'job' in

232

Zagreb was all Gisela had said. The reward – ten thousand Deutsche marks, a false passport to get him safely over the border, and a ride back to Berlin in Konrad's car.

Germany was his second home. He'd lived there five years before the war summoned him back to Bosnia. He'd worked building offices and hotels, installing air-conditioning.

And Gisela? She was 'home' too. She'd said she'd be glad to have him live with her again. Had another 'protector' these days, but the man was gay, and wouldn't get in the way.

Gisela. She was the only woman he'd ever felt tenderness for. The only one he hadn't needed to hurt.

The blue number 6 tram took him from the monotonous towers of Novi Zagreb, across the River Sava into the classical mid-European splendour of the Lower Town. He got off in Republic Square. The sun was breaking through, the warmth of spring in the air.

The Dubrovnik Hotel was part Austro-Hungarian, part modern, a confusing place where guests had been known to get lost. Pravic walked through the lobby and into the small bar. He didn't notice Konrad at first. Looking older than when he'd last seen him a few years back, he hugged a corner like a shadow. The raising of an eyebrow finally caught Pravic's attention.

Konrad got up and walked towards the door, ignoring him. Pravic followed a dozen paces behind. They crossed separately to the other side of the square. A pedestrian zone with trams the only traffic, a fountain splashed at one end. Konrad headed for a bench encircling the base of an ornate lamp standard.

'Good thing you sent me those passport photos,' he declared when Pravic joined him. 'Wouldn't have recognized you with short hair and glasses. Gisela sends her love.'

Tourists were rare in Zagreb since Yugoslavia became

synonymous with war. One or two climbed the steps to the old town from this square, taking pictures on the way. Most were couples, but there was one man on his own, with a British Airways bag over his shoulder, and the broken nose of a rugby player.

The lone tourist wandered across the square, looking as if he was trying to get his bearings. Then he took the cap off his camera lens and adjusted the zoom to its maximum focal length.

The two men on the bench almost filled the frame. The younger, short-haired one seemed a little startled at something he was being told.

11.10 am.
Split, Croatia

'We've got file footage of Tulici,' the American reporter told Lorna. 'And we'll take shots of you three driving down the road together.'

'Uh-oh. That's not too clever,' Lorna cautioned her. Journalists always assumed too much, particularly the female ones. 'You draw attention to us like that, and somebody might say – hey guys, what's going on here? It's going to be tough enough as it is, getting Vildana out of the country.'

'We'll be sneaky. Nobody'll see us. Don't you worry about it.'

The camera team from CNN were packing up. Vildana stood on the balcony overlooking the sea and stared back into the room, bewildered, excited and frightened by the attention she'd been getting that morning.

It hadn't been Lorna's idea to tell the world that she

was smuggling the only eye-witness of the Tulici massacre out of the country. She'd been instructed to do it in an e-mail message from Larry Machin in Boston. He'd already told CNN headquarters in Atlanta they could have the story exclusively if they undertook not to broadcast it until Vildana was safe.

'Tell them it's because CareNet uses state-of-the-art computer technology that we've been able to place the kid so fast.' That was the message he wanted her to put across. 'Publicity like this could bring in millions in donations.'

The camera team had taped Lorna tapping away at her notebook computer, with Vildana watching uncomprehendingly while covering her birthmark with a hand. The woman had asked about the threat to Vildana's life, but Lorna had refused to say how she'd brought the girl to Split, and rejected a request for an interview with Vildana herself.

Lorna hated the publicity machine, but Larry Machin was not a man to be crossed.

'This is the number of the Atlanta newsdesk.' The CNN correspondent handed her a card.

'Call them collect as soon as you're safe, so they can transmit the piece. Okay?'

'Okay.'

'And you've not talked to any other media, right?'

'Right.'

'Great. Well thank you Lorna. And thanks Vildana. Good luck!'

She shook hands all round. The cameraman and recordist clattered out of the room with their equipment. The correspondent followed, then turned in the doorway.

'Oh, I meant to tell you I'm flying back home to the States tomorrow,' she said. 'Anything you want me to take for you? Letters maybe?'

Lorna thought for a moment.

'Oh my God, yes! The camera! Larry wants pictures.'

Her Nikon was on the bed and she'd forgotten to use it.

'Can you give me a few minutes to take some shots? No. I've a better idea. Your office is here in the hotel, right?'

'Sure. One floor up. Room three-two-eight.'

'Give me ten minutes and I'll bring you an envelope with a film in it. Okay?'

'No problem. I'll be editing for the next couple of hours, anyway.'

Lorna plugged in the flash and showed Josip how to use it. Then she put her arm round Vildana and they posed at the table with the computer.

Josip took two shots, but then couldn't wind on any further.

'It is finish,' he suggested, passing her the camera.

'Fine. We've got enough. Thanks.'

She took back the Nikon, rewound the film and removed the cassette. Then she closed her fingers round it, remembering it contained shots of Alex taken in the Bosnian village where they'd met.

She despatched Josip to ask at reception for envelopes, then scrawled a note to Machin, telling him what was on the film, and asking him to post the pictures that weren't of Vildana to her sister in Boston. Then she wrote another note.

Dearest Annie,
You will NEVER guess who the guy with the beard is, standing next to me in a couple of these photos!
His name begins with the letter 'A'!!!
See you soon. Lorna.

Josip returned, successful. Lorna addressed the envelopes, put the one for her sister inside the one to Machin containing the film and hurried down the corridor to the stairway.

She nearly collided with Alex coming out of the lift.

'I'll be back in a minute,' she said hurriedly, walking briskly down the corridor.

As arranged, she had telephoned him last night. He'd told her about his gloomy meeting with Mike Allison, who reckoned Bosnia Emergency had been all but crippled by the publicity surrounding McFee. He had also said that he knew of a way to put a stamp in her daughter's passport.

Alex found the door to her room open.

'Morning Josip. Hello Vildana.' He smiled at the girl and gave her a hug. Vildana almost looked excited and had colour back in her cheeks.

Lorna returned breathless.

'Okay,' she panted. 'What's next? I've got so much to do before the ferry tonight. Vildana has to have some clothes.'

The girl looked nervous again, not understanding what was on offer but sensing tension.

'As I said on the phone, I think I can fix that passport for you, Lorna,' Alex reminded her. 'But there are some things I need to buy. Can I borrow Josip for half an hour? And your Land Cruiser? My boss has nicked my Lada.'

'Sure.' She gave him the keys. 'See you in a while. Not too long, huh?'

Josip knew the town well. They toured dry-cleaning establishments until they found one prepared to sell them di-ethylene glycol. Translating the chemical name proved beyond Josip's powers, but asking for ball-point pen ink remover produced the desired result.

They were back in the hotel within the hour, after stopping at a toy shop to buy a child's paintbrush.

Alex took the two American passports into Josip's room. He'd never done this before and didn't want people watching. He'd been told the technique by a minder at the safe house where MI5 had hidden him after the pull-out from Belfast.

First he opened the passport of Lorna's daughter. No stamps. Looked totally unused.

Julie Maria Sorensen – born 18th July 1980.

Nearly fourteen now, but the photo was younger. Pretty kid. Dark hair, like Lorna had said. Not much else that resembled Vildana. Hope immigration don't look too closely, he thought. Curiously vacant expression. The girl hadn't been looking at the camera.

He spread open Lorna's passport. Her photo had been taken in a studio, hair immaculate, soft lighting, just the hint of a smile. Not her, the style. Done to please her husband probably. He wondered if he was still around.

He flicked through the pages until he found last Saturday's entry stamp to Croatia. He checked his materials. Bottle of fluid, brush, writing paper, tissues.

He dipped the fine-pointed brush in the liquid and dabbed off the excess. Steadying his hand, he painted the Glycol in a thin coat over the black ink outline of the entry stamp. Then, replenishing the brush, he traced the letters of the word 'Split' and the date.

He observed his work. Every bit of ink covered.

'Here goes,' he murmured, pressing the sheet of writing paper firmly onto the moistened page. He lifted it off again. A perfect negative image left by the Glycol-softened ink.

He opened the second visa section in Julie's passport and laid the writing paper face down. Then he used his thumb to press the image onto the page.

He lifted off the paper. The image was faint, but readable. A perfect replica of an entry stamp.

Just one problem. The Glycol had left a stain on both passports. He dabbed with the tissue, but the stain remained.

He took them back next door and showed them to Lorna.

'That's amazing. Where'd you learn to do that?' she asked suspiciously.

'Never mind. Do you have a hair-drier? See if those stains will come out. If they don't, your best bet may be to drop the whole passport in the bath. It'll be such a mess by the time you dry it out, nobody'll know what's what.'

She looked irritated, as if he'd created more problems than he'd solved.

'Okay, Josip, let's go shopping now,' she announced. 'Vildana needs a warm coat, a nightdress and a tooth-brush. And anything else she sees that she wants. I'm going to try to put a smile on that little face.'

She hustled them all out of the bedroom and locked the door. They took the stairs to the ground floor. Alex followed uneasily. Lorna was being deliberately distant.

Downstairs she handed her key to the receptionist then headed for the big glass exit doors. In the middle of the large lobby she turned to Alex.

'Well,' she said with a switched-on smile. 'I guess this is goodbye again.'

Her eyes were like glass, free of any decipherable expression.

'What d'you mean?' he asked, stunned.

'I imagine you're going back up to Vitez in a day or so,' she went on.

He knew his distress was plain for her to see – and she was savouring it, he realized suddenly.

'I really can't thank you enough for what you did getting Vildana down here. *Made up for a lot*,' she added pointedly.

239

'But I'm not sure that I am going back to Vitez . . .' he mouthed, desperately. She was casting off, leaving him behind.

'Fate did us all a good turn this time, huh?'

This time.

'If we hadn't met up like that, Vildana probably wouldn't be here,' she continued, slipping an arm round the girl's shoulders.

'But hang on a minute . . .' Alex said, wishing they were out of earshot of the others.

'Alex, I don't *have* a minute,' she replied fractiously. 'I've got to get that kid sorted out – that's all I'm interested in right now.'

'Yes, but we can see each other later then . . .'

'Later, I'm going to Frankfurt, and then home to the States.'

He felt as if she'd just kneed him in the groin.

'Lorna, I . . . I really do want to see you again,' he said lamely. He was conscious of Josip watching them.

'Oh, you do? I'm not sure that's such a good . . .'

Then she appeared to relent.

'I tell you what. I'll give you the number of CareNet in Boston. They can pass a message. Maybe you'll come to the States one day.'

She pulled a calling card from her pocket and handed it to him.

'Bye,' she said, walking away. 'And good luck.'

She hung on to Vildana using the girl as a shield.

Dumbfounded, Alex watched as they climbed into the Land Cruiser and drove up the ramp towards the town.

Lorna shook like a leaf, terrified she'd overdone it. She responded to Josip's street directions on autopilot.

She had worked it all out in her head last night, while lying awake listening to Vildana's snuffly breathing.

Yes, she ached to have him back, but no, it wouldn't work until they were quits. Until she had made him feel something of the pain that *she* had felt all those years ago.

Nineteen

Alex stalked back to the Park Hotel, seething. Angry at Lorna, and at himself for standing there like an idiot, letting her go off that way. That's what came of being too considerate with women, he thought. Should have just grabbed her and told her what's what. Instead he'd let her dump him like some pickup at a disco.

Mike Allison was waiting for him at a table beneath the palm trees on the sun-speckled terrace.

'Ah, there you are,' he said, pointedly not getting to his feet. 'Wondered where you'd got to.'

Alex pulled out a white-painted, metal chair and sat down without responding. Allison was a good five years younger than him, the type of ex-soldier who couldn't forget he was officer class.

'Thought we'd have a bite here. They do sandwiches.'

'Fine.'

Allison twisted round to look for the waiter.

'Never there when you want them. If you see him come out, give him a wave.'

'Sure.' Alex's chair faced the French windows that led to the kitchens.

'I've been talking to Vitez this morning,' the Major continued. 'I saw Moray's body off on the C-130, then went to UNPROFOR and called Alan Clarke-Hartley on the army "comms".'

'Oh yes?'

'I can tell you we're in deep doo-doo up there. The HVO are claiming we've been using our truck to smuggle the "Muj" in and out. Usual crap. But the bottom line is I've got a lot of work to do patching things up with the locals. And I think it best if you aren't around when I do it.'

'I see.'

The waiter approached and they ordered club sandwiches and beers.

'Yes. The trouble is people will link you with Moray. They probably think you were both perverts. It's all rumour control up there. Truth only makes up ten per cent of what people believe. If that.'

Alex nodded. If he was being given his cards, it was no more than he'd expected.

'So, this is what I've decided,' Allison continued. 'Tomorrow morning there's another of my trucks arriving from England. You can give us a hand stuffing the boxes into the Bedford and then push off back to England if you like. The chap who drives the bread van out from Farnham can come up to Vitez with me. He's bringing a camera. We'll get some new pictures of our aid being distributed and hope it counteracts the lousy press we got over McFee.'

'And ... how do I travel to England?' Alex asked flatly.

'You can have the return half of my air ticket, if you like. I'll get it transferred into your name.'

The sandwiches arrived.

Alex lay on the bed in his room staring at the ceiling. In the hours that had passed since Lorna drove away at the Hotel Split, he'd reached a firm conclusion. However resistant she might be, he needed her and he was going to have her again.

It wasn't a pretty sight, looking back on his life. There seemed to be a trail of human suffering lying in his wake that resembled the work of a joy-rider in a parking lot.

There was still time however, to create something good, something lasting from it.

The problem was *how* to get Lorna back. He'd ruled out returning to the hotel to tell her what he felt. Nothing would be accomplished while she still had Vildana to hide behind.

In the meantime there was also the question of Milan Pravic. A mass-murderer on the loose who had to be stopped from killing again.

He checked his watch. Four o'clock – three p.m. in London. It was time he let Roger Chadwick know what he'd found out.

He dialled the number he'd been given. A voice he'd never heard before answered and took a message. He replaced the receiver and waited for the call back.

Ten minutes was all it took before Chadwick's sonorous tones boomed down the line.

'Nice to hear your voice,' Alex volunteered.

'Oh, dear. Things must be bad,' Chadwick quipped.

'You know what's happened. . . ?'

'Of course. It's been all over the papers and the TV. You have my sympathy, dear boy.'

'Thanks. Well the result is I've just been fired. My days as a charity worker out here are over, I'm afraid.'

'Oh dear. That's a pity, but I have to say I'm not surprised. Did you learn anything useful?'

Alex told him about Father Pravic. He also mentioned the existence of Vildana, but without revealing his own involvement in her escape from Bosnia.

'A witness! You *have* done well. The UN will be delighted if they ever catch the blighter. Where's the girl now?'

'Don't want to say any more at the moment,' Alex stalled. The last thing he wanted was to tell Chadwick about Lorna. He'd never hear the last of it. 'I'll call you again on a *secure line* in a few days' time.'

'Mmm. All right.' Chadwick sounded impressed by his security-speak.

'As to Pravic, or the Scorpion as his brother so descriptively calls him – it looks as if he's done a bunk. No one knows where to. But Roger, the man's really dangerous. He's got to be found. He sounds like a psychopath and his brother says he'll definitely kill again.'

'Well as long as he does it in Bosnia, I don't suppose anyone'll be too fussed,' Chadwick mumbled.

Alex winced.

'Not fussed? Slaughtering women and children?'

'We-ell it's not really *our* problem, is it? We're not the world's policemen any more. You've done your best. *We've* done our best as UK Limited. I think I'll pass the baton back to the UN War Crimes people in the Hague and let them take up the running.'

'You wouldn't be so bloody blasé if the bloke was on the loose in Hampshire,' Alex growled.

'But he's not, is he?'

'I don't know. He could be anywhere.'

'Got a description of him?'

'Fair hair and blue eyes, not very tall. That's all.'

There was a pause from the other end in which Alex thought he heard a sigh.

'Bloody Bosnia,' Chadwick muttered. 'We'd all love to leave them to it, but they won't let us. So what do you suggest – as our man on the spot?' he added grandly. 'We're still happy to pay your exes if you think there's anything more you can do.'

Alex hesitated.

'Give me a day or two to think, and I'll get back to you.'

'Fine. Oh by the way, when you return to England there's some good news for you,' Chadwick continued, perkily. 'Might put a smile on your face. It looks like the Provos are heading for a cease-fire.'

Alex replaced the receiver. He'd given hardly a thought to the IRA in the last few days. Their threat to his life had almost ceased to be real.

There was a knock on the bedroom door.

'Yes?'

'It's Mike. Time to go down to the Travel Agent and get the ticket done. You'll need your passport.'

Of course. His ticket home. He swung his feet to the floor. Half-past-five.

The walk to the harbour took twenty minutes. Clustered at one end of the palm-lined promenade was a small parade of travel and souvenir shops. It didn't take long to re-issue the air ticket in Alex's name.

Young couples in jeans and T-shirts strolled by the water's edge. With the preserved remains of the old medieval town as a backdrop, they could have been on the French Riviera if it weren't for the stench of sewage that rose from the oily waters of the port.

'Gorgeous bloody women in this country,' Allison purred. 'Fancy a drink at one of those cafés to take in the view?'

He was right about the pretty girls. There'd be plenty to look at.

Suddenly, realizing where he was, Alex had a different idea. He glanced at his watch. Nearly half-past-six.

'No thanks. There's a friend of mine going on the ferry to Ancona tonight. Think I'll try to catch her before she gets on board. . . .'

Allison lifted one eyebrow then set off on his own.

Alex hurried towards the docks, suspecting he might already be too late. The ferry sailed in less than an hour.

It was further than he'd remembered to the terminal. He began to run. Dock workers waiting at a bus stop watched nervously. When people ran here, it often meant trouble wasn't far behind.

A short line of trucks still queued at the customs barrier, but no Land Cruisers.

A quarter to seven. Must have missed her.

He walked to the police pole. Without a ticket he could go no further. Two hundred metres beyond the control point, the lights of the ferry's upper deck sparkled in the dusk.

He saw figures on deck. Dark shapes taking a last look at the floodlit ramparts of the old town. He strained to make them out. Two tallish forms with a smaller one between them. Might be Lorna. Might not.

Convincing himself it was, he waved. We'll meet again soon, he decided.

He hung around until the ship sailed, then made his way back to the promenade. The evening was mild, a temperature they'd have called 'summer' in Scotland. The crowds on the promenade had grown. Couples flirted at the cafés.

He ambled through the bustle, relishing its sensuousness. He took a seat at a restaurant whose tables spilled onto the pavement. He wasn't particularly hungry, but he'd eat something.

While waiting for service, he pulled the airline ticket from his pocket and studied it carefully for the first time. The flight was tomorrow afternoon. Split to Zagreb, then Zagreb–Frankfurt, and Frankfurt–London.

Frankfurt! They'd made it easy for him.

Twenty

The man with the broken nose sat in his rented Golf, parked at Zagreb's Pleso airport in a position where he could see the planes landing. At this time of night the place was almost deserted. No more scheduled flights were due in.

Martin Sanders was more nervous than he had been for many a year. As a department head with the British Secret Intelligence Service, it wasn't often he did field work any more. The activities of the Ramblers were so secret however, they were compelled to keep the use of subordinates to a minimum.

Parked nearby, Marcel Vaillon from the DGSE was keeping an eye on the terminal building. Everything depended on their identification of the target. Without that there could be no killing.

The advance intelligence the CIA had gleaned was skimpy. They had the Iranian's name, but their only photograph was a family snap of him as a bearded youth, taken at the time of the Islamic Revolution. They knew he'd be on this flight, but didn't know where he'd meet his contact.

Information on the Russian was zero. No name, no data whatsoever. He must, they assumed, already be in Zagreb. Waiting somewhere with his lethal sample.

For a jumbo jet to fly from Tehran, the hotbed of Islamic fundamentalism, to this the capital of militantly

248

Catholic Croatia, was an odd event, but no odder than many that had happened in the former Yugoslavia.

The flight was arriving in the dark of night and would leave again before dawn. Few people would ever know the plane had been here. Official sources would deny it.

Balkan politicians had turned somersaults in the past few days. The Bosnian Croats and the mostly Muslim Bosnian government forces, who'd fought so bloodily over territory, had cemented their cease-fire by signing a confederation agreement. Pooling resources again to kill Serbs, instead of each other, had finally made sense to even the most stubborn.

As a spin-off from that agreement, Croatia had given permission for Iran to re-arm the BiH Armija. The guns were being ferried through airfields on the coast, to be driven through Croatian territory into Bosnia.

Tonight's flight to Zagreb was the pay-off to Croatia – a plane-load of explosives and ammunition, a gift from the mullahs, which the Croatians wanted for the renewal of their own battle with the Serbs.

On the return flight to Iran, the cargo would be much smaller but potentially much more lethal – a sliver of Russian plutonium.

Sanders had the car windows down, listening. At two minutes to midnight he heard the roar of turbofans as a 747 flared out for landing. Through night-vision binoculars he watched the white-painted jumbo taxi to the far side of the airfield. No markings on it. No airline logo, no giveaway fin-flash. Vehicles clustered round the plane, their tail-lights forming a ruby crescent.

He picked up the rented telephone and dialled the number of Marcel's mobile.

'The guests have arrived,' he said cryptically.

'I thought so,' the Frenchman answered. 'A car has just arrived at the terminal.'

They disconnected.

Sanders started the engine, switched on the lights and

motored slowly to the car park exit. He paid the sleepy attendant with a wad of devalued Dinar notes then drove on and stopped just short of the terminal. He pretended to be consulting a map.

The 'car' was a minibus. Might be for the aircrew, but there was no other vehicle in sight. No taxis at this time of night. If Akhavi had an appointment in town, the bus could well be for him.

Vaillon was closer. The final identification would have to be his.

Sanders drummed his fingers on the wheel. Too many uncertainties for his liking. Desperately under-resourced the whole operation was. Had to be, when officially the Ramblers didn't even exist.

Three minutes later a lone figure in a dark suit emerged from the terminal, accompanied by the uniformed driver of the minibus. Too shadowy for Sanders to make out, even through the glasses. Maybe Vaillon had more luck.

His phone rang.

'Yes?'

'Cannot be certain. But I think,' Vaillon's voice.

'I'll go for it then?'

'Yes.'

The minibus began to move. Sanders slipped the Golf into gear and took station about fifty metres behind, heading for Zagreb.

Vaillon would remain at the airport in case someone else looking like Akhavi emerged, or the Russian arrived. If the rendezvous was on the airport itself however, they were screwed. No way they could take them out.

Sanders followed the minibus for fifteen minutes, then called Vaillon again.

'Crossing the Sava by the Freedom Bridge.'

'Nothing new here,' Vaillon acknowledged.

The minibus turned left onto Vukovarska then right

into Miramarska, Sanders letting a taxi slip in between himself and the van.

Left and right past squares and fountains, then the target vehicle pulled up at the Martinova Hotel.

Sanders stopped at the kerb. Parking no problem at this time of night. Lights out and onto his feet running, keeping in the shadows. He punched the buttons of the phone. A different number this time.

'Ja?' A German voice answered, the man Sanders knew simply as Dunkel.

'Hotel Martinova. *Zehn Minuten*.'

'*Jawohl!*'

Voices on the phone, that's all they were. They'd never met. Never would. Dunkel hadn't even been told who he was working for.

Sanders pushed through the swing doors into the hotel. The man he'd followed from the airport stood at the reception desk holding one of those large black leather bags used by pilots.

Sanders' heart missed a beat, terrified he'd followed the wrong man.

Iranian? Certainly looked it – dark hair, dark-framed spectacles, small moustache, and wearing one of those collarless shirts under a suit that was almost black.

But was it Akhavi?

Sanders walked up behind him as casually as he could. He hovered half a pace from the desk. There was just a night clerk on duty.

Hearing him, the Iranian snapped his head round. Fear in his eyes – a good sign. Sanders smiled.

'Good evening,' he purred.

The Iranian nodded and turned back to the desk. Sanders moved a little closer. The clerk had the reservation details already printed and pushed forward a form for the Iranian to sign.

'You pay by credit card?' the clerk asked in heavily-accented English.

251

'Mmm.'

'I make print?'

He made a wiping gesture with his hand. The Iranian understood and pulled an American Express card from his pocket-book.

Sanders lurched forward, making a grab for a brochure from the display on the counter.

'Sorry,' he murmured, brushing against the Iranian.

Just a quick glance. Enough to see the name Akhavi on the card.

He backed off a pace and pretended to read the brochure.

'Room 610. Sixth floor,' the clerk said. 'Is a letter for you. Have you baggage?'

'I don't need help,' Akhavi answered, reaching out his hand for the key and the envelope.

'Elevator is over there,' the clerk added, pointing to the left.

Sanders rested his hand on the counter and watched Akhavi walk away.

The clerk coughed. 'Can I help you, sir?'

'Yes. I want to know if a friend of mine has checked in already. A Herr Dunkel? From Germany.'

The clerk shook his head.

'Could you look again, just to be sure?'

The clerk wheezed with annoyance, but glanced down at the register. Sanders peered past him at the room keys hanging on their hooks. 612 was missing, but 614 was there. Close enough.

'There is no reservation for that name,' the clerk grunted.

'Oh dear, oh dear. Must be the traffic. I'm sure he'll turn up. Are you sure he hasn't reserved room six one four? Always goes for that number if he can. Some stupid superstition.'

'Is no reservation!'

'Okay, okay. I'll leave a note anyway.' He snapped his fingers, irritably. 'You have some paper?'

The clerk gave him a sheet and an envelope.

'Plenty room, if your friend he come. *Nema problema.*'

Sanders sealed his note, scribbled Dunkel's name on the outside and pushed it across the counter.

'Where's the toilet?'

'Sir?'

'The toilet. The washroom,' Sanders repeated, rubbing his hands together.

'Round the corner. Next the bar.'

The clerk pointed.

'Thanks.'

Sanders followed the directions but ignored the *Gospoda* sign.

He was in luck. Stairs next to the toilets led up to a mezzanine floor. He climbed them, pushed on a door marked *Izlaz* and found the emergency stairs.

He climbed two more floors, then listened. Silence. He took the phone from his pocket and called Vaillon again.

'It's our man. Definite,' he said. 'Hotel Martinova, room six-ten. Our boys are on the way. They'll be in six fourteen.'

Then he rang off.

Sanders continued up to the sixth floor. Easing open the door to the corridor, he slipped past Akhavi's room. No sound from inside. He turned back and hid behind the exit door, waiting and watching through a crack.

Down at the reception desk, Konrad signed the name Dunkel, giving an address in Munich. He paid cash in advance for the room and left his false passport so the clerk could complete the documentation.

Konrad and Pravic waited for the lift. The clerk glanced at them knowingly. The one who'd registered looked to be nearly sixty, but his blonde, blue-eyed companion was younger. Picked him up in a bar shouldn't wonder.

Konrad led the way along the silent sixth floor corridor. He stopped at 614, his key slipping into the lock. Pravic crept forward to check the other numbers. 610 was two doors further on.

Inside their room, Konrad unzipped his bag and carefully removed the equipment. Pravic watched uneasily. Konrad had told him only the bare essentials of what this job was about. Just enough to know why his particular skills were needed.

Poisoning was not the way Pravic liked to kill. Too remote, too uncertain. When he'd murdered a man for Konrad in Berlin six years before, it had been with a knife.

He saw the strain on Konrad's face. He'd refused to say who they were working for, but he guessed it was somebody in Zagreb. There'd been two phone calls with instructions.

Pravic placed a chair in the entrance lobby, beside the bathroom. Above his head was a wire grill and a humming fan. He found the control for the air-conditioning and turned it off. Then he climbed on the chair and lifted the grill which was nearly a metre square, turning it diagonally to lower it through the aperture.

'What do you think?' Konrad asked under his breath.

'Maybe okay,' Pravic whispered, stepping to the floor again. 'Old hotel. Plenty space.'

His German was halting, but adequate.

From Konrad's tool kit, Pravic took a torch, a screwdriver and a drill.

'Help me,' he said, locking his hands together in a stirrup to show what he meant.

Konrad stood beside the chair, and gave him a leg up into the ceiling space.

For years Pravic had worked with ventilation systems, but fear of these cramped spaces never left him. The gap concealed by the false ceiling was just half a metre high, its metal frame and crawling boards built for access.

Pravic shone his torch upwards. An aluminium duct extended in from the corridor. From its open end he felt the cool draught of fresh air.

The fan, when switched on, sucked air from the room, mixed in the fresh supply, then blew it back into the bedroom through a vent.

Every room the same – including 610.

Pravic wriggled into the roof space. Separating him from the void above the corridor was a square access panel, held in place by four screws. He removed them and the panel came away easily. Then suddenly it slipped from his grip, thudding onto the ceiling below him.

He froze. Beneath him Konrad swore, then switched on the television to drown his noise.

Two doors down, Dr Hamid Akhavi dialled the room number written on the note he'd been given at reception.

'Pavel?' he asked timidly.

'*Da.*'

'Hamid. In room six hundred ten,' he said in heavily-accented Russian.

'I'll come up.'

Three minutes later they were shaking hands and embracing.

'I'm very pleased to see you, my friend,' Akhavi said.

'I too.'

They embraced again, their first meeting for four years.

'How much time do you have here?' Kulikov asked.

Akhavi looked at his watch. Ten minutes past one in the morning.

'The car comes at four.'

They sat and Akhavi offered an orange juice from the minibar. The Russian would have preferred something stronger.

255

'You weren't followed?' Kulikov asked.

'I don't think so. An Englishman downstairs – I believe he was drunk.' His lips pouted with distaste.

He asked about Kulikov's family. Time was short, but the social courtesies his culture had taught him could not be by-passed. Eventually he was ready to grasp the nettle.

'So, you have brought me something?' he asked.

Sanders had seen the Russian arrive, carrying a large Samsonite briefcase. He descended two floors on the emergency stairs, then dialled Dunkel's number.

'*Sie sind zusammen,*' he announced softly when Dunkel answered.

Konrad put the phone down. Same mystery voice that had summoned him to this hotel. English accent.

NATO? Was *that* who his employer was?

They are together. The code they'd agreed. The clock was now ticking.

Konrad grabbed a mask, hooked the strap over his head and settled the soft rubber over his nose and mouth. Then he breathed in sharply to test the seal.

He laid out the artists' airbrush, the propellant canister and its connecting tube. Beside it, the screw-top jar containing the lethal, light-brown fluid.

Take great care, Kemmer had said. One tiny splash of the liquid could mean himself being victim to the same delayed-action death he'd chosen for the men in room 610.

Konrad pulled on surgical gloves and unscrewed the lid of the jar.

Blood pounded in Pravic's ears as he squeezed between the ducts in the dark void above the sixth-floor corridor.

With hardly room to move, hardly space to breathe, panic came in waves, drenching him in sweat. He cursed Dunkel for making him do this.

Above his head ran the big square duct feeding air to the rooms. First spur to the left for 612, the next for 610. Just a few metres more . . .

Yet . . . the deeper he crawled, the further he got from his escape hatch, the more Pravic feared that the demons in his soul would emerge from their caves and cripple him.

He rested for a second, trying to shut out memories of the voices and smells, which had always been precursors to the childhood abuse that had warped his mind.

Sometimes darkness triggered these flashbacks – at night he tried to keep a light on when he slept. Sometimes confinement did it, like in this tunnel where cobwebbed pipe work scraped his back as he inched along the boards.

The fear was so strong now he wanted to retch. Fear of being trapped, of his child body being pinned down by a weight so much heavier than its own. It was all coming back – the smell of his father's spirit-laden breath on the back of his neck, the hoarse panting in his ear, the pain as his feeble attempts to resist were overpowered, and the humiliation as the drunkard's fat prick spurted stickily between his thighs.

Then they were gone, the images swirling back into their Hadean mists. This time the waking nightmare had been over quickly. Sometimes the revulsion lingered, destroying his control.

He waited for his heartbeat to settle, then wiped the sweat from his eyes with a shirt sleeve. He had to press on.

At the next joint in the ducts he followed the pipe to the panel for room 610. Muffled voices growled beyond the plasterboard. He heard the whirr of the fan.

He pushed the twist-drill against the panel and turned

257

the handle. Slowly. Quietly. The material was soft. Didn't take much to make a neat round hole.

Then he backed away with his tools, feet first towards room 614.

/

Konrad dripped the brown liquid into the reservoir of the paint sprayer. A quarter of a litre was all it held. As he stopped the flow, a couple of drops spilled onto the tissue he'd laid out to catch them.

He held his breath. Then, steadying his hands, he screwed the cap back on the jar, which was still half full. He wiped the rim with the soiled tissue and placed the refuse in a polythene bag. Finally he screwed the reservoir onto the stem of the air brush.

'Psst!'

Pravic's head hung down from the vent in the lobby. Konrad passed him the second face mask and a pair of rubber gloves.

'Make sure it fits,' he warned. 'Mask must be tight. Understand?'

Pravic grunted. Then Konrad handed him the air brush and the propellant canister in a bag.

'Don't connect the air until you are ready,' he reminded him.

Pravic looked irritated. He knew exactly what to do and didn't like old fools like Dunkel telling him.

Two doors down, Dr Hamid Akhavi had also donned rubber gloves. Plutonium's toxicity made it foolish to touch it with bare hands.

The sample was smaller than he'd expected, like a segment of an orange. But from its colour and its weight he knew it was the real thing. Twenty pieces like this and he could make an atomic bomb.

'We still must analyze it,' he said, trying not to show his excitement.

He packed the plutonium back in its container then went to the bathroom to wash his gloved hands. As he dried them on a towel, he looked up sharply, hearing a creaking from the ceiling.

He listened again, but there was nothing more. Must be the ancient plumbing, he decided.

'There is still a problem, Pavel,' he said, returning to the table and pulling off his gloves. 'Your price is . . . unjust.'

Kulikov bristled. He hated the bazaar mentality of the Islamic world.

'Twenty kilos is a lot of plutonium, my friend. It would take you decades to produce in your own reactors.'

Akhavi held up his hands in acknowledgement.

'Of course. But my country simply cannot pay one hundred million dollars. Already the nuclear programme starves our economy. The reactor contracts with your government and with the Chinese, they are not cheap. And the machinery. . .'

'You too must understand something, my friend. There are many people I must pay. A whole shift of the security personnel. Senior officers who will arrange transportation. Border officials . . . the list is long. And the risk to me is great. If I'm found out it'll be the firing squad.'

They looked at one another. They both knew there was truth in each other's position. They guessed too there was room for manoeuvre. What neither could be sure of was how much.

'What is your offer, my friend?'

'Twenty million.'

The Russian exploded with derisive laughter.

Pravic heard the outburst through the plasterboard, and

froze, terrified he'd been discovered. An angry Slavic voice boomed through the ceiling panels.

A fresh tremor of panic rippled the length of his body. He dug his nails into his palms, puncturing the thin rubber gloves.

Then he heard two voices. Anger directed at one another, not at him.

He breathed again. Short quivering breaths.

Do the job, he told himself. Then the passport would be his. A passport to freedom.

He pressed the nozzle of the airbrush into the hole he'd drilled. A tight fit. Then he connected the propellant can with the tube. He eased the mask over his nose and mouth, the rubber slippery on his sweaty skin.

He held his breath, pressed the button on the spray and held it down. With the torch lighting up the reservoir he watched the brown liquid disappear into the conditioned air of Room 610.

Outside in the street, Martin Sanders re-parked his car to overlook the hotel entrance. He wanted a photo of the Russian if he could get one. He guessed the silver-haired smuggler might be on the flight to Moscow at eight-fifteen in the morning.

Vaillon also waited nearby, his task to follow the Iranian back to the airport.

Akhavi and Kulikov shook hands, not because they'd agreed a price, but because they knew they'd *have* to eventually. Thirty million was as high as the Iranian had been prepared to go.

They were ready for the next phase – the proving of the sample at the desert laboratories. Then they could plan for shipment and delivery.

Kulikov eased open the door, looked both ways and

slipped back to his room. In his hand the Samsonite briefcase which had held the plutonium sample was now packed with $100,000 in used notes.

Dieter Konrad cleaned the equipment with the bactericide Kemmer had given him. Every piece of tissue he'd used, every part of the spray, he placed in a plastic bag and sealed it.

The half-full flask of brown liquid he encased in 'bubble-wrap' plastic to protect it, then stuffed it in his bag to be disposed of later.

Pravic watched, emotionally drained. The precautions Dunkel was taking alarmed him. He didn't even know what it was, this lethal substance he'd administered, and he had a lurking fear it could have contaminated him too.

'You go now, Milan,' Konrad announced. He sounded tired and flat. 'I'll stay until the morning. It will be less suspicious. Ring me at the Dubrovnik at ten. By then I will have decided when we go to Berlin. Maybe tomorrow. Maybe the next day.'

Pravic hesitated. He trusted no one.

'You have the passport?' he demanded.

Konrad frowned in irritation.

'Yes, but not here. I'll give it to you tomorrow at the hotel.'

He saw the suspicion in Pravic's ice-blue eyes.

'Don't worry.'

After Pravic was gone, Konrad lay on the bed and closed his lids. To rest and to think, but not to sleep. That was impossible. It always had been after sentencing someone to death.

Twenty-One

Colonel Irwin Roche eased his Opel Vectra forward.
He'd got used to a manual shift since being in Europe
and liked it. He was even considering giving up on
automatics when he returned to Milwaukee.

The line of cars leaving the base seemed slow today, or
maybe his wish to get home was stronger than usual. Not
that he wasn't always happy to see Nancy and the twins,
but tonight they were expecting a new arrival.

The woman from CareNet had called that morning to
say they'd be arriving late. Very late, probably. Lorna
Sorensen, that was the name she'd given. Didn't know
when they'd get here, but he'd looked up the map and
Ancona was a hell of a long way south.

The queue of automobiles surged a little. He waved to
the duty man at the guard post, and then he was through
to the public highway. He took the slip road down onto
the Autobahn and eased into the slow-moving traffic.
Always solid at this time of day, and in the mornings.
Fortunately the next junction was his turn-off, so he
never had more than a few minutes of it to put up with.

The village of Pfefferheim had hardly existed twenty
years ago. Built as an overflow for Frankfurt, there were
two other USAF families renting houses there. Well-
built, spacious homes with a basement and a good-sized
yard, it suited them well. And Nancy liked living 'on the
economy' instead of in family accommodation at the Air

Base. She saw enough of the place as it was, working there part time in the welfare office.

It was the arrival of Nataša in their household a year ago that had transformed Nancy's life. A twenty-one-year-old refugee from Mostar, she was just one of hundreds of thousands of Bosnians taking refuge in Germany until peace let them return to their homes.

The Roche family fed and housed her, and in return she drove the kids to school, picked them up again, and helped with their care. Nancy had relished the chance it had given her to work again. And the Colonel enjoyed having a pretty young woman around the place.

Irwin Roche was a self-confessed computer-freak. He used a Unix system on the base to plan loads for the giant C-5 Galaxies that tramped back and forth across the Atlantic. But in his own home it was his Compaq PC that occupied much of his time. While Nancy and the kids watched TV in the evenings, he plugged into the Internet, communicating with cyberspace addicts all over the world.

Most of the Newsgroups he subscribed to were trivial, but he'd stumbled across ‹alt.childadopt.agency› one day, while scanning a Usenet directory. Fascinated to see how the communications highway was being used, he read e-mail from agencies seeking American homes for the victims of war and disaster in Africa, and what used to be Russia. It had set him thinking.

The Roche family had had it good. Better than they were entitled to expect perhaps, looking at all the misery in the world. One night in bed, he told Nancy what he'd been thinking. Shouldn't *they* be offering the comfort of their home, and the security and warmth of their family, to a child whose life could be transformed by it?

Nancy had responded with silence at first. She was just getting some of her own life back, now the twins were ten and Nataša was here to help. But then she'd begun to look at the TV news in a different light. All those

263

suffering kids – she'd felt so helpless about them before. Maybe the two of them *could* do something. Maybe they *should*.

Then just at the beginning of this week, Irwin had seen the computer message about Vildana. The girl needed 'an angel' the e-mail had said. He'd pulled Nancy away from the TV and showed her the screen of the Compaq.

Within minutes they'd decided. Minutes later he'd e-mailed an offer to the agency.

Things had moved fast. It turned out that CareNet had contacts at Rhein-Main, and the next day he and Nancy were given a grilling from a fellow colonel. They must have passed, because two days later they'd been signed up.

The twins were pretty stunned at their decision. Bound to be when their even, predictable young lives were about to face the unknown.

Nataša had wept for a day. They weren't too sure why.

Roche eased the Vectra into the garage. Scott and Ella came running round from the yard.

'When's she coming, have you heard?' they yelled.

'Late. Real late. But in time for breakfast tomorrow, I guess.'

Innsbruck, Austria
5 p.m.

It was crazy to do the drive to Frankfurt in one day. Innsbruck was only half way and they'd been on the road since 8 a.m. Lorna was exhausted. She'd hoped doing the journey in one burst would be the best way to minimize its effect on the kid. Vildana had slept for much of the journey, so perhaps she'd been right.

264

She'd had to let Josip share the driving; on motorways he was less of a liability, with no narrow gaps and mountain tracks to negotiate. It had given her time to think.

About Alex. She missed him desperately. Wanted to run back to Split and tell him she hadn't meant to brush him off, that she'd just needed to hurt him a *little*, to show him he couldn't remain unpunished for what he'd done all those years ago.

The next step was up to him. She'd shown him he couldn't just snap his fingers for her to come running, but she'd also given him a way to contact her if he *wanted* to.

The Battle of the Sexes business – it was a game she'd never been good at. Never known how far to go, when to resist, when to give in. She pushed her fingers through her hair and kneaded the tension from the back of her neck, terrified she'd got it wrong.

Passing Vildana off as her own daughter had worked well at the frontiers. Their passports had merited just a cursory glance, and at Split, the stamp that Alex had created had passed unnoticed.

It was illegal what she was doing, of course, but it would be for the Roche family to sort matters out with the authorities later. She was just the delivery girl.

They'd stopped for lunch on the Autostrada near Verona, Vildana's pale face blank-eyed with bewilderment. She had hardly eaten anything. Lorna could imagine the terrors the child must be going through, travelling halfway across a continent to live with strangers.

At Innsbruck they'd taken another short break, and Lorna telephoned CNN. It was lunchtime in Atlanta: the girl on the newsdesk had been expecting her call.

'Great!' she'd said. 'You're happy we run the story in the next World News in a couple of hours?'

'Sure. We'll be in Germany by then.'

Lorna would have liked to see the programme, but

there would be no chance of that with another six hours of driving ahead of them.

The next stretch of road cut northeast through the Tyrol to the German border. Josip was at the wheel. Lorna looked out at the hills in the fading light. Still plenty of snow on the upper slopes. She used to ski most winters. Last time had been with Rees in Colorado. They'd left Julie in the care of her sister Annie for a couple of weeks.

Sometimes she envied Annie. Not often, but at times like this, when life became so convoluted.

Annie had met Joe at College, a good, Irish boy. They'd married soon after graduating, and produced five kids. Just like that, with no doubts raised, questions asked, or mind-shaking problems presenting themselves. Joe and Annie had never faced a crisis in their lives, as far as Lorna could see. Not a single one! Yet for her, crises were like milestones, popping up with alarming regularity.

And now she was in the midst of one called 'Alex'.

Frankfurt International Airport
6.20 p.m.

Standing by the carousel, Alex gathered up his bags from the Croatian Airlines flight, found a trolley and passed through into the terminal building.

Two hours wait in Frankfurt before the British Airways connection to London, which he wasn't planning to take. He could think of only one reason for returning to Britain just now – Kirsty. If things had changed and she needed him, he would go back. For a while anyway.

Leaving Bosnia had turned his thoughts once more to

the place and the people that had been 'home' for twenty years. He still had obligations there which he couldn't ignore. Had to find out if the woman he was married to wanted him back.

He wheeled the trolley to a bank, changed a 20 Deutsche mark note into coins, and found a telephone.

He rang East Lothian and spoke to Kirsty's brother, who'd just got home from work.

'Och, it's good to hear your voice Alex,' he said. 'And so close, you could be in the next room.'

'How's Kirsty?' Alex's throat was dry.

'Och, about the same. Not been able to pull herself together much. The doctor's still giving her tablets.'

'I see. Does she ever talk about me?'

He heard a sigh at the other end of the line.

'No. She does not.' Another sigh, then, 'I *could* tell her you rang, but it may be better not to, frankly. But what of yourself? They had pictures of you on the television earlier in the week. You were refusing to answer questions about that monster from Edinburgh. Must ha' been awful. We felt so sorry for you getting mixed up in such a thing.'

'Aye, well it's all over,' he said, slipping back into his lowlands accent. 'I'm in Frankfurt now and don't expect to be going back to Bosnia. I'll be here a few days. Maybe ring you again in another week or so?'

'Grand if you would.'

He rang off. Fifteen Deutsche marks left. Should be enough for his next call. He fumbled in his pocket for Lorna's card. It was well past lunchtime in Boston.

'CareNet, Bella speaking.' A nasal voice, a slight echo on the line.

'Hello. I'm calling from Frankfurt, Germany,' he said hurriedly, watching the phone counter tick away the Pfennigs. 'I need to get in touch with one of your people over here, Lorna Sorensen? She should be arriving in Frankfurt today or tomorrow, but I don't know where she's staying.'

'Oh, let me just check . . . Who is this?'

'My name's Alex Crawford. I'm an old friend. I've just been with her in Bosnia.'

'Sure, hold the line please, Mr Crawford.' There was a click and the sound of Vivaldi. Ten Deutsche marks gone already.

'I'm sorry, sir,' Bella said, back on the line, 'we don't know where she's staying in Frankfurt. She hasn't told us yet.'

'What about the address of the family who are taking the child? Vildana, you know?'

'Oh that's confidential information, Mr Crawford. We can't give that out to anybody,' she replied stiffly. 'I tell you what. I could e-mail her if you wish.'

'E-mail? Send her a message, you mean?'

'Uh-huh.'

'Okay then . . . Just say Alex is in Frankfurt and has to see her . . . I'll ring again tomorrow to see if she's told you where I can contact her.'

'That's all? Just – Alex is in Frankfurt?'

'Yes. No! No, one other thing. Write . . . write this: *Alex says he loves you.*'

'Oh, that's cute! You want me to *e-mail* that?'

'Sure. I'll ring again tomorrow.'

The phone cut. His money was out.

Bavaria
7.10 p.m.

At the border post between Austria and Germany, the Bundesgrenzschutzpolizei received a daily update of names. Some belonged to undesirables to be denied entry to the Bundesrepublik, others were of felons to be arrested.

New that morning was the name of Milan Pravic of Bosnian or Croat nationality, wanted for questioning on suspicion of having committed crimes against humanity.

The cream Mercedes with the Berlin plates slowed to a halt. Two passports were held out for inspection. Two passports were returned, and the car accelerated away again.

With his fair hair, Pravic passed easily as a Pole. His photograph had been inserted expertly into Marek Gruszka's passport, stolen in Berlin.

They'd left Zagreb in the early afternoon, the journey broken by a brief diversion to a forest, where Konrad burned the contaminated tissues he'd brought from the Hotel Martinova. Then he'd dug a small, deep hole and buried the spray equipment. The jar containing the remains of the lethal, brown liquid stayed in his blue sports bag in the boot of the car.

Konrad wasn't sure why he had kept the anthrax bacilli, but something in the back of his mind was telling him the stuff might be of further use to him before long.

It was getting late and he had done enough driving for one day. Anyway, he was hungry. He saw a sign for a motel and swung the Mercedes off the Autobahn.

Pravic had slept for long stretches of the drive north. It had helped him avoid conversation with the German. Dunkel was not a man he'd ever liked or trusted.

The motel was a shabby, single-storey construction, but it would do. It was on the edge of a small town where there would be places to eat.

Konrad parked out of sight of the lobby. He sent Pravic to check in first, so they'd not be seen together. The rooms they were allocated were next to each other, however.

Pravic threw his bag on the bed and, out of habit,

switched on the television. A few minutes later Konrad tapped at his door.

'I'm going to find somewhere to eat,' he announced. 'You want to come?'

Pravic avoided his eyes and shook his head.

'Not hungry.' He'd seen a machine that dispensed sandwiches and beers in reception.

Konrad shrugged and drove off, glad his invitation had been declined.

The Bosnian lay on the bed and jabbed at the remote control. He flicked through a dozen cable channels but nothing held his attention. Eventually he left it tuned to the leather-clad dancers on MTV.

What he was looking for was news. Any channel that might tell him whether the world cared enough about the Tulici massacre to come looking for him.

He knew there'd been questions asked by the UN in Vitez. He knew the politicians of America and Europe kept mouthing off about war crimes. He knew too that one Muslim girl had survived the attack and could probably identify him. What he didn't know was whether legal wheels were turning, whether there were people out there who were planning to send him to prison.

His stomach rumbled. Time for some food. He locked the door behind him and walked round to the lobby. The receptionist changed his note for coins.

He selected a *Schinkenbrot* and three bottles of Pilsner. He also bought a newspaper which listed the television programmes.

The ham was good and smoky, and the beer nicely chilled. Some things they did well in Germany.

He took off his shoes and trousers and stretched out on the bed, his back propped against pillows. He flipped through the TV listings. There was News at Nine on a German satellite channel; he checked his watch. Half an hour to go. He flicked to a game show.

They made him smile, these stupid programmes.

Greed so coyly concealed. Reminded him of the nervous punters who paid Gisela 300 DMs an hour to whip and humiliate them.

He became engrossed and remained so for the next half-hour, switching over too late to see the start of the news. He swore at himself for missing the headlines. The first items bored him – German politics. News about Bosnia came ten minutes into the programme. He moved to the edge of the bed to see the screen more clearly.

The Serbs were shelling the mostly Muslim enclave of Gorazde.

It was a part of Bosnia that didn't interest him. No Croats there. But the fact that it was Muslims getting pounded gave him some pleasure. The pictures showed Serb guns, Serb tanks thumping their ordnance into the houses spread out in the valley below. His main interest was to see what weapons they were using.

He felt in his bag for the pullover in which he'd wrapped his Crvena Zastrava M70 9mm pistol. He extracted it, unclipped the eight round magazine, slid back the slider and checked the barrel was clear.

The presenter reappeared in vision, saying parliamentarians were complaining about the cost to German taxpayers of supporting so many Bosnian refugees. There'd been a debate in the Bundestag. A picture of the chamber appeared behind her.

Then the background changed. A photomontage of a girl, her hands covering her mouth – and a computer screen.

'*The American CNN TV reports that the computer network "Internet" is now being used to find homes for Bosnian war orphans.*'

The screen switched to CNN's video report, dubbed with a commentary in German.

'*This girl is called Vildana. She's being cared for by American aid worker Lorna Sorensen and is the sole survivor of the horrific* massacre at Tulici three weeks ago in which forty-four Muslim women and children died.'

Pravic caught his breath. He cocked the empty pistol.

'Vildana witnessed her own family being murdered, but miraculously managed to conceal herself from the killers. The United Nations War Crimes Tribunal in the Hague plans to use her evidence to convict the men responsible – if they can find them.

'Lorna Sorensen used the latest computer technology to link up direct from Bosnia to a child adoption service run by the American CareNet agency on the Internet communications highway. As a result, within just a couple of days Vildana has been found a new home in Germany. The identity and location of her foster family are being kept secret, for her own safety.

'Now football. . . .'

Milan Pravic stared motionless at the screen. Then a low growl shook the bottom of his chest and percolated upwards until it erupted from his lips. He pointed the empty pistol at the screen and pressed the trigger.

One little girl! One miserable child standing between him and freedom. And she was here in Germany.

He tossed the weapon on the bed, leapt to his feet and paced the room, angry and afraid.

Half an hour later, Konrad returned from the restaurant, went straight to his room and began to undress. He was in his underwear when Pravic knocked at his door.

'Who is it?' he shouted.

'Milan.'

'What do you want?'

'Left something in the car. I need the keys.'

Konrad hesitated, suspecting for a second that Pravic might drive off in it. He contemplated getting dressed again to go out to the car with him. What the hell. He opened the door a crack and passed out the keys.

Pravic walked out to the car. In his left hand he held two screw-top bottles of fruit juice he'd bought from the

272

machine in reception. He put them on the ground and opened the trunk of the Mercedes. Tucked at the back, wedged in place by a tool box to stop it falling on its side was Dunkel's blue sports bag. He undid the zip, reached in his hand and pulled out the jar of lethal brown liquid.

He emptied one of the fruit-juice bottles onto the ground, then, covering his nose and mouth with a handkerchief, he unscrewed the top of Dunkel's jar and decanted its contents into his bottle. Finally he filled the jar with juice from the other container, screwed the cap back on and replaced it in the bag.

Saturday 2nd April, 1.35 a.m.
Pfefferheim near Frankfurt

Nancy Roche had made fresh cinnamon bread, thinking that something warm and sweet to eat and drink would be a good way to welcome Vildana to her new home. The CareNet woman had rung again to say they'd be arriving after one o'clock.

All afternoon she'd been re-organizing the house – the twins were having to share again for the time being. She'd set up a cot for Ms Sorensen in Nataša's room and another in the living room for her translator. They'd asked to stay until Vildana had settled in.

For the past twenty minutes they'd been sitting around the kitchen table fidgeting, the twins refusing to go to bed. Then they saw headlights outside.

They opened the front door and gathered excitedly round the Land Cruiser, their eager stares answered by three, blank, exhausted faces.

Lorna twisted her mouth into a smile and got out of the car.

'Hi, I'm Lorna,' she said wearily. 'And this is Vildana.' She helped the girl from the back seat and stood with her arm round her.

'Hi, Vildana. Welcome to our family,' said Colonel Roche, shaking her hand. 'Does she speak any English at all?' he asked, turning to Lorna.

'Well no, but . . . Vildana? D'you remember?'

The girl could hardly keep her eyes open. Josip prompted her gently.

'I am vair 'appy . . .' she whispered.

'Hey! That's great!' Nancy declared, giving her a hug.

'I taught her that on the way here,' Lorna confided. 'Boy, that was a drive and a half!'

'You must be wrecked. Let's get you and your stuff inside,' Roche said. 'Scott and Ella can give a hand.'

Nancy settled Vildana on a stool at the kitchen breakfast bar and confronted her with a plateful of food. Vildana latched onto Nataša as soon as she discovered she was from Bosnia.

Lorna carried her laptop into the house.

'If you want to go on line, I've got everything you need in my den,' Roche told her.

She thought for a moment. She should e-mail that they'd arrived safely, and pick up her messages . . . Too tired, though. Leave it until the morning.

She stood in the kitchen doorway and watched Vildana slowly warming to the attention she was getting. It brought a lump to her throat. In the past few days the girl had begun to feel like a daughter. Now she was handing her over to someone else . . .

Still, she thought, at least she'll be safe here.

Twenty-two

Although Gisela Pocklewicz earned her living by inflicting pain on others, she knew it was *she* who was the real victim. The child of a prostitute, there had never been any equality of the sexes in her world. Experience showed women were born so they could be used by men. No point in fighting it.

Her personal relationships had done nothing to change that outlook. She saw them as barter deals – she gave sex, the man gave protection.

Milan Pravic had been generous with the security side of things during the two years they'd lived together and he had demanded little in return. The relationship with him was the closest she'd ever come to loving a man. A strange, damaged creature who seldom looked her in the eye, she'd caught glimpses of the fire that burned inside him. It had drawn her, but she suspected that if she tried to discover what fuelled it, she could be fatally burned.

Excitement at the thought of his return to Berlin had switched to anxiety in the last few days. He had told her he was coming here to hide, but had refused to say why.

She had her suspicions, knowing the hatred that smouldered in his soul and the violence he was capable of. She'd watched the TV pictures of Bosnian atrocities, fearing he could be involved. In the jungle she inhabited, men killing each other was fair enough, but if Milan had murdered women and children . . .

She had missed the small, inside-page paragraphs of

the newspapers reporting that the UN War Crimes Tribunal wanted to question him about the massacre at Tulici.

It would be evening soon, and this being Saturday, she would be busy. The apartment where the clients came was two blocks away from the one where she lived. Paying two rent bills was hard, but it preserved her sanity. The fee Dunkel had given her would ease things for a while.

Konrad dropped Milan Pravic at Alexanderplatz in the centre of Berlin. His contract with the Bosnian now complete, he headed with relief to the apartment in Lichtenberg where his wife would prepare him dinner.

Pravic found a phone that took coins and rang Gisela.

'*Schätzchen*!' she shrieked. 'You're in Berlin? Why not here? I was expecting you. Are you coming?'

'Have the police been?' he asked gruffly.

'Police? No. Why?' Her suspicions and her fears deepened.

'Never mind. Meet me in the Café Luxembourg in fifteen minutes.'

'But . . .'

'Just do it!' He banged the receiver down. She wouldn't defy him.

He ducked from under the hood of the booth. It was still daylight in the huge, bleak square where winds, deflected by the tall 1960s slabs, eddied round small groups of refugees wrapped against the unseasonable cold.

He plunged into the dank warmth of the U-Bahn station. It was two stops to Rosenthaler Platz, the train crowded with the last of the afternoon shoppers.

Strange to be back. Such orderliness after the devastation of Bosnia.

He heard his own language. There were tens of

thousands of Bosnians in Berlin. Muslims mostly. Odd to think that in the Lašva valley he'd have shot them full of holes.

Gisela was at the bar, waiting, dressed in black as always. Short skirt, pullover and a little jacket. Cropped black hair, black eyelashes caked with mascara.

Gisela was frightened by now. She'd planned to greet him with a kiss and a hug but when he walked through the door, she changed her mind. The expressionless look, the close-clipped hair and glasses, the cold eyes nervously checking every face in view – this wasn't the man she remembered. There'd been a sea change in him.

Without a word, he gripped her elbow and hustled her to a table in a dark corner.

'What's up? What's the matter?' she protested.

'I want a beer.'

Gisela gestured to the waitress. When the order was taken and the girl moved away, she slipped her hand over Milan's.

'Aren't you even going to say hullo to me?'

Pravic ignored her, pulled away his hand and downed half the glass.

Once or twice before she'd known him like this, caged by some obsession, unable to relate to her or to anyone.

'Why did you ask if the police had been round?' She was desperate to know.

His scowl convinced her it had been a mistake to ask. For two full minutes he said nothing.

'You know someone who has computer?' he asked suddenly, eyes boring into her.

'Why? You want to buy one?'

'No. I need someone who use computer to read messages.'

'What for?' she asked.

He grabbed her hand and crushed it until her eyes watered.

'Don't ask things . . .' he growled. 'Just tell me! You know someone?'

She kneaded her knuckles. She'd never known him this manic, this dangerous.

'I don't know,' she sniffed. 'I'll have to ask around in some of the other places. Not this bar. Don't know anybody who comes in *here*.'

She guessed Milan had chosen Café Luxembourg so that no one would recognize them.

'You *must* find person tonight. Someone who can do Internet,' he demanded.

'Internet? What's that? Anyway I can't do anything tonight, love, I'm working,' she protested, heedlessly.

He leaned forward, gripping her hand again. Gisela saw the flames; knew they'd consume her if she wasn't very, very careful.

'Tonight, you work for me,' he breathed. 'You want . . . I pay.' He pulled a wad of notes from his trouser pocket.

'You don't need that, Milan*chen*,' she soothed, trying to calm him. 'I'll sort something out. Somehow.'

She'd got clients booked, but there'd be gaps when she could slip out to the bars and look around. There *were* people who did computer stuff. Con-men and fraudsters. Just a question of finding them.

'You coming home with me?' she queried, eager to get on with it. 'You can watch the television and I'll ring you there when I've found someone.'

He shook his head and tapped the table.

'No. You come *here* when you find.' He looked at his watch. It was still early, Berlin's nightlife only just starting. 'At eleven I come back to Café Luxembourg and wait.'

'Aren't you staying with me tonight, then?' she pouted, feigning unhappiness. Privately she didn't want him in his present state.

'No.'

'Where, then? Where will you sleep?'

Another woman? Not likely. Milan had shown little interest in sex in the two years they'd been together.

'I find some place. Then I come here and wait. But, Gisie ... you *must* find me someone with computer Internet. Understand *must*?'

She understood. She left her drink half-finished.

8.25 p.m.
Frankfurt

Alex climbed the stairs to his second-floor room in the dingy hotel, feeling he'd wasted a day.

The previous evening he'd taken the S-Bahn from the airport to the Central Station, found a cheap bed, then got drunk in one of the smoky, apple wine taverns in Sachsenhausen.

This morning he'd spent nursing his head. Hadn't had a hangover that bad for years.

With the transatlantic time difference, there'd been no point in phoning Boston again until mid-afternoon, but the wait had been like watching paint dry.

He'd phoned at three-thirty, not knowing if the CareNet office would be manned on a Saturday. Bella had answered again. Sorry, she'd said. No e-mail from Lorna yet.

He'd called again at half-past-eight. Still nothing, but Bella offered to message Lorna with his hotel phone number. She sounded sorry for him, which made him suspect he was making a fool of himself after all.

He'd bought some German newspapers, then sat in a Macdonald's picking at the text with his school German and a pocket dictionary. In the *Frankfurte Allgemeine* a headline had caught his eye. *Selbstmord in Leipzig* – Suicide in Leipzig.

Siegfried Kemmer, a microbiologist in Leipzig University's Department of Veterinary Medicine had hanged himself, it said. University authorities blamed depression at his being made redundant, but his daughter claimed there were other reasons outlined in a suicide note she'd not been allowed to see. The police spokesman denied there'd ever been such a note.

Kemmer, the paper reported, had worked on dangerous pathogens, including *Milzbrand*. Alex thumbed the dictionary.

Milzbrand m. (med.vet) – Anthrax.

The stuff of germ warfare. He remembered that experiments with it in the fifties or sixties on some Scottish island had made the place uninhabitable for decades.

Odd to put the story on the front page like that. It was almost as if the paper sensed it was on the trail of some huge scandal.

Inside he'd found Bosnian news. Rumblings in the Bonn parliament – fears that with over 200,000 Bosnian refugees in the country, the war might come to Germany. Uproar that in a few days' time Bosnian Muslims were holding a political rally in Munich, to be addressed by militants from Iran and Lebanon.

Not surprised they're worried, he thought. Europe's worst nightmare was the prospect of the Bosnian war spreading.

He'd hurried back to the hotel after his meal – in case Lorna rang.

The Roche household slept until mid-morning that Saturday. After a huge brunch, Lorna sat in the big kitchen watching Vildana learn to make brownies. She had to hand it to Nancy Roche; the woman had handled the kid with panache. Welcoming without being overpowering, motherly but without smothering her.

The Roche twins were finding it less easy to adjust to the newcomer in the nest. Vildana was a couple of years older, and they seemed to suspect the girl's arrival might downgrade their own position in the family.

Nancy had begged Lorna to stay the weekend – to provide continuity, she'd said – and since Lorna's own plans were vague, she'd agreed.

Larry Machin, her boss at CareNet had telephoned at 2.00 a.m. He'd forgotten the time difference and wanted to check she'd arrived safely. He told her the agency had no plans for another run into Bosnia for several weeks, so she could stand the operation down and come home.

Josip appeared at her elbow, his suitcase packed and his anorak over his arm. Time to take him to the airport for his early afternoon flight back to Zagreb.

In the noisy drop-off zone on the departure level, she thanked him profusely for all his work and for his sweetness to Vildana. He insisted on a farewell kiss. It turned out to be rather more than a peck on the cheek, but she was content to indulge him for once.

'Bye, Josip. We'll give you a call when we go back to Bosnia, okay,' she waved, climbing into the Toyota. It wouldn't be *her* going back there, she'd decided, whatever Larry Machin said.

On the drive back to Pfefferheim all she could think about was Alex. She now had a real fear that she had driven him away.

Later that afternoon, Irwin Roche felt a little surplus to requirements, the task of settling Vildana in having been taken over by the women in his household. Fidgeting, he watched from a distance as the girl was shown the family photo albums to give her an idea of what life would be like in America. He retreated to his

281

den. Then around five, he emerged again and sought out Lorna.

'Sure I can't interest you in using my computer,' he grinned. 'Check your e-mail, maybe?'

'Hey thanks, I forgot! I'll never get the habit.'

He led her into his small study and confused her with talk about megabytes and baud rates. He sat her in front of the keyboard, then backed out of the room.

'I'll leave you to it. Give a shout if you need help.'

It was the same Windows system she was used to, so she was soon through to her mailbox on the Internet. Two messages, the screen said.

Saturday morning.

Lorna. Somebody dropped in your letter today with the film. Great! Larry'll be orbital when he hears. He thinks the CNN report was great. Not seen any checks yet, though! Getting the shots printed today, then I'll deliver the rest to Annie personally.

The guy who called yesterday has called again. Sounds real sweet. Hope you got the last message I sent you. Does he have a chance??? He's calling tonight too, so I could pass a message if you want. In strictest confidence, of course!

Bella.

Lorna's pulse quickened. What last message? She hit the return key.

Friday nite.

Lorna. Some guy called from Frankfurt, saying he's got to see you. Said his name was Alex. He's in Frankfurt and wants to know where you are? He said he LOVES you! Let me know what to say to the poor man!

Bella (a.k.a. Cupid)

Lorna stared at the screen in disbelief. She read it again. And again.

Alex had followed her to Frankfurt! Her face twitched into a grin.

She began to type a reply. Bella should still be in the office at this time. Then she stopped herself.

Hang on, kid, she told herself. You're doing it again. Running, the minute he snaps his fingers.

She dropped her hands to her knees. He'd come this far, she calculated, he'd not give up that easy. Let him sweat just a little longer.

She clicked on the mouse and logged off.

Iran

Dr Hamid Akhavi had felt the first shivers last night when he'd reported back to the Minister for Energy in Tehran. He'd put it down to lack of sleep and the long flight to and from Zagreb.

Back home now in the secret desert compound near Yazd, his wife had put him to bed. This evening his symptoms had worsened. Soaring temperature, pains in the chest and a cough that racked his body. His wife wanted to call the doctor, even if it was the middle of the night, but Hamid persuaded her to wait to see if he was better in the morning.

Nizhnaya-Tura, Russia

Colonel Pavel Kulikov felt on top of the world. The down payment he'd brought back from Zagreb meant he could begin distributing the hard currency that was the life-blood of his illegal activities.

At the Strategic Rocket Forces weapons dismantling site east of the Urals, work had ground to a halt in recent days because of equipment breakdowns. Lack of spare parts was rapidly reducing the whole process to chaos, a situation that he could only welcome. Chaos gave corruption more to feed on.

Removal of plutonium from the plant would have to be a gradual business, to prevent its absence being noticed. Could be months before he'd have enough for the first shipment across the Caspian Sea to Iran.

His journey back from Zagreb had been painfully tedious – an eight-hour delay in his connecting flight from Moscow to Sverdlovsk. At one point as he'd sat waiting for the flight, a tickle at the back of the throat made him wonder if he was getting a cold. But it went away as it usually did.

He didn't often get ill. Not surprising, considering all the vaccinations he'd had as an officer responsible for the security of dangerous weapons.

Berlin, after midnight

Pravic had been drinking schnapps with beer chasers. He'd found a cheap room to stay in and had returned to the Café Luxembourg by eleven. It was a dull place with prints of old Berlin on the walls, trying to be respectable in an area of sleaze. There was only one other customer and the manager wanted to close for the night.

The wait for Gisela and the alcohol on an empty stomach had turned his anxiety to anger. If the barman tried to throw him out he would take him by the throat.

At twenty minutes past the hour Gisela pushed through the door, flustered and short of breath. Pravic tried to read her face through the blur.

'Quick,' she whispered loudly. 'The man's waiting up for you.'

Pravic abandoned the rest of his beer. The manager hurried over with his purse. Pravic peeled a couple of notes from the wad and pulled Gisela to the door.

'It's in Wedding. You'll need a taxi,' she told him when they were outside in the street. She handed him a note with the name and address. 'A bloke I know rang him from the bar and asked him to help. Said he owed him a favour.'

'This man can do Internet?' Pravic growled. His voice was slurred.

'That's what he said. Look, there's a cab over there.' She waved and the Mercedes turned towards them. 'Will you ring me tomorrow?'

'What you mean? You come with me!'

'I can't, Milan.'

'Yes. You come.' He gripped her arm.

'Milan . . .' she protested. 'I told you. The bloke in the bar fixed this up as a favour.'

Pravic hadn't understood what she meant.

'A favour . . . it means I've got to do *him* one in return. . .'

He let go of her arm and ducked into the car. Gisela watched it speed away, terrified something monstrous was fermenting in the mind of her one-time lover.

The taxi turned up Chausseestrasse. At each set of red traffic lights, the driver thumbed through his street plan trying to locate the address.

Fifteen minutes after being picked up, Pravic was deposited outside a small apartment house with plaster flaking from the walls. The panel of bell-pushes hung loose, but when he pressed the button next to the name he'd been given, there was a quick response.

'Yes?'

'You are expecting me,' Pravic said, anxious not to give a name. 'For the computer.'

'Yes, yes. Third floor.'

The door buzzed and Pravic pushed it open.

The man was wearing a dressing gown. From the small hallway Pravic caught a glimpse through a gap in a doorway. Satin sheets and the leg of a female.

'*Aber, mach's schnell, Heini.*' The woman's voice was a whine. The man closed the bedroom door and led Pravic into a living room cluttered with cardboard boxes. On a table next to a reading lamp was a computer.

'So what's this about? What do you want?' the man asked, irritated. 'Let's be quick. I've got things to do.'

'You can do Internet?' Pravic asked, looking down at the floor.

'Go on-line? Of course. But what do you want?' He switched on the equipment, glancing curiously at his weird visitor.

'You see, I am from Bosnia,' Pravic began, trying to look sincere. 'My family all killed. Just one survive. A girl. My sister's child. Some people bring her to Germany just now because they think she has no family. They use Internet to find new home for her. Because they think there is no person of her own family to look after her. But they wrong. She has me. Now I must find her. Her name Vildana.'

Pfefferheim

Lorna couldn't sleep for thinking that Alex was nearby. She just wasn't made for the games she was putting herself through.

The house was quiet, the Roche family and Vildana all sound asleep. She tiptoed into the Colonel's den and powered up his Compaq. He wouldn't mind, she told herself.

She'd worked out what to say in the message to Bella, intending to type it quickly and send it. But the 'mail' message flashed, telling her there was something new for her.

Bella again.

Saturday nite.
Hi Lorna! Listen. You've got to do something about this guy Alex. Put him out of his misery. He called again and left a phone number. Sounds so cute. If you don't want him, I'll have him!

Lorna wrote down the number, her heart thumping. She'd ring him first thing in the morning.

Twenty-three

Sunday 3rd April, 10.15 a.m.
Frankfurt

'Hotel Sommer. *Guten Tag.*'

'Good morning, room 313 please.' Lorna hoped the tremble in her voice wasn't too noticeable.

'*Zimmer dreihundert dreizehn. Ein Moment bitte.*'

Not five star, she deduced from the telephonist's lack of English.

'Hello?' Alex's voice.

'Is that Alex?' she asked, unnecessarily.

'Lorna?'

'Sure. I got a message from Bella. What've you been saying to her? She sounds real turned on!'

'I was beginning to think she was keeping it to herself,' he laughed nervously.

'Hmm ... So what are you doing here, truly?' she asked, still playing dumb.

'Truly – I've come to see you. Where are you?'

'It's a place called Pfefferheim. It's where Vildana's new family live.'

'Is she okay? Does she look happy?'

'Everything's great so far. She can say "more please" in fluent English!'

Alex laughed.

'So, shall I come out there?'

'No ...' she answered hesitantly. 'But I tell you what. I've a couple of hours free today. Why don't I come downtown. Leave these good people on their own for a while. Name a restaurant and you can buy me lunch.'

She heard a clonking of the phone at the other end while he wrestled with something.

'Just looking in the guide book. There's a place here that sounds okay. It's called *Bistro Tagtraum* which means "daydream". Sound suitable?'

'Do they do vegetarian?'

'Potato and ginger soup.'

'Okay. Give me the address and I'll see you there at 12.30.'

11.35 a.m.
Autobahn A4 – the road from Berlin to Frankfurt

They'd been on the road since eight. The five-year-old VW Polo was Gisela's car, and she was driving, because Milan had never learned how.

He had told her nothing about his meeting with the computer man. Just telephoned her at four in the morning to insist she drive him to Frankfurt. She had protested, but hadn't refused. She knew what he was capable of, remembering what he'd done to clients who'd got rough with her in the old days.

He'd hardly spoken on the journey. Just sat there beside her, staring at the road ahead, holding onto the handles of a sports bag wedged between his feet. They'd stopped once for petrol and to use the toilets, but that was all. Questions about why they were going to Frankfurt had been answered with silence.

He'd taken her hostage. Not with chains, but with the unspoken threat of violence if she refused to do what he said.

She was an emotional hostage too. Despite his weird

behaviour since returning to Germany, she felt strangely sorry for someone so clearly in torment.

Iran

Hamid Akhavi was lifted from the ambulance onto a stretcher trolley and wheeled into the small, two-ward hospital. The physician who'd ordered him to be brought there from his home was a worried man. His medical facilities at the desert site were minimal. Above all, he had no pathology laboratory. A sample of Akhavi's blood was already on its way to the hospital at Yazd, to be cultured overnight. Perhaps then he might have some idea what this illness was that had struck down one of the most important scientists in Iran.

Overnight Akhavi's cough had worsened further. By first light there were specks of blood in his sputum. His last words to his wife before the ambulance arrived had been to beg her to contact his sister in Tehran to tell her what was happening to him.

They were cut off from the outside world at the desert site. No personal phone calls permitted. To ring her sister-in-law, she would have to arrange to be driven to the PTT in Yazd. She didn't quite trust Hamid's sister, always suspecting she was more political than was good for her. Political in that she had contacts with Iranians abroad, Iranians who called themselves the Resistance.

Ealing, West London

Martin Sanders lived alone in an immaculately decorated, two-bedroomed, Victorian terrace cottage within a stone's throw of Ealing Green and the Underground station.

His well-travelled looks ensured he was never short of female company when he wanted it. But having any of the delightful creatures actually living in and interfering with the way he did things was out of the question and always would be.

The phone call from Rudi Katzfuss had been unexpected and had interrupted the preparation of the *entrecôte au beurre d'olives* that he'd decided to cook for lunch. They'd never had to summon an emergency meeting of the Ramblers before.

The BND man hadn't said over the phone what it was about of course, but insisted they assemble on Monday evening in Munich. Couldn't be sooner because of the time it would take Jack Kapinsky to get over from Washington.

Before he went, Sanders would check with the photographic branch and get some copies of the photos he'd brought back from Zagreb. Might be useful.

Frankfurt-Sachsenhausen

Alex had telephoned the restaurant to book a table, and arrived to claim it ten minutes early. He ordered a little jug of Mosel. By the time Lorna joined him ten minutes late, he'd ordered another.

'Sorry,' she breathed, allowing him to kiss her on the cheek, 'couldn't find anywhere to park.'

She was wearing fawn chinos and a white shirt, covered by a knitted waistcoat in olive-green. Round her neck was a long, thin gold chain. The waiter brought Mosel for her too.

'This looks nice,' she offered, looking round at the simple decor, and the menu chalked on a board. The trouble was she doubted she'd be able to eat, the way her stomach was churning.

'*You* look nice too,' Alex bubbled. 'In fact you look just as fantastic as the first time we met.' Nerves always made him go big on compliments.

'Maybe you should get your eyes checked,' she smiled, putting her hands up to cover the lines on her face. She kept glancing away, not trusting herself to look into the bottomless darkness of his eyes.

'Did . . . did your office pass on my message?' Alex asked. 'All of it, I mean.'

'I don't know what all of it was,' she shrugged, feigning ignorance.

'The bit that said "I love you"?'

'Oh, that old thing,' she joked. There was an edge to her voice. 'Sure. But don't worry, I didn't take it seriously. I try not to fall for the same trick twice.'

Alex felt his face redden. Maybe it was still war and she had come here to twist the knife.

'Why don't we order some food,' he suggested quickly. 'Then we can start this conversation all over again.'

Lorna dabbed at her hair with her finger tips as she looked up at the blackboard. She *was* still at war, but the battle was inside her own head.

She chose the soup and a spinach and goat's cheese lasagna. Alex went for the same. The waiter moved off.

'So . . .' Alex said, fumbling for a place to begin. He pulled out his cigarettes, then remembered he'd reserved a non-smoking table for her sake. He put them back in his pocket.

'So. . . ?'

He took a deep breath.

'Would it help if I said "sorry" for what happened in Belfast? Like an official apology?'

She chewed her lip. She felt as if she were caught in quicksand.

'I don't know whether it'll help. But I guess it's nice to hear you say it. If you mean it,' she added a little too pathetically.

She'd been through a lot, he could see it clearly sitting across the table from her like this. She wore the vulnerability of someone not sure where the next punch was coming from.

'Tell you what,' he suggested, 'why don't we pretend we've never met before?'

Her look said 'you have to be kidding'.

'Hi. My name's Alex Crawford,' he began, smiling theatrically.

There was a gleam in his eye which made Lorna suspect this was a game she was not going to enjoy.

'I'm aged . . . oh, somewhere in the middle of life,' he continued. 'I was born Alex Jarvis, but it's been Crawford for twenty years, for reasons beyond my control. I've been married for eighteen of those years. We've lived in Scotland.'

At the revelation of a wife her eyelids flickered. A good sign, he decided.

'Her name is Kirsty. She was a widow when I met her. She'd been married for just three years to her first husband, then he died in a climbing accident.'

He took a deep breath.

'Now it's your turn.'

'I'm not sure I'm up to truth games,' she told him huskily. 'If that's what this is?'

'If you refuse to play, it means I have the right to ask you questions,' he pressed.

The waiter thumped soup bowls in front of them.

'Okay. So what d'you want me to say?' she boxed, desperate for him to reveal more than she did.

'Tell me about *Mister* Sorensen.'

'Oh, that. Well . . . after I got back from Belfast twenty years ago, I found there were some nasty men who wanted to kill me? You know the sort of guys I mean?

293

Well, they got paid some money to lay off, but I had to go hide someplace, like you. You may remember I was a qualified attorney already, and somebody fixed me a job at a practice in a small New England town called Shelburne Falls.'

Alex saw anger flicker in her eyes. He guessed why. 'Somebody' would have been her father, the man whose influence she'd spent much of her life trying to escape.

'And there I met a guy called Rees Sorensen, who was one of the partners in the firm where I worked. We got married. We lived in a white-painted, clapboard house with maple trees in the yard, and I had a daughter called Julie. Now you,' she concluded. 'Your turn again.'

Too brief for him. Too sanitized.

'Is Rees still around?'

'No,' she said flatly. 'Leastways, not around me. And that was cheating.'

He smiled, but only for an instant. The hard part lay ahead. It felt like walking into a tunnel not knowing what time the next train was due.

'Well . . . what else shall I tell you?' he swallowed. 'Um . . . Kirsty, she had a child, by her first husband. A boy . . . called Jodie. And I helped her bring him up. He was a lovely lad. I thought of him as *my* son. Unfortunately, a few weeks ago, he was killed . . . There was an accident – his first parachute jump. His mother believed it was my fault for letting him do it, so she turned her back on me . . . Which is one reason I ended up in Bosnia.'

Lorna swallowed. She could see it was no trick this time. The pain in his eyes reached out like floodwater.

'I'm so sorry,' she heard herself say.

She'd wanted him to be punished, and now she knew he had been, but in a way more devastating than she could ever have wished.

'Now you,' he insisted. He wanted to know everything,

to lay the whole past out in the open, so they could put it behind them.

She dipped into her soup, not ready to say more.

'You still love Kirsty?' she pressed.

'Now who's cheating . . .' He took a deep breath. 'The answer's yes, but there's love and love, isn't there. Kirsty and I just happened to need what each other could give . . . at the time we met.'

It had sounded callous, but he could see she knew only too well what he meant.

'Tell me about Julie.' He saw a cloud pass over her eyes.

Lorna felt she was fighting for breath. In the past she'd blamed him for all the disasters in her life, but she couldn't any more. Not now she knew what he himself had been through. She bit her lip and steeled herself.

'Julie's thirteen. She's autistic – can't relate to any-body. I gave up my job to look after her and managed it until the beginning of last year, but it was real hard. She was like a . . . some sort of porcelain figure under a glass dome, you know? I could look at her, I could touch the *glass*, but I couldn't reach *her*.'

She chewed her lip again.

'Julie never learned to talk. A couple of years back she began to develop, physically. All the same feelings as a normal kid in puberty, but didn't know what to do with them. She got so moody and hollered all the time, I couldn't handle it any more. Rees – he wasn't Julie's real father, but that didn't matter to him – well, he decided to put her in a home for the handicapped.'

She grimaced, close to tears.

'It broke me up. It broke us up too. Rees and I split.'

Alex expelled the breath he'd been holding. Strange parallels in their lives.

'That's terrible. I'm so sorry. She's still in the home?'

'Oh yes. As happy as she'll ever be.' Her fingers

twisted and untwisted the gold chain round her neck. 'I always carry around with me a few things that were hers. Like this chain. And her passport. That's why I had it with me in Bosnia.'

'I wondered.'

Suddenly she sat up straight and folded her arms.

'You know something?' she remarked. 'This is a pretty heavy conversation for people who've only just met. You treat all your women like this?'

'No. Only the vegetarians.'

She laughed. Inside, she was smiling.

2.05 p.m.
South of Frankfurt

Milan Pravic had the map spread across his knees and told Gisela to take the next turning from the Autobahn. Pfefferheim was just a few kilometres away.

'What do we do when we get there, Milan*chen*?' Gisela asked for the third time. 'I'm really tired, I tell you.'

Still no answer. He was looking for signposts.

Gisela was certain of one thing – whatever Pravic had in mind to do in Pfefferheim it was evil. Somebody was going to get hurt.

For the last two hours it had been raining. Pools of water lay in the uneven side road as they drove through pinewoods towards the village.

'Stop! Stop here,' Pravic barked suddenly. He pointed to the right, where a muddy track led to a clearing in the trees. Gisela swung the wheel and they bounced to a halt.

'Why're we stopping?' she asked, irrationally fearing he'd decided to kill her.

'Further a little. Away from the road . . .' he gestured. Her fears grew.

'Why, Milan? What for?' she wailed.

'Here. Here is okay.'

Gisela looked over her shoulder. They were invisible from the road. Pravic got out and walked to a point where the ground was particularly soft. He dug his fingers into the earth and returned with a handful of dirt. Then he crouched down at the front of the car, smeared some onto the number plate, then took the rest to the rear to repeat the process.

He stood back and inspected his work. Satisfied, he wiped his hands on the grass, and got back into the car.

A few minutes later they passed the sign marking the village boundary.

'*Mühlweg*,' Pavic announced. 'Ask someone where it is.'

'Going to see someone there?' Gisela pressed. 'Some friend of yours?' She felt close to hysteria.

Again, no answer.

They were entering the centre of the village – half-timbered houses, a church, a small shop selling bread and groceries, and a telephone kiosk.

'Stop,' he growled, pointing to the right. He'd spotted a map of the village mounted in a timber-framed glass case beside the church.

He got out and studied it.

A voice niggled inside Gisela's head, a voice urging her to run, to jam her foot down and drive off, leaving him there without the sports bag which he'd nursed throughout the journey as if his life depended on it.

She depressed the clutch and engaged first gear. Pravic heard the crunch and looked round with stiletto eyes. She slipped it back into neutral. Couldn't do it. Hadn't the guts. If she left him now, he'd chase her to the end of the earth to get his revenge.

Revenge. That was the fire that burned inside him, the fire she'd never dared probe.

He got back in and closed the door.

'Two turnings on the right,' he told her, and waved his hand to show they should move on.

'Second on the right?' she checked.

'Mmm.'

There was nobody about. Never was on a Sunday afternoon in these dormitory villages. All at home watching television or sleeping off their lunch.

Gisela turned the car where Milan had said. New houses here, VWs and Opels parked on driveways.

'Left here.'

She obeyed, driving slowly. Two children on bicycles careered past on the pavement, wrapped up in anoraks against the rain.

'Now right.'

Mühlweg. She read the sign on a post at the junction.

'What number?' she asked.

'Just drive. I look.'

The road sloped upwards. About a dozen houses, then it curved to the right. Larger homes now, with garages. She motored slowly past them. Pravic suddenly craned his head round. The house he was looking at had its garage door open and a Vectra parked inside.

The road brought them round in a circle, back to the junction with the sign.

'And now?' she asked.

'Again up the road, but not far. I tell you when.'

Up the gentle rise, the curve to the right and the bigger homes . . .

'Here. Stop. Switch off engine.'

She did as she was told. They'd parked beside a plot that had not been built on yet. She looked up the road ahead. Three houses down was the one with its garage door open.

Lorna turned the Land Cruiser into Mühlweg and as she
rounded the bend at the top of the slope pulled out to
avoid a VW parked by the curb. Alex noticed it was a
woman behind the wheel of the Polo.

He felt wrung out after the catharsis of their lunch.

'Nice houses around here,' Lorna remarked. 'Similar
to what Americans have at home. I guess that's why
they're popular with USAF families. Say, I wonder if
Vildana'll be surprised to see you? Or maybe she thinks
we're all part of her new, extended family.'

'It'll be great to see her again. She's a sweet kid.'

It had been Lorna's idea that he should come out to
meet the Roches. He was delighted, particularly since it
meant they would be together.

'Here we are.' She stopped the Toyota on the drive in
front of the garage doors.

Irwin Roche appeared in the porch, grinning.

'Hi. You're back. And it's stopped raining. Oh, hi to
you too, sir,' he added, seeing Alex for the first time.

'This is Alex Crawford,' Lorna announced. 'He's the
guy who smuggled Vildana out of Bosnia in the back of
his truck. You remember I told you?'

'I certainly do. Let me shake your hand, sir. That
must've been some hair-raising drive.' He looked at Alex
with something like awe. 'So, I guess it's you I have to
thank for our beautiful new daughter ...' he added,
laughing.

'How's she doing?' Alex asked.

'Great. Just great. Ella's going to take her for a bike
ride when the rain stops – which I do believe it *has*!' He
held his hand out flat, then turned back into the house,
shouting for his daughter to come out with Vildana.

'Nice guy,' Alex whispered to Lorna.

'Nice *family*,' she replied.

Within seconds they'd all bustled out of the house into the front yard, with Irwin pulling his wife by the arm so he could introduce her to Alex.

'Hey, Vildana,' Lorna shouted, as she ran past with the twins, chased by Nataša. The girl stopped at the sound of her name and looked back. All self-consciousness about the strawberry mark on her face had evaporated.

'Look who's here!'

Fifty metres down the road the engine started in the Volkswagen. In the hubbub of bicycles being retrieved from the garage, no one heard it.

'It's Alex!'

A smile spread shyly across Vildana's face as she recognized him. Alex gave her a hug.

'Good to see you,' he grinned. Nataša translated.

Vildana grabbed hold of a pair of handlebars that had been thrust at her, then she and Ella wheeled their bicycles out to the road.

'Watch out for that car,' Nancy shouted.

Alex glanced up. A muddy, white Polo creeping towards them. Just a car, yet something about its slowness made it menacing.

Suddenly bells rang in his head. The woman driver was dithering like a kerb-crawler – why? Her male passenger stared like a snake at the girls wobbling on their saddles – why?

His limbs tensed. The man's eyes – the eyes of a killer . . .

He leapt forward, but too late. A fist snaked from the car window like a cobra's head, gripping a cold, grey automatic.

Two sharp cracks. The weapon kicked twice. Vildana's bicycle clattered to the tarmac. Alex ran towards the car, which tore off with a squeal of tyres. For a micro-second the gunman's eyes met Alex's. Then the car was gone. As it turned the corner of the road, a woman's scream shrilled through the open window. Alex stopped.

Gisela heard the scream, unaware it was from her own throat.

'Go! Quick, quick!' Pravic yelled, yanking the handle to close the window. 'And shut up woman!' He hit her on the shoulder with the pistol.

Shaking with shock, Gisela accelerated out of Mühlweg, back through the centre of the village.

'You ... you ...' she babbled, sobbing, 'Milan, you shot a *girl!* That girl on the bike ... Why? What you do that for, eh? Tell me! Tell me!'

'Shut up!' He scrabbled with the map, trying to work out the way back to Frankfurt as his mind played back what he'd seen. He'd hit her. Yes. Killed her? Didn't know. Aimed for the heart, but the girl had turned.

'Why?' she screamed at him. 'Tell me why!'

Irwin Roche sprinted to where Vildana had fallen. The girl's legs were twitching with shock.

'Vildana! Oh my God, what's happened?' Lorna hollered. The twins began to scream.

'She's been shot,' Alex mouthed. 'They've bloody well shot her!'

'No ...' moaned Nancy Roche, arms hanging limply by her sides.

Roche knelt on the ground, pressing on Vildana's shoulder.

'Scott!' he ordered calmly, 'get that T-shirt off and bring it here fast.' The child began to obey.

Alex dropped down beside him. Vildana whimpered like a wounded animal.

301

'Jesus!' he gasped, seeing the blood oozing from under Roche's fingers.

'Somebody call an ambulance,' the colonel shouted.

His wife dived back into the house. Nataša began to cry.

'Hit in the pectoral,' Roche said to Alex out of the side of his mouth. 'I wasn't watching. I thought it was a backfire. Where's that T-shirt son?'

The boy dropped it in front of him then backed away, colour draining from his face at the sight of all the blood.

'You've got to fold that into a dressing, right?' Roche told Alex. 'Then press it onto the wound. Can you do that?'

'Sure,' he answered, grateful that Roche had taken charge.

'We've got to stop the haemorrhage, so press hard.'

The girl moaned with pain.

'Sorry,' Alex winced, fearful of pressing too hard. 'Feels like something's broken in there.'

'Probably a rib. But keep pressing while I see if she's hit anywhere else.'

Alex felt the girl's body quiver, saw her eyelids flutter as she teetered on the edge of unconsciousness. Behind him he heard Ella and the Bosnian girl comforting each other.

Roche gently probed Vildana's chest and stomach, then ran his hands down her legs.

'Seems okay,' he said half to himself. 'Nataša!' he called. 'Get over here and talk to her, will you? Tell her she's going to be okay.'

Nataša didn't move.

'Nataša? Come on, honey,' he repeated soothingly.

The girl kneeled beside them, but turned her head away.

'She'll be okay, I mean it,' Roche said, touching her on the knee. 'It's just a flesh wound. So quit that crying, for her sake, okay? You have to calm her. And somebody go in the house and get Nancy to find a blanket.'

Lorna hurried inside and reappeared with the one she'd used on the sofa last night.

'Alex,' she murmured breathlessly, her lips close to his ear, 'do you think that was . . .'

'Pravic?' he breathed. 'Can't be. Not here. You think?'

'But who else for Pete's sake?'

'You two know something?' Roche demanded. 'Hey, don't let up the pressure on that dressing,' he added.

Alex pushed down again.

'It's the reason we got her out of Bosnia . . .' Lorna gulped. 'Because some guy wanted to kill her. And now this happens! I can't believe it!'

'Did he follow you here, or what? And who the hell is the guy?' he asked angrily.

'He's called Milan Pravic. He's the man who led the Tulici massacre,' Alex answered flatly. 'They call him the Scorpion.'

'Scorpion?'

'Yes. Apparently he got the nickname when he was a kid.'

'But if it's him, what's he doing here in Germany?' Lorna demanded. 'And how did he know where to find Vildana?'

'You tell me,' Alex replied.

Milan Pravic told Gisela to take the airport turning. And to wipe her face. Her cheeks were streaked with mascara.

She pulled a fistful of tissues from the box on the parcel shelf.

It was his silence that terrified her. The calculating silence on the drive from Berlin, when he'd been planning the death of a child. The sullen silence when she'd demanded to know the reasons why. The cold silence now as he worked out what to do next. What to do with *her*.

'Drive into the car park,' he ordered as they crossed the airport perimeter.

He'd buried the gun under some clothes in his bag.

She pulled a ticket from the entry gate and the barrier lifted. He told her to drive to a floor where there were empty spaces and few people about.

She knew then that he was going to kill her. Knew it with a terror and a certainty that clenched her stomach into a ball and made her gag. She thought of stopping the car near some businessmen loading luggage into their sleek BMWs. She thought of getting out and running. But she knew it would be too late. Knew that at the first tiny sign of her doing something to cross him, that gun would be out of the bag and the bullets hammering into her back.

All she could do was grovel, beg him to spare her life.

'Here,' he pointed at a row of empty spaces. Nobody near. No witnesses.

She stopped the engine. He lifted the sports bag onto his knees.

'Milan*chen*, sweetie . . .' she began, desperately.

'Listen! You . . . you don't understand, Gisie . . .' He fumbled for the words. 'Nobody in Germany . . . nobody in *world* understand why I must kill! In my country we fight for life – Christian peoples fight Muslim peoples. Muslim men I must kill, because they think they can fuck arse of Croat peoples!' He jerked his middle finger upwards. 'Muslim women why kill? Because they make sons who fuck arse! They Turks!'

A mad ramble that made little sense to her, she let him bleed the poison from his soul.

'And if they in Germany, I kill also.'

'But that was only a girl?' Gisela whined. 'Couldn't have been more than twelve. Why her?'

'*Tulici*,' he murmured. 'Muslim girl. From *Tulici*.' He fell silent, as if no other explanation were needed.

Tulici. Gisela knew well the significance of that name. Knew the crime she'd just helped him commit was nothing to what he'd already done. The nightmare was true; the man she'd almost loved was a monster, a practitioner of genocide.

He pulled open the zip of his bag and gripped the gun. Gisela gulped.

'If you talk to police, I kill you too,' he growled.

'No, no,' she babbled. 'I'm your friend, you know that. I'm not talking to the police. I promise you, I don't want to tell *anyone* about today. I wasn't here, even.'

'That's right. You were not here.'

He nodded repeatedly to reinforce the point. The hammer clicked as he fingered the pistol.

'Now I go. You make car clean again. Then you drive to Berlin and find friend who will say you were with him last night and today.'

'But what if the police stop me?'

'Take the Bundesstrasse. The police will look on the Autobahn.'

'And you? Where are you going? Back to Bosnia?'

Silence again. Shouldn't have asked. He still had his hand on that gun.

He pushed open the door and got out. Then, clutching his bag, he leaned back in.

'Remember, Gisie. If you my enemy, I kill you.'

He'd stated it as a matter of fact. He closed the door and she watched him walk towards the exit.

The police sealed off the road and pavement around the house in Mühlweg with striped yellow tape to keep the press out. Both the newspapers and the local TV had been tipped off about the shooting.

In the road just metres from where Vildana had been

305

gunned down, detectives recovered two 9mm cartridge cases.

Nancy Roche and Nataša had gone with Vildana in the ambulance. The paramedic had congratulated the colonel on his first aid. Probably saved her life, she said.

The Hessen State Police, who'd answered the 110 call that Nancy had put in, decided to call in help from the Bundeskriminalamt. The shooting of a Bosnian was political and needed the Federal specialists from Wiesbaden.

A Kommissar was on his way, but it would be an hour before he arrived. In the meantime, patrol cars were searching for a muddy, white, VW Polo, possibly driven by a woman, registration number unknown. Unfortunately, the police pointed out, the Polo was one of Germany's most popular cars, and white one of the most popular colours.

While the police went from house to house, seeking witnesses, Irwin Roche despatched the twins to watch TV, then hustled Alex and Lorna indoors and sat them at the kitchen table, so they could tell him exactly what all this was about.

'Oh God ... what have we done?' Lorna sighed, cupping her head in her hands. 'I brought Vildana halfways across Europe, just so she could be shot at.'

Alex clasped and unclasped his fingers, kneading his knuckles. By now he was convinced the gunman must have been Pravic. So close, just metres from the man the world was hunting, the man *he'd* been hunting, and not known it.

In his mind he kept trying to improve on the meagre description he'd given the police – cropped fair hair, male, in his thirties, grim, grey-blue eyes – it wasn't much.

'I still don't understand how Pravic knew where to find her,' he murmured.

Suddenly Roche blushed scarlet.

'O . . . h, oh boy,' he said, getting up from the table and heading for his den.

'The Internet,' Lorna moaned. 'Must've put his address on an open message on the bulletin board. You're not supposed to do that. Anything confidential should go e-mail direct to CareNet.'

They followed Roche into the den. The modem bleeped as it made the connection. A few keystrokes and he was into ‹alt.childadopt.agency› on the Usenet. He selected the 'Children available' item from the menu. The most recent messages came up first. Some of them offensive, some from cranks, some saying that adoption on the Internet was God's gift to child-abusers.

He kept typing 'back' until he came to the response he'd lodged to Lorna's request for an 'angel' six days ago.

'Oh my! Look at that,' he sighed.

There at the top of his offer of help was his home address, street number and everything, instantly read-able by any of the Net's thirty million subscribers.

'How could I be so stupid?' He thumped the screen with his fist.

Alex led Lorna back to the kitchen, while Roche logged off.

'I still don't get it,' he murmured, 'I mean, how would Pravic know about the Internet?'

'CNN. They filmed a report on us,' Lorna answered, her voice heavy. 'My God, Alex, what have we done? Not *you*, but me, Larry Machin, CareNet. So busy being clever, instead of *saving* Vildana's life we may have *lost* it!'

Milan Pravic found a dank stairway which took him two levels down in the airport car park – the floor where the rental agencies kept their vehicles.

He walked past a small office and a line of sparkling

automobiles. Must be a toilet here somewhere for the staff.

He found the door and pushed inside. It smelled of urine, as if drunks had given up their search for porcelain and used the walls. He tried the taps on the washbasin. They worked. Hot water too.

He unzipped the sports bag and pulled out a towel and a sachet of hair colourant shampoo. Dark chestnut.

He draped the towel round his shoulders to protect his clothes, then wet his hair. He rubbed in the shampoo and rinsed his hands. A quick look in the mirror, then he picked up his bag and retreated to one of the cubicles. The instructions said wait ten minutes before rinsing.

Two floors up, Gisela washed clean the number plates of her car, using water from a bottle she always carried in the boot. Then she re-parked it near the exit and behind a pillar, so that if Milan came back to check on her, he would think she had gone.

She walked as casually as she could down the long passage to the terminal and located a phone booth.

Her fingers hovered over the dial pad. 110 would get her the police. An anonymous message perhaps, to tell them he was at the airport?

She dismissed the thought. Not on. Not if she wanted to live a little longer.

She pulled an address book from her handbag. Time to find a friend she could trust. It wouldn't be easy. Loyalty was a rare commodity in the circles she moved in.

Kommissar Günther Linz had intended to spend the afternoon watching athletics on television with his wife who was a gymnastics teacher, but the weekend duty man at the Wiesbaden HQ had gone sick, so when the alert came from the Hessische Landeskriminalamt they'd telephoned Linz at home.

The word 'Bosnia' linked with crime in Germany made him shudder. With hundreds of thousands of refugees here from all the Yugoslav ethnic groups it wouldn't take much to spark civil war on German streets.

And now the attempted murder of a child. Bad news. Very bad.

As he took the Pfefferheim turning off the Autobahn, he jabbed at the radio button to catch the six o'clock bulletin. Wanted to see what the media had dug up on that Leipzig can of worms.

The way he'd heard it from the police rumour network, the suicide note left by the microbiologist had been dynamite. The Leipzig police had passed it straight to the intelligence agencies who'd slapped a national security classification on it and demanded sealed lips. Now the BND were claiming they'd 'lost' the letter.

The 'pips' of the time signal. He turned up the volume.

'. . . *Frau Erika Schmidt, the daughter of the dead scientist, claims in an interview in tomorrow's* Bild Zeitung *that her father told her some of the old Stasi security police were still functioning, and that he'd been ordered against his will to produce dangerous bacteria for them. . . .*'

The Stasi still functioning? No chance. Impossible after the way it had been taken apart after unification. A judicial Commission was still sifting the files looking for people to prosecute on human rights charges.

If there were Stasi men still operating, they were freelancers. But freelancers using *anthrax*? He shuddered again. And working for whom? The BND? Not their style . . . On the other hand, they *had* gone out on a limb with that plutonium business.

He pushed the 'off' button.

A uniformed officer stopped him at the turning into Mühlweg. He showed his pass and was waved through. Locals clustered in groups of two or three on the pavements, watching the comings and goings. Must have shaken up a dull Sunday, Linz thought.

Relieved to see him, his opposite number from the Hessen police shook him warmly by the hand.

'The hospital say the girl will live. The bullet missed her heart by this much.' The Inspector held his finger and thumb so they almost touched. 'By the way, they're all foreigners here. Americans and British. Not much German between them.'

'Then I can practise my English a little,' Linz replied.

Alex stood up to greet the tall, limping newcomer with the pepper-coloured hair. The wariness in the policeman's close-set eyes told him this was a man who preferred facts and certainties to supposition.

Irwin Roche had summoned the help of an interpreter from the Rhine-Main Air Base, a bespectacled school-teacher.

Helped by a large pot of fresh-brewed coffee, they explained the background to the shooting that afternoon. Linz listened, interjecting sometimes in English, sometimes in German.

Lorna spelled out how CareNet used the Internet as an adoption agency, then Roche took Linz into his den to demonstrate.

'So, any person who has a computer can connect to this?' he asked, intrigued.

'All you need is a modem and a subscription to an Internet server.'

'So, anyone who saw the report on the news could have had the idea to connect to this Internet and could

310

find out that Vildana was staying in your house?' he pressed.

Roche blushed again.

'It was incredibly stupid to put my address, I know that. . . .'

'*Ja*, but my point is that *anybody* could do this. Any crazy person with a computer . . .'

'And a gun,' Alex added. Linz seemed to be questioning Pravic's involvement.

'Of course. But I must look at all possibilities,' he said dismissively. 'Tell me, does the computer make a record of the people who have connected up and read these messages?'

'Unfortunately not,' Roche replied. 'There's no control over the "net".'

'That is a pity.'

Back in the kitchen, Linz began to make notes.

'It was you who brought the girl into Germany illegally, Frau Sorensen?' he asked without looking up.

Lorna glanced in alarm at Alex. He shook his head.

'I'm not prepared to comment on that.'

Linz took her answer as an admission.

'Vildana's a persecuted person and could apply for asylum here,' she added simply.

Linz didn't react. It wasn't a point worth pursuing. Any foreigner entering Germany legally or illegally, had a right to stay while an asylum application was processed.

'Milan Pravic lived in Germany for several years,' Alex said. 'His brother told me it was Berlin. Wouldn't there be some record of him there? A photograph maybe?'

'It's possible. The Landeskriminalpolizei in Berlin can check that. Today of course is Sunday, so they cannot get at the Municipal register until tomorrow. We have access to the Bundesverwaltungsamt computer in Köln – where the records of "black sheep" are kept, guest workers who will not get their visa renewed because they've broken the law. But they have nothing on Milan Pravic. I have already checked.'

He frowned.

'What do you know about this person?' Linz asked.

'He's a mass murderer and maybe a rapist, Herr Kommissar,' Alex snapped. 'Comes from a small village in Bosnia. His brother's a priest. Not much love between him and Milan. The man's a psychopath.'

'But perhaps has not used computers much . . .' said Linz frostily. He suspected the Englishman was something of an amateur psychologist, a species he disliked.

Alex ground his teeth.

'You understand, Herr Crawford, that there is not much evidence yet,' Linz continued. 'Maybe the ballistics department will get some information from the bullets. Or maybe the girl saw the face of the man who shot her.'

'All Vildana saw was the front wheel of her bike,' Lorna replied. 'I was watching her.'

'I don't think you've quite understood about Pravic, Herr Kommissar,' Alex continued. 'Let me tell you what his own brother said about him. He said killing's like a drug to Milan. Particularly when his victims are Muslim. He'll kill anybody who gets in his way. And given the means, he'll commit murder on a scale that'll make the Tulici massacre look like a minor road accident!'

Linz blinked at the intensity of Alex's words.

'Then we must pray for some luck in finding him,' he added calmly. 'I would like to know where to contact you if I need to talk to you again.'

Alex gave him the number of the Hotel Sommer.

'And you, Frau Sorensen? Where will I find you?'

Alex's and Lorna's eyes met for no more than a second, but it was long enough.

'I'll be with him,' she said.

They spoke little on the drive into Frankfurt, Lorna's hands gripping the wheel for support as much as to steer the car. Personal decisions were beyond her now. The puppet-master Fate had taken control again.

Her mind gyrated, sifting and sorting the words and happenings of this long day, but they were as hard to hold onto as leaves in the wind. The baring of souls in the bistro had opened old wounds then seared them. Now, the sharp crack of the gunshots, the clatter of handlebars on concrete, the sight of the blood-soaked rag pressed to Vildana's chest – all snapshot images clicking round in an endless loop in her brain.

Alex took in little as they drove into town, his mind filled by the eyes at the window of the white Polo. The cold, blue-grey eyes of a man who'd assigned himself the right to snuff out the life of another human being.

Any man who had such arrogance over life and death would try again, once he learned Vildana was still alive. They'd need a new hiding place for the girl when she was released from hospital. Above all, Pravic had to be found. He had to be stopped.

They would need a new hiding place? Who? Whose responsibility was Vildana now? The Roches', Germany's – or Lorna's?

He turned his head to look at her. Lorna's chin jutted in concentration as she drove, her blonde hair short and wavy like a Pharaoh's. Now that he knew what she'd been through in those lost years, he could read it in the hollowness of her cheeks, in the lines round her mouth.

She sensed him looking at her and flashed a smile that peeked from her face as nervously as a kitten sniffing the air.

Their eyes locked for little more than a second, just long enough to confirm agreement as to what would happen next.

Words weren't needed. They'd be superfluous, dangerous even. Words analysed things too much. If the two of them were to talk about the pact their eyes had just made they'd find a reason for setting it aside. They'd have to conclude that on a day of such shocking, murderous events, it would be wrong to pursue pleasure.

She parked the Land Cruiser in a multi-storey. He took Lorna's small suitcase from the back seat and carried it two blocks to the Hotel Sommer.

The desk clerk handed him the room key without comment. Then when the couple disappeared into the elevator, he changed the figure 'one' in the occupancy column of the register to 'two'.

They stood close together in the lift, their bodies touching, but not their hands. Slowly he bent his head and their lips brushed with the lightness of feathers.

The elevator stopped and the doors opened, but for a moment their eyes stayed on each other, neither wanting to break the spell.

His hand shook as he fumbled with the key. Like a cat, she rubbed her face against his shoulder, her breath halting and uneven.

Inside the room, he dropped the suitcase beside the wardrobe, then held her by the waist. She slipped her arms round his neck, threading her fingers through his hair.

His mouth crushed against hers, their lips and tongues re-discovering the taste and territory they'd once known well.

She pulled back from him, her eyes wild and hungry. She stroked his beard, trying to familiarize her hands with the unfamiliar.

'Maybe . . .' she breathed, 'maybe *that*'ll have to go.'

'What, now?' he asked.

'No.' Her mouth widened into a smile. 'Not now. Later. A lot later.'

She slipped off her knitted waistcoat then crossed her arms, taking hold of the hem of her shirt and pulling it over her head. Alex did the same with his pullover. They dropped the clothes on the floor.

He kissed her bare neck and shoulders, his hands tingling at the feel of her smooth, soft skin, the soapy perfume of her flesh borne upwards by her body heat. She was so thin, he could feel her ribs. He ran his fingers down the ridges of her spine, remembering their geography. Then with a little twist he unclipped the strap of her bra and slipped it forward.

Lorna tossed back her head and closed her eyes to heighten the sensations shooting through her body. His tongue's caress hardened her nipples. She breathed in sharply, clasping his head as if it were the most precious thing on earth and ran her fingers up the soft, sensitive skin behind his ears.

She felt his hands start to work on the belt of her jeans.

'Hang on,' she panted, 'you've still got your shirt on.'

She tugged and pulled at the buttons, breaking one of them, then pushed the shirt back over his shoulders.

She rubbed her body against the thick mat of hair on his chest, remembering. Remembering how fine-tuned his flesh had been when they'd met that second time in Belfast, how addicted she'd become to what he did with it.

He had the belt undone and slipped his hands under her knickers, cupping her small buttocks, his fingertips reaching to feel the hot moistness underneath.

They pulled apart to throw off the rest of their clothes.

Lorna threw the duvet onto the floor and lay down on the smooth white sheets. She covered her breasts with her hands, conscious that they weren't as firm and shapely as when he'd last seen them. But then, he wasn't the same shape either, she realized, seeing the slight bulge of his stomach when he knelt beside her on the mattress. She looked up at his beaming face as his hand caressed her stomach and teased through the tufts of her bush.

'You're as gorgeous as ever, Lorna,' he breathed. 'D'you know that?'

A silly grin spread across her face.

'So are you,' she purred.

She took hold of him and pulled him down on top of her.

Twenty-four

Annie Lowell, née Donohue, slit open the hand-delivered letter and pulled out a pack of photographs. She frowned. For her? Some mistake, perhaps. Then she unfolded the single sheet of writing paper accompanying them and recognized the writing of her younger sister.

'Hey, it's from Lorna,' she smiled, realizing then that the scenes in the shots were Bosnia.

Always close, she and her sister. Two years between them in age, but as children they'd been like Siamese twins when it came to coping with the tyranny of their father.

It was a brilliant spring morning in New England, maples and birches exploding with yellow-green life. The Lowell children were back at school after a few days at home because of bad colds. Annie had the house and the day to herself.

An uncontrolled appetite for muffins and donuts had left her with hips and thighs that were painful to joke about, but she had a ready Irish smile, lively brown eyes and tawny hair almost down to her shoulders.

She took the letter back to the kitchen and poured herself some of the coffee she'd left to brew. Then she sat down and read.

Dearest Annie,
You will NEVER guess who the guy with the beard is, standing

317

next to me in a couple of these photos! His name begins with the letter 'A'!!!

See you soon. Lorna.

What was she on about? Never got sensible letters from her any more.

She riffled through the prints until she found two that showed a bearded man standing uneasily next to Lorna. Certainly didn't recognize him.

She read the letter again.

His name begins with the letter 'A'!!!

'Oh my God!' she shrieked. 'That's not possible.'

She looked again at the pictures, then stomped to her husband's den and pulled a box file from the bookshelf. She returned to the kitchen and opened the lid. Inside were hundreds of photographs, dating back years, all the prints that had never merited being pasted into albums.

Her heart was thumping so much she feared a coronary. She dug deep in the box, guessing anything from so long ago should be at the bottom. She stirred the prints like a cake-mix, but didn't find what she was looking for.

'Come on, Annie, you're being stupid,' she scolded herself. 'Go systematic.'

She began again, removing each print individually, checking and stacking them into piles. Eventually she found it.

Hands trembling, she held the print taken in Belfast in 1973 next to the new ones.

'Oh my God!' she howled.

The beard had fooled her. Older now, jowlier, bigger gut, but the same man.

'A for Alex!' she hissed.

She took the new pictures to the window and held them to the light, looking for signs on Lorna's face of the bitterness she'd harboured for the Englishman for so many years. Lorna certainly didn't look happy in the photograph. The smile looked fixed.

The two sisters had always confided in each other. She remembered Lorna crying over the stocky, unsophisticated boy she'd fallen for in a London pub in the nineteen-sixties. She had been broken-hearted at having to leave him and return to college in America.

She remembered too the ecstatic phone call from Belfast ten years later, announcing they'd met again. Then, just a week or two after that, the betrayal.

Annie had never shared Lorna's belief in fate; when she learned Alex was spying for the British, it hadn't been hard to conclude that he had engineered the meeting to make use of her.

Was he doing it again? What use could she be to him this time? Lorna wasn't involved in anything *sensitive* these days. No longer had anything to do with the Cause.

Annie read the letter once more. No clue from Lorna as to what she felt. No reason given for sending the photos. Just those ambiguous exclamation points. It was almost as if after twenty years of pledging to get her own back on Alex, Lorna couldn't decide what to do, now she had the chance. As if she was asking for help . . .

Mister Alex Jarvis. Annie knew what *she* would do to him. Cut his balls off.

But it wasn't down to her. Not down to Lorna, even. When revenge was personal it was almost always wrong. There were bigger issues to be considered. This was one for the organization, for the boys with long memories who would've given their right arms during the last twenty years to know the tout's whereabouts.

She picked up the telephone and dialled her husband's number. Joe had sat on the Irish Republican fundraising committee for over fifteen years. They'd both of them been involved since soon after the British troops went in. Campaigning, lobbying. Joe would know what to do.

He'd have a feeling for the mood amongst the Provisionals now there was a cease-fire on the way.

Joe was in a marketing meeting, but his secretary pulled him out. He listened silently as she explained, then gave his answer in a couple of sentences.

She padded back into the den, took an envelope and writing paper from Joe's desk and returned to the kitchen. She slipped one of the photos inside the envelope, keeping the other back for herself. For at least ten minutes she just sat, wondering whether she'd done the right thing after all, talking to Joe.

It was she who'd encouraged her sister to get involved in the Cause. Her thoughts drifted back to 1973 when Lorna had fled from Belfast like a wraith. After the boys in Boston put a contract out, the creature had hidden in cupboards, terrified a knock on the door would be followed by a bullet.

Above all, Annie remembered how Lorna's spirit had been broken by that bastard's betrayal, by the shock that someone she'd loved and trusted could do that to her. Annie had told her sister to forget him, but she never could. Never got him out of her system. Lorna, she guessed, was one of those benighted women who only loved the men that abused them.

Annie picked up the picture again and peered into her sister's eyes. What did she see there? Anger? Hate? Oh, no . . . Not the other thing for heaven's sake . . .

'Lorna, sweetie, don't do it. Just don't do what I think you're goin' to do,' she said to the picture. 'He'll fuck you up again, sure as God made little green apples.'

She began to write. Just a few sentences. Just enough to let the boys know what was what. Like Joe said. Then it was up to *them* what they did about it.

The gun attack on a Bosnian girl in a quiet residential street had made front page news. Armed police guarded her ward in the recently-built hospital and the media were beating a path to her door. The TV had portrayed Vildana as a tragic war victim, gunned down by the man she was trying to bring to justice for the murder of her family. The story had touched hearts around the world.

The Universitätsklinik was the accident and emergency hospital for a swathe of semi-urban landscape south of Frankfurt. A white-painted, five-storey block, extending each side of a central entrance that served ambulances and visitors.

Alex and Lorna asked at the main desk for directions to ward 4F. The receptionist assumed they were journalists and told them coldly they'd need to speak first to the hospital administrator.

'And he's not let anyone see her all morning,' she added briskly.

'We're not press, we're family,' Alex answered in German.

'Really?' She'd heard the same story four times that morning. 'The police won't let you in.'

Alex took Lorna's arm. 'Come on, we're wasting our time.' He led her to the elevators.

As the doors opened on the fourth floor, they almost collided with photographers being nudged away by a police officer. Along the corridor two more uniformed men from the Kriminalpolizei stood guard outside room F.

Alex struggled with his school German to explain who they were. One officer went inside and reappeared with Nancy Roche.

321

'Hey, it's good to see you guys!' she exclaimed. Her tanned skin looked grey and pinched with exhaustion. She led them into the four-bed ward and closed the door again. Vildana was dozing in the far corner. Two other beds were occupied by children, one alone, the other with a mother in attendance.

'She's sleeping, thank the Lord,' Nancy whispered. 'It was a terrible night. She was in a lot of pain when the anaesthetic wore off. Nobody got any sleep. Nataša is totally washed out; I sent her home at eight this morning, after a nurse came on who's from Yugoslavia. She looks in once in a while. Say, have they caught the man yet?'

'Not that we've heard,' Alex answered. 'Kommissar Linz hasn't rung us.'

Anyway they'd been too pre-occupied to enquire.

'Vildana's scared out of her wits. Thinks he'll chase and chase until he finds her.'

'She's probably right,' Lorna agreed. 'The man's a monster.'

They looked across at the sleeping child. She had one hand up to her mouth, half obscuring her birthmark, the thumb resting on her lips.

'She's a sweet kid,' Nancy murmured, shaking her head. 'So young, and suffered so much already. Now look, are you guys going to be here a while? Can you give me a couple of hours to flop, to go home and take a shower?'

Lorna and Alex looked at one another and nodded. 'Sure, why not.'

'That's swell of you. One thing, some Bosnian refugee centre has been in touch, just making sure someone's taking responsibility for Vildana. The police say they're bona fide, but I'm a little anxious. Scared they'll take her away from me I guess,' she grimaced nervously.

'And you don't want that. . . ?' Lorna asked, checking. The woman could have had no idea what she was letting herself in for when she agreed to take Vildana.

'No way,' Nancy replied, startled at the question. 'She's *my* girl now. Leastways, so long as that's what *she* wants,' she added. 'See you in a couple of hours then?'

'Sure. Take your time,' Lorna said, squeezing her arm.

She and Alex sat down beside the bed, watching the rise and fall of Vildana's breathing. Her right breast was covered by a thick, white dressing.

Such tiny breasts, Lorna thought, little more than buds. And now there'd be a scar, another physical one to go with those that they couldn't see, in her mind.

Half an hour later, with Vildana still sleeping, Alex descended to the lobby telling Lorna he'd find them some sandwiches. His main aim however was to telephone MI5.

'What are you doing in Frankfurt, dear boy?' Chadwick's voice, suspicious.

'Just checking you'd read your papers this morning . . .'

'And the rest . . . TV, radio, the story's getting a huge play over here. But . . . were you *there* when it happened?'

'Well yes . . .'

'Why? How?'

'I helped smuggle the girl out of Bosnia. Came here to see how she was settling in with her new family . . .'

'Good heavens! You're a canny bastard. Didn't mention any of that when you rang from Split.'

'It was still rather sensitive, then.'

'Well, tell me something. That Lorna somebody-or-other mentioned in the *Times* – she's not *Lorna*. . . ?'

'Good Lord, no,' Alex lied. 'Sorensen's her name. Nordic background, I think.'

'Mmm . . .' Chadwick was unconvinced. He'd seen a photo of her in the paper. 'You're sure it *was* Milan Pravic who shot the girl?'

'Can't think who else would do it. Certainly fitted the description.'

323

'I see. Who's handling it for the Germans?'

'A Kommissar called Linz. From the Bundeskriminalamt.'

'Oh I know Linz. Met him not so long ago at an Interpol bash. Maybe I'll give him a ring. I'll tell him you're a friend of mine . . .'

Alex rang off then bought cheese rolls and mineral water from the stall in the lobby. He also picked up the *Frankfurte Allgemeine* and *Bild Zeitung*.

Back in the ward he scanned the stories that had been written about Vildana.

'It says here she was smuggled into Germany in the trunk of a car belonging to an American adoption agency,' he translated. 'Says it's thought the killer tailed them all the way to Frankfurt.'

'God! Who gives them this stuff?'

'Better *that* than the truth,' he commented wryly.

'Do they name him?' Lorna asked.

'Not directly. There's a lot about Tulici. Mentions the UN asking European police forces to hold Pravic if they find him. Oh, Kommissar Linz is quoted. Says he has no idea who the gunman was. Appealing for more witnesses – all that crap.'

Vildana stirred. She saw Lorna, made an attempt at a smile, then winced with pain. Lorna fussed with the pillows and the girl closed her eyes once more.

It stirred memories for Alex, sitting by a child's hospital bed. Jodie. He'd broken an arm once, riding his bike into a wall. Only ten at the time.

Alex turned back to the papers. Leipzig again – the mystery suicide. A new twist . . . A Zagreb woman was critically ill with pulmonary anthrax. The hotel where she worked as a cleaner had been closed to be disinfected.

'Extraordinary story, this,' Alex muttered.

'*Now* what are they saying?'

'It's not about Vildana, this one. It's about a scientist

324

in Leipzig University, who committed suicide last week. The official line is that he was depressed at being made redundant. You know, a man whose work meant everything to him? Well, his daughter tells a different story. She said her father had hinted about being forced to hand over supplies of lethal bacteria to some thug from the Stasi, you know – the old East German secret police?'

'Really?'

'The papers have been nibbling at it for days. They're saying the bacteria could've been anthrax, and *now* there's a girl dying from the disease in Zagreb.'

'Zagreb! For Pete's sake, why Zagreb?'

'Dunno. But anthrax isn't exactly as common as 'flu, so there's some suspicion it came from the lab in Leipzig. And now, the papers say there's a cover-up going on. They claim the German intelligence agencies know all about it, but aren't saying.'

'Wow! That's some story!'

Voices in the corridor outside, then Kommissar Linz walked in, dressed in his green raincoat and carrying a slim briefcase.

He limped across to the corner bed and shook their hands formally.

'*Guten Tag, Herr Crawford. Frau Sorensen.* Your hotel said you were out, so I hoped you would be here.'

'You have news about Pravic?' Alex asked.

'Yes and no.' He rested the briefcase on a chair, opened it, and pulled out a photograph about seven inches by five. 'They wired this from Berlin this morning.'

Alex took it from him, a blow-up of a passport photo, blurry black-and-white. Man in late twenties. Thick, fair hair, pale eyes. A sullen, brooding face. No trace of a smile.

'Well? Have you seen this man before?' Linz asked neutrally.

'Is it him?' asked Alex.

Linz shrugged, saying nothing.

Alex held it out so Lorna could see too.

'I never saw the guy's face, that's the trouble,' she said, exasperated.

'You?' Linz asked again, turning back to Alex.

'I don't know. I remember the man as older. His hair was trimmed short, I think. When was this picture taken?'

'Maybe six years ago.'

'Mmm. The eyes look similar. Not quite what I remember, but similar. But then I don't suppose he was about to try to murder someone when this picture was taken.'

Linz took the photo back.

'You told me the car was driven by a woman,' he went on. 'You heard her scream. Did you see her face? You think you'd recognize her?'

Alex looked pained and shook his head.

'When we drove into the road, the car was parked there and I think I saw dark hair through the driver's window. But that's all. Why? You've found the car.'

'The police in Berlin have found a woman that Pravic used to live with. And it happens that she owns a white Volkswagen Polo.'

'Aha. Fantastic!' Alex smiled.

'But she claims she has not seen Pravic since he went back to Bosnia two years ago. She also has two witnesses who say she was with them for the whole weekend, and another who says the car has not been away from its parking place for days.'

'Oh. Not so good.'

'But since the woman is a prostitute and her friends have convictions for fraud and drug dealing, we're not necessarily convinced by her story,' he concluded.

This man can be quite droll, Alex thought.

'So, *Herr Crawford*, I would like your help in putting her to the test. She is being brought to Frankfurt this afternoon. I will arrange an identity parade at the police headquarters this evening. At about seven? You could be there?'

'Surely. But as I said, I didn't see her face.'

'Maybe there will be something you can recognize. We will try. It's the best chance.'

He was on the point of replacing the photo in his briefcase, when he noticed that Vildana was awake and watching them. He smiled at her, and hesitated.

Lorna guessed what he was about to do.

'Please don't show her that . . .' she interjected. 'Not just now.'

Linz nodded. She was right. There was no need. Not yet.

6.25 p.m.
Munich

Martin Sanders took a taxi straight from Munich's Franz Josef Strauß Airport to the hotel near the Victualenmarkt. No special hired car this time. There'd be no ramble, no wine tasting. This was an emergency.

He paid cash for the room as usual and went up to it to wait. Katzfuss had said he would make contact.

The Leipzig business had been hot gossip at Vauxhall Cross before he left London. Snide little speculations about what their German counterparts in the BND had been up to. 'Wouldn't happen here, old boy. At least, if it did, we'd make damn sure nothing slipped out.'

Little did they know, Sanders brooded.

He sat on the austere easy-chair in the corner of his room, reading the William Boyd he'd bought at the airport on the way out. Twenty minutes passed, then Katzfuss rang, giving the name of a restaurant five minutes walk away.

When he reached it, Jack Kapinsky and Marcel Vaillon were already sitting with the German at a table in an alcove. Photos of old opera singers cluttered the walls of the place.

'*Bonsoir*, Martin,' the Frenchman said, extending a hand. 'Jack has just told us that Akhavi is on the way out, but there's no word on the Russian yet.'

'Hmmm,' Sanders grunted, squeezing onto the bench next to him. Assisting in the probable death of two men had given him no pleasure.

'Is this place clean?' Kapinsky asked petulantly. 'It's just I thought the Ramblers had rules not to meet near walls.'

The American's nostrils twitched as if they'd detected an unpleasant smell. Getting ready to pass the buck, Sanders thought.

'I think no one will hear us, gentlemen,' Katzfuss replied dismissively. 'I am sorry to have to call this extra meeting, but there is a crisis.'

'Your guy's fucked up, hasn't he,' Kapinsky snapped. 'Killed a Croatian chambermaid!'

The deep lines on Katzfuss's face gave him the appearance of an angry Boxer dog.

'I believe you Americans have a phrase . . . Collateral damage?' the German growled.

'Come on boys and girls,' Sanders intervened. 'Let's *try* to be grown up. We're all in it together.'

'Get on with it, Rudi,' Vaillon said.

A waiter hovered. They looked quickly at the menu, he memorized their choices and left them in peace.

'All right. So . . . When we met two weeks ago,' Katzfuss reminded them, 'we decided the Russian and the Iranian should be eliminated by a freelance with experience. We agreed this person could use whatever means. Yes?'

They nodded. Even Kapinsky.

'So . . . we made conditions – that the *wi*ctims should die only after they return to their own countries. For this, the agent decide to use a biological weapon – anthrax. Unfortunately the man who supplied the bacteria was not reliable any more. He killed himself, leaving a letter telling what he had done. He told also that Herr Dunkel – that is the cover name of our agent – that Dunkel was previously with the Stasi.

'The civil police in Leipzig read the letter. *They* pass it to internal security, BfV, who tell us at the BND. *I* tell them this is *w*ery sensitive, and the letter must disappear, but already it is too late. The newspapers learn from the police what it said.

'So . . . now the newspapers and some Bundestag representatives ask what is the connection between the security services and Dunkel, and the death of Kemmer in Leipzig and the almost death of a woman in Zagreb.

'Most of that you already know. But there is something else, gentlemen . . .' Katzfuss's face sagged like a deflated balloon. 'Yesterday I meet with the man we call Dunkel . . . He told me that he had help in Zagreb. Maybe you two saw the other man?' he asked, glancing at Sanders and Vaillon.

'Yes. But I don't know his name,' Sanders replied, reaching into his pocket for a small envelope.

'That was a pity,' Katzfuss sighed. 'Dunkel brought this man back to Germany. On the way, during the night at a motel, he stole from Dunkel's car the remains of the liquid containing the anthrax. . . .'

'Wha-at?' Sanders erupted.

'God almighty, Rudi!' Kapinsky exploded. 'I thought you said your guy was a pro . . .'

Katzfuss's embarrassment was painful to see.

'*Ja*, Dunkel *was* a pro,' he shrugged. 'Some years ago.

Too many years perhaps. But the worst thing is the *name* of the man who now has the anthrax. It is Milan Pravic . . .'

'Bloody hell!' Sanders spluttered. The other two frowned, trying to place it.

'Responsible for the murder of more than forty women and children at Tulici in Bosnia last month,' Katzfuss continued. 'Wanted for the attempted murder yesterday, here in Germany, of Vildana Muminovic, the only witness to the massacre.'

Silence at the table. No one breathed. The food arrived.

'*C'est incroyable!*' Vaillon hissed after the waiter had gone again.

'Your *old pro* hires a genocidal maniac to help out with the Zagreb job, and then lets him walk away with a bottle of *anthrax*?' Kapinsky howled. 'My God, Rudi! What's going on here?'

Sanders opened the envelope and pulled out the photograph he'd taken in Zagreb, showing Pravic and 'Dunkel' sitting in the big square near the Dubrovnik Hotel.

'That's him,' he said dismally.

'This, I didn't know you had it,' Katzfuss said, grabbing it from him.

'Always take holiday snaps. Never know when they might come in handy.'

'The police must have this. As soon as possible,' the German continued.

'Give that to the cops, and they'll want to know where it came from,' Kapinsky complained. 'Then they'll *know* the BND's involved.'

'Jack, the police must have this picture,' Katzfuss insisted. 'And they must be warned that Pravic could kill thousands of people with the anthrax!'

'Are you crazy?' Kapinsky hissed. 'The Ramblers will

make headlines all over the world. Just think what'll happen in each of our countries when people find out what we've been doing. Putting out contracts to assassinate people without the authority of our governments! Using *biological weapons*. Do you know what Congress will do? I'll tell you. They'll have the excuse they've been looking for to close down the whole fucking Company. The CIA will be dead in the water!'

'I have to agree with Jack, Rudi,' Sanders added quietly. 'The political repercussions don't bear thinking about.'

'They are right,' Vaillon concurred.

'But the risk of what could happen here in Germany? We cannot permit this. Pravic has killed who knows how many in Bosnia, for the reason that they are Muslims. Even if the *w*ictims have never been to a mosque in their lives, they must still be killed because of their culture – that is what he believes. In Germany we have hundreds of thousands of Bosnians. Many, many so-called Muslims.'

He wiggled his fingers to indicate inverted commas.

'My friends. The situation is most urgent. This week there is a target here in Germany that Mr Pravic might find too tempting to resist. On Wednesday – the day after tomorrow – in Munich, there is a Muslim political rally. More than one thousand Bosnians, Turks, Iranians, and Lebanese meet in a sports hall to listen to speeches from Islamic Fundamentalists. Already the police in Munich think neo-Nazis will try to break up the meeting. But if Pravic . . .'

'You're right,' Sanders agreed. 'The risk is appalling.'

'Suppose he can spray the bacteria in there? Five hundred dead? A thousand? Then the questions from the Bosnian Muslims in this country – you knew about this man, why didn't you stop him? Why you let him murder Muslims? You Germans are still Nazis, still with the

Croats, like in Third Reich. . . ? It would be *Bürgerkrieg*. A Bosnian civil war in Germany.'

Marcel Vaillon nodded, reminded of France's own problems with Algeria.

'You are right Rudi, but so are we,' he insisted. 'Of course your police must have this picture and know the danger. But *we four* must not be exposed. Maybe there is a way.'

He turned to the SIS man.

'Martin, in our last meeting you said the UN Tribunal asked for British help to find Pravic. So, now you have some success, don't you?' He tapped the photo. 'Send them this. Say it was taken by a British UN soldier. Tell the UN to give it to the German police immediately. They won't know where it comes from.'

Like laundering money. Sanders picked up the print and studied it again. Easy enough to mask out Dunkel and the background.

'Then Rudi, you must warn the police Pravic could have been in Zagreb when the hotel worker was infected. Say the man is a mass murderer and may have an anthrax weapon. If they ask how you know, you tell them you don't, but it is a guess.'

'That's fine, but what about Dunkel?' Kapinsky intervened. 'He's the crucial figure that connects Pravic with Leipzig and with us. If the police identify Dunkel and he talks, then he could spill the whole bag of maggots.'

The other three nodded.

'Already I tell him he must eliminate everything that links him to Pravic and Zagreb,' Katzfuss replied, knowing that it wouldn't be enough.

'What I'm saying Rudi,' Kapinsky stressed, 'is that *Dunkel* is the key to keeping us out of trouble. And he's *your* problem, Rudi. You have to get to him before the cops do. And you have to take him out.'

A uniformed woman officer led the way into a small, grey-painted, airless office at the headquarters of the Kriminalpolizei. Irwin and Nancy Roche were already there, looking anxious and drawn. So was Nataša. One wall was made of glass. Beyond it Alex saw another room, furnitureless and empty.

'In a minute you will see six women through the glass. They cannot see you. Each woman will carry a card with a number,' Kommissar Linz explained. 'Do not talk to each other about what you see. If you think one of them is the person who was driving the Polo yesterday, write down her number and give it to me.' He handed each of them a notepad and pen. 'Are you all ready?'

They concurred.

'*Anfangen bitte!*' he said into a microphone projecting from the wall. He dimmed the lights.

'Not too close to the glass,' he cautioned.

A few seconds later the women filed in. All had short, dark hair, some black, some brown. Three were in short miniskirts, three in trousers.

'Tough looking bunch,' Alex commented.

'Please! No talking,' Linz repeated.

Alex looked at each face in turn, hoping some detail might jog his memory – the cut of the hair or the line of the jaw. The trouble was they were standing face on. When he'd seen the woman's profile yesterday, he'd been looking down at the Polo from the high-up passenger seat in the Land Cruiser.

'Can you get them to sit on the floor and face to the left?' he whispered.

Linz nodded. He pushed the button on the microphone again.

'*Bitte, setzen Sie sich auf dem Boden und nach links gucken!*'

333

Reluctantly the women complied, the ones in the miniskirts objecting strongly.

'Now let's see,' Alex breathed. There were only two possibles, numbers four and six. Couldn't be sure about either of them. Both had hair that was almost black, both were heavy in the chest and fat in the thigh. He wrote both numbers on the paper.

'She could be one of these two,' he whispered handing Linz the note.

'But you are not sure?' he checked.

'Impossible. I didn't see her full face in the car.'

Linz grimaced. Without a positive identification they were sunk. The Roches shook their heads, as did Lorna.

'*Danke schön!*' Linz shouted into the box.

He accompanied them back to the main entrance.

'Sorry that wasn't much help,' Alex said. 'The woman's still denying everything, I suppose?'

'Such women are in the habit of telling lies to the police. It is easy for her. But she is frightened, that's for sure. Of Pravic probably. What woman would not be? But without evidence we cannot hold her for long. We will ask her some more questions this evening, then tomorrow she must go free.'

'Which one was she, by the way?'

Linz turned to look at him. He knew he shouldn't answer, but an idea had just come into his head.

'Number four.'

Alex faltered.

'Damn! If only I'd been sure . . .'

'There may be something more you can do . . .' Linz said, stopping just short of the swing doors. He took Alex and Lorna to one side, while the Roches waited. 'I would like to talk with you on the telephone tonight, after I have spoken with Fräulein Pocklewicz. You'll be at the Hotel Sommer? At about eleven o'clock?'

'Certainly.'

They shook hands, then Linz disappeared back into the building.

On the steps outside, the Roches turned to Lorna.

'We have to have a talk,' Irwin told her. 'You and I, we've got some hard thinking to do. We have to decide what's best for the kid, I mean.'

Lorna could see some embarrassment in Roche's eyes, signs of a weakening resolve.

'Beginning to change your minds about Vildana?' she asked bluntly.

'No . . . but we want to know a little better what we're letting ourselves in for,' he explained. 'I mean we have two kids of our own, and we're surely not going to do anything that'll screw up *their* lives.'

'No. No, of course you can't. I understand. But why not wait and see how things pan out in the next few days, huh? Vildana will have to stay in hospital for a while yet.'

'Sure, sure,' Roche concurred. 'Just wanted you to understand where we're coming from.'

Nancy Roche looked pale and awkward.

'Don't get us wrong,' she stressed. 'As I told you in the hospital, she's *my* girl so long as *she* wants it and . . . and as long as my family do too.' She pulled her mouth into a thin smile, but it did nothing to dilute the anguish in her eyes. 'Anyway, I'm going back there now. So's Nataša. We'll stay the night again if she needs us to.'

Lorna gave her a huge hug.

'Don't worry. I understand,' she whispered.

11.05 p.m.
Hotel Sommer

For a long time after making love, Alex and Lorna lay

335

side by side, their bodies just touching. They were conscious of each other's breathing but said nothing, each pre-occupied with their own thoughts. In the background the soft strains of a Mozart piano concerto tinkled from the radio.

Lorna turned on her side, tucking her cheek into the dip of his shoulder and resting her hand on his stomach. It felt so strange lying there with him. Strange, because it was hard not to believe that she had vaulted back in time, wiping out the years of pain and anger.

'You know something, mister?' she said, throatily.

'What's that?' he breathed.

'You're kind of good at this. In fact if there was an Oscar for screwing, you'd get my nomination.'

'Well thank you! You're not bad either . . .'

She gave a little snort of laughter.

'On second thoughts, the nomination depends on you shaving that beard off!'

'There's always a catch . . .'

'Hey, you remember the first time we did it?' she asked meanly. 'On my Mom's carpet?'

'Eighteen and overexcited,' he replied. All over within seconds, as he recalled.

'You were so embarrassed,' she giggled. 'And you remember what we used to talk about in those days?'

'Not really. I was only after your body.'

'Oh sure. You remember all that teenage stuff. Why are we here? The world stinks but you can't change it, so let's drop out, get stoned and watch it all go by? We used to sit out on Hampstead Heath in the moonlight and talk about this life and the afterlife, about God and ghosts. And fate.'

'Fate I remember,' he conceded. 'Your whole life written down beforehand in some doomy book. You still believe that?'

She was silent for a moment.

336

'Maybe. Maybe not. What d'you think's written in Vildana's book?'

'A lot more misery . . .'

'Don't say that. You think the Roches will adopt her?'

He thought about it. The odds were about evens, he reckoned.

'If the police catch Pravic quickly, then it might work out. If he stays on the loose and the Roches have to live with the knowledge that he's out there, then I'm not sure they could handle that.'

The telephone rang, startling them.

'God, what now?' Lorna gulped, picking up the receiver. 'Hullo?'

'Mrs Sorensen?'

She recognized the voice of Kommissar Linz.

'Yes, hi there. You want to speak to Alex?' She suspected the policeman was more comfortable talking to a man. She passed the phone over.

'Good evening, Kommissar,' Alex answered. 'Has the Berlin woman told you anything?'

'Nothing. Nothing. Tomorrow morning at nine I must release her, but I have an idea. Will you help me?'

'Of course, if I can.'

'Then would you and Frau Sorensen be here tomorrow morning? I want *you* to speak to Fräulein Pocklewicz after she leaves. She may talk to you if you say you're not the police. Tell her you recognize her from the car, but won't tell the police if she agrees to help you. Maybe take her to the hospital to see Vildana – she is a woman. Use tricks if you think it will persuade her to reveal to you where Pravic is now.'

'A long shot, isn't it?'

'*Ja*, but it is the only shot we have. Except one. A new photograph. I will show you in the morning. You can be here at eight-thirty?'

'No problem.'

337

'Oh, and by the way, Herr Chadwick in London sends a big hello.'

'Oh yes. Yes, thanks.'

He leaned across Lorna's warm body to replace the phone on its rest.

'What was that all about?' she asked, running her fingers down the hard muscles of his back.

'He's fixed us a date,' he replied. 'With a prostitute.'

3.35 a.m. the same night
Berlin

Karina closed the door to her room in the brothel and locked it. It had been raining all evening. Bad for trade. Only three punters since seven o'clock. Not even enough to pay the rent.

She'd changed from her working clothes into trainers, black ski-pants and a large purple sweater. Out in the street, she held a plastic bag above her head as protection against the downpour and began to run. It wasn't far to the cosy little flat with the large bed that she shared with another girl in the same profession.

Dieter Konrad hardly recognized her through the rain-smeared window of the stolen Audi. But the doll-like hair and the look of her backside as she ran convinced him. He drew alongside, then wound down the passenger window.

'*Fräulein Karina!*' he shouted. She stopped and bent down to peer inside.

'Oh, it's you. What do you want?'

'I want to do business,' he replied, trying to smile.

'What, another sodding passport? Piss off!' She walked on, feeling the cold rain soak through her sweater.

338

Konrad eased the car forward, keeping pace.

'Look, I said no!' she shouted, halting for a second time.

'Not a passport. Business. You know.'

'What? Sex?' she began to laugh. 'You?'

'*Ja!* And this time I won't argue about the price!'

'Switch the light on.' She stuck her head through the window to get a better look at him. 'What are you up to?'

'You know.'

She saw his cheek twitch and mistook it for lust. She remembered he'd been wanting it when he came to the apartment the other day.

'Why didn't you come into the house?' she demanded, shivering as the rain drenched her back.

'I get embarrassed,' he replied glancing down. 'Didn't want that old madame to see me. Anyway, get in out of the rain while we talk about it.'

Karina was wary about cars. If this was someone she'd never seen before, she wouldn't get in. But it was cold, she was getting wetter by the second, he'd said he wouldn't haggle over the price and it had been a slow night.

'Okay, but don't put it into gear.' She got in, leaving the door slightly open. 'All right. So what did you have in mind?'

'Straight sex,' he shrugged awkwardly.

'Not without a condom, and I'm not carrying any around with me.'

'But I have some.' Konrad pulled from his pocket the packet he'd got from a machine in a bar round the corner.

'Oooh, proper little boy scout!' she said, huskily. 'Where then, if you don't want to trick in the apartment?' She glanced over her shoulder. The car was a hatchback. He'd folded the rear seats down and covered the floor space with a yellow tartan blanket. 'Thought of everything, haven't you?'

Now, she decided, let's see whether he's serious about not haggling.

'It'll cost you two hundred,' she announced coldly, opening the door wider as if to get out.

Konrad winced.

'I know I said I won't argue,' he whined, 'but that's taking advantage. And if you're fair with me, I might come back and see you again. It could be good business for you.'

'Are you married?' she asked out of the blue.

'*Ja.*'

'But she doesn't like doing it any more?'

'Menopause, you know?' he answered, turning away from her. He saw two people walking towards them on the opposite side of the road. Better be quick.

'So?' he asked.

'One hundred then. In my hand, now.'

'All right, but close the door. It's cold.'

He slipped the car into gear and drove off, juggling his wallet against the steering wheel. He passed her the 100DM note.

'The Tiergarten, right?' she insisted. There'd be other hookers around there. Safety in numbers.

Konrad headed down Friedrichstraße trying to control the sickness in his stomach, ticking off the preparations he'd made, wondering if he could go through with it when the moment came.

'Have you done this sort of business before, handsome?' Karina asked, resting her hand on his crotch. He brushed her away.

'No. Haven't needed to,' he replied brusquely. There was double meaning in what he'd said.

He turned off Unter den Linden, round the back of the Reichstag, and headed into the broad, tree-lined avenue that crossed the unlit park of the Tiergarten.

One kilometre away, the distant, floodlit erection

commemorating Prussian wars formed a priapic background for the whores at work in the vehicles parked in pools of darkness between the street lamps.

Konrad halted the car in a free space, a hundred metres from the nearest stationary vehicle.

Karina unzipped his trousers and slipped her hand inside.

'You'll have to do better than this,' she smiled, feeling the flaccidity of his organ.

'I think it will be easier if we get in the back,' he explained, removing her hand from his underpants. He took off his jacket, then they opened the doors, turned their backs to the wind and rain, and climbed into the rear.

'Fucking cold out there,' Karina shivered. 'Some poor sods will be out in the bushes.'

She looked at him. He seemed awkward. Perhaps it really was his first time with a whore.

'What now?' she asked, hugging herself. 'You're the customer. You have to say what you want.'

'Take your clothes off, then.'

She pulled down the side zip of her ski-pants, then removed them together with her knickers. She lifted her sweater up under her chin then lay back on the blanket exposing her breasts.

'Take your sweater right off,' Konrad insisted.

'Aw, come on. It's too bloody cold. Get your pants off and let's get on with it.'

Konrad loosened the belt of the trousers and eased down the zip again. Then he half-slid, half-rolled until he lay on top of her.

'Oof,' she gasped as his weight drove the air from her lungs. She reached down with her right hand. He pulled it away again.

'Not just yet,' he said, unable to stop the shake in his voice. 'I like to take my time.'

He stretched her left arm out to the side.

'What's going on?' she asked, as she felt him slip a band over her wrist.

'Don't worry,' he soothed, pressing together the Velcro straps he'd attached to the seat belt mount earlier. 'It's just my little game.'

Suddenly she began to kick. She was a lot shorter than him and powerless under the bulk of his spread-eagled legs.

'No fucking games! Get off me you bastard!' Her left hand jerked and pulled, but the strap held it. 'Help! Help somebody!'

With his right hand Konrad peeled a pre-cut length of adhesive carpet tape from the back of the front seat and slapped it across her mouth. With his left hand he fended off the nails clawing at his eyes.

Using both hands now, he pinioned her right arm with a second Velcro strap, Karina's eyes almost bursting from their sockets. Her lips and tongue pushed and twisted to dislodge the tape muffling her screams. Konrad ripped off the tape, stuffed a ball of paper into her mouth, shoved a hand under her chin and slapped the tape back in place.

Karina's head shook in a frenzy, her panicky breath sawing through flared nostrils. Then, with a fresh length of tape he pinched them closed.

'I'm sorry,' Konrad whispered, his fingers feeling on each side of her neck for the throb of the carotid artery. Sensing the pulse through his thumbs, he pressed with all his strength.

'Believe me, I did not want this . . .' he added through clenched teeth.

Her nut-brown eyes stayed locked on his until her lids began to flicker and she blacked out. Slowly her face turned a purpley blue.

Twenty-five

Tuesday 5th April, 7.20 a.m.
London–Heathrow Airport

The BA 214 from Boston landed ahead of schedule.
Chauffeurs and minicab drivers on the early shift hovered outside the arrivals hall holding name cards.
Amongst them was a short man with a florid complexion,
wearing a grey suit, white shirt and dark, nondescript tie.

Inside the hall, Liam Doyle carried his shoulder bag
through immigration and customs in a daze. He'd done
the sensible thing on the flight across the Atlantic,
turning down all offers of alcohol, but despite that he had
a thick head this morning and eyeballs that felt as if
they'd been smeared with Vaseline. He wore a light
trench coat over a midweight, brown suit. His curly, grey
hair was brushed across the top of his head to cover a
bald patch.

Things had happened so fast yesterday afternoon,
he'd hardly had time to think. The letter delivered to the
Committee office by the older Donohue sister, the phone
call to Belfast to tell them about the photograph, and the
plea from Nolan that it be brought across overnight by
hand.

He emerged from the baggage hall and followed other
passengers past the waiting faces. Then he paused to
read the name boards held by the drivers.

'That's me,' he announced, approaching the short
man with the florid face.

'Mr Doyle of Emerald Finance?' His accent was from
south of Dublin.

'That's right.'

The driver offered to take his bag, but Doyle refused. They walked to the car park and were soon on their way round the perimeter road to the north side of the airport.

'It's another hour before your man gets in from Belfast,' the driver explained. 'I'll bring him to you at the hotel.'

'I guess that gives me time for a shower,' Doyle remarked in his softly sterile New England voice.

The Post House was one of the older Heathrow Hotels. Not as plush as some, but cheaper than most and reassuringly anonymous. The driver hovered by the desk while Doyle checked in, waiting to learn his room number.

'Nine-two-three,' the man from Boston announced. 'You'll bring him straight up?'

'Just as soon as his plane lands.'

The Belfast flight was twenty minutes late, due to a glitch in the security checks when they were loading the luggage.

Tommy Nolan felt as tense as a brick, but forced his face to relax as they filed past the Special Branch men who watched all arrivals from Ulster. He avoided eye contact and passed without trouble.

Deadly job. The Met bastards couldn't hope to remember any but the most current of mugshots.

Nolan's involvement with the Provos had declined since the 1970s when he'd been a company commander in the Whiterock area of Belfast. The breakup of the structure into cells had left him on the sidelines.

Nolan wore a dull, tweed jacket and baggy, bottle-green cords. He had crinkly, black hair which always looked greasy, and a broad, stress-worn face with watery brown eyes that made him look older than his forty-four years.

By day he drove a taxi, by night he hogged a seat in Dunphy's Bar, talking about the old days. Talking too, often as not, about his younger brother Kieran, shot dead by the RUC during the failed Long Kesh jail break in 1973. More than twenty years ago, but after a few jars it still felt like yesterday.

In Republican Belfast, Tommy Nolan was known as the man who'd pledged to 'top' the tout who'd put his kid brother in Milltown cemetery, but in twenty years had failed to find him.

Last night's transatlantic phone call had been pure adrenalin. The man he'd sworn to kill had finally broken cover. Just in the nick of time before they called an end to hostilities.

The man in the chauffeur's grey suit had no need of a name card this time. Nolan was his cousin.

At the Post House Hotel, Nolan went alone to Doyle's room. Had to hammer at the door because the American had fallen asleep.

'You Tommy?' Doyle asked bleary-eyed, opening it on the chain.

'That's right.' Nolan replied in his tortured Belfast brogue.

'Sorry, sorry,' Doyle yawned. He slipped the chain and pulled the door wide. 'I guess I just passed out. I'm flying back this afternoon, so I'm staying with Boston time. And according to my brain, that means I should still be asleep.'

Nolan's head hurt from the Bushmills he'd drunk to steady his nerves last night. He didn't want conversation, just the picture.

'This is the shot,' Doyle announced, handing him the photograph taken on Lorna's Nikon. 'Pretty good, huh?'

Tommy Nolan held it in his shaking hands. Hard to reconcile this middle-aged, bearded figure with the lanky twenty-eight-year-old whose picture he'd kept in the tin box under his bed.

'Is that *her* with him?' he growled.

'It certainly is. But she wasn't involved, right? *She* was betrayed by him just as much as you were.'

'So what's she doin' with him here then?' he demanded, smacking the print with the back of his right hand.

'Posing for a picture, that's all. *She* was the one who sent it to us, don't forget . . . Just like she did with the last photo, the one from 1973. She's not to be touched, okay?'

Nolan reined in his feelings. He'd always reckoned the Donohue woman just as much to blame for his brother's death as the man Jarvis.

'And this was in Bosnia, you said?' Nolan asked. 'There's no ways I'd go *there* to look for him.'

'You don't have to. As I told you yesterday, he's in Frankfurt, Germany. Annie Donohue made some check calls with Lorna's office. The guy's been leaving messages for her. Here's the name of his hotel and the phone number.'

He handed Nolan a page from a notebook.

'Can't say for sure he's still there, but you can easily check.'

Nolan felt a nervous bubbling in his guts. The trail that chilled so many years ago was hot again. The blood throbbed painfully in his temples.

Half-an-hour later, the Irish driver parked outside a terraced house in the West London district of Chiswick and rang the doorbell of a ground floor flat. A man in his mid-twenties with dark hair and designer stubble let them in. The driver made the introductions.

'Michael McCarthy – Tommy Nolan.'

'Hello.'

'Are youse Michael or Mickey?' Nolan asked matily.

346

He wasn't at ease with the new generation of hard young men who ran the operation on the mainland.

'Michael's my name,' McCarthy replied coldly. He led them into a cluttered back room adjoining the kitchen.

'A quick cup of tea, Michael, and I'll be out of your hair,' the driver muttered, gravitating towards the stove.

'Fix it for all of us, will you?' McCarthy pulled chairs from under a dining table that had been picked up cheap at an auction.

'We'll talk the business after he's gone,' he whispered, jerking a thumb towards the kitchen. 'How was your flight? No bother?'

'Och, none at all.' Nolan looked round the room. A clothes airer propped against the radiator had a woman's underwear hung out to dry. 'Nice place. Youse got a wife, then?'

The younger man looked away and ground his teeth. They'd no idea of security these old boys. Didn't understand the rules of war.

'Listen Tommy, all you need to know about me is my name. Right?'

Nolan felt bruised. Just trying to be friendly. He shrugged.

'As you like.'

They sat in silence until the tea came. Then for the five minutes it took the driver to drink it, they nattered about horse racing and football.

When the latch closed behind him and they'd heard the car rev away, Nolan pulled the photograph of Alex from his jacket pocket. McCarthy gave it a cursory glance, then spread open a road atlas of Europe.

347

Frankfurt
8.30 a.m.

Kommissar Linz looked as if he'd slept little, his top shirt button undone and his bow tie crooked. Lorna wanted to straighten it, but restrained herself. He'd taken them to an interview room on the ground floor of the police headquarters.

'At nine o'clock, Fräulein Pocklewicz will walk out of here,' he explained edgily. 'I will come to the door with her. Then it is up to you. We have given her a train ticket to Berlin. She may go direct to the station, so you have not much time.'

'And she's still admitting nothing?' Alex queried.

'She has not said one word since yesterday afternoon.'

'Then I doubt she'll speak to us.'

Linz opened a folder, preoccupied. 'Does this picture help?' he asked. He produced a computer print of two identical faces, one wearing spectacles, the other not.

'That's him!' Alex exclaimed. 'Without the glasses.' The cold, hard eyes left him in no doubt. 'He's the man who shot Vildana. This is Pravic? Where did the picture come from?'

'The United Nations, so they tell me.' Linz looked sceptical. 'Our computer experts removed his spectacles for him.'

'But where was it taken?'

'They will not say. But . . . but I can tell you that since last night the interest in Herr Pravic has grown,' he added enigmatically.

'Really? Why?'

'New information. From the intelligence agencies. They think he will try to attack Muslims in Germany . . . maybe with some chemical weapon,' he explained vaguely.

'*What*? Bloody hell!'

'*Ja*. It is not easy to believe. But this morning I must go to München.'

'He's been seen there or what?'

'No. But tomorrow one thousand Muslim Fundamentalists meet in that city. It could be the perfect target for him. Now I must show Fräulein Pocklewicz to the door. I give you my mobile number to call if she tells you something.'

He handed Alex a card.

Rain was pelting down outside on the broad pavement. Alex wore his Barbour and tweed cap, Lorna the anorak she'd used in Bosnia. They looked like hillwalkers who'd wandered into the city by mistake.

'This is crazy,' Lorna complained, as the rain soaked her sneakers. 'She'll tell us to get lost.'

Linz appeared at the door of the monolithic police station. Alex recognized the woman from the identity parade. Linz reached out his hand, but she turned her back on him.

'What are you going to say to her?' Lorna hissed.

'Whatever I can find the words for, in German ...' Alex muttered.

As Gisela tottered away on her high heels, shoulders hunched against the rain, Alex fell in beside her, Lorna at his shoulder.

'*Fräulein Pocklewicz?*' he began, touching her on the elbow. '*Ein Moment, bitte! Darf Ich mit Ihnen sprechen?*'

She stopped, startled.

'Now what?' She looked them up and down. 'The Kommissar's let me go.'

'Ah, but we're not the police,' Alex explained in German. 'You know Vildana? The girl who was shot? We are the people who got her out of Bosnia. We thought we were bringing her to safety, then this happened. The thing is, we're scared that Milan, your friend, will try again to kill her.'

'I don't know anyone called Milan,' she replied doggedly. She pulled her arm free. 'Piss off.'

She stomped away, terror growing. Too many people after her. Pravic, the police – and worst of all, Dunkel. She'd heard that a man of his description had hung around her house most of Sunday. And now these two weirdos, clinging like leeches.

'Look I know you were there . . . I saw you,' Alex snapped. 'You were sitting in the car, down the road from the house. Before the shooting.' He spat out the words in chunks ignoring the complexities of grammar. 'You had those earrings on.'

It was a guess, but he seemed to recollect the Indian-looking bangles. With luck she wouldn't remember anyway.

She faltered, putting a hand to her ear, then marched on again.

'Don't know what you're on about,' she muttered, looking round for a taxi.

'You want the girl to be killed?' Alex shouted.

Gisela ignored him.

'That's what'll happen unless Milan is stopped.' He got her by the arm again. 'You may be the only person who can save her life, do you know that?'

'Fuck off! I can't even save my own life, let alone anybody else's.'

She looked petrified, vulnerable.

'Is that it? You're scared he'll kill you if you talk?'

She didn't answer.

'Don't you see? If you help us get him locked up, you'll be safe.'

'Look, do something useful, will you?' she answered eventually. 'Tell me where the sodding station is.' They'd reached a crossroads, that was devoid of signposts.

'We'll take you there. In a taxi,' Alex answered.

Lorna had understood nothing except that the woman wasn't co-operating.

'We need a cab, quick,' Alex muttered to her out of the side of his mouth.

'Look, I've told you . . .'

Lorna hailed a cream Mercedes and it pulled into the kerb.

Alex put his arm round Gisela's shoulders. He could see her resolve was weakening.

'Come on. You're soaked.'

The rain had turned her hair into a mop of black string. Grudgingly she let herself be nudged into the car.

'Zum Hauptbahnhof, bitte!'

They slid onto the back seat, the hooker wedged in the middle.

'Who *are* you?' she demanded.

'As I said, we were in Bosnia,' he whispered, suspecting the driver might be Yugoslav. 'I met Milan's brother there. He is a priest, did you know that?'

'He never talked about his family . . .'

Progress. At least she was admitting she knew him.

'You remember the Tulici massacre?'

Oh yes, she remembered. And how Pravic had used Tulici as an excuse for shooting the girl. She nodded.

'Milan did it. Killed all those women and kids. That's what his brother thinks. The UN wants to put him on trial. You know that? We work for the UN . . .' Alex added quickly. 'Not for the police, you understand. Whatever you tell us, we won't pass it on to the police, I promise.'

He saw her suck her lower lip to stop it trembling.

'But I don't know where he is . . .' she said plaintively.

'Okay, but we'll talk, yes? At the station. A cup of coffee?'

'Na, wenn Sie wollen,' she shrugged.

Alex nodded to Lorna. They were getting somewhere.

Three minutes later the taxi pulled up by the main entrance. They'd been almost within walking distance.

They sat on high stools, their coffee cups perched on a

351

little shelf. Gisela's hands shook. Normally she carried speed in her bag, but she'd dumped the tablets down the toilet when the police came for her yesterday morning.

'Where did you last see him?' Alex asked.

She held the cup of sour liquid in both hands and sipped. Her head was like spaghetti. Couldn't think straight any more.

'Frankfurt Airport,' she replied. 'He could be anywhere by now. Maybe back in Bosnia even.'

'Did he say anything about wanting to . . . to kill more Muslims?' he probed.

'He's at war with them. That's what he said. Even here in Germany.'

Alex translated this to Lorna.

'So Kommissar Linz may be right about Munich!' she exclaimed in dismay.

Alex wasn't so sure. There was something about the effort Pravic had made to find Vildana . . . The man must be *obsessed* with the need to kill her. A fixation that would still be there, once he realized the girl wasn't dead.

He turned back to Gisela. 'By now, Milan must know that Vildana's still alive,' he suggested in German. 'What do you think he'll do about it?'

In her mind, Gisela heard the shots again, felt the back-blast, remembered the certainty that he would kill her too if his survival depended on it.

'He won't forget her. He'll be back for the girl, wherever she is,' she said chillingly.

'So we've got to stop him, right?' Alex implored. 'You *must* help us.'

'But what can I do?' she snivelled. 'I tell you I don't know where he is!'

'No. Okay. I understand.' Then he remembered what Linz had said. 'Tell me, does Milan just have the gun, or . . . or something else perhaps? Some chemical, *poison* maybe?'

Poison? The word shot through her like a glass-sliver. Her pencilled eyebrows bunched in consternation.

Last night in the isolation of the detention cell, kept awake by the wailings of drunks, dark, disjointed thoughts had marshalled in her mind, linked by some invisible thread. The thoughts were to do with Dunkel, with the Stasi, with Leipzig, with Zagreb and with what she'd read in the papers about the scientist Kemmer who'd killed himself.

'What d'you mean, poison?' she queried.

'I don't know. Something that could kill hundreds of people at once.'

The spectre in Gisela's mind took on flesh.

'Why? Why do you ask about that?' she asked querulously.

Alex hesitated. Had Linz told him about it in confidence? Too late now.

'The police think Milan has some biological weapon and he'll use it in Munich. There's a big meeting of Muslims there tomorrow. *Fundamentalists*.' He said the last word in English, not knowing the German.

Gisela stared at the wall. The thread in her head tugged itself from the tangle and formed into a word.

'*Milzbrand!*'

'What?' Alex gaped.

'What's she saying for God's sake?' Lorna nudged. 'Can't you translate?'

'Anthrax! She's talking about anthrax,' he whispered. 'You remember the story in the paper yesterday?'

He turned to Gisela again, incredulous. 'Pravic? He has something to do with that anthrax business?'

Gisela nodded dumbly, then corrected herself by shaking her head.

'I don't know. But I think it's possible.'

'How? What's the link between him and the Leipzig man?'

She turned her head to face him.

'Herr Dunkel – he's the link. Don't know his real name, but he came to see me two weeks ago. I've known him many years. Used to be Stasi. Used to pay me to find people who would steal things, people who would kill, if the money was right. This time he asked me to find Milan. Needed him for some job in Zagreb; wouldn't tell me what. When he came again a few days later, he'd driven up to Berlin from Leipzig.' Gisela covered her mouth with a hand. 'I shouldn't be telling you this.'

'Go on. I won't tell the police – unless you want me to.'

'The papers say the man in Leipzig was forced to make anthrax for some old Stasi people . . . Dunkel was Stasi. Last week he met Milan in Zagreb. Now the papers say there's a girl dying from anthrax there.'

Gisela shivered with fear. Dunkel had fouled up, that was clear. Now he wanted to silence anyone who could give him away. That's why he'd been looking for her on Sunday.

'What's she saying for Christ's sake?' Lorna demanded.

Alex translated.

'But anthrax is lethal!' she exclaimed. 'It's the stuff they thought Saddam Hussein would use in the Gulf War!'

'And it's what Linz must have been talking about.' He turned back to the hooker. 'Milan never said anything about anthrax?'

Gisela snorted.

'He told me nothing. When he got to Berlin, he was crazy. Not like when I knew him before. Just wanting to kill.'

'But my God! With anthrax he could kill a thousand people at once! A thousand Muslims. Gisela, you've *got* to tell this to the police.'

She shuddered.

'You don't understand. Look, these people have long memories and long arms. I'll never be safe if I grass.'

Alex rubbed his eyes.

'So, let's just go back over this.' Had to get his mind straight. 'If you're right about the anthrax, then that Muslim rally in Munich is the sort of target Pravic would go for, yes?'

'How should I know?' she shrugged. 'Maybe if it was to do with Tulici . . .'

'Why do you say that?' he growled.

'Tulici's what matters to Milan. He seems possessed by what he did there, don't know why. It's almost as if he was *relieved* by all the killings he'd done.'

'And . . .?' Alex sensed some fog beginning to clear.

'I'm saying the idea of killing the girl made him crazy. Like as if her death was the final bit of something. Something he can't be free of until she's dead.'

Agitated, Alex grabbed Lorna's arm. 'Vildana . . . She thinks he'll go for Vildana again.'

'But surely she'll be safe in the hospital with the police there . .'

He nodded. Then a cold hand gripped him. *Safe?* What were they saying? A gunman might be stopped by police barriers, but bacteria wouldn't!

'Lorna . . .'

'I know. I just thought of it too.'

Alex touched Gisela's still damp shoulder. 'We must go to the hospital. You'll come with us?'

'What hospital?' She stared at him wide-eyed.

'The Universitätsklinik at Sembach on the south side of Frankfurt.'

She gasped.

'It's a new hospital, yes? Maybe three years old?'

'Could be. Why?'

The blood drained from her face.

'That was his last job. Before he went back to Bosnia to fight. Milan helped install the ventilation in that place!'

Alex pounded through the entrance lobby and hammered on the 'up' button of the elevator, Lorna a few seconds behind. No police in sight, and only one of their vans parked outside. Had the lawmen stopped worrying about the hospital because of Munich?

Gisela had refused to come. If Pravic *was* here, and he saw her, she'd be dead.

'Come on, come on!' Alex thundered at the slowness of the lift.

'Let's take the stairs,' Lorna suggested.

'Maybe . . . hang on though. Here it is.'

The doors closed behind them.

'There must be a thousand people in this hospital,' Alex panted. 'Patients, staff, visitors. My God, it's terrifying. He could be pumping the stuff in this very minute.' He glanced up nervously at the ventilation grill on the roof of the lift.

'Shouldn't we call Linz? You've got his mobile number,' she said.

'Better to talk to the police here first.'

On the fourth floor they pelted down the corridor towards ward F. As they approached Vildana's room, a green-uniformed officer got up from a chair, unbuttoning the flap of his pistol holster.

Alex slowed to a walk. A different face from yesterday, young, suspicious, hostile.

He explained first who they were, then mentioned Kommissar Linz, Pravic and anthrax in a jumble of semi-comprehensible German.

A second officer emerged from the room. These men were sentries, unversed in the complexities of the case. They stared at Alex as if he'd landed from Mars.

'Who did you say you are?' one of them asked.

'The name's Crawford. We rescued her from Bosnia, the girl in there. Colonel Roche . . . is his wife here? She'll tell you who we are.'

He made to push open the door, but his way was barred.

'Your I.D. please . . .'

'Look, for heavens' sake, this is terribly urgent. You must search the hospital!'

The second officer held up a radio and mouthed into it, while the first studied Alex's passport.

'Kommissar Linz knows me. He knows what I'm talking about,' Alex insisted. 'Can you call him on that radio?'

'Linz? Linz?' They shook their heads.

'From Wiesbaden. The Bundeskriminalamt.'

'Ah. We are from Hessen. We have no connection.'

'The card!' Lorna whispered. 'In your pocket.'

Alex pulled it out. 'This is the number of his mobile. He's on the way to Munich.'

'Yes, but for a telephone you must go downstairs. In the main entrance.'

Alex grabbed Lorna's arm and hustled her back to the lift.

'I don't *believe* this,' he hissed. 'Whatever happened to ruthless German efficiency?'

'Come on, they're only rookies,' Lorna soothed. 'Call Linz, then we'll talk to the administrator.'

Downstairs they discovered the phones took cards, not cash. Lorna scuttled to the newspaper stand to buy one.

After a minute she came running back.

'We can only buy cards at a post office!' she howled.

'Come on!' He led her towards the reception desk.

Just then two more policemen marched through the revolving doors. He guessed the officers on the fourth floor had become suspicious and called them in to see what he was up to.

Alex stopped in his tracks.

'Time to split up,' he breathed. 'Get hold of the administrator. Tell him what's happening. Use the phone to call Linz. Get the official wheels moving.'

357

'And you?' Lorna asked.

'I'm going to look for Pravic!'

'For God's sake be careful!'

He turned her towards the rapidly approaching policemen, then slipped through a doorway to the emergency stairs.

'Excuse me,' Lorna shouted, blocking the path of the officers, 'do either of you gentlemen speak English?'

Alex ran up two floors, then entered a wide corridor identical to the level where Vildana lay. A strong smell of disinfectant. He walked briskly to the far end. More stairs. He was aiming for the roof. No clear plan, but that's where the air-conditioning must be.

Crazy to be searching for Pravic on his own. What would he do if he found him?

He reached the top floor, then a spur of stairs took him to a fire exit on the roof. A push on the bar and he was out onto flat asphalt, edged with a low wall.

He was at one end of the hospital now. Looking back towards the middle of the building he saw a square brick construction that he guessed must house the winding gear for the lifts. Next to it were the ventilation fans.

His heart pounded from the exertion of running up the stairs – and with fear. He stood there bemused, half expecting to see the killer doing something with the machinery, though he had no idea what.

Anthrax. Was it a liquid? A gas? A box full of microbes? He'd assumed it would have to be fed into the air supply, but he didn't *know*. Guessing. In the same way he was guessing Pravic would be here and not Munich.

Overhead a 747 climbed noisily out of Rhein-Main, heading east. From somewhere below, the siren of an arriving ambulance. Alex felt ridiculous suddenly. Here he was playing the sleuth without even the humblest qualification for the job.

'It's only in the movies that they end with a roof chase . . .' he reminded himself.

Now what? Better check since he was here. Awkwardly, feeling as if some hidden eye were watching him, he began to walk towards the fans.

He felt absurdly exposed. If Pravic *was* here, and he still had his gun, there'd be nowhere to hide.

The technical manager at the Universitätsklinik Sembach had his office on the ground floor. It was an untidy room cluttered with filing cabinets, and on the wall behind his desk was a board from which hung the keys to all the maintenance spaces in the building.

He stared quizzically at the man hovering near the door, whose blue overalls were so crisp they could have been bought that morning. The surprise visitor carried a toolbag, seemed to be sweating a lot, and had just announced that he'd come to test the fire dampers.

Milan Pravic had never been good at bluff, but this time it *had* to work. The last thing he wanted was to have to use the gun and alert the whole place to his presence. The man behind the desk was the same technician who'd organized the handover when the constructors finished building the hospital twenty-six months before.

The manager tapped a pen on the desk. He'd not been expecting this visit, but it was perfectly normal to have random checks on the system that closed the ventilation in the event of a fire. And even though the man claimed to have left his I.D. card at home, he distinctly remembered his face.

He plucked a bunch of keys from the panel behind him and held them out. Pravic grabbed them, grunted his thanks, then walked briskly back to the main entrance lobby.

Lucky so far.

Now he had to find the girl. The TV and the papers

hadn't revealed which ward she was in, and it wasn't a question he could easily ask.

Using the main stairs by the lift lobby, he ascended floor by floor, peering into each main corridor looking for signs. On the fourth he found them. Two policemen, chatting. Outside a ward.

His neck prickled at the thought of being so close, the same way it had in Pfefferheim. She was the last. The end of the line. With Vildana Muminovic dead, Tulici could breed no more monsters to torment him.

His nights were still haunted by his childhood terror of that place. Living half a kilometre away on the same side of the valley, he'd walked through Tulici every day to reach his school. An undersized runt of a boy, a misfit even amongst his own, he'd been picked on by the youngsters there. Frail for a teenager, he'd been mocked for his weediness and skulking ways. Once, three boys and three girls had taken him to a cow barn, stripped him, rolled his hairless body in slurry, mocked his immature genitalia and urinated on his face.

One final score to settle and Tulici would have paid the price.

The chief administrator of the Universitätsklinik was in his thirties, chubby-faced, wearing a shiny, grey suit and spectacles with fashionable, bright-red frames. He listened to Lorna with an expression of growing disbelief. One of the police officers stood watchfully by the door.

'My English is not so good,' he responded when she'd finished. 'You tell me the name Kommissar Linz. He I know. So you telephone him, and then I will speak.' He pushed a phone across the desk.

'Good,' Lorna sighed. Sense at last.

She dialled the number. Linz replied within seconds from his car on the autobahn heading south. Lorna talked for two minutes, listened for less, then handed the phone back to the man with red spectacles.

Linz had heard her story without comment. He'd told her he would call the Hessen police for reinforcements and head for the hospital himself. Lorna almost wept that he'd taken her so seriously.

The administrator's cheeks seemed to sag as he listened to Linz's voice. He pulled off his glasses and wiped sweat from his eyes with a handkerchief.

'*Ja, ist gut, Herr Kommissar. Machen wir.*' He put the phone down. 'He say we must search the hospital,' he explained.

The policeman by the door told him they'd have a hard job, with only four officers on duty. The administrator scratched his head, grabbed the phone again and dialled an internal number.

'*Könnten Sie bitte sofort hierherkommen?*' he asked. He listened for the acknowledgement, then replaced the receiver. 'The technical manager,' he explained sombrely. 'He will come.'

He flopped back in his chair and puffed out his cheeks. His carefully brushed hair looked ruffled.

'This cannot be true,' he gabbled. 'I have three-hundred-and-eighty ill peoples here.'

Up on the roof, Alex stepped warily behind the whirring fans. Nobody here and no sign of anything being tampered with. Daft. He'd been jumping to conclusions. The *wrong* ones. He began to suspect Pravic was miles away.

Hang on . . . If fresh air was sucked in here it had to be pumped to the wards through ducts, which probably passed into the building via the lift shaft, judging by the location of the fans. Better head down again. There was more to check if he was to be sure.

A fire door identical to the one at the far end of the

roof opened when he pulled it. Back on the main staircase, he descended to the fourth floor. Vildana's floor.

He emerged into the lift lobby, from which the ward corridors stretched in two directions. Beside him were the double doors of the elevators. His eye was caught momentarily by a maintenance man in blue overalls opening what looked like a broom cupboard on the far side of the lobby. At his feet was a tool bag. Alex looked away, stepping forward to see along the corridor to ward 4F. Still there, the two policemen. Looking bored.

Maintenance man? Jesus! He was a couple of steps from the cupboard. The man had opened the door and was disappearing into it.

Couldn't be Pravic, though. This man had dark hair.

Then the man turned to check no one was watching . . .

Their eyes met, this time. And locked. The killer's eyes. Fear washed over him, such as he'd never felt before.

The cold, pale eyes of the Scorpion.

Pravic froze. The face opposite was familiar. Dangerously so. Images of the Pfefferheim pavement forty-eight hours before. A man with a beard, running after the car. He recognized him.

In a second he propelled himself from the doorway, just as Alex turned to shout the alarm, jerked the pistol from his overalls and pressed its barrel into Alex's chest, throwing a hand over his mouth.

'*Komm mit!*' he growled, wrestling him towards the maintenance room. Alex struggled, but a sharp prod from the barrel quietened him. Pravic shoved him inside, followed, then pulled the door shut.

'*Du sags nix, Du machs nix!*' The voice hoarse, the gun barrel jabbing. He pointed to the ground and told him to sit.

Pravic stared hard at the hunched figure on the floor,

as if the intensity of his look might penetrate the man's mind. *Who* was he? *Why* was he here? Was he the man who had adopted the girl?

What to do with him, that was the question ... Couldn't let him live. But a gunshot would give him away ... Best to beat his head to pulp, maybe. He turned the pistol in his hand ...

Alex felt the bare concrete cold beneath his backside, his heart thudding, his head slumped. *Avoid eye contact.* The words a mantra, like at the ambush in the canyon. Nothing else to cling to. But he sensed Pravic's intentions, cringed in anticipation of the blow.

He waited. Then he inched his stare up from the floor. Saw the grubby black combat boots beneath the blue trouser legs. Took in the tight confines of the maintenance space, two metres wide and a metre deep. Blinked in the glare from the bare bulb in the ceiling.

Pravic relented. There'd be noise if he beat the man. He'd keep him cowed. Less of a risk.

He transferred the gun to his left hand, backing away as far as space would allow. No time to lose. He reached into his bag and grabbed a rechargeable electric drill. Had to press on. Nothing, *nothing* must prevent him from doing what he had to do.

Behind him a square sheet-metal duct passed from ceiling to floor – the down pipe from the fans on the roof. High up, an extension branched at right-angles – the air supply to the wards.

Alex saw the black power tool. For a moment he thought Pravic was going to use it on him, to puncture his brain. In the tight, claustrophobic box, with the ventilation roaring in the ducts, his mind and his guts turned to treacle.

Had to do *something*. Not just his own life at stake. Hundreds would die if the madman wasn't stopped.

Run for help? No chance. Pravic would cut him down. Grab the gun? Crazy even to think of it.

Pravic kicked against a stack of bricks cemented to the floor as a mounting block. Still with an eye on Alex, he stepped up to reach the high, horizontal duct. He glanced away just long enough to locate the drill bit against the panel, then began to cut a hole in its side.

His ears just centimetres from the air pipes, the noise thundered like the fire that had scorched through the homes of his tormentors in Tulici three weeks ago. At the time of the attack, he'd imagined those flames, the executions and the bitter-sweet defilement of the young woman would be enough to erase the taunting memories, and stop the mocking voices in his head. But it hadn't been. Silencing them needed one last act.

The hole finished, he stuffed the drill back in the bag, then reached further in, feeling for soft rubber.

Alex saw the gas mask and gulped. An object turned by history into the definitive badge of evil. The moment had come. Pravic was about to commit a monstrous, silent massacre – unless Alex could stop him.

'*Mach's nicht!*' he croaked, lamely. 'Don't do it. Think of all the innocent . . .'

'*Halt's Maul!*' Pravic snapped, pulling the mask over his head.

Alex looked into the goggled eyes, watched Pravic crouch by the bag. Saw the paint-sprayer – and the deadly brown liquid that swirled inside its clear, plastic reservoir.

He held his breath, as if the very nearness of the anthrax spores meant death. He had to stop him. *Had* to! He tensed his legs.

Pravic stood up, his overalls glued to his sweaty back. He remounted the bricks and aligned the sprayer with the hole. Alex's movement caught his eye. He clicked back the pistol hammer. If it was the only way to ensure he could complete his task, he'd shoot.

Then suddenly, with a moan like an exhausted beast,

the ventilator fans died. Silence, total silence that rang in their ears.

Pravic remained on the mounting block, frozen in disbelief, finger on the trigger of the spray, its nozzle pressed to the useless duct.

Then he cursed, long and low, the guttural Serbo-Croat muffled by the rubber of the mask.

With the fans safely shut down, the technical manager led the two nervous policemen to the fourth floor. He knew exactly where Pravic would have gone.

A radio check had revealed that the Landespolizei reinforcements were still five minutes away, but they couldn't wait for them.

He'd identified Pravic from the photo they'd shown him. Pity he hadn't seen it earlier. Nobody had thought to tell him there was a maniac on the loose.

Lorna shivered uncontrollably now she *knew* the killer was in the building. Pravic was up there somewhere – and so was Alex.

The police cluck-clucked when she told them about him. Interfering civilians. A foreigner at that.

They asked her to wait with the administrator in his office. She gave them a minute's head start. Then, making the excuse of needing the toilet, she rushed from the room and headed for the stairs.

The technician and the two policemen were silent with fear as the elevator carried them to the fourth floor.

The doors slid open. Two figures crossing the lobby, heading forward F. Pravic pushing Alex in front of him, the gun at his back.

A nod from the manager. The police drew their guns.

Alex heard the clunk of the lift doors but dared not turn to look. His hands were bound behind his back with adhesive tape. Pravic was a hair's breadth behind him. And the pistol bruised his ribs.

'*Halt!*' A policeman's shout. The hollow bark of a man whose only authority was his uniform.

Pravic hooked an arm around Alex's neck, and spun him as a shield towards the voice, levelled his automatic and fired. One policeman buckled, clutching his chest. The other stumbled back into the lift where the hospital technician had already sought cover.

Alex strained against the choking arm, ears whistling. The shot shook him, hammered home the danger he was in. Pravic jerked him sideways into the ward F corridor. Police outside the ward. Police in the lift lobby. More on the way. They'd *never* let this madman through. They'd gun him down for sure. Shoot them both if they had to . . .

He heard rough shouts – warnings to staff to stay in their wards.

Milan Pravic stared left and right. Out of sight of the lobby, now. There'd been two police in the corridor. Gone. Ducked into doorways. A gun, an arm and half a face was all he saw of either of them. His heart thumped.

He knew he was cornered. But not finished. He had the gun. He had his shield. And above all, he had his *need*.

His ears still rang from the crack of the shot. In his head the ringing turned to voices, girls' voices from inside ward F. Had to get in there to stop them. To silence their derision. There must be no more snickering from Tulici, ever again.

Lorna panted up the last flight and pushed open the

glass-panelled door to the fourth floor. She'd heard the shot, feared the worst. Hand to her mouth, she saw the sprawled policeman, gasped at the pool of red spreading from his chest.

Footsteps on the stairs behind her. A nurse pushed past and ripped open a sterile dressing to press on the policeman's wound.

'Alex?' Lorna called. Half shout, half whisper. Bewildered.

Hearing her, the technical manager rushed from the lift, and hustled her back to the stairs. She twisted from his grip. He gave up, scrambling through the doors to save himself.

The second policeman growled into his radio, ignoring her. He checked his wounded colleague was in good hands, then edged up to the corner of the corridor, gun arm extended.

Lorna took in the scene and understood. Pravic must be metres away. Down the corridor which led to Vildana's ward. And for the police to be so cautious, there must be someone with him . . .

Alex.

Full of dread, she stepped round the nurse and the body on the floor. Heedless of the risk, she edged forward.

She glimpsed Pravic. Saw his arm tight under the chin of a hostage. Saw who the hostage was. Saw the gun at his temple . . .

'Ale . . .' she screamed. The cry died in her throat as the policeman barged her back out of sight.

'*Zurück! Sind Sie verrückt?*' he hissed, shoving her through the doors to the stairs, then returning to his watch.

Alex felt the gun hot against his jawbone.

He'd caught a glimpse of Lorna. Why had they let her through?

She mustn't see him die. Mind spinning. Stupid thoughts suddenly important. The end. For him the pain might be quick. For her it would linger.

In his ear, the Bosnian's breath in jerky spasms. He sensed Pravic's nerve go.

'Drop the guns or I kill him!' Pravic screamed. Fear in his voice. No wish to be a martyr.

Me neither, Alex thought.

Inside ward F, Vildana stared at the door, transfixed by the shout in the corridor outside. The same voice she'd heard on that day of death, cowering in her hidey-hole behind a cupboard. The shouts, the laughter, the gurgle of the madman who'd ripped open her mother's belly with a hunting knife branded on her memory. The Scorpion. He had come for her, like she always knew he would.

Nancy Roche kneeled on the floor beside Vildana's bed, clutching the girl's hand. Two other children in the ward, both crying. Between the metal bed legs Nancy watched the police officer braced by the door, his right arm extended into the corridor. At that moment she trusted his invincibility in the way a child trusts its father. Had to.

But if he failed? If the crazy Bosnian blazed his way into the ward? What if *she* was the last barrier between Vildana and death? Would she sacrifice her own life if she had to? Would Irwin want that? Scott and Ella?

She sank closer to the floor, checking how much room there was under the bed.

The young policeman pressed his forehead to the door jamb, eye in line with the Heckler und Koch that had become an extension of his arm. Poised to kill a man for the first time in his life. He remembered the certificate on the bedroom wall at home. Top of his year for marksmanship. But paper targets were different from an armed man.

He saw the gunman edge closer, his back to the corridor wall, hugging the Englishman like a security blanket. A clear sight of Pravic's head, for just two seconds, that's all he wanted. All it would take to snuff him out, to pop the balloon with a bullet, just like the display shoots on open day at the police college.

Alex heard his own breath rasp, felt the tape sear his wrists as he struggled to loosen his hands. Could be dead within seconds unless he did something. Powerless though. Tipped back on his heels. Unable to use weight and strength.

Just needed one chance. One chink of an opportunity . . .

A moment's glance from the police marksman to his companion in the doorway opposite. A nod of agreement. Beyond Pravic at the corner to the lift lobby he saw that the third man was ready too.

Deep breath.

'*Lass' ihn los!* Let him go! Let him go now!' he yelled.

Pravic started. He jerked on his hostage's neck. Alex gagged. Pravic swung the gun left and blasted plaster from the wall by the door to ward F. The marksman ducked inside.

'*Herr Pravic!* Drop the weapon!' From the lift lobby now.

Herr Pravic, Alex seethed. Why so bloody formal? Why not *arsehole*? He wrenched his head to the right. Ten metres away, a face and a gun edging round the wall.

He understood. Saw their tactic. To prod and confuse like picadors in a bullring, twisting Pravic one way, then

369

the other, in the hope he'd expose enough of himself for a hit.

A dangerous tactic, that could kill *him* in the process.

So, Pravic was to be stopped at any price. Never to be let into that ward. Even if the hostage died in the process . . . Alex had nothing to lose.

The gun muzzle crushed the lobe of his ear.

'Let him go, Herr Pravic!' The voice from the left. The word. 'Let the hostage go!'

'Herr Pravic!'

From the right, now. The lift lobby. 'Throw down the gun!'

Pravic trembled, blinded by flashing images from the past. Taunts. Prods with sticks. The stones flicked in his face as he ran to school.

'Let him go!' The lobby end again. 'Have sense! You're surrounded. No way out, Pravic!'

Oh yes there was! He'd learned to fight back. Learned that if you asked for mercy, they pissed on you.

He aimed the Zastrava at the lobby corner.

Alex felt Pravic tense to absorb the kick of the gun. He tensed too. Ready.

The shot cracked and ricocheted off the walls. A split-second only in which to act.

Alex reached back with his trussed hands and grabbed for the soft, sensitive offal of the gunman's genitals.

Pravic buckled instinctively, grunting with surprise.

With the sudden weight-shift, Alex had leverage. He locked his chin onto Pravic's arm and buckled his knees. As he fell forward, with Pravic hooked to his neck, he jinked, turning the Bosnian's back towards ward F.

Marksman of the year for 1992 saw his chance.

Four shots. Four shuddering jerks to the Bosnian's body. Then Alex felt a stabbing pain in his spine. He crumpled to the floor, with Pravic's twitching bulk on top of him.

Lorna banged open the doors to the lobby and sprinted after the policeman as he thundered down the corridor.

Bodies on the floor. Uniforms clustered round. A policeman's boot stamped down hard. Crushed by its heavy sole, a hand clutching a gun.

She couldn't speak. Didn't dare ask.

Face pressed to the shiny floor by Pravic's body, Alex tasted blood. Wetness trickled to his mouth from the back of his head.

Words in gruff German, then Pravic was pulled off him. Alex rolled onto one side, wincing at the pain in his back. One look at the dark red dribble from Pravic's mouth told him the blood he'd tasted had not been his own.

'Alex!'

He looked up – Lorna was kneeling beside him. He smiled up at her, seizing her hand, and holding on to it as if it were life itself.

Twenty-Six

On the long, hard drive from Calais Michael McCarthy had stayed at the wheel of the British-registered Mondeo. Didn't trust the moody, hungover Nolan.

They'd found beds at one of the new, plastic hotels that did cheap rooms near an autobahn junction west of Frankfurt. He'd dropped Nolan there, then driven to the airport and left the Mondeo in the long-term car park.

At the arrivals terminal, he rented a VW Golf using a stolen driving licence, paid cash for three days' rental, then took the car for a short familiarization spin before returning to the hotel.

He knocked on Nolan's room. Heavy feet, then the door wrenched open.

'Will you fockin' look at this, Michael,' Nolan howled, heading back into the room and pointing to the television.

'What, then?'

'Youse can get *Sky News* here, that's fockin' what!'

'So?'

'So your man's only on the fockin' news!' Nolan was apoplectic.

'What you on about, Tommy?' He grabbed his arm. 'Count to five. Then tell me.'

'It was himself! Your man Jarvis, only his name's Crawford now. It was shown on *Sky News*, but it happened here. In Frankfurt. At some hospital. He stopped some madman murdering hundreds of people

372

with anthrax. They's calling the bastard a hero!'

'When did you see this? Are you certain about it?'

'Just a few minutes ago. And of course I'm fockin' certain. It'll be on again in a wee while. You'll see.'

McCarthy perched his backside on the dressing-table unit. Didn't change anything.

'Did they say where this hospital was?'

'I don't know. I didn't get it anyways. You'll see for yourself in a minute.'

Nolan sat on the edge of the bed, crumpled and out of his depth. He'd only once been out of the British Isles before, a fortnight in Tenerife one year when he'd won a bit on the pools.

'Not getting cold feet, are you Tommy?'

'What? Not on your life.'

Not convincing. McCarthy could see he'd have to put some bottle in him. Hadn't brought him all this way just to have him cop out at the last minute.

'What's he done?'

'Eh?' Nolan looked up, confused.

'What's he done to you this fellow, that you've wanted to kill him for the last twenty years?'

'He's a tout. You knows that. He put my brother Kieran under the earth.'

'Exactly. I know that. You know that. So don't you forget it tomorrow when you've got the nine millimetre pointed at his head.'

Belsize Park, north London

In the comfort of his suburban home, Roger Chadwick watched *News at Ten* with deepening unease. It was all there. The bloodstained hospital corridor, the press conference with Alex and Lorna. Big close-ups, their names broadcast for everyone to hear.

'Oh God,' he breathed. The IRA cease-fire was certainly expected, but it wasn't yet in place.

'Something the matter, dear?' his wife asked, glancing up from her crossword.

'Yes. I think there might be.'

He got up from the soft armchair, crossed the hall from the living room to his study and picked up the phone. Better have a minder or two on the first plane to Frankfurt in the morning.

Lorna Donohue! It *was* her, after all. Why the hell had Alex lied to him? Not hard to guess.

After his call to Thames House he stared up at his well-filled bookshelf, thinking. By the time his men got to Germany and found their way around, it would be mid-morning. The thought made him uncomfortable. A vital few hours left uncovered.

He tried another call, to the German Bundeskriminalamt in Wiesbaden.

No reply to Kommissar Linz's direct line and he had no other number. Better get Thames House to pass a message through the BKA duty officer.

Alex was the person he most needed to contact, but the idiot hadn't told him where he was staying.

Harz Mountains

Dieter Konrad sat alone in front of a fire of crackling spruce. Normally he loved the quiet of his isolated retreat in the Harz. Trees all around, nearest neighbour half a kilometre away. But tonight the silence deepened his fear.

The man he knew as 'Schiller' had ordered him here this morning. Telephoned him at the Berlin apartment, breaking the agreement not to contact him there. His wife had asked questions.

The mystery murder of Karina the prostitute had been on the morning radio news. There'd need to be two more deaths before he felt safe. Gisela Pocklewicz and most important of all, Milan Pravic.

It was after midnight, but there was no point in trying to sleep. Not while his mind still saw the disbelief in the whore's bulbous eyes as he'd choked her to death.

Strange that with a handful of murders to his credit, *this* one should affect him so deeply. The difference was it had been personal this time. Had to kill Karina with his own hands, to save his own skin. And worse, much worse, she was somebody he had *desired*.

The ring of the telephone made him half leap from the chair.

Rudiger Katzfuss and Martin Sanders weaved through the forest on the deserted 'B' road, headlamps bouncing off the light bark of silver birches. Sanders at the wheel of the big BMW, Katzfuss on the phone.

'Schiller here,' said Katzfuss. 'We're on our way to see you. Can you pack a bag with enough things for a week?'

'Why? What's the matter?'

'We've got wind that the press are on to you. We've decided you'd be safer, and so would we, if you were in one of *our* houses. Pick you up in about ten minutes?'

Konrad grunted an acknowledgement and rang off. Katzfuss held the phone out so he could see the dialpad in the light of the reading lamp. He pressed the 'secrecy' button. The line would stay connected, but silent.

Konrad stood by the phone staring at it. Why? Why at this time of night? *How* could the press be on to him, unless the BND themselves had tipped them off. No one else knew that Herr Konrad and Herr Dunkel were the same person. Not even his wife.

Perhaps the press had been on to *her*. He picked up the receiver again. She'd be asleep at the flat in Berlin-Lichtenberg, but never mind. He had to know.

No dialling tone. Just a hum and a crackle. He pressed down on the rest, then up again. Dead.

'*Ach, Du Liebe,*' he gasped. '*Nein!*'

He flung open the front door and stumbled towards the Mercedes, guided by light spilling from the house. He felt with a finger for the escutcheon and inserted the key. Stupid habit keeping it locked. No need to out here.

Ignition on. Wait for the diesel light. Come on!

A flick of the key and the engine rumbled. He stabbed at the light switch, crunched into first and accelerated down the hundred metres of narrow gravel towards the road.

Headlights! Turning in towards him.

'*Gott o Gott!*'

Full beam. Dazzling. No room to pass. Trees either side. He stamped on the brake.

Sanders braked first, then sprung from the door running into the darkness, reaching into his shoulder holster for the pistol.

Katzfuss, heart pounding, walked slowly to the driver's door of the Mercedes.

'Weren't you going to wait for us, Herr Konrad?' he asked when the window was down. Konrad looked old and very, very scared.

'Something happened to my telephone ...' he explained lamely. 'I don't know what's going on.'

'Not working? Never mind. There's one in the house we're going to. It's not far from here. Bag packed?'

'No. I . . .'

'Better be quick. These journalists work through the night. Back the car up. You'll come with us in ours.'

'Us?'

'Yes. I have a friend with me. There's another colleague at the safe house. We'll all be staying there tonight. A little cramped, but we'll manage. *Gemütlich!* Here, I'll help you reverse.'

He walked to the rear of the Mercedes, took out a flashlight and guided Konrad back up the drive. Sanders slipped behind the wheel of the BMW and followed closely.

Ten minutes later they headed north on the Bundes-strasse. Sanders gripped the wheel of the BMW in total concentration. He knew what he had to do, knew it was something he'd never done before, knew if he allowed himself to think too much, his nerve would crack.

In the back, Konrad sat beside Katzfuss, gripping the sides of the small case perched on his knees. They drove for less than fifteen minutes, then turned onto a mud track. Konrad knew these woods. The way led to a lake where he'd fished for pike.

No houses here. He was sure of it.

'So,' said Katzfuss, struggling to sound calm, 'we're here. Just a little walk.'

'There are no houses here,' Konrad croaked, frozen to the seat.

'It's a fishing cabin. You haven't noticed it before? Well that shows what a good safe house it is. Come along. It's three minutes.'

Katzfuss got out of the car. Sanders hovered in the darkness, shining a torch on the ground.

'What are you waiting for Herr Konrad? Someone to carry your bag? It's not that sort of place,' Katzfuss laughed hollowly. So did Sanders.

377

Konrad opened the door. Legs like lead, throat desert-dry. Somewhere in this murk death lurked. He could smell his own fear. Should he run? They'd shoot him for sure. Maybe if he played along with them there was a chance. Just a chance . .

Katzfuss led the way, flashlight lighting up the mud of a path. Konrad next, then Sanders, shining his torch forward.

The smell of decaying weed told Konrad they were within metres of the water.

When he'd fished for that pike here, months ago, he'd identified with it – a predator in a pool of torpidity. Sensed that one day he too would swallow a hook disguised as bait, because like the fish, decades of trickery had not equipped him to avoid the trickery of others.

As they squelched deeper into the blackness he knew the end had come. He tasted the salt of tears. His eyes began to blur. All he'd wanted was to live out his days in the peace of the forest, doing no one harm any more. His wife would be asleep in their warm, soft bed, knowing nothing about what he'd done in the past. He prayed she never learned the truth.

'Shh!' Katzfuss held up a hand for them to stop. Pitch black all around, he shielded the beam of his torch. 'Something's wrong. There should be lights in the house.'

They listened for a moment, none of them breathing.

'Wait here a minute,' he said. 'I'll go on alone.' He trotted forward out of sight.

Sanders raised the beam of his torch. It caught Konrad's head as he turned his fearful face towards him. He fired the bullet smack into the Stasi man's temple.

Twenty-seven

Alex and Lorna stepped out of the Hotel Sommer at
eleven minutes to ten. The media had been phoning
non-stop that morning. Time to check out.

The press conference had alarmed him. All those
close-ups – no question now that his cover had been
finally blown. Just had to pray the IRA were watching
football instead of the news.

Alex carried their two bags, and Lorna their coats. A
watery sun shone that morning, but rain was forecast.

Opposite the hotel, the VW Golf had been parked on a
meter for more than two hours. McCarthy sat with his
gloved hands on the wheel, Nolan fidgeting beside him.

When he recognized the man he'd come to kill, Nolan
gulped. Never seen him in the flesh before. Under the
coat folded on his lap was the heavy Springfield pistol
McCarthy had retrieved from beneath the floorboards of
the house in Chiswick.

'I'll not do it here,' Nolan declared, nervously. 'Not
with all these people about.'

'Course you bloody won't,' McCarthy snapped.

There was no way he was going to let this old man
cock things up and get them jailed just as peace was
breaking out in the six counties.

'We'll follow them.'

379

He started the engine, slipped out of the parking bay and crawled along the kerb.

Lorna took the road south, towards the airport.

'How's your back?' she asked, looking at Alex with concern.

The muscle he'd pulled yesterday when falling to the floor of the hospital with Pravic on top of him was still painful.

'Not too bad. I get a twinge when I move.' He pushed the switch on the dashboard radio. 'Let's see if there's any news of Mr Pravic.'

He already knew that surgeons had spent much of yesterday afternoon removing the police bullets from his back. They'd given his chances of survival as fifty-fifty.

Alex turned the volume up high. The news in German was always read too fast for him. Loudness helped him pick out the words.

The economy and European Union were back on top of the agenda. The fate of the Bosnian Croat who'd nearly committed mass murder in a Frankfurt hospital was the third story.

'Still alive,' Alex translated. 'They use the word *beständig* which I think means stable.'

'Pity,' Lorna remarked. 'They don't have the *chair* in Germany, do they?'

'No. He'll probably end up in some asylum with nurses fussing round him.'

They were heading for Pfefferheim for what they intended to be the last time. Vildana was being let out of hospital that morning and Lorna wanted to check the Roches were still committed to her, before she pulled out and left them to it.

Last night, after the police had finished their questions, after the journalists had completed their interviews and after Alex had told the hotel desk not to put calls through to their room, he and Lorna had talked.

Not about the future. They'd leave that to fate. They'd talked about the missing years, realizing how little they knew about each other now, how little they'd known before, even when they'd been together.

Last night they'd begun to build the framework of something, without yet knowing what it was. In the days ahead they planned to add shape and texture until it took a form they could understand.

They didn't talk much more on the way to Pfeffer-heim.

They didn't notice they were being followed.

Frankfurt Airport

Martin Sanders bought a fistful of German newspapers from the bookstall in the Duty Free area then sat down to drink a cup of strong coffee. He flicked through the pages to ensure there were no alarming headlines. He felt uneasy, sickened by what he and Katzfuss had been forced to do to protect the secrecy of the Ramblers.

In his head he had the draft of a letter to his SIS Chief, resigning from the group. In it there'd be a recommendation that the concept of 'black' multinational security operations be abandoned. Too much risk of soured relations when things went wrong.

The lake was ten metres deep where they'd dumped Konrad's body. They'd towed it out behind an inflatable which they'd stashed there earlier, then sunk it with iron weights. With luck it would never be found in such murky water.

The word *Milzbrand* featured in the headline in the

Frankfurte Allgemeine. Kommissar Linz from the Bundeskriminalamt was quoted saying he had no idea where Pravic had got the anthrax bacillus, and would question him closely if he survived his wounds.

The journalists could *speculate* as much as they liked that it was from the Leipzig Veterinary Laboratory, but with both Kemmer and Konrad/Dunkel out of circulation, they'd find it hard to *prove* the connection. And the media were getting nowhere with the death of the chambermaid in Zagreb. The Croatian authorities were refusing to reveal who'd been booked in the hotel at the time and had even begun to deny it was anthrax that killed her.

Sanders put down the paper. The concourse bustled with business people rushing for their flights. Men and women for whom Bosnia, plutonium smuggling and anthrax were of little more than passing interest. Best to keep it that way.

And they would, unless Pravic talked.

Pfefferheim

Nancy Roche couldn't hold back her tears. Everything had been too much in the last few days. Lorna hugged her and found her own eyes moistening.

Vildana sat in a chair by the kitchen table, her face pale, her dark eyes blank, her right arm in a sling. The twins and Nataša sat with her, gently easing her back into the world of a family.

Irwin and Nancy led Lorna and Alex to the living room.

'We just want you guys to know that the Roche family's in this for the duration,' Irwin announced formally. 'Nancy and I talked it over with the kids last night. Whatever it takes, Vildana has a home with us for as long as she likes.'

'That's just great,' Lorna grinned, clasping his hands.

'And something else you need to know,' he went on, 'I've put in for an early transfer to the States. We thought it best to move Vildana back home just as soon as we possibly can.'

'That's a swell idea. Couldn't be better.'

'What's the hospital saying about Vildana?' Alex said.

'Has to go back in a week to have the sutures out,' Nancy explained. 'But otherwise she should be okay. Shoulder will be sore for a while, and it could be months before she gets any strength back on that side. But the long-term looks good.'

'And when we get home we'll see what can be done about that birthmark,' Roche added.

'Sure. She's real keen on that,' Lorna confirmed. 'Say, could I ask you for one last favour?'

'Anything.'

'Just to use your computer. It'll save me setting up my own. If I can e-mail all this to CareNet, then I can sign off the case!'

'Come on. I'll set it up for you.'

Nancy turned towards Alex when her husband and Lorna had left the room.

'What are your plans? You're going back to Bosnia?' she asked.

'No. I doubt that,' he replied. 'No, Lorna and I plan to go off for a few days. We're going to dump the Land Cruiser at the US Air Base, rent something cheap at the airport, then drive up the Mosel and find a pretty village to stay in.'

'Gr . . . reat!' Then she tilted her head in curiosity. She'd never quite worked out their relationship. 'You two, you've known each other for some while?'

'You could say that. On and off.'

Kommissar Günther Linz was late into his office that morning. Hadn't got to bed before two last night. He'd asked for the witness statements from the hospital and Pravic's charge sheets to be ready on his desk by noon, so he could approve them before they were presented to the magistrate. At eleven-thirty when he arrived, the documents were already there.

The message sheet from the overnight duty officer had been buried underneath them. When he discovered it, he blanched.

A fax from MI5 in London telling him the Englishman Crawford was on an IRA death list . . . Unbelievable! Two agents were on their way to Frankfurt.

He looked at his watch. The British Security Service people would be landing at the airport any minute. He had nothing for them. Didn't even know where Crawford was. And the crucial time gap that had worried Herr Chadwick – he'd done nothing about it.

He rang the Hotel Sommer. Crawford had checked out. He rang the Roche house in Pfefferheim. Crawford *had* been there. But he'd left with the Sorensen woman just two minutes ago. Heading for the airport, according to Frau Roche.

He picked up the internal phone. Better get a car from the anti-terrorist team to intercept the Land Cruiser at the Rhein-Main base.

'Here we go!'

McCarthy prodded Tommy Nolan in the ribs. The white Toyota four-wheel-drive was on its way towards them down Mühlweg.

'You okay?' he checked. For the past couple of hours Nolan had been sighing and sweating like an old sow.

Nolan grunted.

'Does that mean you're ready, then?'

'I'm ready,' Nolan croaked, unconvincingly. He wished he'd had a drink to make it easier. Only done this once before. A soldier, off-duty in a pub, twenty-two years ago. On his conscience ever since. Sick with fear then. Sick with fear now.

McCarthy slipped the car into gear and cruised slowly out of the village, watching in his rear-view mirror as the target came up behind them. He'd spotted the ideal place on the way in. An opening in the pinewoods, with a muddy track leading into a clearing. Drive in there and they'd not be visible from the road.

They'd do it quick. Take the tout a few yards into the forest. If anyone heard, they'd think it was someone shooting pigeons. He glanced at Nolan. White as a sheet.

'You're not goin' to throw up are youse?' he hissed, fearful that Nolan would bungle it and get them caught. 'Just remember your wee brother! A wee kid. And what the fucker did to him!'

'Oh aye,' Nolan growled. 'Don't worry. Don't worry.'

He was close to wetting himself with nerves. Getting even with the bastard had been easy enough when it was just words over a pint in Dunphy's. But in the cold, sober daylight of a bewilderingly foreign land, knowing whether he was doing right wasn't so simple any more.

Lorna pulled out to overtake. The Golf dawdled annoyingly in front of them. She was impatient to put Pfefferheim into the past.

'Shit!' she hissed, as the VW began to accelerate, swerving to the middle of the road to block her. 'I hate guys like that. Some creep with a small prick trying to show he's tough.'

Alex put a hand against the dashboard to steady himself.

'Keep cool. Don't let him get to you,' he soothed. 'We've got all the time in the world.'

But the sudden acid burn in his stomach told him different. The tightening of the chest, the pounding pulse – that terrible clamminess was back. Like the day Jodie died, the certainty something was desperately wrong.

A kilometre from the village already. No more houses. Just trees.

'What's the bastard doing?' Lorna cried, scared now.

The VW slowed, hogging the line in the middle of the empty road.

'Alex! What do I do?'

He stared mesmerized as the Golf eased further out then slipped back, its rear overlapping the front of the Toyota. Two men in it.

'Shit! We'll be off the road!' Lorna screamed.

Brake lights dazzled. The Golf just inches in front. Lorna stamped the pedal and wrenched the wheel to the right. A gap in the trees. A muddy track as an escape lane.

The Land Cruiser jolted over the rough ground, halting twenty metres from the road. In the mirror she saw the Golf stop and reverse in behind them.

'Alex! For Christ's sake – who *are* these people?'

He turned. Both men piling out of the VW, heads in thick, woollen sock masks, hands gripping guns.

Lorna's door burst open. A fist reached in and dragged her to the ground. She screamed.

'Oh God, no,' Alex gulped. The masked face at the window stared unblinking. A gloved finger beckoned. 'Not now. Not after all this.'

The gunman pulled open the door.

'Time's up, Mister Jarvis!' he growled, the Ulster twang unmistakable. He pointed deeper into the woods where Lorna was being frogmarched by the older man, his gun pressed to her spine.

Alex stumbled from the car. Stupid, stupid! Dropped

his guard. After all those years . . . All those little tricks, those superstitions he'd believed would keep him alive . . .

Now he was like the stag in the Highlands, the beast that thought itself invincible. One moment's inattention, then caught by the cross-hairs of the gun.

They were herded into a circle of pine trees, two people swept up years ago in a struggle they'd never really understood, called to account for their deeds twenty years on.

'You's the bastard . . . what touted . . . on my brother!' The older man panting between the words, ignoring Lorna, concentrating on Alex. Nolan, circling like a hyena, jabbing at the air with his Springfield, not too close, not quite looking him in the eye.

McCarthy backed away, watching the road. The score to be settled here was a personal one. Had to be done by the man with the grievance.

'What are you on about?' Alex croaked, playing for time.

How had they found him? Not the TV, surely. Too soon, too quick for that.

'Don't gimme that, *bastard*! I knows who you are, *Alex!* For twenty fockin' years you's had it coming. An' now you's fockin' goin' to get it!'

He levelled the gun. Bloodshot eyes through the slits of the hood.

Anger boiled in Alex's guts. Fear too. What to do? Confront or comply? Challenge - or beg for mercy?

'No...o!' Lorna screamed, interposing herself, hands outstretched as if to stop the bullets. It *can't* happen, she thought. Not now . . . Not after everything . . .

'And as for youse . . .' Nolan growled at her, 'come over here. Come on. Out the way!'

He grabbed her by the shoulder, spun her round to face Alex.

'Will you tell him or shall I?'

'What? What d'you mean?' she croaked.

Alex gasped, a black, black thought erupting in his head. It was revenge they were after, sure enough. But *whose* revenge?

'What d'you mean?' Lorna's voice, high-pitched, the squeak of a bat.

'Your wee snap? He doesna know about it?' Nolan goaded, plucking the photo from his coat pocket and letting it flutter onto the ground between them.

'Annie!' she gasped. 'Oh my God! Annie, how *could* you?'

She'd forgotten her sister's husband was still a firm supporter of the IRA. She turned to Nolan, eyes brimming with tears.

'N-n-no!' she stammered. 'You're wrong, you're wrong! *I* didn't . . . You think *I* sent *you* that picture? No. That wasn't for you! No, listen. It's *over*, all that. He's paid already. Been punished. Suffered . . . just as much as you or I, or anybody!'

'Shut your mouth!' Nolan's resolve was shaky enough as it was. He could do without her pleading.

Alex had to know. Had to be sure this wasn't Lorna's doing. A tit-for-tat betrayal.

'Why now, Tommy?' Alex's voice hard and crisp. The use of the name was a gamble. It was the one he'd heard the minders talk of. 'What good will it do?'

Nolan flinched. Anonymous he was an executioner carrying out orders. But 'Tommy' was personal. One to one. Man to man.

'Shut your mouth, youse! You's been sentenced. By the army council. Twenty fockin' years ago!'

'Twenty years! A long time, Tommy.'

Had Lorna set him up? Faked *everything*? Was she pretending still?

'We's don't forget,' Nolan snapped. But he couldn't forget the weariness either. Weariness of war.

'That's your trouble, Tommy. But you'll have to learn how to if you want peace.'

Alex shot a glance at Lorna. Deathly pale, mouth gaping. No fake. He was sure, almost. She looked destroyed by this.

'How many hundreds have you boys killed in those twenty years?' Adrenalin pumping, now. Fighting for his life. 'Soldiers, police. Women out shopping. *Schoolgirls.*'

He saw Nolan flinch.

'Suppose every one of your victims had a big brother wanting to get even. There'd be nowhere *you* could hide . . .'

He saw the eyes blink, the weight shift from foot to foot.

'What d'you mean *schoolgirls?*' Nolan spluttered. 'Those was accidents. A mistake. We admitted it.'

'Oh yes. Like me and Lorna meeting in Belfast – that was an accident. Getting mixed up in your troubles – that was a mistake. I'll admit it too.'

'Don't give me that! Youse were different!' But Nolan was rattled. A wedge was being driven between his bluster and his resolve.

'There's a cease-fire coming. You know that?' Alex pressed.

'Don't be so sure . . .' Nolan countered. He didn't like this. Wanted the man to shut up.

'Killing me won't help.'

'Fockin' shut it!'

'Not if the Provos want to be taken seriously. Not if you want to be political. Kill me and you could wreck everything . . .'

Alex gulped. Maybe that's what they wanted. Maybe these two hoods had instructions from the hard men to wreck the peace process.

'Fuckin' get on with it, Tommy!' McCarthy's voice a growl from ten yards back. The swish of intermittent traffic on the road. With every second the growing danger they'd be seen.

Nolan raised the pistol level with Alex's mouth. First pressure on the trigger, sweat trickling into his eyes. Aim for the chest. It'd be easier to look at . . .

'Look me in the eye Tommy if you're going to do it.' Alex's throat bone dry. Heart galloping. 'And tell me why. Tell me what good it'll do. Tell me who'll thank you for it . . .'

Nolan forced his gaze higher. Just for a second. Just for long enough to register the face of the man they'd called a hero on TV. The man who'd helped save the life of a kid and hundreds more. Someone who'd suffered as much as any of them . . . so the Donohue woman had said . . . What had she meant? Too late to find out, now.

'I've forgotten your brother's name . . .' Alex's tone softer now.

'Kieran . . .'

'He wouldn't thank you. All that killing, all that hate – didn't get *him* anywhere, did it?'

'Do it Tommy!' The yell from behind.

Alex plundered his memory for everything the minders had told him about Tommy Nolan.

'You don't have to, Tommy,' Alex whispered. 'Don't let *him* tell you what to do. He's only young. What does he know . . .'

He saw the gun shake in Nolan's hand. Heard the wheeze of the breath.

'You *can* forgive, you know,' Alex persisted. 'Like the mother of the soldier-boy you shot?' Gambling again. Gambling he'd remembered it right. 'She forgave you didn't she? Said so on TV the day of the funeral . . .'

Slowly, inch by inch, Nolan's arm dropped down. With his free hand he plucked the sock mask from his head, then used it to wipe the sweat from his face. He turned and looked at Lorna.

'Stupid bitch!' The word flung at her like a gob of spit.

Nolan stumbled towards McCarthy, the Springfield hanging limply at his side.

'Couldn't fockin' do it,' he spat. 'Couldn't pull the friggin' trigger.'

'Jesus fucking Christ!' McCarthy exploded. What a waste of time. Risking everything – and for what? He thought of stepping forward, doing the job himself. But what would be the point? It had been Nolan's grudge.

'Get in the shagging car!' he growled.

McCarthy pulled his pocket knife out. He paused by the Land Cruiser, crouched by the nearside front wheel, then jabbed its spike into the tyre.

The hiss of escaping air jerked Lorna from her trance. She turned to see the doors of the VW slam and the car speed away.

Unsure of his legs, Alex stepped forward, bent down to the carpet of pine needles and picked up the snapshot McFee had taken in Bosnia.

He held it in his shaking hand. His face and hers, smiling tensely, neither sure of the other one's thoughts.

'Not bad . . .' he croaked. 'Considering.'

Lorna flung her arms round his neck, quivering with relief.

'I . . . I never thought,' she stammered. 'Sent it to my sister with a note saying we'd met again. What I meant was – *isn't that unbelievable!* She must have imagined I meant something else.'

'I guess she must have,' Alex replied, holding her loosely.

For more than a minute they leaned against one another, each conscious of the other's breathing, thoughts circling like moths round an oil lamp.

'Is . . . is that it, d'you think?' she asked suddenly.

Alex looked up through the crowns of the pine trees. Flecks of blue visible through the grey of the sky.

'I believe it may be . . .' he murmured.

The poltergeists had been exorcized.

'Do you know what I'd like to do now?' she asked.

Alex looked over at the stranded Land Cruiser, praying the spare wheel was inflated.

'Vanish,' she said. 'With you.'

Epilogue

Dr Hamid Akhavi died from pulmonary anthrax the following day, but the Iranian authorities never made it public.

Colonel Pavel Kulikov's life was saved by the vaccine he'd been given in 1991. Finding that his contact with Iran had been cut, he began to look for other markets for the stolen plutonium.

Milan Pravic recovered from his wounds and was transferred to a remand prison to await trial for the attempted murder of Vildana Muminovic. Kommissar Günther Linz continued to hope that before long he could persuade him to reveal where he'd obtained the anthrax bacillus. The United Nations War Crimes Tribunal in the Hague announced its intention to prosecute Pravic for the crime of genocide. Two days later he was stabbed to death in a knife fight with another Bosnian prisoner.

The Ramblers were disbanded. There are no records to show that the group ever existed.

Also in Arrow by Geoffrey Archer

JAVA SPIDER

A British minister is taken hostage in the South Pacific. The kidnappers' grim video of him is relayed to London by satellite TV. His captors say that if the minister is to live Britain must stop its lucrative weapons sales to Indonesia's repressive armed forces.

Islanders thrown off their island by Indonesian troops to make way for a multinational mining operation seem to be behind the kidnap. But when undercover investigator Lew Randall is sent to Indonesia, he's aware that in a land of masks, nothing is what it seems.

Peeling back the deception layer by layer, he uncovers an international intrigue of nightmare proportions, and a web of corruption that spreads to the top of his own government.

Randall is not alone. Working beside him, but with an agenda sharply at odds with his own, is TV reporter Charlotte Cavendish. *Her* aim is to expose injustice, *his* to find and free the politician. Together they penetrate a world where torture is a tool of power and life is cheap.